JUST FRIENDS
FOR NOW

A laugh out loud romantic comedy

LUCY KEELING

Friends Book 4

Choc Lit
A JOFFE BOOKS COMPANY

Choc Lit
A Joffe Books company
www.choc-lit.com

This edition first published in Great Britain in 2023

Cover art by Berni Stevens Cover Design

ISBN: 978-1-78189-534-4

This has to be for you, wonderful reader.
Thank you for waiting for this one.
I really appreciate your support.

ACKNOWLEDGEMENTS

To Leonie and Lucy, you go first this time. Thank you for being with me every step of the way, every draft, every edit, every message, gif and bottle of Prosecco. Thank you.

To my online support network: Laura from Tangents and Tissues, Jayne H, Emma J, Zoe A, Lucy M, Bettina H, Ritu B, Lyndsey G, Caroline K, Kiley D, Amisha J, Jen R, Sarah B, James H, Becca R, Anita F, Abi Y, Donna G, Sue B — thank you so much. Thanks as well to all the support from the Chick Lit & Prosecco Facebook group. And everyone that has ever contacted me online to say nice things about my books, or just cheered me on, you have no idea how much I appreciate it.

Thank you as well to my real-life support network: James, Kids, Mum, Charlie, Aby. Michelle, Helen, Nic, Nic Nic, Emma, Matt, Andi, Big Red, Barlow, Helen, Jo & Mary, Sarah & Twin, Yvonne, Michelle B, Clare R.

Thanks as well to Rachel Dove, who somehow managed to become both.

Thanks must go to my editor and my wonderful publishing team for their endless patience and support.

Thank you as well to the incredible Choc Lit team Tasting Panel readers who made publication possible: Margaret

Marshall, Laura Sumner, Alison Bilham, Jo Elliott, Donna Morgan, Michele Rollins, Linda Middleton, Janice Butler, Jenny Mitchell, Dimitra Evangelou, Honor Gilbert, Bee Master, Lisa Vasil and Jo Osborne.

Thank you to you, dear reader, for taking a chance on me. I am and will always be so grateful.

PROLOGUE

Paige looked around her bar, business was steady but not busy. The background music a soothing accompaniment to the Mancunian accents around her. The vibe of Barbarella was unique and welcoming. The eclectic mix of light fixtures scattered around the bar bright enough to light up an otherwise rainy afternoon. But her mind was quiet. Too quiet. A nice rush of students, or maybe a large group of day-drinking mums, would have been ideal. A distraction of any sort would be appreciated. Anything that would take her mind off the fact that today marked two weeks since she first noticed her mojo had completely disappeared. Two long weeks in which each passing day her mood darkened, as the fear increased, that this may not be a temporary problem.

The little insights she'd had about how her friends were, what drinks people wanted to order, hints and clues about how her day was going to pan out. Vanished. It was two weeks ago when the signage for the new bar down the road had gone up, and that was when she'd known for certain it was missing. She'd given herself some time, a few days at first, then a week, and she'd been jetlagged from visiting Mya in Vegas which could have played a role, but now at two weeks, Paige was finally forced to admit that her mojo had gone.

She didn't even have her friends to distract her. Mya was still in Vegas with Smithy apparently looking at casino expansions or something. Polly was doing super-secret song writing work in LA but was due back soon, and Sophie had nipped down to London doing influencer stuff. She could mither Bailey and Marcus, but she knew she wouldn't.

'The new bar down the road looks cute,' Belle said as she wiped down the tables nearest the bar.

Paige appreciated the break from her internal dwelling but this particular topic wasn't going to help. While she didn't know exactly when she'd lost her mojo, she did suspect it had been around the time the new bar owner had rocked up. 'It's called Lulu, and it's going to be an Instagram type prosecco bar. We don't need to worry.'

'Oh, I'm not worried. She seems nice though.'

Paige didn't want to ask who, didn't want to give any more time to thinking about Melanie, but she didn't get that choice.

'Melanie, right? Sophie said she was lovely when she came in here when you were in Vegas.'

Belle's expression was open, clearly looking for more information. 'You must have seen her at the Neighbourhood Business group thing right? When they were pitching for the lease?'

Paige sighed, knowing when Belle wasn't going to leave something alone. 'Yeah, it's Melanie and Louisa and they've got a really clear business concept. It's why she, I mean they, got the lease.'

'And . . . ?'

'And what?'

'She's cute too, right?'

'Belle?'

'Yes, boss?'

'Get back to work now, please.'

Belle grinned before spinning around to grab more glasses, and Paige tried to think about anything other than her mojo or Melanie. She looked at the rotas instead, always a sure-fire way to keep her brain occupied.

CHAPTER ONE

Three months later
Paige

The name displayed on her phone finally disappeared and a notification of a missed call flashed up in its place. Her phone immediately lit up again; this time from a caller she actually did want to talk to. Simultaneously, her phone pinged the reminder she was due at the Neighbourhood Business Alliance meeting in fifteen minutes. With a quick glance around the bar she noted everything seemed to be in order. And so, with a quick wave at her bar staff, Paige answered the call as she strode out of Barbarella, phone to her ear.

'Book darling, how are you? Sorry if the line is terrible, we're sailing, you see. So, I'm going to be . . . and then we'll . . .'

'Hang on, where are you?' Paige nearly tripped as she concentrated more on what was being said than avoiding the puddles filling the pavement in front of her.

'I'm on the—Hang on.' The voice on the end of the phone abruptly stopped and Paige hated to admit that she had no idea what was going on. Again. Still.

She moved further into the street until she was out of the way of the other pedestrians frequenting the Northern

Quarter with their hustling and bustling. Paige pulled the phone away from her ear. She was still connected, what was going on? The idea that ignorance is bliss was laughable, and with every day that passed she lost a little more of the belief that this was a temporary blip.

Paige pulled her phone back to her face. 'Hello?'

There was a rustling sound, a muffled thank you and then . . . 'Bloody Hell, Kevin. What the hell do you call this? I asked for a Tom Collins. This is all Tom and no Collins. Come on, Flower.'

'Gran, you were saying . . .' prompted Paige as her feet now began punishing the pavement, all too aware of how Connie, her gran, preferred her drinks.

'Yes Book, I'm on my way to you. I should be disembarking and dockside, what day is it now, Tuesday? Right, I should be on the dock tomorrow. Then I've just got to make my way up there from Southampton, so unless I find the man of my dreams between there and Manchester, I should be with you in no time.'

Paige didn't know what to process first. There was every chance her gran *would* find the man of her dreams between wherever the hell she was and Manchester. It had happened before. Her gran had been spending the last five years getting over the end of marriage number five, her widowhood taking her across the world. Several times over in fact. The rather substantial inheritance had provided Connie with enough money to live the rest of her life on a permanent cruise and, as much as Paige missed her gran, she couldn't complain too much as it had also given Paige the money to set up her bar.

'But hang on, where are you staying?' Paige asked, worried about the possible response.

'With you, of course. But don't worry, you won't cramp my style. We'll sort out a hooking-up system so that we don't disturb each other.'

Paige smiled at the same time as her stride slowed and shortened. Her gran was coming home. She'd help. She'd

4

know what to do. As it really sunk in, Paige could feel her muscles loosen. Connie would make it all better. And as for the hooking up, well, Paige very much doubted there would be any issues there, at least from her side. Paige had been pretty absent on that front for a while now.

'So, make up the spare room, make sure Mr Higgins knows I'm on my way. I can't wait to meet that ball of fluff, and round up all the eligible bachelors, it's time for me to get husband number six. Or do you think a woman this time? Maybe I should consider a wife, do you think that might work? I'm not sure I could do without the man meat.'

'Yeah OK, Gran,' Paige said shaking her head quickly. 'That's too much information. Do you have a rough idea of when you'll be here?'

There was a little tut over the phone. 'Why don't you guess?'

Paige sighed. 'Come on, Gran.'

'Your doodah still off then?'

'Yes,' Paige conceded reluctantly and with no small amount of petulance.

'Maybe it's a good idea I'm coming back now. Maybe it's to help you get fixed back right again.'

Paige very much hoped that was the case.

'Have you met someone?' Gran continued.

'What do you mean? I meet people every day, I run a bar,' Paige pointed out.

'You know exactly what I mean, and your being obtuse tells me I'm right. The only time I ever lost my doodah was when I met your grandad.' Connie's voice fell into a soft sigh at the mention of her first true love.

'I don't think you're on the right track there, Gran'—and if an image of Melanie in her pencil skirt and heels popped into her brain that was a coincidence and nothing to ponder further—'but, it would be incredible to be working properly again so if you can help me, well, I'd . . .' Her throat tightened and for one scary second Paige really thought she was going to do that thing she'd seen other people do sometimes

5

— and cry. Instead, she cleared her throat, and added, 'I'd really appreciate it.'

Paige clung on to that hope that Connie could help her as she pushed open the door to All The Beans. She quickly waved at the staff behind the coffee bar, getting the nod that she was allowed to go through towards the staff room.

'Hmm. Yours might be broken but mine's just fine. So, I think I should be there by Friday at the latest. I suspect an intense but short-lived romance somewhere between Southampton and Birmingham, which will be lovely. Thank you, Kevin — no, wait there.'

Paige could hear her gran twirling the glass in her hand, the ice cubes clinking against the sides, before she took a drink. 'It'll do, thanks Kevin. So, gather the girls. We'll have a party night on Friday. I'm going to need to nap Friday afternoon on the account of my shenanigans, disrupting my sleep patterns.' Connie slurped her drink again.

'OK Gran, but look I have to go, I'm about to go into a meeting.' Paige took a seat at the large but informal and well-worn table.

'You sound thrilled by the idea. Love you, Book.'

'Love you too, Gran.'

'Pssshh, I've told you it's Connie in public.'

Paige laughed. 'OK, fine, love you Connie. I'll see you soon.'

'Oh, I get the feeling this meeting might be quite interesting for you after all. Have fun. Don't do anything I wouldn't do.' That didn't really leave a whole lot.

The loud beeps in her ear signified that Connie had already gone. Paige sat up straighter in her chair, and looked around the room, seeing the lockers, the notice board and the big health and safety poster. She was looking for something, anything to stop her falling back into her bad mood as she waited for the other members of the Neighbourhood Business Alliance to show up.

If her mojo was working properly she would have known the right time to set off and would not have been so bloody early.

If her mojo was working she wouldn't have ended up stomping the whole way here like a stroppy teenage speed-walker.

Hopefully it would be a quick meeting, and in no time she would be back in her apartment, snuggling up with Mr Higgins, the only male she'd ever loved, watching something in the Disney family. She hoped. She didn't know though, and the reminder, the constant reminders that she was broken made her head ache. As she frowned she realised her jaw was clenched tight.

Then Melanie came in.

Of course she did.

Why did she have to look like a librarian all the time? The wire glasses were trendy, but come on? Her hair was scraped back so fiercely that Paige couldn't be sure if it was dark blonde or brown, curly or straight? Not that it mattered. But she also didn't know how long it was, again it didn't matter, and the sudden image of Melanie letting her hair down until it landed and swayed around her was completely unnecessary and completely not relevant, not to mention cliched as hell.

'Hi.' Melanie smiled warmly and sat down opposite, but Paige didn't miss the look of nerves that passed over her face as she settled on the seat.

Paige nodded, unable to unclench her jaw. It was all she could bring herself to do at that moment.

Clearly wanting to fill the awkward silence that Paige had created, Melanie continued awkwardly, 'Louisa couldn't make it today, so you've got me instead. Not, you've got me, I just meant the group, you know?' She laughed a little and the sound settled in Paige's head, unwelcome but unmoving; a laughing earworm.

Paige nodded in response, urging her jaw to relax, watching as Melanie pushed up her glasses on her nose. There actually wasn't any further for them to go and Paige wondered if that was a nervous tell.

'We don't have to make small talk, you know? The rest of the group will be here soon.' Paige inwardly cringed as soon as the words were out. Aiming to put Melanie at ease, instead her words had been tainted with her frustration.

Melanie gifted Paige a tiny and absolutely not real smile, her lips tight, before looking away as she grabbed her iPad out of her bag, and maybe it was the smile, or the efficiency, or the librarian nature, or the lack of mojo but Paige's bad mood was now all encompassing and she had no idea how to make it better. She should have said nothing. Like the proverb said if you can't say something nice don't say anything at all. Her gran had never believed that, saying instead that if it needs to be said then say it. But what could she say?

'What did you do with my mojo?'

Then again it probably wasn't Melanie, it might not have anything to do with Melanie, just a coincidence then, just weird timing. Something that started around the first time she saw Melanie at one of these meetings. Maybe the lack of mojo was Melanie or maybe, God forbid, she was just 'normal' now. Her head dropped at the thought. Maybe instead of rage she just needed to adapt? But that didn't feel right. Paige had always been a fighter; it was the way Connie had raised her.

Paige looked up again as Councillor Houghton sat down and she knew she had to regain her focus as the meeting was about to begin. If she didn't pay attention, she'd end up with random tasks next to her name again in the minutes.

CHAPTER TWO

Melanie

As Melanie power walked down the street towards All The Beans, she knew that she was very much done, and that was very much unlike her.

She usually had endless amounts of, whatever the opposite of done was, but today was proving particularly challenging and she was doing all she could to make sure that her failures weren't visible to anyone else. The toothpaste her four-year-old nephew had spilled on her earlier, gone, vanished, in the rushed five minutes she'd had in the car to shimmy out of her skirt and to put on the replacement. The fact that the bar had ran out of prosecco for the bottomless mimosas served at brunch, no problem. She'd managed to run to Tesco and grab what she could, even if it did make her look bad to the cashier who was questioning why she needed to buy three boxes of the stuff before 10.30 a.m. on a Tuesday morning. Oh, and the disappearing napkins that the driver swore he delivered that nobody could find. Yep, done.

And now, several hours later, this. The Neighbourhood Business Alliance meeting.

She had only seconds to check her appearance on the glass door outside before stepping in, but she knew her hair was slicked back into its tight bun, and her black pencil skirt was neat — and clean.

Rushing into the coffee shop as quick as her heels allowed, she waved at Kazim behind the counter. Although she wasn't able to stop, she quickly pointed to her eyes then at his and grinned at his professional looking eyeshadow blending.

'Go on through, I'll bring your oat milk latte in.'

Melanie waved her thanks, hoiking her bag further up her shoulder and cursing when she realised that there was an unexpected high-pitched whine coming from within. Looking through her bag at the same time as elbowing and hipping her way through the door, she discovered that her mostly adorable nephew Alfie, had left his *PAW Patrol* toy iPad in her bag. He was no doubt trying to be cute, thinking she might need it for work . . . but where the hell was the off button?

Finally managing to turn it off, she quickly shoved it back into the depths of her bag before entering the staff room, come meeting room. She grabbed a seat, sat down and dropped her bag to her side, before then rising slightly to sort out her skirt. She sat herself back down, straightened her back, and placed her hands gently on the table in front of her, all the time trying to take slow steady breaths. She hoped that she projected calm, confidence and perfect punctuality. But when she looked up she noticed that there was only Paige in front of her.

Her heart stuttered, her breath nearly came out in one go, and Melanie put it down to the fact that she was finally stationary after running around all day. And although her heart was often doing strange things around Paige it could all be easily explained. Just like at these meetings; that first one they'd been presenting their business idea and hoping they'd get the lease, and then the next one, being the new girl – yeah definitely nerves. And when they'd been awarded the lease and she'd gone to Barbarella to say hello, and her heart had gone all jittery then, she recalled she'd had an extra latte that day, so that was clearly down to too much caffeine.

'Hi.'

Oh so smooth. Open with a classic. Well done, Melanie.

A nod. A bloody nod, that was all she got? Oh, and now Paige was glaring at her. Yup, that seemed about right for the day.

Melanie looked at the clock on the wall: just another hour in her company and then she could go back to work, check on her bar, check on her business partner, check on her sister, make sure that they would be getting the prosecco order delivered. Presuming that all the wait staff were in, she could even be in her apartment by nine p.m., if she was lucky. Which at this point, she already knew she was not.

Looking up she noticed that she was still being glared at. What was Paige's problem?

But more to the point, where the hell was everyone else?

The glaring and the silence was too much, and as usual Melanie opened her mouth having no idea what was about to come out.

'So, Louisa couldn't make it today, so you've got me instead. Not, you've got me — I just meant the group . . . you know?'

Another nod from Paige, and a slightly toned down glare. Melanie swallowed and pushed her glasses further up her nose.

'We don't have to make small talk, you know? The rest of the group will be here soon,' Paige said.

Wow, rude much?

Melanie was surprised at how closely she'd come to saying that out loud. Instead, she used Paige's simple nod technique and crossed her legs before looking back down and grabbing her iPad out of her bag and immediately opening up her to-do list app.

She had a list on there she shared with her sister for childcare and diary planning, and another that she shared with her business partner, Louisa. Logging onto the coffee shop Wi-Fi she refreshed it to see if there was anything new on either.

'Here you go, Melanie.' Kazim put her drink on the table, and Melanie smiled up in response.

'Thanks Kazim, your make-up really is gorgeous today.'

'Thanks'—he turned to look at Paige—'it was one of Sophie's tutorials.'

Melanie watched Paige's reaction closely, believing that Kazim had meant Sophie Bowman, the very famous make-up artist and influencer, who also happened to be one of Paige's best friends, or at least that's what Sophie had told her, when Melanie had run into her at Paige's bar a few months ago.

And there it was.

Paige's smile. It was only there a second. A blink and you'd miss it type thing but it hit Melanie right in the gut.

'Enjoy your drink. I'll be back in a minute.' Kazim turned briefly back to Melanie before walking back out to the main coffee house area. She smiled at him as he walked away and then her gaze naturally fell back to Paige and she caught her eye and no not her eye, her glare. Again. Seriously?

Before she could say anything the chair of the Neighbourhood Business Alliance, Councillor Houghton came in and sat down.

'Sorry I'm late. Where is everyone?' he asked, settling himself into his seat. He wore what Melanie would class as a standard council suit. It was smart but there was nothing special about it, however Councillor Houghton was helpful to have on the board and helpful to their local businesses as he could sometimes share council insights on issues, planning permissions, that type of thing.

The only problem was that Councillor Houghton saw himself as the next Jeff Bezos, always pushing them for the next big thing, the next big investment, trying to fulfil his own ambition that his sixty-plus years had yet to burn out. To be fair though, he did also lend that energy to their community, and that was part of the reason why getting a lease around here was so hard. The Neighbourhood Business Alliance worked on the belief that a high tide floats all boats and they had clearly worked hard to cultivate a thriving community that felt more like a village with indies and organisations working hand in hand, while still being within a busy city.

Students working in a coffee house, were the same students that drank in their bars at night. The mums using the yoga studio were also more likely to use the smoothie stall. And those that had bottomless brunch in the morning could carry on drinking all day along their row of establishments in their Manchester community, before heading to Spinningfields or Deansgate to keep on drinking and dancing into the small hours.

The popularity of the community meant that when a site became available it was highly competitive and surprisingly the Neighbourhood Business Alliance had, well if not the final say, a very strong sway in deciding who got the lease. And now, after the most stressful few months of her life, here she was part of the illustrious Neighbourhood Business Alliance.

'We'll give 'em five minutes and then we'll crack on.' Councillor Houghton's voice was deep and with a proper thick Mancunian accent. He spoke with authority and although not so much now, Melanie had been intimidated by him at first. Then the door opened, and more people started making their way in. Melanie looked at her to-do lists, cursing when she saw that the breakfast club Alfie attended before school, had some necessary training that meant it would be closed next Monday.

She made a note to talk to her sister about that.

Melanie did all of this between nodding and smiling at the other arrivals, and studiously ignoring any further glares that Paige sent her way.

'Right then, I think we'll begin if you're all ready?' Councillor Houghton announced to the six people now sat around the table.

'I was hoping that more of you would be able to attend today but let's make do. Can I ask that you all get in touch with the rest of the group and explain what I'm about to share with you? I'll email out as well but word of mouth will be better for reasons I'm about to explain.'

Melanie came out of her lists, opened up her notes app and looked up at the Chair.

'I called this extraordinary meeting because I've been privy to some information. There are some serious investors currently in town. That's not uncommon, we know that, but they're looking at our community in particular. I think we need something different to really drive new people towards our little corner of the city and so I suggest all of us club together and get an artist that can do a huge mural or something that really demonstrates what we're about. I mean it's unlikely we can ask Banksy — right? None of you have any connections?' He paused, and Melanie realised he was serious. 'No? Worth a shot. But I think if we get an artist to come and get a feel for our little community, they'll be able to get a cracking mural done in no time, something that symbolises who we are. Drives the people to us. Shows the investors how things are done around here. What do you think?'

'Well, that was a lot to take in, Patrick,' Brian from the local deli said.

'How much are we talking?' Lydia from the seafood restaurant asked.

'Well, I don't have the figures yet, but I may be able to secure a grant.'

'What about if we get a local artist that wants to get involved, that way we can continue to support our local community?' Melanie asked, as she continued to type notes.

'Yes,' Councillor Houghton began with more than a touch of hesitancy, 'but we don't just want some teenage gobshite that thinks just because he can tag, he can create art.'

The faces around the group all looked up at Councillor Houghton's outburst.

'Sorry, sorry, we're having some trouble with graffiti and it's annoying a lot of voters. And so annoying me. But yes, I agree if we have someone local, that's talented and would like the opportunity, we could offer excellent exposure.'

'Exposure doesn't pay the bills though, we still need to pay them,' Paige added, sending her glare straight at Councillor Houghton, who appeared to handle it better than Melanie did.

'Well of course. Let's see if there's anyone that meets the criteria first though yeah?'

'How do we do that?' Paulo from the tattoo shop asked. 'I mean I might have some contacts, can call up some people maybe.'

'What about if we each put posters in our windows, oh and flyers and tell our customers about it, get the word spread within the local community, put it on our socials?' Melanie casually suggested.

'That's an excellent idea. If you could pull something together that would be great. I have a contact at a printer so just send me through your final design and I'll sort the rest, OK? Great, thank you, Melanie. I knew you'd make a great asset to our community. So, moving on, is there any other urgent business?'

Melanie sat stunned for all of a second, before opening her to-do list and creating a new list heading, and adding a bullet point that just read, "*design a flyer and poster*".

Did she have design experience? No, but she did know that Canva existed so that was a start. Did she have the time to do this? Also, no. Did she have someone that she could pass this off to? In a word, no. So, on the list it went, and Melanie would make the time, just like she always did.

Once she'd finished typing away she tuned back into the conversation; they were talking bins. The Neighbourhood Business Alliance always ended up talking about bins. Bins or parking.

She caught Paige's eye again, expecting to see a glare but all she saw was confusion.

Yeah, you and me both.

CHAPTER THREE

Paige

Paige left the coffee shop, her mood absolutely none the better. Listening to the usual complaints about the bins was as boring as it sounded, even if she did completely agree and every now and again spend a good fifteen minutes ranting to her cat Mr Higgins about them.

Walking into Barbarella, she saw Belle by the optics putting away some clean glasses, and India clearing some tables. There were a few other staff members scattered about, but it was quiet for now; it would pick up in an hour when the nine-to-fivers finished and needed a quick drink before going home or cracking on for a big night out. But seeing that she could excuse herself, Paige did exactly that and, with a wave, took herself straight through the bar, and up to her flat. It wouldn't be fair to impose her mood on her team.

But Connie would be here soon, and Paige wouldn't have to pretend with her that all was OK. Paige didn't want people to worry, so while friends knew she was off, they didn't know just how badly, and nor would they.

Grabbing the kettle and forcing the tap down with a little too much power, the water shot out and sprayed Paige's

T-shirt. She slammed the lid down and put the kettle on. Reaching for a mug it hit the counter with force. Paige winced, half expecting to have broken the thing. With a sigh she tried to sort herself out. This stropping about wasn't a good look. Instead, Paige began making kissy noises for Mr Higgins. He clearly knew she was in a mood though, as he was nowhere to be seen. Figures. Placing her brew on the coffee table, Paige turned on her TV and sourced the only thing that would boost her serotonin. After a minute, Disney Plus was loaded.

She stuck on her favourite, *Hercules*, and sank back into the cushions, waiting for her very first crush to appear on screen. She'd emptied her mug of tea before the appearance, but there was Megara.

Mr Higgins jumped up on the sofa. 'Oh, there you are. I thought you'd run off to find another family.' Mr Higgins responded by strutting up to her, turning around and sticking his bum in the air and his tail in her face. 'Yes, thanks for that.'

Eventually he settled on the sofa next to her and looked up at her.

'What?'

Mr Higgins said nothing, obviously, but continued to stare.

'I'm not feeding you yet.'

Still nothing.

She waited, sure that her cat, that she'd had since he was just a few weeks old, would look away. But he didn't and the look he gave her sliced through Paige like only a cat's look could.

'Fine. Yes, I am in a bad mood again. No, I still don't know what's going on. How do people put up with this shit?'

Mr Higgins dropped his head and with it, his rather forceful gaze and rested his head on her lap, indicating in her mind that she should keep talking.

Reaching out to slowly stroke down his spine, she quietly admitted her pain. 'I know I didn't know *everything*. I wasn't that good, but this is . . . Well, it's scary.' She continued the strokes as Mr Higgins purred his encouragement, whether to continue talking or stroking she wasn't sure but she carried on with both, knowing that Mr Higgins would never tell her secrets to anyone. Well, he hadn't to date. 'Hell maybe I never really *knew* anything before. Maybe it was all non-verbal cues, unconscious vibe pick-ups. But then why did it stop? Where did my mojo go?'

Her head fell back to the sofa, just as her apartment door knocked from the bar side.

'Like now, I should know who that is, or at least suspect.'

Mr Higgins looked up at her and then at the door and back again.

'Yes all right, I know and you know that it's Sophie. This one doesn't count.' Mr Higgins hopped off and went to his tower.

Paige walked over to the door. The bar staff simply didn't allow anyone other than her best friends to the door, so no psychic mojo had been needed. Mya although due back soon was still in Vegas, and Polly would have texted first.

'Oh no,' Sophie said as soon as she entered the flat. 'Are you OK? I'll put the kettle on, unless you want something stronger?' Sophie's tone was overly gentle.

'Stop worrying, I'm fine.'

'The glare on your face says otherwise. I'm texting Polly.'

'Why do you need Polly?'

'You're watching *Hercules*, and Mr Higgins is lording it up in his tower. That tells me you're feeling a little odd, needed comfort, and that you've talked to Mr Higgins so much he feels like a human and that his rightful place is residing in a tower.'

'What? When did you get so insightful?'

Sophie grinned and shrugged her shoulders. 'Well, Belle downstairs said you were in a definite funk when you passed through the bar, so that may have been a clue, but *Hercules* confirmed it. Though I would have been more concerned if you were watching *Tangled*.'

'Why?'

'Because of your Rapunzel obsession.' Sophie shucked off her coat and bag, putting them both on the kitchen table.

'I'm not obsessed with Rapunzel.'

Sophie grunted, and made a fresh brew while Paige settled herself back down on the sofa, watching Megara reluctantly fall for Hercules.

Sophie came round from the open-plan living space and sat down beside Paige. 'Enough,' she proceeded to say.

'What?'

'Enough with this. Lately you've either been moping around, or you've been pissed off and grumpy. Enough.'

'No I haven't, and don't pretend like you understand.'

'Yes, you have. Don't get me wrong, you're never one for all the warm and fuzzies but enough. You've temporarily lost something; it will come back to you, of course it will. Now stop being a dick in the meantime.'

'Is this tough love?' Paige asked.

'Yep. I'm trying to channel you. I'm thinking to myself what would Paige say if it was me.'

Paige couldn't but breathe out a little chuckle and give a little nod. Sophie was a hundred percent correct; Paige could be called upon to cut through the niceties and get to the point.

'So, wise Sophie, what do I do?'

'The same thing all of us do, of course — wing it and hope for the best. Make it up as you go along if you have to, or you could try and make a plan, but enough now.' Sophie lay her hand on Paige's arm.

Paige grunted. 'Have I really been that bad?'

'Yes,' Sophie said without any hesitation.

Paige thought it through. She'd been so sure she had been successfully keeping this from her friends so as not to worry them, but clearly not. She had been a little growly lately. And fine, yes, she had been rude to Melanie. She'd known it at the time too. Yes, Paige wasn't naturally one for the warm and fuzzies but she usually tried not to veer straight into bitch.

'I think I have some amends to make,' Paige said on a sigh.

'Let me guess, to Melanie?'

Paige deliberately kept her eyes on the screen while the muses onscreen summarised how Meg really felt. Even if she wasn't going to admit it to herself.

'You're like a school kid in a playground that doesn't know what to do with their feelings. You like her, so talk to her. Have you even had a proper conversation yet?'

It had been enough that she could acknowledge she'd been off earlier; she didn't need to go any further. 'Do you know someone that can help with poster and flyer design?' she asked.

'Yeah, and so do you,' Sophie said without questioning the sudden change in topic.

'Who?'

'Bailey's sister, Seb. Remember she did all my invites and seating charts?'

'Would she do a simple poster and flyer as a favour?' Paige asked, a plan forming.

'I'd say. Did you hear that her last work was for Lady Gaga? She's mega successful now, so yeah, she owes me. Let me send her a text.'

Sophie bent down towards her phone, tapping furiously. 'When do you need it by?'

'As soon as possible. If she's on then I can send her the brief. And we can print them locally. It's just the design. And do you know any local artists that could do a huge wall mural?'

'Erm no, I don't think so. I'll keep an ear out though. Why, what's going on?'

'The Business Alliance are looking for an artist to do a mural that best represents our corner of Manchester — something to do with city investors.'

'Uh-huh,' Sophie said with a nod as she continued typing on her phone.

'Anyway, Melanie suggested we advertise for an artist locally, and she got lumbered with the task of creating posters and flyers.'

Sophie paused and looked up at Paige. 'You know that helping like this is really nice.'

'Shut up, or I won't do it.'

Sophie grinned and looked back down at her phone. 'I really like her, by the way.'

'Who?'

'Melanie. When I came back from my honeymoon, you know, when you had all swanned off to Vegas? I met her then. She was really lovely. She even asked for a selfie.'

'Oh, she's a fan of yours, is she? Internationally world-renowned influencer? I'm surprised you still hang out with us plebs.'

'How else am I going to get the content that best resonates with my people?' Sophie raised an eyebrow before bursting out laughing. 'Having said that I've gone and got myself invited to a royal engagement celebration or something . . .'

'Seriously?'

'Yeah, just the evening-do part, but I can't make it — it's Barbarella's psychic night and I promised you I'd be here for that.'

'Soph!'

'What?'

'It's a psychic night in a bar in Manchester. They happen all the time. What the hell? You were invited to a royal event!'

Sophie laughed. 'Honestly, I'm not even really sure what it was but look without sounding bigheaded, I get invited to lots of things these days. But I need to remember who I am. It can be a weird space, and I've felt a little lost at times, but you, Marcus, Polly, Bailey, Mya and now of course Smithy, well you're my family. You keep me grounded and real and it reminds me that real life is more important than my pseudo influencer life. I'm not complaining. I love it, it's hard work, the perks are incredible. But I need you guys. So yes, I will always pick a psychic night in a bar, a girly booze up at Polly's, or hell, travelling around the world to support Mya on her quest for global domination, over some big influencer thing. It's what we do. And you don't have to say, because of the warm and fuzzies, but you would do the same in a heartbeat. You've been there for us every step of every day, no matter the drama, the event, the excitement. I have your back, Paige. We all do, whatever happens.'

Paige threw her arms around Sophie, unaware before that point how badly she'd needed to hear that. And just as quickly, Paige pulled away.

'Right then, well if we can get the flyers and posters sorted then that will go a long way to making me look less like a bitch.'

'Then you can tell Melanie you like her.'

'I do not. I barely even know her.'

'That's true, she could be a right cow. I mean I doubt it but maybe she puts brown sauce on her bacon butty? Maybe she sleeps with socks on? Maybe she hates Doc Marten's? She hates cats?'

'She might not be attracted to women,' Paige said before she could stop herself.

'Oh, she definitely is. It's on her Instagram bio,' Sophie said with a huge grin, before turning her phone towards Paige to show the bio in question. Paige studied it closely.

'I knew you liked her!'

'I don't know her,' Paige said again, growling as she pushed the phone back at Sophie as she got up and started putting down some food for Mr Higgins.

'Sure you don't,' Sophie said with a little chuckle as the door knocked with a rhythm that could only be one person. 'Polly's here, let's see what she thinks shall we?'

Sophie got up to let Polly in, and before any welcoming pleasantries were passed, Sophie cried, 'Polly, what do you think Paige's deal is with Melanie?'

'Oh, erm.' Polly looked over at Paige, who was already scowling in response.

'Come on. Don't worry she's not *really* bitey today, she just hugged me. Go on.'

'Well, I get the impression Paige would quite like to know Melanie a little better.'

'That's subtle,' Sophie said. 'But yes, that's what I think too. But with a tad more banging.'

CHAPTER FOUR

Melanie

Despite the Tesco dash yesterday they were still short on prosecco. So Melanie had asked some of her team to go out and find more. She had the supplier on the phone now, an AirPod in one ear, her phone on her shoulder under the bra strap so that she could tend the bar at the same time as doing everything else.

Thankfully, her colleagues appeared with six boxes of prosecco they'd sourced — as long as they got a delivery tomorrow that should get them through.

'Thanks everyone, I really appreciate it. Go put it in the back and then I need you out front as quick as you can. Thanks again.'

As they disappeared, the most unexpected person appeared at the entrance — and was now heading in her direction.

'You know I've never been in here before. It's very . . . erm . . . shiny. And flowery.'

Melanie mentally rolled her eyes, refusing to give Paige the visual satisfaction. Paige might have dropped the grumpy glare, but Melanie was professional through and through, and needed to be. A lot rested on the success of this venture.

'What can I get you? Or are you here to admire the aesthetic?' Shit, she hadn't actually meant to say that. Why did Paige have this effect on her, and why was her stomach all tingly, and nervous?

'Ms Curzon, are you still there?' The voice in her ear disturbed her thoughts.

'Yes, yes! I'm here. Is it all sorted?'

Melanie saw a look of confusion pass over Paige's face, so she pointed to her AirPod, and mouthed sorry. Not that Paige deserved it necessarily, but she hated being rude.

'Can you confirm your order again, please?'

Melanie pressed her lips together and took a breath, preparing to repeat herself for the fourth time. 'Tomorrow, I need twenty boxes of prosecco, and then my regular twice weekly order that you deliver Tuesday and Friday. Yesterday's of course never turned up. It's a standard repeating order so I don't understand where the issue is?'

'Yes, it would seem that the standard ordered was cancelled. So, you want that rolling delivery back on, and you want it on Tuesdays and Friday's, yes?'

'I don't understand how it was cancelled, but yes please. The problem I have right now though is that I didn't get yesterday's. I need it.'

'Well we can get ten boxes to you tomorrow and have the standard delivery sorted out, starting from next Tuesday. I'm sorry for the inconvenience but that's the best I can do.'

'Fine. Fine. Thank you for sorting it out.'

'No problem. Thanks for your call.'

'Thanks, bye.' Melanie scooped her phone from its bra holster and ended the call.

'Sorry I just need a minute — is that OK?' Melanie asked. Paige nodded.

Somehow Melanie could tell that this nod was slightly less aggressive than the others, leading Melanie to wonder if Paige had a nod for all occasions. But she didn't have time to ponder that.

She went to the trusted to-do app and calculated that they would still be three boxes short to get them to the end of Saturday. Not a problem if the delivery came early on Saturday, but as they had bottomless brunch on offer, and bookings already taken, it wasn't a risk she could afford to take. She opened up her list and added a note that they needed to secure three more boxes of prosecco ASAP. Hopefully her business partner, Louisa would pick up on that.

She quickly switched over to her family list and saw she was looking after Alfie that night. Of course, she was. Not that he wasn't a joy to look after, and most likely would already be in bed, but, no actually it was OK because she could use that time to do some more admin for the bar — oh wait no she'd have to spend the time designing that damn flyer.

Temporarily halting her brain from going any more haywire, she added a quick note and a reminder to come back to it again later, before turning back to Paige. 'Right, sorry about that. What can I do for you?'

'You having problems?' Paige asked.

Melanie couldn't tell from her tone what Paige was getting at and Melanie's heckles rose, a wave of defensiveness taking over. It was a very physical feeling, as were most of her feelings around Paige. She felt her spine straighten, her resolve strengthen.

'Nothing that I can't handle,' she said with a genuine smile, because she would sort it; that's what she did now.

Paige nodded. 'No doubt.'

Another nod. What did that mean? Was she being sarcastic? Sincere? What game was she playing? The Paige in front of her now was not the same one that had sat in front of her in yesterday's meeting.

Paige looked around. 'I know you're busy, but do you have five minutes?'

Melanie studied her again, trying to figure out what she wanted. Her blonde hair long on the top but undercut underneath. Her piercings that went all around her ear, and the small stud just under her full bottom lip. Her forest green eyes bright against the paleness of her skin were giving nothing away, as they held her own, and Melanie felt her heartbeat increase. Really heart? You're so easily swayed by a pretty face. Melanie shook her head, her brain kicking in. She didn't know Paige. She could be a complete weirdo, and if the way her moods fluctuated so wildly was any indication, then Melanie knew she needed to be wary. But then she saw something in Paige's face. Could it be she looked disappointed? Was she expecting Melanie to refuse?

'Look, don't worry. It's no problem. I'll see you later.'

Melanie realised that Paige had misinterpreted her head shake. 'No, it's fine. Stop. Just hang on.' Melanie glanced around at the staff. 'Ari, can you cover the bar, please?'

Ducking around the pillar that separated the bar from the floorspace, Melanie came around and gestured to Paige that she follow. Taking them to a quieter corner, Melanie sat down at the table, rising once to adjust her skirt before retaking her seat. Pushing her glasses up her nose she waited as Paige sat. The silence started to stretch out.

'So, Paige what do you need?'

Melanie watched as Paige's shoulders tightened, and she played with her hair, running her hand through the strands. Then she grunted and grabbed her phone from her back pocket. Opening something up she placed it on the table and moved the colourful bespoke Lulu drinking glasses out of the way before pushing the phone towards Melanie.

Whatever Melanie might have guessed was on there, it wasn't what she saw.

'Did you make this?' she asked.

'No but I have a friend who's a designer. I thought . . . Well, I thought . . . It might . . .' Melanie waited as Paige's words got quieter, sharper and grumpier. 'Help. I thought it might help. She's done them in several sizes for different posters, flyers, and socials. She'd done something similar for someone else, which is why she was able to get them done so fast.'

Melanie picked up the phone and zoomed in on the image. It was a perfect flyer to get the attention of a local artist. Grungy and yet arty, sure to attract the attention they needed, and more to the point, a million times better than anything she could ever have come up with. 'Some of the details, such as contact details and deadlines might need changing. Seb is more than happy to make any changes we need. And she'll do them quickly. She's really good.'

Melanie nodded in agreement. This really was fast, but then, Melanie supposed that a *girlfriend* might well turn something around just like that. There was little doubt in Melanie's mind that Paige was a lesbian . . . So, her girlfriend then, presumably, had done this incredible work for Paige as a favour, as couples were supposed to do, to help each other out and look out for one another. With a purposeful breath, Melanie refocused on the image. And if Melanie's spirits rose slightly at the prospect of crossing this off her to-do list they sunk with the girlfriend realisation, and really, they had no right doing that.

'If you give me your number or your email address, I'll send them over to you and then you can send them over to Councillor Houghton. Like I said, I guessed on the deadline and the contact details — I've just used the Business Alliance's email — so if that needs changing just let me know.'

Melanie handed the phone back over to Paige and recited her number. It didn't take long for the images to come across.

'Thank you. You didn't have to do this . . .' Melanie paused for a moment and pushed her glasses back up her nose. 'Why did you?'

Paige opened her mouth to say something, but instead she nodded once, and stood up. 'Don't worry about it. See you later.'

And before Melanie could even utter a thanks, Paige was gone.

Melanie looked down at her phone, studying the images for the poster again. They really were good. Melanie's mind drifted off a little as she conjured up what Paige's girlfriend might look like. She wasn't really getting far with that, so instead she wondered what Paige might be like as a girlfriend. She didn't get far with that one either, because as gorgeous as Paige was, all Melanie had seen so far, was a mercurial attitude, a myriad of head nods and sullen silence, and that was not attractive at all.

She glanced down at her phone again and back to her messages.

Her message from Paige.

She had Paige's number.

Her brain knew that this was something or nothing, that it was helpful to have a neighbour's number on your phone, and she could have gotten it through the Business Alliance contacts info if she needed it, but Paige had given Melanie her number. Was it odd to be slightly excited that she had Paige's number?

Her brain jumped in with a solid 'yes'.

For all her strange misplaced giddiness what difference would it make? Why should she even care? Paige was only going to give her whiplash if she contacted her again. But she saved the number anyway, as peers and neighbours it would no doubt come in useful. Best to keep it civil. She opened up her emails and quickly sent the images to Councillor Houghton, and with none too small a flourish she opened up her to-do list and virtually crossed it out with a strange mix of satisfaction and sadness.

Right, back to prosecco.

* * *

'Found these outside,' Louisa said, three hours later, with more than a little strain.

Louisa was walking in ready to hand over. Her best friend and business partner looked all business apart from a box under each arm which Melanie immediately ran to help her with. Louisa predominantly worked from four to close, while Melanie tended to oversee the set up, brunch through lunch to four. In an ideal world at least that's how they would like to work it. But life was never ideal and the pair of them spent every spare minute of the day at Lulu if they could. It was important to both of them that they made it a success. It was still early days but it was mostly steady, and they had the Instagram walls to thank for that. The plan was that the Instagram niche would bring in the customers and their amazing food and drink would ensure they returned.

The main entryway was bright pink and eye-catching with a neon sign on the wall. But that theme continued throughout and every bit of space had been utilised for influencers, and wannabe influencers. There were bright silver angel wings spread across the wall at the back, several neon signs hidden amongst foliage on another wall. The best part was that each wall was temporary and could be updated as per the latest trends. The walls of course were only accessible to paying customers. It was genius really, at least for now until they'd established themselves more firmly, it meant a steady stream of traffic. But that only worked when they had drinks to offer, and while Melanie could talk most people into an Aperol based drink, the prosecco really was essential.

Which is why Melanie's face lit up when she saw Louisa with another two boxes.

'There's two more, I'll just go grab them,' Louisa said before disappearing out the back again.

Melanie searched around the boxes for some sort of invoice, delivery note or something. But there was none to be found, and despite being around prosecco as often as she was, she didn't yet believe in a magical prosecco fairy.

Louisa slowly walked back in with another two boxes and put them on the side. Melanie hunted around again. Still no paperwork.

'Where did these come from anyway?' Melanie asked.

'There was someone at the back with a trolley load, they just explained that they were for us, and before I could ask any more questions they'd gone.'

'But who would just magic us up some prosecco? Surely, they need paying? Maybe our suppliers just had some extra and felt bad for us?' Melanie wondered aloud.

'Ah, well in that case it will turn up on the next invoice. So how did the Neighbourhood Watch meeting go yesterday?'

'Neighbourhood Business Alliance and, you're going to the next one. I somehow managed to get roped into designing a flyer.'

Louisa rolled her eyes. 'You'll never know peace.'

Melanie grinned at the accuracy. 'Well, now that I don't have to worry about prosecco, I'll leave you to it. Dan is just prepping the evening bar snacks in the kitchen, last I checked it was all in hand. All your wait staff are present and working well. By the way, Cleo is all signed up and ready to start next week. I think this might be our first night without any pr—'

'Don't dare finish that sentence you jinxy cow! Right get gone — you got Alfie tonight?'

Melanie nodded as she hurried out from behind the bar and through the back, shouting as she went, 'Yeah I need to head over there now.'

'What about food? Will you eat?' Louisa asked.

'I'll grab something at my sister's, don't worry.'

'Make sure you do.'

Melanie reappeared, her jacket slung over her laptop bag and purse, her phone in her hand once again retrieved from her bra strap.

'Why are you taking your laptop?' Louisa asked.

'I need to work on some of the admin and marketing.'

'What you need to do is unpack.' Melanie scowled and so Louisa carried on. 'I did the budget balancing earlier, by the way, and a few other outstanding bits and pieces like the insurance check up and—'

'Did you update the—?'

'Yes, I updated your bloody to-do list. Go.'

'OK that's great. At some point I need to sync that up to our forecast . . .'

Louisa sighed but said nothing. She knew, just as Melanie did, that there were lots of things that needed doing. Perhaps when they were more settled it would get a little easier. Melanie quickly opened up her phone, pressing her emails by mistake as she did. She stood still as she read the message. She glanced over most of it, until she got to the bottom.

"Thank you for being so speedy with this. It really is appreciated. And clearly with that sort of ability and work ethic you'll be the best person to lead on this project. I'll send you over the details re budget and scope."

What the . . . ?

Her legs wobbled as if the email carried actual weight.

So now she was organising the whole art project was she? What was the saying? If you want something doing, give it to a busy woman. Melanie walked round the back to the tiny private car park, jumped in her car, threw everything on the passenger seat, before setting off.

'I can't fit it in, I'll have to say no. But then we're new to the Alliance and I probably need to show my worth.' She straightened her glasses quickly before putting both hands back on the steering wheel and continuing to talk to herself. 'But this could be a huge project — how would I even . . . ?' Stopping at the lights she pulled at the bobble in her hair. 'No, it's not possible . . . but then I would have more influence. Maybe I could then sway the group as to where the mural actually goes. No no no. I don't have time to think about this now. Focus, Melanie.'

With that Melanie gently shook out her hair, straightened her glasses again, and pretended she hadn't even seen the email from Councillor Houghton and made her way to her sister's house.

CHAPTER FIVE

Melanie

'Oh my God, I can't believe I haven't been in your bar before. This is influencers' heaven. Oh hi.' Her new guest quickly stopped talking, probably at Melanie's shocked expression. Well, she really hadn't been expecting Sophie Bowman, influencer extraordinaire, to walk into her bar. It wasn't that they hadn't met before, in fact Melanie could still cringe over their first meeting. She'd gone to Barbarella to re-introduce herself to Paige, thinking that it was the right, polite thing to do. Paige wasn't there and instead Melanie had fangirled herself into a corner. Torn between immediately wanting to hug Sophie, having watched enough of her videos and her daily socials to believe that they were already best friends, and complete and utter dumbfounded shock.

With a shake of her head she realised she wasn't faring much better this time around either. Luckily some of the Friday lunch crowd were clearly fans, and so, Sophie was in the middle of taking selfies and smiling politely, making perfect small talk. Admiring eyeliner on one person, giving tips to another. Until finally, Sophie was released and Melanie had composed herself into a relatively normal human being.

'Hi!' Melanie was stunned at the sound of her own voice, having never heard it screech in welcome quite like that before. She straightened her already straight glasses and did a little cough before trying again, 'Hi.'

Sophie grinned, and Melanie noticed that her grin was just a little wider than the one she had shared with her fans.

'Hi. How's it going?' Sophie asked as she perched on the barstool. The bar wasn't quite set up for lots of people around it like Paige's was. It was smaller with limited seats, the focus being the tables where people could eat brunch, lunch, and then nibble on high-end bar snacks for the rest of the night, while drinking copious amounts of prosecco, and of course taking lots of selfies. But still Sophie perched and Melanie didn't really know what to do, or more specifically, she didn't know what to say.

The break in conversation was just getting to the point where Melanie was about to fill it with whatever unfiltered thing was first to come out of her mouth before Sophie carried on.

'I'm really sorry we didn't get chance to talk properly when you came over to Barbarella that time, and I'm even more sorry that I haven't been in here sooner, because this place is unreal. I mean, I've seen some of it on the ol' 'gram but, it's really clever. I feel inspired.'

'Thanks. I mean I can't take all the credit. Louisa, my business partner — we worked on it together.'

'Oh,' Sophie said, 'just business partner or . . . ?'

Melanie answered before she even really processed the personal nature of the question. 'Just business partner and you know, friends. Nothing more. Nothing more with anyone actually. There isn't time. I mean before you got with Marcus, I'm sure you were the same, right? Just so busy spinning so many plates.' Melanie quickly shut up when she realised she'd compared herself to mega influencer Sophie Bowman.

Sophie smiled warmly, like Melanie had seen her do hundreds of times before. 'I get it. But, I'm here with a purpose, well two now actually. No, wait, three. Maybe even four.'

'Well er, how can I help?' Melanie asked wiping down the bar as she did so, but also wondering if she would need her phone to make notes.

'The first thing is that I think you should come over to Barbarella tonight, if you can? I imagine it's pretty hard when you run a bar?'

'Louisa does the lates,' Melanie said to explain the situation.

'Great, so we'll see you later then, yeah? Brill.' Sophie had carried on and Melanie realised that in trying to explain the situation she had inadvertently agreed to socialise. She grabbed her phone, and while Sophie was talking, made sure she wasn't on Alfie duty. A very quick glance showed her she was. She quickly put her phone down not wanting to be rude as Sophie continued talking.

'Second, I would love, love, love it, if I could come in one time, maybe early morning, and take some pictures in front of your influencer walls? Maybe I could be really cheeky and set up a little table and use one of your walls as the back-drop while I do my make-up? Better still, I could give you a makeover, what do you think?' The sheer joy radiating from Sophie's face was what Melanie imagined being blessed by an angel would feel like.

Melanie was lost for words but that was OK, Sophie carried on. 'And not that I think you need it at all because I'm sure your business is booming but of course I'd tag you and your bar into it all. In fact, you could tell my viewers all about yourself and the bar while we're at it.'

Melanie's jaw dropped. That would be amazing. That would be incredible. That would be the boon that most small businesses could only dream of. It was so generous. It was a little overwhelming. What would that mean? Would they be too busy? No, they'd make it work. They'd be foolish not to. Right?

'Can I take your silence to mean yes, or have I offended you? I'm so sorry. I wasn't trying to imply that you need a makeover, in fact' — Sophie put her hands on the bar and leaned forward — 'your make-up is gorgeous. You'll have to tell me what lipstick that is.'

Sophie sat herself back down on the barstool.

Melanie licked her lips and finally found her voice. 'Oh my God, I'm such a huge fan, and you want to give me a make-over, and do it in my bar, and you want to know my lipstick!'

Sophie was still grinning. 'It'll be fun.'

Melanie quickly fanned her face. Best. Day. Ever.

'Do you want to have a think about when we could do it? If you message me on Insta — no, wait, don't do that. I might miss it, or my PA might bin it. Erm . . . Tell you what, here's my personal mobile. Please do not give that to anyone. Text me your availability and we'll get it booked in OK?'

Melanie took the card that Sophie had scribbled on. 'Wow, thank you and yeah of course.'

'The other reason I'm here is that I think your goals are great and I think everyone should have them. Unfortunately for me, for a little while I let my career ambition rule my life until there was no life to speak of, just work, work and more work. So unsolicited advice here, just try and hold on to those things you enjoy and the people you love.'

Melanie immediately thought of her sister Emily, her nephew Alfie and Louisa and knew that she would always have them, and she didn't have time to wish for anything more.

'Which brings me onto the final reason I'm here . . .' Sophie paused and Melanie watched as Sophie spun her engagement ring around on her finger. 'I erm . . . well, it's about Paige.'

'What about Paige? Is she OK?' Melanie asked.

'Yeah, well she's grumpy but that's, well that's what I wanted to say. She's lost something important to her, and it's making her a bit tetchy. Well, tetchier, she's always a bit tetchy.' Sophie shook her head. 'No, wait' — she let out a laugh that sounded a little forced — 'I didn't mean that. She's not always tetchy. In fact, most of the time she's lovely.'

Melanie didn't mean to, but she could feel her eyebrows raise at that one; she doubted even Paige's own mother would use the word lovely.

'Yeah no, that's not quite right either. God, I'm making this worse. Look, Paige is good, OK? That's all you need to know. She's a good person, one of the best. I've known her for years and she's one of the kindest, most selfless people I know. She's also a huge supporter, of well, everyone. She's good. She's great. She's one of the best. I've already said that. Sorry. It's just that she can sometimes come across short. Or a little grumpy but that's not really her.'

'I'm sure her partner would agree with you but are you trying to sell her, or — I mean, what does it matter what I think about Paige?' Melanie was genuinely confused by Sophie's obvious nerves. To be fair, in Melanie's mind, Paige took up a lot of head space, more than she should. Rightly or wrongly, she was there for at least a small part of every day. Like when she opened up the bar and she could see Barbarella down the road. And maybe occasionally when she looked at her phone and realised that at any point she could just text her and that filled her both with giddy butterflies and weighty gut daggers. But that was in her own head, so back to the original question, why would anyone else care what she thought about Paige?

'Oh no, she doesn't have a girlfriend at the moment. And well it doesn't, I guess. I just . . .' Sophie paused as her eyes ran over the room. It looked to Melanie like Sophie was searching the room for the right words. There was a neon sign in the fake foliage that said "freedom", but as Sophie turned back round, that clearly wasn't it.

Sophie sighed. 'Forget I came here.'

Melanie's disappointment was immediate.

'No, I don't mean forget the whole thing. I mean forget about the Paige part. We're still good for the rest, right?'

Melanie slowly nodded.

'Great, so text me, yeah? Don't forget.' Sophie stood up and grabbed her bag and turned towards the door. 'And we'll see you tonight, right? Anytime from eight will be fab. See you later.'

And before Melanie could even protest, Sophie had run out the door.

Melanie opened her phone. She could always ask her mum to watch Alfie for her. If Melanie asked rather than her sister then it might be more likely. Or she could just not go. It's not like she had the spare time. If she was looking after Alfie or more specifically being in the same house while he slept, then she could get more work done. Going to a bar to just drink and hang out, when was the last time she had done that? Could she do that? Did she want to do that? She really didn't have the time. But the temptation was so great and it really had been so long.

Walking through the bar round the back, through the coats and bags, and then the boxes of neatly piled up prosecco, she finally made it into the tiny cramped storage room that doubled as the office as her mobile continued to ring. Maybe she wouldn't pick up.

'Hello Melanie, you all right?'

'Hi Mum, I'm good. But listen, I need a favour.'

Her mum's tone immediately dropped. 'What is it?'

'Can you watch Alfie tonight?'

Her mum groaned. But Melanie didn't fall for it. She knew the groan was aimed at her sister rather than at her only grandson.

'Is this you asking or your sister?'

'It's for me actually. I've been invited out for drinks and—'

'Yes. No more words needed. I'll be at your sister's for seven so I can put the only decent man in my life to bed with a bedtime story.'

'OK great. Thanks, Mum.' Melanie was a little perturbed with the speed that her mum had agreed when she knew Melanie was going out but decided not to look a gift horse in the mouth.

'See you later, darling.'

'Bye Mum, love you.'

'You too.' So, it looked like Melanie was going out tonight, with a bunch of people she didn't know. But it was only down the road from work and twenty minutes in a cab from her flat.

Well, she knew Sophie, even if that was mostly her online persona. But it didn't seem that different from her real-life persona. Oh God, Melanie really hoped it wasn't. She knew Paige of course, although which Paige she would get tonight was anyone's guess, and she probably wouldn't get more than a nod anyway. Maybe she would get a glimpse of the Paige that Sophie saw. Hopefully it wouldn't be Business Alliance grumpy nod Paige. Not to be confused with the I've called in a favour to help you out grumpy nod Paige.

Either way, Melanie was already nervous. Besides, this was how people made friends right? They went out and met up with people?

Only to lose them again when they pick sides. She couldn't stop the thought that flashed through her brain, leaving behind its streak of pain. Melanie shook her head, and began gathering up drinking glasses, wiping down surfaces, anything to keep her mind from progressing that train of thought. But Melanie suspected that was why her mum had been so quick to step up for babysitting duties; no doubt hoping that Melanie was starting to heal, starting to live again.

CHAPTER SIX

Paige

'Book!' Paige looked up at the same time as the soothing rumble of her gran's voice broke through the bar. 'There you are, kid. Come here then.'

Paige was immediately jogging out from behind the bar. She wrapped her gran into her arms, realising only in the moment, just how much she had missed her.

'You're in a bit of a mess, my love, aren't you?' Connie said, pulling back to study Paige more closely.

Paige rolled her eyes but didn't comment further. Her throat was actually a little tight, the relief at having her gran with her, making her unprecedentedly emotional.

'Right, come on, lead the way,' Connie said as they fought over who was going to carry her suitcase. In no time they were sat at the kitchen table in Paige's apartment, cups of tea in hand.

'You're going to need to get some of that oat milk in, Book,' Connie said before taking a sip.

'Sorry Gran, didn't realise you'd changed your milk?'

'Not for me, love.'

Paige chose not to ask. If her own mojo was working she would know what Connie meant.

'Come on, you've barely said a word. How bad is it?'

Instead of speaking, Paige moved her palm over the table for Connie's close inspection.

'So, there's nothing, no intuition, no guesses?'

Paige shook her head. It still hurt to admit. But she had to ask the question bothering her the most. 'Is it for good?'

Connie put down her cup and picked up the offered hand. 'Let's have a look then.'

Paige's jaw was clenched, her shoulders nearly immobile as Connie moved her hand around looking closer at different parts. Paige could feel all the various rings her gran wore as they pressed against her. She'd always been the same ever since she could remember, always covered in silver and gold, precious gems, and wearing bright colours.

'You help and very rarely ask for anything in return. Maybe letting people a little closer wouldn't be all that terrible.' Paige rolled her eyes, but Connie continued. 'Helping is good, but you must make sure it's aimed in the right direction. Book, this is important. You find fulfilment in helping others, it's your love language. But make sure you aim it at the right place.'

'Gran.' Paige didn't need the full reading, she needed the answer to that one question. Then they were going to move on and try to forget all about it.

'She's trying to get in touch again, isn't she?' Connie asked.

'It doesn't matter,' Paige said, through a very tight jaw.

Connie sighed, and paused, no longer looking at Paige's hand, even though she held it tightly. Instead, she studied her face and it was too much for Paige. She quickly let go and jumped up. 'I need to get a shower. The girls are all coming to the bar tonight. They'd love to see you if you can join us.'

'Book,' Connie said. 'Paige,' she said more softly. 'Your mum is still going to keep contacting you until you talk to her, you're long overdue closure.' Paige still said nothing as Connie got up and approached.

'I think it's temporary. I believe you'll be back to your fully functioning self again soon.'

Paige stilled but didn't turn. 'Do you *know* or do you believe?'

'Love, we both know that sometimes they're the same thing.'

Paige went to walk away, but at the last second, she turned and reached for Connie, finding her arms wide open.

'Two hugs in one hour, I'm honoured.'

Paige squeezed her tightly, taking in the scent of Chanel No 5 and then let go. 'Yeah, that's your lot, old woman.'

'Right, well I need a shower and to find some glad rags then, don't I?'

'Thanks for coming, Gran.'

'Always Book.'

* * *

Paige was making her way over to her friends sat as they were, in their usual spot but she couldn't stop her eyes from canvassing the scene. As much as Paige loved that they all hung out in her bar, it wasn't exactly relaxing. Connie would refer to it as a busman's holiday. She couldn't hang out the same when she was making sure all the staff were around. Checking to see what the wait time at the bar was, seeing dirty glasses on the tables. But she would try and make the most of it, because she was grateful that her friends were with her. It had been ages since they last hung out together, and even now they were still missing Mya and Smithy. Paige tried not to sigh at that, but it was only just held in. The fact they hadn't been able to hang out was symptomatic of them all going through major life changes.

Then as she was scanning the bar, she saw Connie emerge in skinny jeans and killer heels, a turquoise shirt, her silver hair swept up off her face with a bright pink scarf, and her mood immediately started to lift as she watched Connie make her entrance.

'Darlings!' Connie called out.

'Here she is,' Paige muttered, watching as her friends one by one jumped up and hugged her gran as she kissed cheeks, patted backs, passed compliments. Then they were all settled and seated and Bailey and Marcus were properly introduced.

Paige was not at all surprised to see how quickly Connie had become one of the gang. She had always been charming, hence the husbands, but she also had the ability to make you feel like she was rooting for you. It had been nearly four years since Connie had been in Manchester. She'd been the guest of honour when Paige opened the bar, being that it was her living will that enabled it to happen, and all of her friends had immediately fallen under Connie's spell, and by the looks of things that hadn't been forgotten.

'Oh Polly, you did good there, girl,' Connie said, and while the words were aimed at Polly, Paige couldn't help but notice Connie looking at Bailey like he'd come to save her from a fire, and if she wasn't mistaken, she thought she saw Bailey blush. That was new. Clearly a first time for everything.

'Thanks, Connie,' Polly said, a slight look of concern thrown to Paige. Paige grinned, knowing she couldn't and would never control her gran. Unable to stop herself, Paige checked out her bar once again. Belle was serving drinks along with India who was showing their new starter the ropes. A number of staff were collecting empties, and clearing down tables, and it was the usual sort of Friday night busy. Paige tried to refocus on what was important. Her friends and her family sat around her. They were tucked away in the far corner of the bar, the overhead light pendants shining down on the table, the fairy lights scattered around the wall behind them. Sophie sat next to her, Marcus on the other side. Beside him was Bailey, and obviously he sat next to Polly. Then there was Connie and finally back to Paige again. Paige tried to soak up the happiness of the situation. Mya and Smithy were due to fly back soon too. Then hopefully Paige would feel it. That sense of contentment.

'Sophie, I must say you are doing so well. I was showing Richard, the Captain on the cruise liner, all your social media. He wasn't as clued up as me so I made sure to subscribe him to everything of yours when he wasn't looking. That's at least a dozen subscribers I've gotten you using that technique, you know, and they won't know how to unsubscribe either so that's a dedicated following for you.'

'Thanks, Connie,' Sophie said.

'I was thinking by way of payment for my input into your business you should maybe see that some make-up products make it my way.'

'Connie, I didn't realise you were on commission. I'll send some stuff around tomorrow, or the day after. Anything in particular?'

Connie delicately shrugged.

'Why don't you come round and I'll do you a makeover?'

'Oh that would be lovely. I really think I could be a YouTube star – shall we say tomorrow?'

Paige grinned. Polly nearly spat out her drink. Sophie nodded with complete sincerity. 'I really think you could. It's been a while since I've done make-up on such . . .' Sophie paused for the right word, the pause a little too long. 'Such a fabulous canvas.' Paige was impressed; that was an incredible save. 'I'd love to give you a makeover. Tomorrow should be fine.'

'That would be great love, thank you. It's a shame Mya isn't here but she was telling me that she had to kick ass in a big meeting with The Suits today to go over . . .' Connie paused. 'What?'

Paige was wide-eyed as she looked at her gran. 'When do you speak with Mya?'

'Oh, we catch up all the time, usually over WhatsApp.'

Paige gave it some thought. They were two peas in a pod personality wise, so she guessed it made sense. She also suspected Mya was acting as Connie's spy, no doubt reporting back on how Paige was.

'Anyway, yes I think a makeover would be just the thing, thanks Sophie.' Connie sipped her drink, and Paige got the distinct impression, gift or no gift, that that was what Connie had wanted all along.

'Erm hi.' The awkward hello came from behind Paige and she swung around so fast at the sound, knowing immediately who the voice belonged to, that she nearly pulled her neck. Why was she here?

Paige was stunned, but Sophie must have shot out of her chair because she was over and on Melanie with a huge hug before Paige had even taken a breath. Paige felt her spine strain and yet she was unable to move from the twisted position around the chair as she watched Sophie wrap her arms around Melanie, and Melanie one-arm hug her in return, but with one of the biggest smiles Paige had ever seen. Not just on Melanie but on anyone. For a second, Paige felt something tug in her chest. It wasn't quite jealousy, not quite resentment. But Melanie had never smiled like that for Paige. The closest she had gotten was when she gave her the designs Seb had knocked up, and even that hadn't been her idea. Then again, Paige hadn't exactly been charming. Hell she'd barely managed nice. Paige needed to sort herself out. What had she ever really done to deserve a Melanie Megawatt Smile? The strange feeling in her chest grew bigger until everything else in there felt too tight and restricted.

'Everyone,' Sophie announced after letting go of Melanie, 'this is Melanie.' And there was something in the way she announced her name, or maybe the eyebrow raise that closely followed it, that made everyone around the table go, 'Ohhhh' in a synchronised way that felt like they had all practiced. Paige scowled at them.

'Here, sit down, I'll just grab another chair,' Sophie said sweetly. Melanie slowly sat down next to Paige and by this point Paige had to spin back around again on her chair. Slowly she repositioned her spine to match up with her legs. But then she realised just how closely she was sat next to Melanie. Their legs were inches apart and Paige would have sworn that even through her ripped denim she could feel the heat of Melanie's skin. Seats were pushed back, shuffled and rearranged until Sophie had positioned herself between Melanie and Marcus. Connie elbowed her in the ribs, and as Paige gasped and turned, Connie winked. Flashing a quick grimace in the universal non-verbal code for shut up, Paige relaxed her face before turning once more, and quickly noticed that it was oddly quiet, and Sophie was giving her a strange look.

'Oh erm, right,' Paige started not quite sure why she was the one introducing Melanie when it was clear Sophie had been the one to invite her. 'So, you know Sophie, and presumably you know Marcus too then?'

'Not in real life,' Melanie responded with an instant blush.

Marcus smiled and leaned forward. 'Lovely to meet you in real life then.' Again, Paige studied Melanie's reaction as she smiled back and returned the sentiment.

'Then we have Polly and Bailey.'

'I'm really going to embarrass myself here, but I saw you guys on Sophie's socials on her wedding day, and immediately followed you, Polly, so I feel like I know both of you too. Congrats on the song writing, by the way, I take it it's going well?'

'Thank you so much, Melanie, you're so sweet. And yes, I suppose you could say that.' Polly smiled, and Bailey nodded.

'It's going so well that she's officially not allowed to say.' Bailey winked at everyone as he threw an arm around Polly's shoulders and kissed her hair.

'I might have signed over one of my songs to someone. It's no big deal, it might not even happen, and I don't want to jinx it so let's just leave it at that?' Polly said before her face disappeared into Bailey's biceps.

Sophie quickly ran round and hugged Polly, before Connie continued, 'And I'm Connie, Bailey's second wife, although he doesn't know that yet, also known as Paige's gran. Nomad of the sky and seas, soon to be internet superstar, and for the next few weeks flatmate of Paige's.'

Sophie and Marcus laughed, Polly tried, and Bailey quickly drank as Connie leaned over Paige and grabbed a hold of Melanie's hand. Paige knew what was coming; she also knew she couldn't stop it. But as Connie not so gently pulled Melanie's hand closer still, turning it so that she could closely study her palm, Melanie really had no choice but to rest her other hand on Paige's thigh or else be toppled off her seat altogether as she was pulled closer over Paige towards Connie.

'Sorry,' Melanie muttered. Paige grunted. Words momentarily escaped her, as all her attention turned to the warm hand burning her thigh. Melanie was still in her work attire of pencil skirt and shirt, and in order to avoid looking at Melanie's legs, Paige instead studied the wall across the other side of the room. Taking a breath, she tried to steady herself, but instead all she could smell was the shampoo that Melanie must use in her hair, which was still scraped back, and Paige still didn't know what it was like when down and for some reason was desperate to know. Was that mango she could smell? Whatever it was, it was delicious, and making her mouth water. She took in a deep breath. Trying to steady her heart, trying to get herself grounded, and not at all to get another hit of her scent. That would be weird. Instead, Connie's voice cut through her thoughts.

'Yes, yes, you see here this line here, tells me you are very successful. Very dedicated. I said the same to you, Sophie, remember?' Connie didn't wait for a response. 'Hmm interesting you see here, you like being busy.' Again, Connie didn't need the confirmation. 'But there's some confusion there, maybe it's not that you like being busy as such. Hmmm. Keep an eye on that. Your love line is interesting too. You've had a hard time before — I have something similar on mine.' Paige focused in on the conversation, hoping she'd misunderstood the reference, as Connie continued, 'But there are brighter times ahead and that love line looks very healthy to me from here on out.'

And with that, Connie let go of Melanie's hand, and Melanie pushed a little on Paige's thigh before she lifted off again to regain her balance and was once again able to sit properly on her chair. Well, once she'd done the ritual of slight raise, skirt adjustment, back down and glasses up face manoeuvre.

'Oh, do me next please, Connie,' Polly asked.

'Remind me to bring my tarot next time, darling.'

'Hey boss, you guys want more drinks?' Belle appeared, and Paige was grateful to have something else to focus on as she stood. 'Yeah, I'll come and help.'

'Hi, I'm Belle.' Belle leaned over Paige, her hand out to shake Melanie's hand. What was with this lot tonight? You'd think they'd never met anyone new before. Shaking hands now? Really? Why were they all being so weird?

'Erm, hi. I'm Melanie.' From the surprise in her tone, Melanie wasn't sure what was going on either.

'Oh, I know, it's lovely to meet you properly. What can I get you to drink?'

Paige studied Melanie trying to use her gift to weigh up what Melanie might say versus what she might want. It used to work with her friends. They might ask for one thing but really Paige knew they needed something else. But with Melanie, she couldn't figure it out. She suspected she was a rosé kinda girl. Maybe prosecco.

She continued to watch as Melanie leaned up, trying to see what was available. 'Oh erm, I'd love an IPA please, whatever you recommend.'

See, Paige hadn't been expecting that, and with the unnecessary and yet still painful reminder that she was broken, Paige didn't say anything else as she followed Belle back to the bar, but her mood, not high to begin with, tanked even further and she felt the sourness returning.

'I like her, boss,' Belle began.

'I'm not sure why you're all being so weird around her,' Paige grunted out.

'You don't?' Belle laughed, then properly laughed, like leaned over to one side laughed.

'What?' Paige asked.

'Oh boss. I hope she's around a lot because this is going to be fun.'

'I can fire you, you know?'

'Yeah but we both know you won't. You never do.' Belle had only just got her breath back.

Even without her gift, Paige knew they were all laughing at her expense, but she didn't want to look too closely at what specifically they found so amusing.

CHAPTER SEVEN

Melanie

Melanie tried to rub her hand on her skirt without anyone noticing but it was sweaty, and she couldn't shift the feel of denim from beneath her fingertips no matter how hard she tried. Melanie looked around the table unable to believe she was actually there. Well for one thing, that she was out, socialising, maybe, possibly, making new friends. New friends that in some cases happened to be internet sensations. But while Melanie had expected to feel starstruck and awkward, she had to say that for the most part everyone was making her feel very welcome.

For the most part.

Paige was sat next to her, not really saying anything unless spoken to and there was a tenseness about her that had Melanie on edge. Connie jumped out of her seat and Melanie watched as she walked purposefully towards the bar, even though Belle had not long since dropped their drinks off. Sophie, Marcus, Polly and Bailey were talking about something to do with gardening and everyone was trying to make rude gardening puns. Melanie had thought of three to do with bushes and one to do with edging but wasn't sure if they were too much, so instead she took a sip of her IPA and let the noise of the bar wash over her. It was a home from home type feeling.

'Erm so, I'm sorry about my friends all being weird.'

Melanie jumped, the shock that Paige was willingly conversing surpassed only by her sudden proximity. Paige had leaned close so that she could talk into Melanie's ear. No doubt because of the general Friday night noise, and background music, but Melanie had to try and contain a shiver the second Paige's breath connected with her neck.

'They're not. I mean . . . Everyone is being really lovely,' Melanie said. Well nearly everyone.

The lack of response from Paige was starting to get awkward, especially considering she hadn't moved back. It was like she still wanted to say more. Melanie slowly put her drink down on the table and turned a little to see Paige better, and immediately wished she hadn't. Paige was frowning at her again. Great, at this rate she'd be back to communicating in nods.

Melanie was about to turn and rejoin Sophie's conversation but her mouth to brain filter malfunctioned without warning. 'Look, if you don't want me here, I can go.' And then the malfunction continued, unrestricted. 'Actually, I have lots to do, not to mention it now appears I'm project managing this whole art thing. So yeah, I can just go. In fact, I need to go.' Melanie reached down to her side to get her bag, a bitter taste in her mouth; a cocktail of disappointment and anger.

But it was the warm hand placed on hers that stopped her in her tracks. Her head shot up to look at Paige, and she found that she couldn't look away, the look on Paige's face like someone conflicted. The frown was still there but there was a wariness to it. 'Please, you don't have to go.'

Paige kept a hold of her hand, the one that had reached for her handbag and with her other she reached to pry Melanie's fingers off, until the handbag landed on the floor.

Melanie tried to study Paige's face to see if she could make any kind of sense as to what was happening between them. It was almost like she was causing Paige some sort of pain. Melanie sighed. She had no idea what she might have done to cause it, but she didn't need to continue to make it worse and more importantly she didn't have to wait around to receive the brunt of it. She'd learnt that lesson the hard way once before. Was only just recovering in fact. But even now, Paige's hand still holding hers, Melanie had to admit her heart was racing at the contact. Her body was stuck in place, unable to move even if she wanted to; Paige's green eyes had her trapped. Which was how she noticed Paige's gaze move to her lips and her pupils dilate.

Woah. Hang on. What was that?

'Paige? Belle and I need you for something, so sorry to interrupt.' Connie's low voice broke through the moment, and Paige was up and walking off towards the bar. Melanie looked down at her hand, expecting to see some sort of imprint on it. Something tangible. Something to help her make sense of what was happening with Paige. Oh, Melanie was attracted to her, despite her best intentions she knew that. But she also knew she could put it to one side. That it was purely physical; that it could be ignored. It wasn't exactly like Paige was winning her over with her smashing personality, was it? All Melanie got were grunts, nods and the occasional sentence. She didn't have time for lust, whether reciprocated or not; it wasn't going on her to-do list.

'Melanie, what do you think?' And just like that Melanie focused instead on what Sophie and the rest of the group were talking about. But her handbag was down and she was staying for now at least.

* * *

Melanie couldn't quite believe she'd gotten all the way to closing time, considering she was opening up her own bar tomorrow morning, and especially considering the less than warm welcome afforded her by Paige. But here they were. Paige and her staff were cleaning up around them, as they all began pulling on their coats and jackets. Melanie discovered she didn't live all that far away from Polly and Bailey so they arranged to share an Uber that would be there any minute. Sophie and Marcus were also being picked up. Melanie watched, feeling a little awkward as one by one they went up to Paige and gave her a hug and a kiss goodbye, before doing the same with each other.

'Will we see you again Melanie, my love?' Connie asked appearing at her side from nowhere.

'Why don't you come down to my bar? I'm only down the road and if you come in for brunch tomorrow, the prosecco's on me,' Melanie suggested.

'You're such a love. Surely you've been snatched up by someone by now?' Connie asked with a nudge.

'No, not wanting to be snatched by anyone to be honest, Connie.'

Connie let out a burst of deep laughter. 'Me neither, but sometimes it's nice to be wrong.'

'Connie haven't you been wrong quite a few times now?' Sophie asked, joining their conversation.

'Yes, five times married my dear, and many more mistakes apart from that, but there's still time for a few more mistakes yet . . .' Connie paused, before leaning over conspiratorially towards Melanie, and lowering her voice. 'Nearly all my mistakes have been worth every second. I can sense a rather amazing mistake for you soon, I think.'

'Oh, you do?' Melanie raised an eyebrow.

'Maybe I'm getting soft in my old age, but I think you should give Paige a chance.'

Melanie had been about to retort, her mouth ready to fire something back, but Connie beat her to it. 'She needs you. And maybe you need her. She can be a grumpy arse for sure. But you've seen that bit. I promise you'll see the other side soon. Don't write her off just yet.'

Before Melanie could say anything further, the rest of the goodbyes had happened, she'd been dragged into hugs from Sophie and Marcus, and Polly and Bailey were waiting for her at the door. Melanie's head was a mess; a combination of alcohol and Connie's words. She quickly turned to glance at Paige, but saw her already head down and clearing things away. Melanie turned back around and walked towards the door, more than ready to get home and to bed.

Once back, showered and in her pyjamas, painkillers taken, water on her bedside table, and her alarm set, she thought over all of the events of the evening. She tried to focus on how lovely Polly, Sophie, Bailey and Marcus were. They'd all threatened to have brunch at her bar soon. Melanie wasn't sure they would, but there was a chance she may have made some friends. Maybe that was wishful thinking from one night out. But then her phone pinged.

Polly: *It was lovely to meet you tonight Melanie, see you again soon x*

Polly really was lovely. Maybe she was right, maybe new friends had been made. Melanie messaged back the same. She'd lost pretty much all her friends when her last relationship ended. She didn't mourn the individual losses but missed having a friendship group. That wasn't easy to create when all her time was devoted to setting up the business or looking after her nephew.

Just as she was about to put her phone on charge and try to sleep it buzzed in her hand.

Paige: *Hope you got home safe x*

The whiplash this woman gave her was unreal. And a kiss on the end. What the hell? But then without warning all the Paige moments from the night replayed in her head. Her hand on Paige's thigh, the hand holding, the looks, the ask from Connie that she give Paige a chance. Well fine, but this would be the last one.

Melanie: *I got home safe thank you for a great night . . .*

She was going to leave it at that. But with a freedom that comes from text rather than face to face, and the remaining alcohol in her system, she went on to type some more.

But maybe next time when you speak to me you could be a little nicer?

She went to press send but couldn't do it. In the end she didn't have to, her phone buzzed again.

Paige: *I'll nip round tomorrow I can help with this art project. I'd like to help. If that's OK?* x

Melanie deleted the message she'd yet to send.

Melanie: *Got home safe thanks for checking. And erm yeah, you know where I'll be . . .*

The question was whether or not to put a kiss on the end. She'd put a kiss on the text back to Polly. She'd probably do the same when she texted Sophie. She was definitely over-thinking it now. Nobody thought a kiss on the end of a text actually meant anything did they? Melanie quickly added a kiss then pressed send before she could do anything else.

What a freaking night.

Phone on charge, she took off her glasses and snuggled down into her duvet, eyelids closed, ears only slightly ring-ing, and took a deep breath. The moment where she talked at length about organisation apps with Sophie replayed in her head and she cringed at her own geekiness — had she really used the term organisational porn about her Pinterest account? Surely that wasn't what actual celebs like Sophie Bowman wanted to talk about was it? Melanie cringed so hard she gave herself a headache. They weren't going to be asking her back to hang out anytime soon.

CHAPTER EIGHT

Paige

'Paige get a shift on, we need to go,' Connie shouted.

Paige sighed as she leaned over the sink, checking out the side of her undercut in the mirror, trying to decide if it needed freshening up. She knew what she was really doing. She was nervous, and she was stalling, because once more she had no idea how the day was going to go, and she hated it. What she did know was that it wasn't fair to take her lack of mojo out on Melanie, and not just because Connie had spent all night last night telling Paige over and over to cut it out.

Tying up her hair into a topknot so that her undercut could be seen more clearly, she then focused on her T-shirt. Tucking it in slightly, before pulling it back out a little. Then she made sure all her ear piercings were straight. And the one below her lip.

She groaned.

This was not who she was. She never cared what people thought of her. She never had this much uncertainty going on in her head. It was chaotic and unnerving, and she longed for some normality. Normality for her at any rate. She studied her face. Still Paige.

'You're a badass. Just go be you, and who cares what anyone thinks.'

'That's right, my love, you're a fighter. It's how I raised you. Now let's go.' Paige jumped out of her skin, not realising Connie had been listening in. She reached forward and pulled open the bathroom door.

'You always listen in at bathroom doors, Gran, like a weirdo?' Paige said shaking her head.

Connie started singing, 'I am what I am' as Paige grabbed her leather jacket, her keys and her phone, then put on her Vans. She was half tempted to text first, let Melanie know about the change in plans, hell who was she kidding, she was always tempted to text her. Ever since she got those digits, the battery life in her phone had dropped significantly, the number of composed and unsent messages could have been turned into a short story.

Me and Connie are both gonna come over if that's OK? She wants brunch, and I want to know how I can help x

Paige studied the message for a minute before Connie nudged her in the ribs and the message was on its way.

'Oops,' Connie said, looking inordinately pleased with herself. 'Come on let's go — it'll be fun.' Connie set off towards the back exit to the apartment, and down the metal fire escape steps.

'Will it though?' Paige shouted as she locked up.

'Oh yes, if you want it to be, today's going to be great.' Connie's smile was somehow both radiant and scheming and Paige wasn't sure if Connie knew something she didn't, but then her phone buzzed in her hand.

Melanie: *Great I've saved you both a table — see you soon x*

And completely without meaning to, Paige let herself relax, just a little, as she smiled at the response.

'See,' Connie shouted. 'Let's go.'

* * *

Together they walked the two-hundred meters down the road until they were outside of Lulu. It was ten a.m. and there was already a queue. Paige went to walk towards the back of the line, when Connie grabbed her arm. 'Don't mind us, we know the owner,' she said before stepping into the bar.

Paige shrugged and followed, keeping her head down as she entered, but her eyes were unstoppable as they searched the premises for . . . her. She found Melanie in the corner by the bar, in what must be her standard work attire of black pencil skirt and shirt, only she was wearing Converse today rather than heels.

Connie made a beeline in her direction. 'Morning love, thank you so much for the invite.' Connie reached up to throw an arm around Melanie and brought her in for a hug.

'Oh hi,' Melanie said her smile widening at Paige over Connie's shoulder. 'How are you both? It's lovely to see you again, Connie. I've saved you this table over here. Follow me.' Melanie led the way, Connie pausing to get something out of her bag, gesturing that Paige follow. Paige absolutely did not stare at Melanie's bum in that skirt. Instead, she focused on the Instagram walls, so much so that when Melanie did stop, Paige walked right into her. She quickly held onto Melanie's shoulders so that she wouldn't run her over altogether. Which actually resulted in pulling Melanie closer to her chest. Paige realised that without heels, Melanie was just a few inches shorter than her own height. Her hair, nearly in Paige's face . . . mango again.

'Sorry.' Paige stepped back, and immediately pulled out the chair and sat down so she didn't have to see whatever expression was on Melanie's face.

'Good morning to you too, Paige.' Melanie chuckled and Paige looked up and saw genuine amusement on her face before she pulled out the chair for a grinning Connie who sat down.

'Can I use your walls for my Instagram, Melanie?' Connie asked.

'Of course. Would you like to order first though? Have a look at our menus.' Paige watched as Melanie moved away to grab some menus from the little pedestal at the front.

'Paige, you're so cool.' Connie laughed, and Paige rolled her eyes, so happy her gran was there to witness her embarrassment first-hand.

Melanie made her way back towards them and Paige had no time to sort herself out.

'It's going to be a little busy with the brunch rush this morning, so I might not get a chance to speak to you both properly, but I'll try,' Melanie said, handing over the menus.

'We don't want to impose, do we, Paige? If Paige can't talk to you about whatever she wants to talk to you about then I'm sure you can catch up another time, can't you? I appreciate you're a businesswoman and we don't want to be getting in your way or be an inconvenience. And we really appreciate your generosity inviting us over here like this.' Connie paused for a split second as her attention moved to the menu. 'Now, can you tell me, do you have gluten-free muffins for the eggs benedict? But also can I have my eggs scrambled not poached, and if it's not too much trouble I would love the sauce on the side, and the smoked salmon on the other side, deconstructed if you will?'

Paige watched as Melanie was momentarily stunned silent before her eyes widened as she tried to take in the complex order. With a quick smile at Paige, that might have been a cheeky little smirk, Paige wasn't sure, Melanie looked back at Connie.

'Absolutely, we can do that. What would you like to drink?'

'I think today feels like a mimosa day, what do you think, Paige?'

'Sure.'

'Paige? What are you going to have?' Melanie asked.

'Can I be really difficult . . . and ask for the eggs benedict, just exactly as it's listed in the menu?' Paige flushed with embarrassment as her little joke, the worlds tiniest joke in fact, failed to land. Connie looked baffled, but then Melanie burst into a huge smile. As in showing teeth, eyes sparkling, Melanie Megawatt Smile.

'In all our interactions I would say, that's the least difficult you've been yet.' Paige couldn't stop the laughter from escaping. She wasn't wrong. 'I'll be back over with your drinks shortly. Connie, go wild with your Instagram. Make sure to tag us in your pics.'

Connie wondered off and Paige looked around. It really was clever, especially for a new business. The food and drink would no doubt keep people here and keep them coming back. But with such a heavy emphasis on brunch they really needed to sort out their prosecco supply.

'Here are your mimosas. Enjoy.' Melanie dropped off the drinks, and then hesitated.

'Erm, thank you,' Paige said, assuming that's what Melanie was waiting for, but then boosted from the earlier megawatt smile, Paige carried on. 'I really do want to help with this art project thing. If we don't get chance to catch up about it today, can you let me know when you're free? Maybe give me a call or text?'

'You don't have to, you know,' Melanie said, and Paige couldn't for the life of her determine what Melanie's expression was trying to convey at that moment.

Paige shrugged slightly. 'I know.'

'OK then . . . Thanks, I'll let you know.' Melanie nodded once before dashing off.

A little while later, Connie sat down and began to show Paige all her selfies, while Paige tried to feign interest. She was only a little disappointed when a waiter brought over their food instead of Melanie. As she predicted, the food and drink were divine. But just as they finished eating, Paige heard a bit of a kerfuffle from the front of the restaurant near the bar, and before she could do anything, Connie was on her feet and headed over, a small smile on her face as if she knew what was going on.

Paige stayed where she was but turned in her chair to watch the proceedings, trying to figure out whether she would need to try and drag Connie out of whatever was happening. Melanie looked stressed, but not nearly as much as the woman next to her. Then Paige noticed the little boy happily stood between them both, a little rucksack on his back, no taller than hip height, who — as Paige watched — immediately took off for the flower wall, and several waiters and customers had to quickly swerve out of his way to avoid him. Melanie and the other woman were still having a heated debate while Melanie looked at her phone, tapping at it furiously again and again as they spoke.

'Come this way, let's get you both out of the doorway and figure this out,' Connie said as she began shepherding them towards their table. They carried on their discussion oblivious to Connie's machinations.

'I can't, Louisa isn't due in until later,' Melanie said, her voice hushed but urgent.

'I thought you were getting a new manager?' the other woman said, as Paige tried to suss who she was.

'Yes, but Cleo is still learning the ropes.'

'I wouldn't ask if I wasn't desperate.'

'But why are they calling you in? You're not even on call.' Melanie almost had a whine to her voice.

'Paige, be a lamb and get the little one, would you?' Connie asked. It took a moment for Paige to realise she'd been addressed. She pointed to herself, and whispered 'me?' Paige knew next to nothing about little kids, it having been a while since she was one or hung out with one. She looked over at him as he began touching the flowers on the wall. Paige wasn't sure how they were put on that wall, but even she could tell he was probably going to pull down a big chunk of the display if she didn't get to him soon.

Walking over to the little man she stopped, completely unsure of what to do next.

'I like these flowers. They smell nice,' he said.

'They're not real, they just smell like plastic,' Paige retorted.

'Nope they smell nice. You should smell them.'

'I'm not smelling plastic flowers,' Paige said as she stood next to him.

He looked up at her then and really stared. 'I like bad smells, do you?'

'No.'

'My name is Alfie, do you know how old I am?'

'Should you be talking to strangers?' Paige asked, eyebrow raised.

'I'm four.'

'That sounds like a great age,' Paige said in all seriousness.

'How old are you?'

'Thirty-one.'

'Wow, that is old. What's your name? What's that on your face?'

'I'm Paige, and what?'

Alfie pointed again, and Paige bent down a little hoping she could guess what he was pointing at.

'That on your lip. It looks like you've eaten a marble or something. I'm not allowed to play with marbles any more after the last time.'

Paige wiggled the piercing under her lip with her tongue. 'This is a piercing.'

'What's a purse-in?'

'This is.'

'What's it for?'

'It's not for anything.'

'Does it give you super powers?'

'No.'

'Can I have a purse-in?'

'I don't know, listen, why don't you come over here where your . . . mum is?' She guessed.

'Oh yay, I hope I get to play with Auntie Mel today, she's the best. She's not the best like my mum is the best, but she's still best. Billy at school told me his dad's the best, but I don't think that's right.' It took Paige longer than she cared to admit to figure out everything he was saying, but still Paige considered it a success that she managed to get him back to their table in one piece and with some reasonable communication. Paige caught the tail end of the conversation the adults were having and was immediately worried.

'. . . so he can't be here. Why don't you come back to mine, ours, both of you? Alfie, I bet you like Disney films, don't you?'

'I don't like some of the bad guys,' Alfie quickly whispered.

'Paige has a cat. Do you like cats?' Connie asked.

'I want to see the cat. Mum, can I see the cat?'

'Well, that's settled. Emily, you can go off to work, Melanie and Alfie can hang out at Paige's apartment, and if the new manager here has any issues, then they can call you and Melanie can be here in five minutes.' With that Connie got up off her seat, grabbed her handbag, and pushed her chair back in. 'Come on then, Alfie, let's go and find Mr Higgins.'

Paige was stood still as chaos erupted around her. But she didn't miss the smile Emily deployed before saying, 'Oh, *this* is Paige', in much the same tone her friends used when introduced to Melanie. But before she could respond, a small hand grabbed hers. A small warm, soft and weirdly sticky hand.

'Come on, let's go,' Connie said leading the way.

So, all back to hers then, yeah? Great.

CHAPTER NINE

Melanie

'So, I guess make yourself at home,' Paige said.

Melanie blinked in shock but took a step forward. Paige's flat was huge and open plan, and so homey. Maybe it was the furniture, maybe it was Paige or simply what a home looked like when it wasn't just boxes, but homey it was. The modular sofa in the middle, the artwork, the rug on the floor, the cat tower. The kitchen table with benches, the gorgeous kitchen, the wooden worktops. She realised that if she could have, she would have designed her own home in a similar way. Melanie couldn't take it all in, but neither could she believe she was actually in Paige's flat, full stop. This was surreal and she hadn't had time to stop and think about it before she was here. Alfie's little hand was already tugging at her to be let go. She'd gripped his hand so tight as they made their way up the metal fire escape steps outside.

'Where's the cat?' Alfie asked, his hand demanding to be let go. Dropping her laptop bag and coat down by her side, she knelt down and began unbuttoning his coat.

'Right, listen there are some rules, OK? This is Paige's home, so shoes off, no climbing on anything, we use gentle hands with everything and especially the cat, yes?'

Alfie nodded seriously, and she couldn't not press a kiss to his squishy cheek.

'Oh don't worry, just make yourselves comfy,' Connie added from the sofa.

'The cat is around here somewhere. If you pick a spot and stay very still he will probably try and find you, but maybe check his tower first,' Paige said as Alfie ran off in the direction that Paige was pointing.

'Is your cat good with kids?' Melanie asked.

Paige shrugged. 'No idea. He's a cat.' She picked up Melanie's coat and bag, popping the bag on the kitchen table before hanging her coat up behind the door. Melanie sank down on the bench and tried to get her brain to catch up and accept what was happening.

'How long will he stay like that?' Paige asked.

Not knowing what she was talking about, she turned and found Alfie stood like a statue next to the tower. It was the most still she had ever seen him. Wow. Shaking her head, Melanie turned back to the table. Right, what was the plan now? She couldn't really impose on Paige and Connie like this. She should go back and get her car and take Alfie to her house. But then if there was an issue, she couldn't just run back to the bar. She couldn't leave Alfie here though either could she? Could she? They were friends, weren't they? Were they? It was only a few minutes away. She didn't know what to do for the best. What if the new bar manager didn't need any help, then they would have just wasted Paige's time for no reason. Surely Paige needed to work as well, right? It must be their busiest day of the week. She really was making problems for everyone and her brain was spinning as she tried and failed to think through all the possible solutions and inconveniences.

'Tea?' Paige asked as she moved around the kitchen.

Melanie shot up and followed. 'No, I couldn't possibly. I'm really sorry for imposing on you like this. Look, I'll get Alfie and take him back to mine. I'm sure everything will be fine with the bar.'

Paige shrugged. 'OK.'

Oh God she really was imposing. This was so awkward. She could wring her sister's neck. But surgeons be surgeons or something like that. She was off saving lives, as she liked to point out every time. She also liked to point out that Melanie said she would be there. That she would support them both. That Alfie wouldn't ever feel the consequences of a parent leaving like they had when their dad left. She had said that and she had meant it. But this wasn't right either. Was she overthinking? She should just go, but oh God what if the fresh grocery delivery didn't turn up? She'd call Louisa and see if Louisa could help. Grabbing her phone, she checked. Nope she couldn't call Louisa. Louisa was taking her girl-friend out for the morning for a little bit of relationship TLC.

'Here. Do you have sugar? And it's oat milk, right?' Paige said pushing a brew in front of her over the kitchen island towards her.

'One sugar please,' Melanie said, staring at the mug, brain spinning.

Paige nodded, adding the sugar, stirring it and passing it back.

Wait how did she know about the oat milk?

'Drink. Then call the manager. Then see what you want to do. What about him, what does he drink?' Paige nodded over at Alfie, and Melanie smiled. Paige sounded like she did at her bar.

'He'd love a shot of tequila but I'm a terrible Auntie and only ever give him milk.' Melanie tried to keep her face straight.

'Alf, you want a milk?' Paige shouted.

'Shh,' he replied, refusing to move.

'Think he's fine. Right, sit down, drink your tea and get your head together. We'll sort it.' Paige didn't even look at Melanie as she walked back towards the sofa and proceeded to hand Connie a cup too before sitting down next to her.

Right so, was she imposing . . . ?

'Melanie, love, just relax. I can feel you thinking from over here. Alfie, what Disney films do you like?' Connie asked.

'I love *Star Wars*. Have you got *Star Wars*?'

'Kid, I've got Disney Plus. Choose your poison,' Paige said.

Melanie stared in fascination as Alfie ran over towards Paige, sat down next to her and looked at the screen.

'You have lots of them.'

'Sure do.'

'Which one is your favourite?'

'BB8.'

Paige nodded at that and put one of the *Star Wars* films on.

Well Alfie certainly looked settled, Paige even looked settled and Connie was grinning.

'Call the bar manager,' Paige ordered not once looking up.

'You're bossy,' Alfie said.

Paige shrugged. 'Sometimes. Shhh, it's starting.'

Melanie slowly turned around, not wanting to miss the interactions taking place on the sofa. It was clear Paige had limited knowledge of interacting with a child, the way she spoke and the words she used didn't change from when she spoke to anyone else. But Alfie clearly had no issue with that at all. And if something pinged near her heart, it was definitely wind and completely unrelated to the two people currently bonding over *Star Wars*. Instead, Melanie did as instructed, and called Cleo.

* * *

It was a good thirty minutes later by the time she'd talked her manager around some of the more intricate parts of the pay systems. But she was relieved to hear the groceries were there, and the booking system that had been playing up all week seemed to be resolved for now. Melanie made sure Cleo had her contact details and then sent a message to Louisa to make sure she was turning up at four like usual. In which case that was two hours-ish.

'Right, loves, I'm off for my makeover with Sophie. See you later.' Connie was quickly gathering her bag and coat and was out the door before anyone could say bye.

'Erm, I think this kid is broken,' Paige said. 'He's also leaking.'

Melanie stood up and saw an image that would be with her forever as one of the cutest things she'd ever seen. It wasn't that Melanie did cute necessarily, but this was too much. She was tempted to take a picture and in fact she very subtly tried to steal a picture as she got closer.

'Firstly, he's not broken, he's napping and what do you mean leaking?'

Paige pointed to the arm on her T-shirt where Alfie had snuggled up and rested his head, drool coming out of his lips.

'Can I move or am I stuck here forever now?'

'Stuck forever I'm afraid. You must never ever wake up a small kid, and their naps have been known to last a minimum of three hours. Alfie is a pro though — he normally goes four hours solid. I hope you're comfy as you're officially that kid's pillow.'

Melanie watched as Paige glared open-mouthed.

'You're messing with me, aren't you?' she said, sounding surprised. What like no one had ever tried to wind her up before?

'Of course I'm messing, hang on.' Walking round to the front of the sofa between the coffee table and the couch she knelt down. 'Right, I'll move him off you and lie him down, but you'll need to scoot out of the way, OK?'

'Sure,' Paige whispered. Melanie tried not to grin. Alfie was out for the count, no talking, moving or otherwise would wake this kid up right now.

Melanie leaned forward and brushed her hand down Paige's arm to the back of Alfie's head. Her other hand went around the back of his shoulders, as she tugged him gently up a little.

'Can you squeeze out?'

Paige quickly moved out of the way and far away. But before Melanie could lay him down flat, a little cushion appeared on the sofa for Alfie to rest his head on, and just as she had him settled and comfy, a blanket appeared and was gently placed over him.

'Should I move the coffee table? Will he roll onto it?' Paige asked still whispering.

'Good idea,' Melanie said as they both grabbed an end and moved it further towards the TV unit.

'How long will he sleep for? Should I pause the film?' Paige asked with complete and utter sincerity, and Melanie felt her heart melt. So yeah, probably not wind, but maybe caffeine again.

'He can sleep as long as he wants and that's for my sister to deal with later tonight. No, wait, hang on.' Melanie opened up her app. 'No, he's with me, in that case no more than half an hour, and no you don't have to pause the film, you can watch it if you want it's not going to disturb him.'

'So, he's your nephew?' Paige asked as they both stood over Alfie.

'Yup. He's cute right?' Melanie watched as Paige shrugged. 'The right answer there by the way is yes, or yes he's the cutest, even if you don't believe it.'

Paige's lips curled slightly to one side. 'He's the cutest.'

'You don't mean it.' Melanie laughed. 'Yeah, I share the childcare with my sister — she's a surgeon.'

'Is there no other parent around?' Paige asked.

'No, my sister had a very intense relationship that ended as quickly as it began, and he left before he knew what he'd left behind. My mum had warned her and well . . .'

'Well, what?'

'Well, my mum adores Alfie, but she has a chip on her shoulder about Emily, saying that she should have been more careful, that having a child could damage her career.'

'But you just said she's a surgeon.'

'Yeah. Mum's not very happy with the men that have been in her life, and I think she feels like Emily should have made better choices. Not to repeat her own mistakes really. Our mum was on her own with us. And I promised I'd help.

Usually, it's not a problem, and my mum will help out with childcare a lot, it's just she's more likely to if I ask than if my sister asks. If my sister asks she's going to get a lecture about wise choices. What about you? Any nieces or nephews?'

'No, it's just me and Connie. And the girls.'

Melanie couldn't decipher Paige's tone. 'Louisa will be at Lulu from four, so if you don't mind us staying here for another hour or so, we'd really appreciate it. But I don't want to impose if you have other things you need to be doing? I can wake Alfie up.' Melanie moved as if to wake him and Paige stopped her.

'Melanie, it's fine. I just need to run downstairs and check everything is sorted down there. Then we can start work on the art project if you like?'

'Erm, yeah that would be a really good use of my time actually.'

Yeah, she knew how she sounded.

CHAPTER TEN

Paige

'So, if you need me, call, OK?' Paige was moving away from the bar already itching to get back upstairs.

'Yeah, I'll call if we need you — but we can handle it, as you well know. So just go have some fun, yeah?' India said with a wink.

Paige dead-eyed her in response before turning around and heading back up the stairs to her apartment, not missing the laughter from her staff behind her; she'd fire the lot of them if they carried on like this. But still she was delighted to see their newest recruit joining in too. The soft music from *Star Wars* was playing, and Paige immediately remembered her sleeping guest and as quietly as she could, closed and locked the apartment door behind her.

Before she could move any further forward, her eyes were stuck on the image she faced. It was hard to describe but for a second Paige felt like she'd been thrown into some weird alternative reality. One in which she had a partner of her own. One that was quite happy working from the big kitchen table. One that apparently preferred to work without shoes on, as they had been haphazardly kicked off. One that was so concentrated with their phone that they hadn't even realised their partner had come home. In this weird alternative reality Paige was struggling not to wrap her arms around Melanie's middle and kiss the back of her neck.

Paige continued to watch Melanie, as she placed her phone on the table and leant over to get something from her bag. Her shirt moulded to her curves as she moved, that hair of hers still tied up and Paige reasoned that it perhaps wasn't Melanie specifically, but instead just a general sense of loneliness. Maybe it was time for Paige to consider dating. She'd put it off for a while, knowing she had other areas of her life that needed focus, mainly her friends, Connie and the bar. She'd also 'known' in the way she used to 'know' things that the timing wasn't right. But now, Paige couldn't rule the idea out altogether, but it did remind her that she wasn't firing on all cylinders, and that was enough to unstick her feet from the floor and move towards Melanie.

She detoured via the couch first to make sure her little guest was comfy. He seemed fine enough, even if he was drooling on the cushions. Then she went back to the kitchen and made another brew for them both, until finally she'd put it off long enough. She went to the table and sat on the bench opposite Melanie. Their knees touching briefly as Paige sat down.

'Thank you,' Melanie said as she took the tea with a smile, and there it was again that weird feeling.

'Right, so what do we know so far?' Paige asked.

'Well, oh hang on.' Melanie picked up her phone again and began scrolling one-handed as the other went up to her head, and for a second Paige was gripped as it looked like she might just take out her bobble and grips and she'd finally find out how long and what colour Melanie's hair was. But no, she ran her hand over her head and back down to the phone.

She must be brunette, it was dark, but were those strands of red she could make out? Maybe the ends were a different colour again? Maybe it wasn't too long and just grazed her shoulders, maybe it fell down near her bum?

'Councillor Houghton has sent over some time-line proposals and apparently Paulo from the tattoo shop has already had some interest; he knew of a few people and got word out locally. But I was thinking we could also approach the local colleges and see if they've anyone on an art program or something?'

'Yeah, that's a really good idea. I have someone in mind too.'

Paige watched as Melanie nodded once. 'We also need to set up a judging panel. It's going to need to be as transparent as possible. If we're doing this, then we need to do it right. I'm not putting my integrity on the line especially as the new girl on the block.' Melanie was frowning at her phone.

'Which also means finding out how much the materials are going to cost, how long it will take and how much we can afford to pay,' Paige said watching as Melanie swapped the phone for her iPad and opened up more apps, before tapping away again.

'We're probably going to need to get press releases and interest and all that as well if we're going to maximise on things,' Melanie said thoughtfully as she once again went to run her hand through the hair that she couldn't get at. Paige wondered if the reason it was tied up was because she would always be running her hands through it if it wasn't? Then Paige wondered if she was being weirdly obsessed about it and went back to the task in hand.

Melanie continued, 'Right, what we need to do is break it down into chunks. All the tasks we need to do now, all the tasks for when we have our artist, and the tasks we need to do for when it's finished.'

There was something in Melanie's tone that Paige couldn't quite place.

'It's going to need several lists. I might even go old school and use a notebook, no, well yes maybe just for notes.' Melanie carried on and Paige realised she was talking faster than normal, and her voice was just a little bit higher.

'You like this stuff, don't you?' Paige blurted out.

Melanie shrugged, but Paige could make out the pink on her cheeks and couldn't hold back her chuckle.

'It's no wonder you get on so well with Sophie.'

'I wouldn't say we get on well, well I'm not trying to say I don't like her, I do a lot, it's just that she's a . . . erm . . .'

'Have you got a crush?' Paige asked as Melanie dug herself further and further.

'No, not at all, it's just that she's . . . you know . . .'

Paige shook her head. 'No I don't know, what is she?'

'Famous.'

Now Paige really did chuckle. She knew Sophie was famous, but she didn't think of Sophie like that at all. 'She still pukes into the toilet and all over herself when she's drunk too much same as all of us. Oh, and you must have seen the video where she poked herself in the eye with her mascara wand and swore like a trooper. Besides, she makes her sex tapes the same as the rest of us . . . only with good lighting.'

'Wait, what?!' Melanie had been laughing, but now she was about to choke on thin air.

'It was accidental but that's a story for another day,' Paige said.

'Wait, have you made a sex tape?' Melanie asked and then immediately covered her mouth with her hands. 'Forget I asked that.' The pink in her cheeks now really stood out.

Paige smiled slowly. 'Wouldn't you like to know.'

Melanie said nothing for a second as their eyes locked.

'Anyway, you were talking about organising?' Paige said, sitting back in her seat and crossing her foot over her knee.

'Yeah . . . erm . . . so yeah.' Melanie coughed a little. 'I'll add you onto my to-do list app. What's your email address?' Paige reeled it off and a notification appeared on her phone. 'You just download the app and then we can both see the schedule and the tasks. That way if you do a task, you can cross it off the list and it will keep us both up-to-date.'

A shuffling sound broke Paige's focus and she shot up to look over the back of the sofa. The traitorous Mr Higgins was currently curled up in a little ball next to Alfie's chest.

'Oh my God, I need a picture of this.' Melanie appeared behind her, and Paige watched as Melanie leaned over the sofa and took a picture. Paige could admit it was pretty damn cute. He never curled up like that when she napped. But admittedly she was somewhat larger than Alfie. Grabbing her own phone, she took a pic and then took a step back and caught one of Melanie taking the photo on her phone. That weird feeling in her chest once again.

'I probably need to wake him up really. Otherwise, he won't sleep tonight,' Melanie said almost to herself as she bent over the back of the couch to stroke her nephew's face.

Realising that she was staring, Paige quickly moved towards the kitchen and tried to find something for her little guest to eat. He probably wanted a snack about now, right? After a couple minutes, she'd managed to find a lightweight glass that wasn't as big as some of the others and filled it with oat milk. She'd also figured he might want a biscuit and made her way to the sofa where a little voice was talking sweetly.

'He's so cute,' Alfie whispered.

'Remember gentle hands,' Melanie said.

Alfie was sat up and stroking Mr Higgins who was loving all the attention as he purred noisily. He almost appeared to be looking at Paige as if to say 'this is how you do it'.

Dick.

Paige sat down at the other end of the sofa and placed the drink and the biscuit on the coffee table.

'Hey Alf, I got you some milk and a biscuit if you want?'

'Thank you Pwaige.'

Well, dammit that was cute.

CHAPTER ELEVEN

Melanie

Melanie disliked mornings the most. When her alarm went off, she was forced to open her eyes and once her glasses were on, she couldn't help but see the boxes she otherwise tried to ignore, and her heart would sink a little further into the duvet. Then she would race to open up her to-do list and calendar as quickly as possible so she was forced into action, forced to start her day rather than unpack literally and psychologically.

Studying her phone, Melanie was relieved to see a standard Wednesday lay ahead. Run, shower, dress, coffee and then to her sister's house to take Alfie to school. From there she would go to the bar, spend an hour on paperwork, deliveries and other essentials, while the kitchen team prepped, before making sure the whole place was reset as the wait staff turned up and then it was doors open and ready to go.

No there wasn't a lot of spare time, but she was occupied and she was productive and that, along with the pressure to succeed, sustained her. However, that morning was different for several reasons. The first being that Melanie kept replaying her afternoon at Paige's house over and over in her mind.

She still couldn't believe it had happened, that Paige had been so adorably awkward and yet caring for Alfie. That she had forgotten herself for a minute and even attempted some cheeky flirting. No, she did not have time to flirt with Paige.

Anyway, the second reason the morning was unlike any other, was that Paige had apparently texted her late last night. The third was a notification of a new video on Sophie's YouTube featuring Connie. Feeling a strange thrill at all three things, Melanie allowed herself some extra time in bed and figured that for today she could cut short her usual running route. But the excitement in her belly was matched with a little ball of anxiety. She looked at the text from Paige first.

Can we put a regular meet up in our calendars for all things art? X

Eeek! A regularly scheduled time slot with Paige made her stupidly excited. Or at least that was Melanie's initial gut reaction, until she reminded herself Paige was very firmly on the 'to not do' list. Melanie was forced to admit, attractiveness had turned into attraction. Now if she could keep it from becoming a crush, she should be fine. She had no idea where Paige was at, but Melanie absolutely didn't have time for a relationship. Her last one had ended a while ago, two years ago to be precise, and the amount of time it had taken up had been exhausting. She looked across at some of the boxes that filled every room of her flat; she knew logically that not all relationships were the same, but yeah. She quickly looked away. Then there was Paige's mood swings. Surely a red flag in and of itself. But then again, her old relationship had been so full of red flags in the end they communicated by semaphore.

Not wanting to think of that she went to her guilty pleasure, opened up YouTube and went straight to Sophie's page and grinned so widely at the preview image of Connie and Sophie. It was bizarre to Melanie that she knew a celebrity, that she knew the woman getting the makeover as well was just too wild. That she had been invited to have one herself inconceivable.

And highly unlikely to happen.

On her priorities list, it kept slipping down. It wasn't that it wasn't a high priority for her; she'd be at Sophie's right now knocking the door down if she could. But Alfie was high up there and the bar was right at the top. They couldn't fail with the bar. For now, her time had to be spent sorting out the actual logistics of owning a bar. They'd sank so much money into it, had so many loans riding on it, and she had something to prove too, but if the customer numbers started to drop or she found herself desperately needing the press then her makeover would creep back up the list, but for now it stayed where it was. And Melanie had to battle every day with the desire to text Sophie. But she wasn't sure if the text was going to say, "*Yes let's book it in, this is when I'm free*", or, and more likely, "*Come in and use the walls whenever you like, but I'm not sure I can fit in a makeover just yet, no matter how desperately I would like one*".

Allowing herself to feel melancholy for one more minute she finally got through the ads and could watch Sophie's new video. After ten minutes of pure giggles and smiles, Sophie felt her mood lift; there was no better way to start her day. Connie had been amazing, her full charming slightly unfiltered self, and Sophie had been her usual funny and lovely being.

With a sigh, Melanie admitted to herself that there was a part of her that longed to be in that group. To be really in it and not just on the periphery like she was now. Seeing Paige, Sophie, Marcus, Polly and Bailey had made her realise what a true friendship group looked like. She'd only realised she hadn't had that before when her old friends had taken a side that wasn't hers. But she'd had Louisa, and that was all she really needed right now.

Still lying in bed, she went back to Paige's text asking to set up a regular art catch-up.

Melanie thought through the options for her response. There was the simple, "*Yes of course, I'll sort out some time later*". Or there was the more, "*You're just desperate to see me again, aren't you?*" cheekiness. Or maybe even, "*Sure my place or yours ;)*" No, she would never.

She wrote out option one, and then before she could stop herself, carried on including all the options, and in a split-second moment of madness, pressed send.

What the hell was wrong with her?

The sent-message anxiety crashed through her body. She rolled over and pressed her face tight into the pillow and groaned. What on earth had she done that for?

Not even looking at her phone she checked the time on her watch. She could fit in a half-route run if she got up now. She quickly got up and dressed in her running gear and set off. She went to grab her phone to listen to music as she would have done normally, but didn't want to face the consequences of ill-advised texts and set off without it.

Forty minutes later she was washed, dressed for the day, and back in the car ready to see her gorgeous nephew; she had only compulsively checked her phone about fifty billion times. But of course, Paige wouldn't be up yet, she wouldn't need to be. Her bar didn't open until lunch. Which meant that Melanie had all morning to feel nervous about it.

Melanie let herself into her sister's house and found her and Alfie in the kitchen, Emily clearly getting her stuff together and coat on ready to leave.

'Morning M, you OK? Alfie is just finishing his breakfast. He needs to finish getting dressed and brush his teeth — we've not had a great start to the day and we're a little behind schedule. Sorry. He's on school lunch again today.'

'No worries,' Melanie said, putting her bag and her phone down on the table. 'Morning, gorgeous boy.' Alfie grinned up at her, his mouth full of cereal.

'Wait, stop. What's wrong?' Emily asked, her hand on Melanie's arm.

'Nothing, I'm fine.'

'No you're not, what is it?' Emily asked a look of concern on her face.

'Nothing, honestly, just go. You don't want to be late for the slicing and dicing or whatever it is you do.'

'Depends on the day, sometimes slice, sometimes prod.'

'Lovely.'

'No, but come on, what is it?' Emily asked, in what Melanie suspected was her doctors' authoritative tone. Melanie's phone buzzed on the table.

'I just sent a text I wish I hadn't,' Melanie said, hoping that wasn't a reply that had just come through.

'Huh?'

'I just text Paige something that . . . I'm just overthinking. Ignore me.'

'Oh, it's about the incredible Paige, is it?' Emily leaned in and spoke quietly, 'Did you send her a picture of your tits?'

'God no,' Melanie said at the same time a little voice said, 'Why do you have a picture of the Twits? Mummy's been reading me that book. Can I see a picture?'

Melanie's mouth dropped open and Emily had to restrain from laughing. 'Yeah Auntie M loves that book too.' Alfie nodded and went back to his cereal.

'Do you really want your son going into reception class talking about tits?' Melanie whispered.

'You heard him as clear as I did, he's going to be talking about the Twits, and the teacher will be impressed his reading is so advanced.' Emily smirked and Melanie couldn't hold in the laugh. Emily spoke again, 'I know we don't get chance to properly hang out. But I am here, you know? If you want to talk about Paige or anything at all. Wait did you send her a picture of your downstairs?'

'No!'

'Auntie Mel doesn't have a downstairs she's in a flat remember.'

The pair of them burst out laughing.

'He's too smart for his own good,' Emily said.

'Just like his mother. Right go, you're going to be late for work.'

'I mean it, but you're right, I'm going.'

Melanie watched as Emily quickly kissed Alfie, told him she loved him, and left, calling down the hallway, 'I think you should send Paige a picture of your twits,' before shutting the door behind her.

'Right then my man, you finished your cereal?' Melanie noticed three things in quick succession as she turned towards her nephew. Alfie had her phone in his hand, it was lit up and now that it was quiet, she could clearly hear a little voice saying, 'Hello?'.

Melanie quickly grabbed her phone and . . . of course.

Of freaking course.

Her stomach hollowed out.

Her brain frazzled out.

It was Paige.

Melanie quickly hung up and immediately regretted it. Hell.

Had Paige called her or had she, or rather Alfie somehow managed to call Paige? Oh God how long had she been on the phone for? Had she heard about the downstairs and the twits? Melanie rested her head on the cool marble-topped kitchen island. She was desperate to let out a swear word but realised Alfie going into school talking about twits and some version of forking hell made it unwise.

A little hand patted her back.

'Are you poorly, Auntie Mel?'

Melanie sat upright and pulled him into a hug. 'No, I'm fine. Right, come on, finish your cereal or you'll be late.'

Melanie gingerly approached the phone like it was venomous, and slowly unlocked it, trying not to spook it. But as she did her phone buzzed in her hand and Melanie nearly threw the phone to the floor.

Paige: *Just calling to say hi but think Alf got there first. Hope you're OK this morning?* x

Well, that was fine. We could all move on from here. That was totally fine. Melanie could actually feel her blood pressure lowering. Everything was going to be OK.

But then she saw the three dots and a second message came through. When she saw it, Melanie seriously considered calling it a day and going back to bed before it could get any worse.

Paige: *I do enjoy the Twits but my favourite is the giant peach* x
And there was a laughing emoji.

'Right OK little man go upstairs and brush your teeth please.' Melanie tried to get herself back on track as he headed to the bathroom.

The only thing to do here was to take charge, then they could all move on with their lives.

Melanie: *Well, you're not having a picture of either so don't worry about it* x

There she was back in control and they could all have a good laugh about this one day. Like the adults they all were.

Three dots.

Oh bloody hell what now?

Paige: *Shame* xx

Melanie pushed her glasses back in place, her eyes wide. What the . . . ?

CHAPTER TWELVE

Paige

Paige was sprawled on her sofa, *Beauty and The Beast* playing in the background, but Paige wasn't watching, rather she had her phone in her hand. Her mind was racing around a single track over and over again. Why had she sent that text? Now if Paige had been able to tap into her mojo, her psychic ability, her gut instinct, whatever the hell you wanted to call it, she would have known whether or not it had been a good idea to send that message to Melanie. But she didn't have that, and didn't know if she'd overstepped, but from the lack of response had to guess that maybe she had.

She still wasn't clear even now, what had possessed her. That she'd just woken up was her excuse. She'd sent it before she could think it through, but the flirting had definitely been building. Right? Or had that been in her head? Her hands fisted as she once again and possibly forever continued to try and second guess every little thing. No, she hadn't imagined it. Maybe now they could outright flirt? Was that what she wanted? Was that something Melanie wanted?

She lifted her head from the sofa cushions as she heard the clonking sound of the metal steps outside and a key in the lock to her flat. As the door opened it let in some more sunshine from outside, along with Connie.

'What time do you call this?' Paige asked.

'You're not my mum, God.' Connie grinned. 'Thank you, I've always wanted to say that.'

'You'll be getting grounded if you carry on,' Paige said.

'Yeah that's too far. So, as predicted the Captain from the cruise just happened to be in Manchester. We went out for tea and then back to his hotel to get reacquainted.'

'Oh.' What else was there to say to that?

'And by reacquainted, I mean, I got reacquainted with his jolly roger.'

'Oh God, it's too early in the morning for this.'

'Well then it was a good job I didn't bring him back here then, isn't it?' Connie strode over to the kitchen. 'You could do with a little action yourself lady, might chill you out a little maybe even cheer you up.'

'Thanks, Gran.' There was no little amount of sarcasm.

'I mean it, I see you and Melanie hitting the sheets sometime soon.' Connie was putting the kettle on, and talking as if this was common knowledge.

Paige sat upright on the sofa. 'I really hope you haven't.'

'It doesn't work like that as well you know or used to know. It's just a series of hunches and suspicions — my gut if you will. But it's telling me, you two will get to it.'

Paige nearly asked, 'And then what?' but very quickly decided she didn't want to know the answer and neither did she know what answer she wanted to hear.

'You look like you need a cup of tea and a hug.' Connie moved towards the sofa and sat down beside Paige, who leaned in a little for what was Paige's equivalent of a hug. 'No, wait, let me go shower first.'

'Gross, Gran.'

Paige's phone lit up as a call came through, and Paige quickly rejected it. Connie sighed. 'And what are you going to do about that?'

'Nothing, she'll get the message soon enough.'

Paige kept her eyes down, not wanting to see whatever expression might be on Connie's face.

'You know she's only going to start messaging me again too,' Connie pointed out.

Paige grunted. Connie was waiting for something else from her. Well, she would be waiting for a long time. As if Connie knew, and let's face it she probably did, she got up off the sofa and changed the topic.

'You make the tea and I'll be right out.' Connie all but ran to the spare room, and Paige grimaced. Were other people's relationships with their gran like this? She doubted it. But she also wouldn't change it for the world. Her gran was unfiltered, a rare gift, and always made Paige feel better about herself. She was the reason Paige had always felt confident, sure of herself and usually confident in her actions.

Until now. And that was the crux of what was going on, she realised. She felt unmoored, lost and it was battering her confidence. Her phone pinged and she looked at it, seeing a strange notification. Realising that it was from the to-do list app Melanie had added her to, she visited the app.

Notification: Louisa has completed task, 'Talk to energy supplier re tariff' and has added a note, click here to read it.

Paige did as it suggested.

Note: Hey Mel, spoken to the supplier they're going to change our tariff.

Why was she seeing all this? It was fascinating. She watched as another to-do action was added.

Action: Set annual reminder to get tariff checked over — Louisa.

Paige spent the next few minutes scrolling around the app, careful not to add or disrupt anything. She saw the tab for the bar, the tab labelled Alfie and the tab labelled art project. Clicking on the last one, she saw a whole host of actions in there. Paige selected two that she could action pretty quickly. One was to put a date in with Councillor Houghton for pertinent updates, and the other was to pick up the flyers and posters, again that needed Councillor Houghton. Scrolling to her contact she called the man in question, who picked up straight away, and then promptly passed her to his PA. After looking in the scheduling part of the app, she found a time that they could both meet with Councillor Houghton, and Paige also agreed a time that she could pick up the flyers.

Then she went back to the app but hesitated before updating it.

Did she need to apologise first for being flirty in the text messages? She had laughed so hard when she'd overheard the conversation. Had she made Melanie feel awkward? Paige rarely had cause to apologise but if felt like she constantly did with Melanie. But then Paige realised that what Melanie would appreciate the most was the help. And so, she updated the app. First by ticking off the boxes next to the actions and adding a note in both.

Note: Agreed a date for us both to meet with Councillor Houghton later this week. I've added it below. Let me know if that doesn't work and I'll change — Paige.

And in the next action she added, *Note: I've arranged to pick up the flyers and posters so consider this one done — Paige.*

Paige went back to the messages between her and Melanie. Scrolling up she read through the last few. Melanie had flirted with her first, hadn't she?

A slight buzz in her hand and there was a new message arrow. She scrolled down.

Melanie: *You're ticking all the right boxes x*

Paige grinned, pleased she'd figured out the key to Melanie's good graces, and maybe even to her flirtation.

Her phone buzzed again.

Melanie: *I meant that in a light teasing way, not in a bossy well done for picking up the right actions on the list type of way.*

A facepalm emoji followed.

Melanie: *I'm really not bossy I was just trying to — I don't know.*

Three dots appeared over and over, disappearing each time as if suggesting Melanie was writing and deleting message after message.

Connie appeared over her shoulder, making her jump. 'Jesus, Gran.'

'I was talking to you, but you were transfixed. Aww, I do love that Melanie, she's the sweetest. Even if she can't flirt for toffee. I'll have to teach her.'

'Wait what, why were you reading that? What do you mean flirting? Do you really think she's trying to flirt?' And why did Paige so desperately want the answer to be yes?

'No doubt she's trying to flirt. I say go for it. Try flirting back and see what happens.'

And then Paige had a complete mind blank.

She typed out, *You're ticking my boxes too.* Connie groaned as if in pain, and Paige realised she was still reading over her shoulder.

'Good Lord what is wrong with you two? You can't send her that. Here, look at this, just ignore the pictures.' Connie held up her phone to Paige's face.

'What do you mean ignore the . . . no Gran, why are you showing me *that*?'

'I said ignore that, you need to read the messages.'

'No Gran, I really, just no. How am I supposed to ignore . . . ?' Paige closed her eyes and pushed Connie's hand away.

'Well fine, I have another idea. Just send her a picture of you laughing. You have to do something, put her out of her misery. I can feel her cringing all the way from here.'

Paige shook her head. That was definitely not her style. The girls might know what to do. But she wasn't sure she could tell them everything, it wasn't really what she did. They leaned on her not the other way around. They would, she had no doubt, she just . . . couldn't that's all, and with every passing second it was getting more and more awkward.

Paige: *Good, I'm happy ticking your boxes x*

'No! God no, you can't send that,' Connie all but barked at her.

She deleted the message. Great, now they were both playing the three dots game.

Paige: *Happy to help you tick off anything x*

With the pressure of a response needed, she pressed send.

Connie groaned, shouting as she walked away towards the kettle, 'You should have just sent her a picture of your boobs, that's what I'd have done.'

Paige stared at her phone as it pinged.

The to-do list was showing a new notification.

Notification: New tab created — Personal.

Notification: New action created — Learn how to flirt.

Paige's smile was slow as it went from one side to the other. That was surely the green light for flirting?

Melanie: *We still need to put some time in for us to meet up. I'm thinking like two or three times a week? X*

This wasn't flirting, but Paige was more than happy to find time to meet up. She looked at Melanie's schedule; they could do one night a week at her sister's while she was watching Alfie. If it was earlier in the week then Paige wouldn't feel so bad leaving the bar. That could work. Then maybe an early one? Paige sent over the suggestions.

Melanie: *Great so I'll see you tomorrow night at my sister's house. Here is the address. I'll be there from five, with Alfie, but Alfie goes to bed around seven if you want to come after up to you x*

Paige: *It's a date see you tomorrow x*

Paige groaned, yeah she really was terrible at this, but she could be better in person.

Maybe.

CHAPTER THIRTEEN

Melanie

Thursday was one of the days she didn't have to take Alfie to school because her sister put him into breakfast club. But it did mean that it was her day to pick him up from after-school club, feed him his tea, and do all the bedtime routine, which usually involved a book or two dozen while her sister did the food shop. Today was going to be different for two reasons. The first was that she was late picking up Alfie because she'd just seen a truly horrible and definitely fake review added to their Facebook page and had to go through it and flag it for Louisa's attention. Secondly, Paige would be joining them, although it wasn't clear if she was joining pre or post bedtime routine. If she came at seven that would give her a couple of hours with Paige before Emily got in. That would be more than enough time; perhaps Paige would only stay for like fifteen minutes. They'd have a professional catch-up and then Paige would be on her way. In fact, she could even ask for Paige's advice about what to do with bad reviews. If they were keeping it professional. Which she assumed they would be after her disastrous attempts at flirting.

Melanie got out the car and charged towards the school, running her hands down her skirt and straightening her glasses.

'Auntie Mel,' a little voice shouted out from behind the gate. She spotted him, so tiny and yet so grown up in his school uniform.

'Hey little man, ready to go home?' She apologised for the two-minute delay and thanked the school assistant as she took Alfie to the car, his car seat a permanent fixture in the back now.

'So erm, I don't know if she'll be coming or not, but my friend Paige might be around later,' Melanie said, figuring she'd best prepare Alfie just in case. What she wasn't prepared for was his response.

'Ohhh. Will she bring her cat? Will she bring her purse-in? Can we watch *Star Wars* again? I liked Pwaige. Can I show her my toys?'

Melanie roughly translated most of it but was unclear about the purse thing. But she really hadn't expected him to be quite so enamoured. Now she was worried he might be upset if he didn't see her tonight.

'Well, I don't know what time she's coming yet bud, you might already be in bed.'

'Oh.' Yep, his disappointment was clear.

'But if that's the case you want me to get her to go tuck you in or something?'

'Yes, please.'

Wow that kid fell hard and fast. She could relate.

Once in and green pasta dinner decided on, all Melanie had to do was battle through the million and one questions from Alfie about Paige, the main question being "what time was she coming?"

Melanie pulled out her phone. She was going to have to find out.

Melanie: *Alfie wants to know if he will see you tonight* x

Melanie put her phone back down on the table and then remembered to move it away from Alfie.

'Right, let's get you in the bath and then you can pick out the books you want me to read. How many are we reading tonight?' Melanie asked as she cleared away his dinner and pulled out his chair.

'I think ten.'

Melanie raised her eyebrows in surprise — it was normally a lot more than that.

'And then Paige can read me a hundred.' That was more like the usual quantity, but really kid you've only met her once?

Her phone buzzed and she went to grab it.

Paige: *On my way be there in ten x*

Melanie: *I've put the door on the latch let yourself in I'll be washing my monster x*

Oh God Melanie really?

Melanie: *Alfie, I meant Alfie, Alfie is the monster x*

Why could she not just text like a normal person? Why did it have to go so wrong? And why with Paige and no one else?

Paige: *See you soon x*

Melanie groaned and chased Alfie upstairs to get him in the bath, and sure enough it was as Alfie was dry and getting into his *Star Wars* pyjamas that she heard the door shut, lock and Paige shouting out a hello.

'We're up here,' Melanie said as she towel-dried Alfie's hair.

'What you sayin?' he asked.

Melanie said nothing and waited for Paige to appear. Alfie shot up out of her lap and ran straight to the bedroom door, hugging Paige's legs. Paige looked startled and awkward, and Melanie couldn't hold in the laughter.

'Did you bring your cat?' Alfie asked as he slowly and only partially unwound from Paige's long legs to look up and ask her.

'No Alf, he lives at my house. He doesn't travel a lot.'

'You brought your purse-in though.' Alfie pointed at Paige's chin.

'Yeah, this comes with me everywhere I go.'

'Huh?' Melanie asked.

'I think he means my piercing. He was asking me about it on Saturday.'

90

'Yeah, her purse-in. I want one. Where can I get pursed?'

Melanie was about to offer some sage auntie advice, along the lines of, "Wait until you're older" but Paige beat her to it.

'Pretty much anywhere, Alf.' Melanie watched as Paige sat herself down on the floor and pointed to her ears. 'I have my ears done, and look the inside bit done too. I've had this one under my lip done, my eyebrow is done. You can pierce pretty much anything.'

Alf looked all serious as he studied Paige's face, and Melanie smiled as Paige let him. Paige only ever spoke to Alfie in the same way she spoke to everyone else, the grunts, the nods, they were all there.

'Will you read me some stories, Pwaige?' Alfie asked, giving the full please face with the eyes and the hands on his cheeks. It was a power move he had perfected in the last six months, but Paige seemed unaffected by it.

'Depends on what books, Alf.'

'I'll show you, wait there. Are these OK?' he asked all serious as he cascaded a dozen books all around them.

'You've got good taste, Alf. I like the Disney books.'

* * *

It was nearly half-eight by the time Alfie had settled and been read all the books. Paige appeared to have endless patience when it came to reading bedtime stories. She may not have done the voices like Melanie, but she had read them all as if they were the most incredible literature that ever existed.

'Can I ask a question?' Melanie started and waited until she had a Paige nod before continuing. 'What do you do about bad reviews on things like your Facebook page?'

'I don't look.'

'What do you mean you don't look?'

'I don't look. Ever.'

'We don't have that luxury unfortunately.'

'No, you probably don't especially given your socials niche. Why, what's up?'

'We've been getting the odd random bad review that's all. I'll just ignore it for now. I don't want to turn it into a bigger thing. Anyway' — Melanie looked down at her phone — 'We've only got about half an hour until my sister turns up. I'm really sorry. That's not going to give us long.'

'No worries let's do what we can and then book in for some more time.' Melanie had to agree, and if the flutters in her stomach were any judge, she was excited at the prospect of spending more time with Paige. Even if they had absolutely no business doing that.

She gestured for Paige to take a seat at the kitchen island and as she went past, Melanie noticed Paige's undercut had been freshened. She also noticed Paige smelt divine, the faintest hint of something slightly spicy, and if Melanie had to guess, it was either Paige's shower gel or shampoo and she almost leaned closer, but held herself back at the last minute. The image of Paige in a shower flashed through her mind, and good God. She needed to pack that in. Paige was on the 'to not do' list, but her mind and her libido had other ideas, because once they were settled on the kitchen island barstools, their knees touching, leaning towards each other, their iPads and phones on the table, Melanie found herself wondering about Paige's long legs. They were almost always covered in some sort of ripped denim.

Paige knocked her knee with Melanie's. 'Won't you need your to-do list if we're doing this?' Paige suggested, and Melanie felt her whole body flush with embarrassment, mortified at being caught checking out Paige, and not at all subtly. But Paige was smirking, her green eyes bright with mirth. Melanie straightened her skirt and pushed her glasses up before reaching for her iPad.

'Right, did you see the erm, the updates from Councillor Houghton? And he wants an update at the Neighbourhood Business Alliance meeting next Thursday.'

'Then maybe he should do it himself,' Paige muttered.

'I think as we know we're not going to get through everything tonight, we should prioritise putting in a second date,' Melanie suggested.

'A second date?' Paige asked.

Melanie kept her head down, opening up the calendar section of the app. Why was she so bad at this? She could talk to people, she did it all the time. But Paige made her feel like every word out of her mouth was loaded and could go off any minute.

'You know what I mean,' Melanie said as she saw Paige unlock her phone.

'A second date then. While I don't mind coming here, Alfie kinda cut into the time a little bit. So why don't we make this a weekly like quick update thing. And we can put another day in with more time, maybe at mine?'

Melanie still couldn't look up. Her breathing was a little fast, but hopefully not noticeably. Paige had just uttered what was possibly one of the sexiest things anybody had ever said to her, and she was sure that Paige had no idea.

A weekly catch-up update date. Oh, it was organisational bliss to know that they were going to regularly catch up. It was more than bliss, it was perfect. As for having a bigger meeting at Paige's flat. Or a second date as Paige had insisted. There was only one thing hotter as far as Melanie was concerned and if Paige suddenly pulled out some post-its Melanie was going to strip off right there at the kitchen island.

'It looks like next Tuesday might work for our second date. Why don't you come round to mine whenever you finish, and we'll get through as much as we can?'

'Erm yeah that would work. Thanks for helping me with this, Paige.' Melanie looked up, her eyes catching on Paige's lips and on that piercing. The piercing that was starting to keep her awake at night. She wanted to kiss Paige and find out if she could feel it against her own lips, and other places. It led to a whole host of imaginings.

'Mel, I'm home,' Emily shouted as the sound of the door, and a person with lots of bags, came from the hallway.

'In the kitchen,' Melanie called in response.

They both watched as Emily finally made it into the kitchen carrying five bags full of groceries in each hand.

'Here,' Paige said and before Melanie had even realised, she was up taking the bags off Emily and putting them on the countertop. Emily raised her eyebrows at Melanie and Melanie shrugged in response.

'You *must* be Paige,' Emily said in *that* way.

'I am, and I should get going. So sorry, but it was nice to briefly meet you.'

Moving back to the kitchen island towards Melanie, Paige reached across for her phone and keys. 'See you Tuesday yeah?' Paige's hand reached up and held oh so softly onto her chin, as she deftly moved Melanie's face slightly to the side. In a blink and you'd miss it type situation that Melanie absolutely did not blink and miss because she wasn't sure her eyelids remembered how, Paige gently pressed her lips to Melanie's cheek. She could still feel their heat and impression as the sound of the front door closing landed in her ears.

Melanie looked around the room, her eyelids still malfunctioning. But then she saw Emily all but melt into the barstool next to her.

'Oh my days, Paige is hot. I mean, like wow. I'm trying to be straight over here and yeah.'

Melanie nodded. 'Yeah, she is.'

Emily came to her senses first and sat up on the barstool. 'Please tell me you're going to do something about that?'

Since when was a kiss on the cheek that freaking sexy? Why hadn't her heart stopped racing yet and when were her eyelids going to get with the programme? What on earth would happen if they did more than that? Melanie wasn't sure, but she suddenly felt like she desperately wanted to find out.

CHAPTER FOURTEEN

Paige

Paige had not been counting down until Tuesday because that would be really uncool. But she was very reliably informed that today was Tuesday and therefore she would be seeing Melanie again, any minute. Which was fine, and she wasn't sure why she kept replaying the kiss on the cheek. Paige absolutely was not the sort of person to do a kiss on the cheek by way of saying goodbye. And while on the one hand that really shouldn't be noteworthy as it was very far removed from the full-on making out that Paige had wanted to do, it had been hot in its own way and Paige hadn't been able to stop thinking about it. She couldn't help but wonder if the second date would be hot too? Or maybe even more so?

Paige just narrowly avoided smashing several glasses as she misjudged the bar top. The same bar top she had stood at every day for the past four years, and she realised she really needed to focus. She felt bad not working tonight as it was; the least she could do was make sure she didn't cause more work in the meantime. Luckily as the manager/owner Paige made sure there was enough staff to cover and she would dip in and out when she could. As much fun as owning and managing a bar was, she preferred the serving customers than the stocktaking, rota scribbling and endless planning. Which reminded her she needed to make sure everything was ready for the psychic night next month. She'd gotten the psychic, it was the rest of the night she needed to prepare for.

'Hey boss, all right?' Belle asked.

'Yes thanks,' Paige muttered back.

'I'm fine too, thanks for asking.' Belle was smiling.

Paige stopped what she was doing and studied Belle. Paige knew she could be short, and some people found her obnoxious, usually the people she didn't need around her but still. She liked her team and chose them with care. 'Are you though?'

'Yes boss, I'm fine, promise,' Belle said with a grin.

'How's the new starters going?'

Paige watched as Belle stood taller, her smile wider, and knew she'd made the right choice giving Belle some additional responsibilities.

'Great, they're all settling in and I've buddied all three of them up. I might need to come back to you with some signposting queries, but we're OK for now. Don't worry boss, I'll keep an eye on them.'

Paige nodded before smiling softly. 'I know you will, Belle.'

'But you don't look right, what's going on?'

'I might be a little distracted is all,' Paige said, turning back to put away the clean glasses.

'Oh right 'cos of *Melanie*.' The way Belle said Melanie reminded Paige of playground taunts.

'No. I just have a lot on what with psychic night and this art thing.' Paige was studying the glasses very carefully.

'Hmm sure.'

'I can fire you, you know,' Paige said, wishing she hadn't bothered interacting. But Belle knew her almost as well as some of her best friends and had in fact taken on a grumpy Paige once or twice before and lived to tell the tale.

'You tell me that nearly every shift,' Belle said with a wink.

Paige grunted.

'Besides, if you fired me you'd have to work more shifts and then you couldn't spend any time with *Melanie*.' Again, the same sing-song taunt.

Paige upgraded to a growl in Belle's direction.

'You certainly wouldn't have anybody to drop off secret boxes of prosecco either.'

Paige spun around, her eyes narrowed. 'I told you not to talk about that.'

'I know. It's why it works so well to wind you up.' Belle's smile was sly. 'You know if she's distracting you, making you almost smash all our glasses, then maybe you should do something about it.' Belle slipped away before Paige could respond.

She could do something about it could she?

Paige allowed her mind to wander for a moment.

'Hey.'

Paige spun around quickly, feeling a little bit flustered at having conjured the person that she had been so vividly thinking about just a second before. She quickly gathered her cool, or what was left of it. 'Hey. You ready for our second date?' Paige asked.

Melanie nodded but didn't say anything further, as Paige led the way towards the private staircase and up to her flat.

'So hopefully we can get loads sorted out today, lots of things ticked off the list,' Melanie said, her voice sounding a little tight as she followed Paige up the stairs.

'What's up, are you OK?' Paige asked.

'Yeah, of course.'

Paige opened the door and gestured for Melanie to go first. Something wasn't right though she was sure of it. 'Is business going well?' she asked, trying a different avenue.

'Yeah.'

'You can tell me you know?'

'I'm sure it's nothing but' — Melanie's shoulders visibly sagged — 'as well as the reviews, we've started getting some strange complaint letters and some voicemails . . .' Her voice drifted away.

'Who would do that?'

'I don't know. I'm sure it will pass. But honestly, I don't even nearly have the time to think about it. It doesn't appear to be affecting business and there's plenty of incredible reviews.' Melanie sighed, and Paige studied her again. Melanie's skin, not quite as pale as her own, seemed to be duller, a little dark under her eyes, and she wondered if that was always there or usually covered by concealer. She made them both a hot drink before they sat down at the table, adding the tin of biscuits that Connie had pulled together along with iPads, phones and in Paige's case, a notebook and pen too.

'Right, so I think let's start with Councillor Houghton. He wants an update,' Melanie said as she straightened her skirt and pushed her glasses up her nose. A move that Paige was quickly associating with Melanie feeling flustered. 'I'll load up the email on my iPad.' Paige moved closer towards Melanie so that she could see the screen, so close they were practically touching.

'Great,' Paige said. There. That's what she was after. That scent of mango, the hit that made her mouth water, and her hands itch, and she felt it right into her very centre. Belle was right, Melanie was distracting.

Paige couldn't help but imagine all the amazing ways they could distract each other, couldn't help but imagine her legs, how smooth her skin would feel under her palms as she moved them up her calves, round the back of her knees, slowly edging higher . . .

'If you look here,' Melanie said before looking up into Paige's eyes and stopping abruptly. She swallowed. Paige saw Melanie's eyes widen, her pupils dilate, and Paige knew hers were doing the same. They were staring at each other now, lost in their own bubble in time. Neither moving, nor saying anything but communicating a whole lot. Paige's stare forcibly moved as she saw that Melanie was looking at her lips and she edged even closer. Paige's brain fractured, part of her trying desperately hard to think things through, to pay attention, the other part of her pushing forward the last few inches until their lips joined.

Melanie's eyes looked back up to hers, her pupils wide through her glasses, a desperate look, her brow furrowed.

'What do you want, Melanie?' Paige asked, hearing her own voice sound like a whispered growl. Their faces were now only an inch apart, their breathing shared. Paige slowly raised a hand to gently stroke the side of Melanie's face with her fingertips until they fell towards her neck where she slowly pressed her hand against Melanie's thudding pulse.

Still Melanie said nothing, but her eyes were back at Paige's lips, and her breathing was hard, and Paige felt it too. Her own heart raced, her blood pounded through her body.

'I can give you what you want,' Paige whispered, closing the gap slightly, their lips just touching. 'But you need to ask.'

Please ask.

Paige was desperate and holding herself back was a delicious agony that she hadn't anticipated. But it would be nothing compared to the agony of Melanie remaining silent. Her body was practically screaming, and Paige felt her fingertips tingle in response, wanting to stroke every single fluttering pulse point, to travel all over Melanie's body. She wanted to follow her fingertips with her tongue. She wanted it all.

But Melanie still hadn't said anything.

It shouldn't have hurt; they barely knew each other. But the lack of response was crushing Paige's chest and she felt slayed. Paige dropped her head, their foreheads touching slightly as she took in a deep breath and went to move away. But Melanie's hand gripped her wrist, keeping it on her neck.

Paige pulled back a little so that she could look at Melanie's eyes.

'Kiss me,' Melanie softly begged.

Their lips met and Paige was revived. Melanie's lips were so soft under her own, and Paige's eyes closed as she took in every hot sensation as Melanie pushed the kiss further with her tongue. Paige moved her other hand until she was holding onto Melanie's face reverently. Melanie's hands were on Paige's forearms, holding her in place, both clinging on as the kiss deepened, as they slowly explored each other. Paige was barely even breathing. But she pulled back a little, and very quickly took off Melanie's glasses, placing them on the table and bringing their lips together once more.

Paige cursed the fact they sat next to each other on the bench; she wanted them to be closer still. She was half tempted to drag Melanie onto her lap but for now at least she was content with each and every kiss hitting a little deeper, burrowing into her body a little further. Paige's blood rushed to all the interesting parts and her thighs pressed close together.

Melanie let out an exhale like a soft groan, her nails now digging into Paige's arms.

'Afternoon, my loves.'

Paige immediately let go of Melanie and shot backwards further down the bench.

'Gran!' she said loudly and with a hell of a lot of frustration as she spun around to see Connie at the door, having clearly missed the sound of her travelling up the iron staircase outside.

'I told you we needed a system in case of any interruptions. I told you I would put a sock on the door. Why didn't you do that? Hello Melanie, love, you all right? Well, I can see I've ruined the mood, so I'll just put the kettle on, hey?'

Paige stared in disbelief as Connie got to the kitchen and just carried on as if Paige's whole world hadn't just been cut apart and soldered back together again. Melanie had quickly put her glasses back on and moved further down the bench too. Her gran was right. The mood was ruined. For now.

CHAPTER FIFTEEN

Melanie

Melanie tried to concentrate as Louisa wrapped up their fortnightly staff meeting. Instead of customers their team were sat at the tables, their breakfast detritus not yet cleared away. These meetings took place early before Lulu opened for brunches at 10 a.m. and they alternated who led so Louisa only had to come in early once a month. Melanie was very glad it was Louisa running it today. They'd both been really clear coming into this business that as important as the customers and the reviews were, if they didn't look after their staff they wouldn't have the rest. And so their priorities were always to make sure staff knew they were valued. It was why Melanie and Louisa knew each of their staff members by name, knew what their home life was like. Not in great detail but enough to know that Trav would more likely need a shift change last minute as he had childcare needs. Or that Ari's mum had early onset dementia and might be late in if her mum had had a bad "do". They were all a team, which is why Melanie felt terrible at not being able to pay attention. She had her iPad in her hands, her business to-do list app open, but she was dipping in and out of focus. Every time she thought she was concentrating, her mind would replay the moment she'd shared a kiss with Paige yesterday.

'Melanie, have you got anything further to add?' Louisa asked, breaking into her thoughts.

'Just keep up the good work everyone, we really appreciate you going the extra mile for our customers.' Melanie hoped she hadn't just repeated what Louisa had said.

'Great, has anyone got any questions or concerns? Any feedback?'

'Yeah, erm. I'm really sorry to mention it but some of us have noticed a couple of bad reviews . . .' Melanie was impressed their staff were checking on reviews, and that they'd felt comfortable speaking up. Melanie had worked in many a hospitality setting where that wasn't the case.

'Thanks, Tempy,' Louisa said. 'Yes, we've seen those too. I don't want anyone to worry. As far as Melanie and I are concerned we're not convinced they're genuine, or if they are, they're very small in number compared to all the raving reviews we get the rest of the time. But thank you for looking. The success of Lulu is down to all of us.' Louisa's voice rang with confidence and the staff visibly relaxed in response. 'And finally, not wanting to put you on the spot, Cleo, but you're our first manager here, and our newest employee. How are you finding things?'

Cleo smiled briefly. 'I feel like I've always been here.'

'Great, I hope everyone is making you feel welcome. We'll be passing rota responsibilities over to you soon. We'll give it another week or so and then all queries will go to Cleo in the first instance. OK everyone, thanks for coming in those of you not working this morning, and thanks Rick for making the breakfast buffet.'

Everyone disappeared and Melanie realised there was at least two items on her iPad she'd completely forgotten to bring up.

'Mel, let's sit down. We have ten minutes before we open,' Louisa said. 'Tempy would you mind grabbing us some coffees please?'

Melanie followed Louisa, until they sat at the small table right at the back of the room. Melanie looked around, watching as everything was cleared away and reset ready to open the doors at ten a.m. There was a small smile on her face as she saw how smoothly everyone worked together.

The coffees appeared a moment later, and Louisa sat back, mug in hand, as she blew the top of it, giving Melanie a kind stare that simply said, 'Spill'.

Melanie didn't know where to start, her head was a mess. They hadn't managed to get through any of the art project to-do list because Connie decided she wanted to get involved and had spent their remaining time relaying all her credentials and why she would be a useful commodity. Melanie was grateful for Paige's help but between the time lost watching Alfie, the time spent with Connie, not to mention the time spent kissing, Melanie could have used that time to actually do some of the tasks, and the number of boxes not yet ticked off was stressing her out. Then there was the kiss.

The kiss.

Oh God, the kiss.

The way Paige had held onto her like she was the most precious thing in existence. The way she could feel Paige's piercing against her lips, and her tongue. The way her heart felt completely restarted. The way her body lit up from within. Oh, it was outrageously hot for a simple kiss.

'What can I do to help?' Louisa asked when Melanie still hadn't said anything. It was the serious tone, the look of concern on her face, the hand that Louisa put on her arm, that hit hard. The plates were not all spinning. Something was going to slip, and it couldn't and wouldn't be anything that would put their business at risk, which included the art project, nor would it be something that would put Alfie at risk either.

'I'm sorry. I'll move the items we didn't discuss today to the next meeting. The prosecco issue is now resolved.' Melanie studied her iPad on the table, scrolling through the list. 'Do you think we should try and get those reviews removed? Maybe put something back?'

'Melanie, I'm not bothered about any of that, are you OK?' Louisa asked, her head tilted to one side.

'Yeah, I've just been distracted but I'll sort it.'

'We were mates before we were business partners. I know we don't get to see each other much outside of work these days, but we're still friends first. If something is going on, tell me.'

Melanie sighed. 'I think I have a lust build up, and it's causing me to lose focus, to lose sight of what's important but I promise I won't let you down.'

Louisa nearly snorted out her coffee. 'How long has it been?'

Melanie raised an eyebrow. Louisa must have a rough idea because she could barely find time to spend with her actual partner, so when would Melanie have found time to find one? Besides she didn't want to admit that there hadn't been anyone since Laura.

'You've been with someone since Laura right?'

Dammit she must have thought her name too hard, like if you say Beetlejuice too many times. She wouldn't utter the name again just to be on the safe side.

'Look, it's fine. I'll deal with it. I'm not going to let you, or us, or this business down.'

Melanie's iPad pinged and she looked down at the message.

Paige: *I think we should make the third date somewhere else so we don't get disturbed and we get some work done? How about we go out for dinner? X*

Oh God. A third date. A third date. But like a third. Date. Wasn't there still an expectation of something on a third date? Shit, this was confusing.

'Ah I see. It's about Paige.' Louisa nodded, like everything suddenly just made a whole lot more sense.

'We kissed,' Melanie said quickly, her brain to mouth filter still faulty.

'Yes! So that's the distraction. Go get some.' Louisa nodded.

'I don't think . . . like I don't have time. I don't see how I can fit her in.'

Melanie realised what she'd said, at the same time Louisa creased with laughter. Melanie reluctantly smiled.

'You say it's lust then you know what you have to do,' Louisa said once she had finally gotten her breath back. Melanie looked around deliberately avoiding her gaze. The doors were open and the customers were starting to pack in.

'Something to think about. Right, I'm off. I'll see you later. But don't forget to text Paige yeah? I'll swing by the cash and carry on my way in — is the list up to date?'

Melanie nodded. 'I'll make sure it is, but you don't have to do that.'

'It needs doing, it's no problem.' Louisa stood up and they hugged. 'Nobody is saying you have to jump into a relationship if you don't want to. But maybe you should see what Paige is offering? And Melanie, if she offers you a relationship it doesn't mean it will go like the last one did.' Louisa squeezed her again before hurrying out the bar.

What would Paige offer? There were too many reasons to avoid a relationship: the timing, the business, her responsibilities. While Melanie knew they were all true she also knew she had yet to sort out her old demons, but rather than think about that, she sat back down and looked at the message on her iPad.

Melanie: *We're not exactly getting much work done are we? X*

She sent it before she could overthink it.

Paige: *That's why I think if I take you out for dinner we can get a lot more done x*

Melanie: *I'm not sure when we could what with our shifts and Alfie and everything x*

Melanie sent the text and then read it back, her stomach sinking. Yes, the art project work needed doing, yes, she did feel like she was dropping some of the plates she was desperately spinning, but her heart clenched at the thought of taking Paige off the to-do list — so to speak. Melanie started typing before she could stop herself.

Melanie: *One last try. Let's find an evening that works and I'll make an early dinner, you can come over and we'll do the art stuff and then you should still have time to get back to work. What do you think? X*

Melanie felt better after sending that. She didn't want to be rude to Paige, and she could use the help, so long as she actually got help. And yes, she didn't want to not spend time with Paige.

Paige: *Third date at yours. Just let me know when and what to bring x*

Melanie: *Let's do tonight then if you can make it work? We need to get to it x*

Oh no. What had she done? What was Paige thinking now? Had she really invited Paige for a third date at her place? Could she have any more obviously said let's have sex?

Melanie groaned and took her glasses off. She rubbed at her eyebrows gently, not wanting to smudge her perfect eyeliner. She picked up her iPad again.

Melanie: *To work, you're coming round to work x*

Paige: *I can work hard don't worry x*

Oh God.

Melanie felt flushed, and now her brain was fried and her body pulsed. She all but threw her iPad on the table as if it had burnt her.

'Melanie, I'm sorry I can't find the full allergy menu — do you know where it is?' Cleo asked.

Shit, she needed to focus. Switching into work mode, Melanie smiled.

'Sure, let me go see if I can track it down, it's probably in the kitchen.' Melanie put her glasses back on, straightened her skirt and tucked her iPad under her arm. Her spine was straight as she clicked on her heels through the restaurant, hoping she appeared calm and in control. Hoping that it might come true.

CHAPTER SIXTEEN

Paige

Paige had seen on Melanie's to-do list that flirting had been crossed off. She wasn't sure if that was good or bad. It was neither of their forte to be fair. Paige had also seen that Melanie should be on Alfie watch tonight, but had called in a favour with her mum, and Paige wished she knew what that all meant. Once again, she mourned for her mojo. She'd have had more confidence.

Paige followed the instructions and parked up at the end of the street, using the app on her phone to pay. She'd guessed at two hours, but who knew if she'd be sent home by that point or not? Paige would have known that's who. Consciously breathing through her cognitive impotence, deliberately choosing not to feel wound up by it, Paige approached the lobby. She would just have to take Melanie's lead. But they needed to talk. It was an all the cards on the table type situation, no more confusion. She buzzed to be let in, and as she waited she had a feeling of low-level static energy running through her. She realised she was excited, that she was experiencing anticipation. Not something she got to feel all that often when her mojo was in full swing.

But with that not knowing came hope. She hoped that they would end up kissing again and maybe even more, but hope was something she could cling on to.

Yes, conversation first.

Work second.

A rather heavy make out session third.

Hopefully.

Paige grinned as she realised, she'd just created a to-do list in her head. Melanie was clearly having an impact and Paige was tempted to add it to the app, but the lift was opening, and she was walking towards the flat. The door opened before she got there and Melanie waved her forward. 'Quick! Come on I need your help.'

Paige rushed forward, the acrid smell of burning reaching her nostrils before she'd even crossed the threshold. She followed Melanie inside, noticing with despair that she *still* wore the pencil skirt and shirt combo and her hair was *still* tied up. Then she saw the black smoke and turned her attention to the open plan kitchen.

'How can I help?'

'It's the oven. I only put it on to preheat and it's done this. I really don't want to set the alarms off and have the whole block evacuated.' Melanie's panic was clear as she opened the balcony door wide.

'Have you turned the oven off?'

Melanie looked at Paige as though she was an idiot which Paige took to mean yes.

'Where do you keep your carrier bags?'

Melanie looked confused. 'Here,' she said grabbing some and passing them to Paige.

'I need tape too.'

Melanie opened and closed a few drawers until she handed her some packing tape. Paige quickly grabbed a chair and reached up to cover the sensors, while Melanie grabbed a tea towel and appeared to dance around the room with it.

Paige kept her smile to herself. Once she was happy the sensors were covered, she slowly opened up the oven door.

There was nothing in there to have caused any immediate damage. She'd been expecting to see some sort of food. Then she spotted the bottom of the eye-level oven and the back of the door.

'Melanie, when did you last use this oven?'

'Why?' she asked out of breath as she continued to ballet around trying to direct smoke to the balcony.

'When did you move in?' Paige tried a different take.

'Erm probably coming up to a year, why?'

This was getting them nowhere.

'Be honest, have you used the oven since you've moved in?' Paige asked.

'Well, erm no, actually.'

Paige had suspected as much. It looked like the previous tenants had used it a lot but never actually cleaned it. Ever.

They'd have to wait for it to cool down and then scrub it. Well more than scrub it — this was probably at RIP level. Melanie appeared next to her.

'That's gross. I swear I'm not that bad.'

Paige looked around, glad the alarms weren't going off. 'You've been here a year?' There were boxes in every corner, and against some of the walls.

'Yeah, I've not had chance to get everything out and sorted.'

Paige raised an eyebrow, there must be more to it. 'And?'

Melanie hesitated, dropping the towel until she could wring it through her hands. 'There was an ex.'

'Ah,' Paige said.

'How long will it take to cool down?' Melanie asked, whether to change the subject or not Paige couldn't be sure, but she went with it.

'Who knows. Why don't we go and sit on the balcony while it cools down?'

'Sure,' Melanie said finally relinquishing her tea towel. 'Oh hang on, I have beers in the fridge, you want one?'

'Sure, thanks,' Paige said. She'd have one but then they needed a conversation.

The balcony contained an outside sofa and coffee table on matting. The sky still held on to the last of its light as Melanie sat down beside Paige and put two craft beer bottles on the table in front of them.

'I haven't unpacked the glasses yet, sorry.'

Paige shrugged; it didn't matter to her. 'Out of curiosity what were you planning on cooking?'

'I didn't have time to shop properly, so I was just going to do a carbonara.'

'Do you need an oven for that?' Paige pointed out.

'Garlic bread.'

Paige nodded and took a drink; it was good beer. She couldn't help herself from looking at the label.

'You can't have them, they're in the middle of signing an exclusive with us,' Melanie said, her gaze not even moving from the horizon, but she let out a soft, tired sounding chuckle.

Paige stayed quiet a moment longer. There was a lot to be said, but she knew or suspected at least that if she waited, Melanie would fill the silence.

Besides it was nice sitting outside with her in the low-level quiet surrounded by nice new looking apartments. There was a shared courtyard in the middle that looked untouched.

Melanie sunk further into the sofa, as Paige untied her topknot letting her hair fall to her shoulders hoping that Melanie might do the same. She looked stressed and tired, surely that would help? But it was armour wasn't it? It was her battle suit for any and all purposes. Battling with customers, with four-year-old nephews, and probably with Paige and everyone else. She must own pyjamas though, she wouldn't sleep in that, and Paige knew she had to find that out for herself one day.

Paige got herself comfortable and that meant moving ever so slightly towards Melanie.

'We got more reviews at the weekend, more voicemails too,' she said quietly.

Paige said nothing but turned her face towards her, hoping she would say more.

'I don't know what to do about it. Even the staff have picked up on them. I think if we don't do something someone might reply or something; they're starting to take them so personally, especially when we know they're completely made up. The gas bill has finally come through and it's about three times higher than we calculated. However, business has been steadier than we'd planned for so far, so we should balance out. But it just means more pressure to keep it going as it is. How long before everyone local has taken their Instagram pictures? I need to design next season's walls, hopefully reuse as much of the stuff we already have. Then there's this art project. We're meeting with the Neighbourhood Business Alliance and Councillor Houghton tomorrow and so far, other than the posters and the flyers which you sorted and distributed, we have nothing else to show for it. And then there's you.'

Melanie stopped abruptly, and Paige was in two minds. Push forward on that conversation and see where the 'and you' part was going. But then again, she could hear what Melanie was saying; she was listening to what was being said and what wasn't. Melanie was stressed. Forcing her into a conversational topic that she clearly didn't want to talk about, wasn't exactly meditative. Not to mention the other things that were going on. The unpacked boxes, the rushing around. No time for shopping? Paige had to wonder if Melanie was actually looking after herself properly. But mostly, Paige had no idea what would happen if she pushed that topic. So maybe ignorance for now could actually be bliss. It was a novel concept for Paige. Instead, Paige remembered what Connie had said about helping. *Helping is good, but you must make sure it's aimed in the right direction, Book'*. So instead of facing a potential rejection, she got her phone out of her pocket and opened up Uber eats.

'You like Greek food?' Paige asked.

'I said I was feeding you tonight, at least let me order something.'

'Greek yes or no,' Paige said firmly.

'Yes, and I want spanakopita please.'

Paige nodded, placing a large order so there would be leftovers and salad to last for a few days. She supposed that Melanie ate at Lulu but she'd never actually seen it.

'Oh gross, I stink of burning,' Melanie said with a shudder, leaning forward.

'Don't worry about it. If you get changed now, you'll just have to walk through it again,' Paige said reasonably.

They sat in silence again, their arms touching, and Paige felt a quiet peace with Melanie as they both sunk heavier into the sofa, the sky darkening and a slight chill in the air. Spring was trying its hardest but couldn't compete with the warm summer nights.

'Hang on,' Melanie said as she passed both drinks to Paige and lifted up the coffee tabletop. 'Here'. She produced a gorgeous soft silver throw and sat back down, getting closer to make sure the throw covered them both. Drinks back on the table, Paige took off her Converse and put her feet up. She threw her arm along the back of the sofa behind Melanie's head but not quite touching. The busy hubbub of Manchester was like a second throw surrounding them both, and Paige felt truly comfortable, hoping that Melanie felt the same.

Paige tried not to sigh as she finished her beer, knowing their reprieve was over and it was time to talk. She was surprised Melanie hadn't spoken yet. She hadn't seen Melanie ever be so still. Then she felt Melanie's head on her shoulder. Surprised, Paige quickly turned her head and saw she'd fallen asleep. Gently and carefully, she took both their bottles and put them on the floor. Before getting comfy again, she gently peeled off Melanie's glasses, putting them carefully on the arm of the chair next to her and then settled back down. Melanie sighed and turned slightly until she was nestled in next to Paige, under a blanket together. Paige quickly took her phone off the arm of the chair and snapped a selfie. She wasn't sure she would have this moment again, especially if they had a talk and it didn't go well.

Then realising that might have been a bit creepy, she sent it to Melanie too. Paige moved her arm until it was lying gently across Melanie's shoulders, resting her own head on Melanie's. She breathed in deeply. Yes, she could smell burning but that mango scent was there too. Paige couldn't recall a time she'd snuggled like this, felt this content. This was the first moment of peace she'd known since her mojo had gone, if not before. But Paige worried that this would also be her last and so she clung on to every second.

CHAPTER SEVENTEEN

Melanie

Melanie's eyes opened to the sound of soft talking and she realised a few things at once. Firstly, that she had fallen asleep. It wasn't that much of a surprise as she hadn't slept properly in so long that she'd become accustomed to catnaps. Except not usually outside, and not usually on the pillow she was currently on. Which brought her to the second thing. She could feel her pillow gently rise up and down, she could feel through her ear and her cheek as her pillow spoke softly. The third was the scent, that spicy scent of Paige's was in her nostrils and it sent waves of lust through her body, or it did until she smelt the smoky undertones too and remembered what had happened. She wasn't quite sure how she had ended up in Paige's arms but that's definitely where she was.

'Great, thanks, I'll be there in a second.' There was a pause and Melanie still hadn't moved. She should have moved as soon as she woke up. Now she was awake and er, snuggling? Would this constitute a snuggle?

'Mel,' Paige whispered as her hand stroked up and down her arm.

Melanie sat up, albeit with reluctance. 'Hey, sorry about that.'

'No, I'm sorry to wake you but the food is downstairs. I need to go find it before he gives it to someone else.'

'Of course.' Melanie moved further out of the way and Paige quickly put on her shoes before hopping up and disappearing through the apartment.

And Melanie needed a damn minute. She could still feel Paige's body beneath hers and honestly it was making her dizzy and breathless. Why did that woman have so much power over her? She'd never been this instantly attracted to someone and for it to get to this level where she felt combustible, it was as new as it was thrilling, and scary, and distracting. She had no idea what to do.

Standing up she hunted for and found her glasses and stretched out her back. Walking through the apartment she was pleased to discover the oven had cooled down, and more importantly, the smell was dissipating. She could close the oven door, take the bags off the sensors and cover the place in Febreze. She was going to add cleaning the oven to her to-do list but she already knew it would go right to the bottom. She didn't cook here anyway. It had waited a year. She had just finished with the air freshener when Paige came back in.

'Hey. Oh, that's better already,' Paige said with a smile and two large bags of food.

'How hungry *are* you?' Melanie asked as Paige turned around, putting the bags on the counter instead of answering. 'So, I need to go get a shower. I absolutely stink of smoke, is that OK? I'll just be in and out.'

Paige coughed a little before answering, then turned and looked at Melanie. 'Yes of course that's fine. Do what you've got to do. I won't eat all the food while you're gone. Promise.'

Melanie swallowed, the look of hunger on Paige's eyes was intense, and Melanie suddenly felt like she was the meal. She ran to her bedroom, grabbed her stuff and quickly hit the bathroom.

Melanie's hands were shaking as she started the shower and got undressed. Not really sure why, as there was a whole wall separating them, but being naked so close to Paige was having an impact. She pulled out all the grips in her hair, followed by the industrial strength bobbles and groaned with pleasure as her hair fell free. She couldn't decide which sensation was better, taking off her bra or taking down her hair. She'd have to wash her hair though, which meant she'd have to be even longer. Pulling open the bathroom door a little, she shouted out, 'I need to wash my hair, sorry, don't wait for me, get started.'

'OK. But don't worry,' Paige said in her deadpan voice.

Oh God now she was talking to Paige while completely nude, with the door slightly open. She quickly closed the bathroom door before she did something stupid. Her mind had parked up at horny station and seemed unable to move. Melanie returned to the shower, and turning the temperature down, hoped that might help.

Ten minutes later, she pulled on her knickers, black leggings, grey vest top and hoody, wrapping her hair up in a towel. She'd held onto her bra, debating whether or not to put it on for at least three of the ten minutes she'd been indisposed. It wasn't comfy and she'd had it on all day. Then she figured that if Paige wasn't there she wouldn't have put a bra on and so why change for other people. But the second the bathroom door opened, she felt a tingle of excitement. The balcony doors were still open, the apartment cool. And it was the coolness of the apartment, and nothing at all to do with being braless around the hottest woman alive, that was making her feel this way.

Melanie really should have made that shower even cooler.

She looked at the little breakfast bar and saw Paige had set it all up. Even managing to find the big plates, and the cutlery which Melanie *had* actually unpacked — she wasn't a complete heathen. All right, she'd needed them for takeaways.

There were cardboard food boxes everywhere and, rather than smelling like an incinerator, the flat now smelt delicious.

As she walked closer she caught Paige's eye, and nearly laughed at her expression. Paige slowly looked up her body, starting with her bare feet, slowly moving up the casual leggings, but then Paige's hot gaze continued, and Melanie smiled, but then Paige looked up to her face and scowled.

'What, what's wrong?' Melanie asked. She'd taken off her make-up, but she didn't think she looked that bad underneath. Her skin was clear and one of the features she was most proud of.

'Your hair.' Paige groaned. 'Just tell me what colour is it? Is it curly? Straight? How long is it?'

Melanie raised an eyebrow. 'You got a thing for hair there or something, Paige?'

'Don't kink shame and no I don't, but' — Paige stepped closer — 'I've never seen your hair down. You scrape it back off your face all the time and I was curious.'

Melanie nodded, but didn't really understand.

Paige stepped back. 'Right, I'll just dish up everything yeah?'

'Sure. Thanks.' Melanie sat down at the barstool, her knees weak. Paige gestured forward, and she saw another beer was open and ready for her. She helped herself, watching as Paige placed a selection of food onto plates, before putting salad into bowls too. Every now and then she licked her fingers as she went. Melanie was transfixed. There was a lot to take in: Paige's arms as she lifted food, spooned it out; her hands as she picked out pastry filled things, her tongue appearing when she licked her fingers.

Paige put the plates down, and then quickly swept up the mess and wiped down before she sat down too, and honestly the whole thing was one of the sexiest things Melanie had ever seen. Finally, they were sat side by side at the breakfast bar. Neither said much as they ate through vine leaves and spanakopita. Melanie watching carefully out of the corner of her eyes as Paige's fingers held the food carefully, her mouth savouring each bite. Melanie was turned on and it was not for turning off.

She ate the salad, the kebab, the rice. There was so much food, and for once she didn't have to eat it quickly, ready to deal with the next problem, the next task, she could savour each and every bite. She felt like she hadn't eaten like this in a long time. Her eyes caught on Paige, licking her fingers clean.

'I think we need to talk,' Paige said, placing an olive in her mouth.

Melanie nodded, not as fully lucid as she would have liked.

Paige licked her lips. 'I could be way off here, but I think we are distracting each other.'

Melanie stilled. Where was she going with this? Was she about to be mortified. Oh no, she was about to say something along the lines of, 'It's clear you have a crush on me, but this is a working relationship.' Melanie was quite sure she would die of embarrassment if that happened.

Melanie carried on eating, preferring to say nothing rather than letting her mouth take over, but it was hard to swallow and her heart raced as she focused on the plate in front of her.

'I would really like to spend the night with you. If you'd like me to. I think . . .' Paige paused, and Melanie couldn't breathe, not until Paige finished her sentence. You think what Paige? That we should leave all the food and go to the bedroom? That we should not see each other in any capacity any more? What? Melanie couldn't remain focused on the plate, she had to look at Paige's face to try and get a sense of what was about to be said.

Their eyes locked. Melanie had to breathe through her mouth, unable to get any of the oxygen in the room into her lungs.

'I think that we might both feel less distracted if we dealt with this like adults.'

Dealt with what?

Melanie forcibly swallowed and wiped her hands and mouth with a napkin, but she still needed the clarification. 'What exactly are you saying, Paige?'

'I'm saying that if you would like to, I can tick something off both our to-do lists. I think a few dozen orgasms should be enough to make us both feel better. Get it out of our system, so that we can focus. Just a tonight thing.'

Hang on. Paige was offering a night of orgasms, a dozen orgasms without the expectation that anything else happen?

'You're offering me a night of orgasms, one night, to get this attraction out of our system,' Melanie said, her face flushing as she heard it again.

'Yes, I think we'll both feel a lot better afterwards, in fact I'm going to work really hard to guarantee it, but only if you want. If you're not interested and I completely misread, then I'm really sorry. But . . .' Paige's voice dropped lower. 'I'm not wrong, am I?'

Melanie lost the power of speech, her throat dry, her body having chosen the more important task of heating her up, of making her ready for the dozen or so orgasms. But Paige needed an answer. Melanie tossed her head back, her towel falling to the ground, threw her glasses on the side, and yanked her hoody off. She was between Paige's legs in a second.

'Yes please, Paige.'

CHAPTER EIGHTEEN

Paige

'Yes please, Paige.'

Those three little words were as powerful as a starting pistol. Paige didn't have time to note the breathy way Melanie had said her name, nor the fact she finally had Melanie out of her armour, her wet hair hanging between them, because Melanie had placed herself so firmly into Paige's body where she sat on the barstool, that she could barely move.

But then Melanie's lips were against her own and Paige's body sparked to life. Her arms wrapped around Melanie's back bringing her in even closer, until their chests were touching. Melanie's hands were tight around Paige's neck, clinging as if to keep her in place as they devoured each other's mouths. Paige held back at first, not wanting to unleash the full force of the passion she'd had building for Melanie for the last few weeks. But then Melanie softly groaned, and her teeth lightly grazed Paige's lips, and Paige knew she was losing control.

'I need you,' Paige whispered, her lips travelling across Melanie's cheek and then down her neck. Paige's breathing was heavy as she tasted and devoured, as she drank in the taste of Melanie and took the scent of her deep into her lungs, the feel of her delicate skin on her lips, licking, sucking and teasing bites as she went.

Melanie let out that whimper groan, her hands moving, one of them holding onto the back of Paige's head, her fingers tangled in her hair, the other on Paige's forearm as she pushed down, driving Paige's hand further down her body.

'What do you want, Melanie?' Paige asked, whispering directly into her ear as she continued to kiss up her neck, finding that spot that made Melanie's back curl as she whined.

'Paige, just give me everything, I want it all.' Panting, Melanie continued, 'Don't hold back. Please.'

'I want specifics. I want a to-do list.' Paige grinned as Melanie squirmed further, her hand pushing down on Paige's arm, until it covered her breast over her vest top, her tight nipple sitting in Paige's palm. Melanie lowered her arms, her back arching, thrusting her breasts more firmly at Paige.

'OK first on the list,' Melanie breathed out. 'Naked. Then . . .' Melanie's speech was lost as Paige began pressing and moulding her breast more firmly. 'Then,' Melanie tried again her breath shaky, her body taut. 'Then orgasms. All of the orgasms. Yours and mine.'

Melanie groaned as Paige teased her nipples, at the same time as she was kissing back down her neck, biting her way to her clavicle, breathing deeply. Melanie's hot skin smelt of mango and of pure Melanie. She licked up the droplets of water from her wet hair as she went. Her hands moved to Melanie's hips, pushing up the vest top so that her hands could feel the heat of her bare skin. Paige's fingertips tingled with every stroke.

'I thought you were supposed to be organised,' Paige said, between kisses, her voice low. 'You have the list all wrong,' Paige whispered into her ear, as Melanie's body continued to undulate under her hands.

'I do?' she whispered, her eyes closed and her head back.

'Yeah. Orgasm first, then naked. If that's OK with you?'

Melanie nodded, her smile wide, as Paige lifted Melanie's vest top straight over her head, not caring if her arms got tangled, as her eyes instead focused on the sight right in front of her. She tongued around Melanie's breast before gently biting the underside, until finally she reached her nipple, sucking it in to her mouth, her hands exploring what wasn't currently being feasted on, as Melanie gasped and twisted. Paige listened to how Melanie responded and knew she was on the right path when Melanie's hand clawed onto Paige's thigh, and she could feel her nails through the denim.

'More. Please, more.' Melanie was panting and Paige took a moment to study her. Her head thrown back, her chest pumping wildly, her hands gripping Paige's shoulders so tightly that Paige could see the muscles in Melanie's arms. Put simply, Melanie was stunning.

Paige quickly looked behind her, hoping there was some space to get Melanie to sit on the countertop, but there wasn't and Paige didn't want to delay any further. Her mouth still on Melanie's breast, one of her hands trailed down her stomach and towards the waist band of her leggings. She pulled back and quickly looked at Melanie, her eyebrow raised.

'Can I make you come?' Paige asked.

Melanie's physical response was to shudder as if asking the question had been as much a turn on as everything else, 'God yes, but only if I can make you come after?'

Paige grinned. 'I'm sure you could.'

Their mouths met again, and Paige's hand travelled underneath Melanie's waistband, over her knickers, feeling Melanie's heat and gently playing with her through the cotton.

'Oh,' Melanie said, her hands no longer able to hold onto Paige, instead holding onto the breakfast bar behind her, rigidly straight, her face pointed up to the ceiling, her eyes closed tight, as her hips moved urgently back and forth over Paige's fingers.

Paige groaned, She could feel Melanie growing more wet even through the cotton and knew that she couldn't hold off much longer.

'Please Paige, I need more.'

Paige kissed Melanie hard, taking her groans and desperate pleas and instead moved her hand, thrusting two fingers into her and pressing down with her palm, pushing against her, and then she began to move slowly in and out.

'Hell Paige, I'm so close. Don't stop.'

Paige had no intention of that, wild dogs couldn't pull her away. She was right where she needed to be, completely in the moment, completely focused on the task in hand as it were. She could feel Melanie trembling, her body rocking onto her hand, taking her in further.

'Yes, yes, yes. Oh yes Paige.'

Melanie's whole body tightened, and Paige felt her fingers squeezed by Melanie's core, her thighs shaking until slowly her body began to soften as she all but collapsed, her legs not able to support her weight. Paige slowly disentangled her fingers, as Melanie's head landed on Paige's chest as she tried to catch her breath.

'Oh my days, that was . . .' Melanie was still breathless and wobbly as she looked up at Paige.

Paige moved closer until she was breathing and kissing and whispering into Melanie's ear, 'If it's just tonight, I want it all. Don't hold back. I want everything. I want you begging, I want you to tell me every little thing you've ever wanted to do or have done. I want all of it.' Paige watched as Melanie's eyes widened, her pupils dilated, and her breath shook again. Paige continued, 'So don't keep anything from me, I want to hear it all, I want to taste it all, I want to feel it all.' Paige spoke at the same time her hand travelled up and down Melanie's body.

'Give me everything,' Paige demanded.

Melanie licked her lips, her body still rolling beneath Paige, but she didn't hesitate.

'I want you to take it.'

CHAPTER NINETEEN

Melanie

Of course, she was going to be late, of freaking course. There were few things that stressed Melanie out more than being late, especially when it could have been avoided. If she hadn't overslept, then her day wouldn't have felt so rushed from the very second she opened her eyes. If she hadn't had Paige in her bed for half the night, perhaps she wouldn't have been quite so worn out, and maybe she wouldn't have overslept. But then again she wouldn't have had the best night of her life. And only part of her regretted kicking Paige out in the first place. But they had both agreed it was a one night thing. Done and done.

Anyway, here she was, living the girl boss dream. Scrabbling around the pavements trying to get everything that had seconds earlier fallen out of her bag that had decided there was no better moment to break. In the bag's defence she had been pushing it to its very limits every day. She even had on her to-do list to order a new one. It probably should have broken a long time ago. But this was far from the ideal time. She reached under a car to try and get her phone, retrieved it with a grunt, before slowly standing up, gingerly holding her bag together and all of the contents she could recover. She was pretty sure she dropped a few tampons but the birds could have them now. As much as she was digitally minded, she still had supplies. Wet wipes, she had 'em. Post-its she had 'em. Nail file. Deodorant and so on. Laptop. In this case yes, she had managed to squeeze her laptop in as well as her iPad as she was hoping to sort out wages. So now she had her bag clutched to her chest, her arms aching with the weight, her head feeling dizzy with the rushing as she tried to jog in stilettos and a pencil skirt to the Neighbourhood Business Alliance meeting, wishing she'd chosen Converse today.

She turned and used her bum to push the door open, not even stopping to say hello to Kazim. She rushed through and made her way to the meeting room, panting as she went, not feeling at all in control of anything. The plates no longer spinning but throwing themselves to the floor today that was for sure.

And then of course there was Paige. Even now, Melanie stumbled as her eyes locked onto Paige's. What had they done? Melanie felt like they'd gotten the attention of the goddess of love after their night of passion. Like she was being punished in some way with constant reminders, dreams, daydreams and longing. Her mind would wander off constantly, and she'd see an image of Paige between her legs, or of Paige naked before her and so on. Her bedroom forever ruined. Whatever they were previously, had they been friends? For argument's sake let's say they had been friends, now it felt odd.

So of course, there she was. And there was a space right opposite. Fine. That was OK. She could be professional, and she could stay focused.

'Ah here she is,' Councillor Houghton called out. 'We wondered where you had gotten to. Right anyway, Charlene as you were saying?' Melanie landed in her chair and tried to carefully and quietly get her things together while listening to Charlene talk about a new retail space that was to become available. Melanie was trying to listen as she knew it was important, but she was still trying to hold her bag carefully so its contents wouldn't spill again. She felt like a crisp eater at the theatre, rustling and chomping all over someone's important monologue.

'Well, will it be the same process as last time?' Lydia asked.

'Yes, yes. The protocol has been set up now. Anyone that wants to let that space will have to present their business proposal through us as we will have some sway. Not a lot, but in some cases enough. Just like we did with Melanie here.'

Melanie's head shot up. She hadn't really been paying attention but now her name was being called out. Shit. What was going on? Melanie was still sweaty from her impromptu stiletto jog. Her shoes were rubbing blisters into her toes, her skirt was awkward, her glasses sliding down her nose and she still held her bag in her hands.

'You know what we don't have a lot of in our part of the world?' Paige asked, in what was one of the few times she'd heard her speak in this forum. 'Charity shop or vintage clothes shop. It would really help with our sustainability and eco priorities.'

'Yes,' Councillor Houghton agreed. 'Yes, let's think green on this. I'll coordinate this end. I dare say some of the unsuccessful applicants from last round will want to try again. But anyway, I'll let you know when we have candidates for interview, and then we can figure out the who's and when's and whatnots.'

Ah, they were talking about when Melanie and Louisa had to come and present their ideas for Lulu in order to secure the lease. Fond memories of the first time she'd been intimidated by Paige. Strange to think it was only about six months ago.

There were nods around the table.

'Right then great, well that brings us to our main agenda item for today, the art mural. Back over to you Melanie for the big update.'

The big what now? She'd seen the agenda, knew she was to give an update, but she'd presumed it was just a quick five-minute job. What in the bloody hell? She tried to swallow but her throat was suddenly dry, her heart racing as everyone turned to look at her. For some reason there was a large attendance today. Of course there was.

Melanie felt sick. All she could hear was the sound of plates smashing around her.

'Well,' Melanie began before clearing her throat. 'I'm afraid there isn't all that much to report. As you know the posters and the flyers were distributed. I've checked the community inbox, and it looks like there have been some erm, responses.' Melanie's voice trailed off. What could she say? That she had planned to do some work last week but her caring responsibilities for her nephew didn't help, or that Connie had waylaid the next time she'd tried to focus on the project. Or maybe she should tell them that her lust had gotten the better of her and any spare time had been spent either imagining Paige naked or being with Paige naked.

The cold sense of dread trickled through her body as she looked at Councillor Houghton's face. She could see his disappointment and her body chilled further in response. This was a familiar and unwelcome feeling, and it was one that she worked hard daily, to avoid. When the dust had settled with her ex, Laura, Melanie had made a promise to herself that this wasn't going to happen again. She swore that she would never be made to feel little, unable, stupid. All the names that she had been called before. Yet, here she was, and for a horrifying second, Melanie thought she was about to cry. But, no not again, she'd worked hard to become someone stronger. She clutched her bag closer, trying to ground herself.

'Well, Melanie . . . Yes . . . Well, I think we had hoped you'd be a little further on by now.' His tone was unwaveringly polite but the reprimand clear, and the murmurs around everyone else in the room didn't go unheard either. The one thing Melanie could not do was look at Paige.

Melanie licked her lips and hoped her voice didn't carry the remembered pain of this feeling. 'Yes, well I'm hoping to push forward and set up the vote, get the press involved, secure our artist. Then we can set up the rest of the stuff from there.'

'Yes well, I have to say Melanie that when we agreed to let you take on the lease I thought we were very clear about what it meant to be part of this community. That lease very nearly went to someone else, you know?'

No, she didn't know, but was now really the time to bring that up? She felt shitty enough as it was. She hadn't even asked to take on this project in the first bloody place. Melanie welcomed the anger, it warmed her up, protected her from the icy shiver down her spine.

'I'll make some progress this week and update you,' Melanie replied.

Councillor Houghton looked thoughtful. 'Perhaps this is a big project in such a small timescale. Do we have any volunteers to help Melanie with this?'

'I'll help.'

'That's wonderful, thank you, Paige. And with your personal style I'm sure you'll be a valuable asset to Melanie.'

Paige said nothing, and Melanie still couldn't look at her.

A what? She would be a what?

'Right then, seeing as how we have more time, is there any other business?' Melanie let the conversation go on around her.

She was in trouble. Grabbing her iPad she added an item to her personal to-do list in capital letters.

"NO MORE SLEEPING WITH PAIGE."

There. She could do that. Hopefully, as planned, they'd banged it out of their system. Besides it was Paige's fault they hadn't been able to do any work. If she hadn't been so interesting to Alfie, if she hadn't had such an interested gran. If they hadn't been so interested in each other there would have been more done, and Melanie wouldn't have to feel like this. But even as she felt out of control, she knew that wasn't true. This was on her, and so it was up to her to turn it around.

Her iPad buzzed.

Reminder: Pick Alfie up from school.

She looked at the time. It was fine, there was time. She couldn't just walk out. She'd make it in time. She had a look at the rest of her schedule.

Reminder: Stock check with Louisa to be done before the 10th.

Melanie already knew. She just knew that today was going to be the tenth. She knew that because tomorrow she was putting the order in with her suppliers for the following month. So of course.

She quickly shot a message to Louisa.

Melanie: *I have Alfie but we need to stock check I'll be there as soon as I can x*

Louisa: *Don't worry I'll try and sort it x*

Plates smashing everywhere, Melanie was surprised everyone else couldn't hear them.

'Great, in that case, thank you, everyone. I'll see you at the next meeting.' Councillor Houghton grabbed his briefcase and quickly walked out the door, talking to Hayley the cake shop owner as he went.

Melanie tried to get her stuff together but it was hard with a broken bag. Getting her iPad that was still out, she put *'Get a new rucksack'* higher on the list.

Melanie looked up as Paige approached her, the room having emptied now.

'So . . .' Paige said.

So? So?! Was that all? Melanie was fuming. Yes, she knew it wasn't all Paige's fault. It was as much hers, but still.

'Listen Paige, thank you for the offer of helping with me on this art project, but I really don't think it's going to work, do you?'

'Why not?' Paige asked quietly.

'Why not? Because every time we tried it didn't work!' Melanie shouted.

'Yeah, but it might be easier now.'

'Easier now?' Melanie whispered. 'Easier now what? Your magical vagina has cleared all the tasks off my to-do list, relinquished me of my caring responsibilities, my business responsibilities, my business loan, has it?' Melanie whisper shouted. But Melanie didn't really do rage, she couldn't ever hold the anger for long. And then she reheard what she'd just said to Paige.

Paige stared at her, clearly not having expected that response. But then her face broke into a smile. 'My magical vagina? Did you really just say that?' Paige laughed properly now and Melanie couldn't help but join her.

'Sorry, I'm just. I'm defensive, I'm sorry.'

'I get it, you're embarrassed about being called out over something that wasn't your fault. You're no doubt pissed off too, right?' Paige raised her eyebrow, her eyes still twinkling.

'Yes. All those things.' Her feelings now vocalised, quickly began to simmer down.

'I'm sorry. I promise I can actually help. I really can.' Paige's hand landed on Melanie's arm, the touch sending a shock through her.

'No, I don't think it will work.' Melanie moved her arm away.

'Look, I will banish my magical vagina back from whence she came. I won't be a problem, I promise.'

Melanie burst out laughing.

'Please let me try again,' Paige said earnestly.

'Absolutely no banging. Lock that magical vagina away.'

'We have to stop calling it that. But yes. No more silly business. It's time to get serious.'

Melanie nodded. 'OK then, fine, one more chance.'

Paige moved towards the door. 'I promise to keep my hands to myself. Hope you can say the same.' She chuckled as she left the room.

Melanie didn't have the same level of confidence. Her mind constantly filled with images and wishes. Unsurprisingly given that it had been one of the greatest nights of her life. But focus, back on track. What the hell had she just agreed to? Again. It wasn't going to work and if it didn't it would be all her fault. She went back to the to-do list.

"REALLY — DO NOT SLEEP WITH PAIGE IT'S NOT WORTH IT."

It wasn't worth it. There was too much at stake.

Her phone pinged.

Louisa: *We've had more reviews.*

CHAPTER TWENTY

Paige

'Right, what's the plan then?' Connie asked as she stood over the hob.

'I'm going to her sister's tonight. There's a five-book max policy in place with Alfie and then we're getting everything set up, contacting all the people that have applied and yeah, just getting our shit together.'

And absolutely nothing else, because I'm apparently not worth it.

Paige moved towards the pot on the hob. 'Who are you making that for?'

'What's this? I thought I could make it for you and Melanie. You can't work on empty stomachs. And I don't think Melanie looks after herself properly.' Connie tutted.

Paige didn't say a word. She just continued to stare at Connie. That was not all there was to it. Mojo or no mojo, that was not it.

'That stare never worked when your mother did it, it's not going to work now either,' Connie said without looking away from the pan.

'She's texted again,' Paige replied.

Connie didn't say anything, and Paige wasn't sure if she wanted to talk about it anyway. She quickly moved on, 'But just so I'm clear, that's the mushroom risotto, right?' Paige asked.

Connie nodded, her spine straightening.

'The mushroom risotto that you swear *has* to have oyster mushrooms, or it isn't worth doing?'

Connie nodded again but slightly more rigid this time.

'The oyster mushrooms that you specifically purchase dried, that you rehydrate using a very specific broth for twenty-four hours, *that* risotto?'

'It's the only way to make it, Errol taught me that.'

Errol was husband number three and mega chef. He didn't last because she never saw him. Or so she said.

'Do you still see Errol?'

'From time to time, we stay in touch,' Connie replied still carefully stirring.

'Come on, Gran, who's coming for dinner?'

'No one.' Connie just stayed focused on the pot in front of her. Paige waited again. 'No one you know, now mind your business,' Connie said, giving in a little.

'Will there be a sock on the door when I get back?'

'No of course not, it's not like that. The Captain has already set sail. This is more of a professional interaction than it is anything else. Anyway, this will be ready in twenty minutes and I've made enough so you and Melanie can eat too. In fact, there's enough for little Alfie to try. Need to start training those palates early, you know.'

'Thanks,' Paige said slowly, still suspicious, sure there was more to it.

Connie finally put her spoon to one side and turned to study Paige. She raised her hand to rest on Paige's cheek just as she'd done ever since she was old enough to remember.

'What's wrong, Book?'

It was the sudden change in direction that caught Paige off guard. 'Nothing. Well, nothing I want to talk to my gran about.'

'Ha! You finally did some fun stuff with Melanie then. About time. The heat between you two. Yikes. You're probably going to want to take some mints with you, this risotto has a strong flavour.'

'Don't worry, that's not on the cards,' Paige said.

Connie removed her hand and quickly turned back to stir. 'Oh, and is that why you're sad? Or is this more about your mum?'

Paige growled out an agitated breath. 'It's not that and I'm not sad.' But she continued, 'Besides we agreed it was a one-night thing. We were just getting too distracted by not doing it. Now it's done and we can focus on work.'

'But you remember your reading, right?' Connie asked quickly, glancing over her shoulder at Paige.

She sighed. 'Of course. I'm going to go downstairs and make sure everything is under control.'

'OK but be back up here in twenty. You need to take the risotto right away else it will get claggy.'

* * *

Paige pulled up outside Emily's house and took a deep breath before grabbing her bag. She'd brought her notebook and pens; they had to get some decisions made tonight. Paige was not going to let Melanie down.

Paige made her way to the main door; it opened before she could get close.

'Pwaige! Auntie Mel already said five books only.'

'Most people say hi first Alf,' Paige said as she offered out her fist.

Fist punched, Alfie continued, 'Come on let's go.'

Paige smiled as she followed this little man with his cute *Star Wars*-themed PJs back into the house.

'Pwaige, come on,' Alfie urged as he started climbing the stairs.

'Hang on,' Paige called back, making her way towards the kitchen. Melanie sat at the kitchen island, iPad already in hand. Paige bent down and kissed her cheek. 'Here, Connie made us dinner. Pop this in the oven, really low heat. I hope you like mushrooms. Shall I go and start the reading?'

Paige ran off before Melanie could say anything else, embarrassment sweeping over her. She'd kissed her on the cheek. Again. She'd been here only seconds and already she couldn't keep herself away. But she'd made a promise. And besides, *she wasn't worth it*. Yeah, she wasn't getting over that one any time soon.

'Right then little man, what books have we got?'

Paige sat down on the floor cross-legged and watched as Alfie ran around picking up books and putting them back down again, until finally he had the chosen ones.

She grabbed the first book off him and expected him to sit next to her. Instead, he stood right in front of her waiting for something.

'What?' Paige asked.

'I can't sit on your knee with all the books.'

'Er, OK.' Paige moved the books to the side and suddenly Alfie made himself comfortable on her. His fingers held onto the rips in her jeans.

'Better now?'

Alfie nodded.

'Right then, book number one. Let's do this . . .'

'Pwaige why do your jeans have holes, did a bear get you?'

Paige snort laughed. 'No Alf I just like them like that.'

'Can I rip up my jeans?'

Paige didn't know what to say so opened up the book and started reading. By book number three she'd noticed that Alfie's head had gotten heavy on her shoulder, and he wasn't saying as much. She didn't get to the end of book three before she could hear little snores.

Once again, she didn't really know what to do. Would he wake up if she tried to move him? She wasn't sure she could get up even if she wanted to.

Shuffling until she could get her phone from next to her, she quietly texted Melanie.

Paige: *Help*

Apparently, that was the wrong thing to text because she could hear Melanie tear arse up the stairs and throw the door open.

Paige whispered, 'I'm sorry. He fell asleep on me and I didn't know what to do.'

'Well maybe don't text *help*. I thought something horrible had happened.'

Paige nodded. 'Understood. But I can't lift him up and my legs have gone dead.'

Melanie smiled. 'I'll grab him and settle him. You try and stand up.'

Melanie quickly reached down and pulled Alfie into her arms, as he murmured in his sleep. Paige slowly stretched her legs out. No, they were gone, but the agony of pins and needles was going to kick in any second.

'Fuck,' Paige whispered as she tried to ignore the pain and stand up.

'Come on, let me help,' Melanie said, pulling Paige's arm up and over her shoulders, her other hand sliding around her waist. Paige's body jolted at the touch. But she leaned slightly on Melanie until the feeling in her legs overtook the pain and she could stand.

Melanie let her go and led the way back out the room, closing the door to.

'What have you brought to eat, it smells amazing?' Melanie asked, her voice still soft as she began walking down the stairs.

'Connie's famous mushroom risotto. Her third husband taught her how to make it. He said that if food was the way to the heart then this was the way to . . .' Paige stopped talking quite quickly.

'Turns out, you've made quite the impression on Alfie,' Melanie said changing the subject quickly.

'Yeah? Why's that?'

'He's been asking Emily when he was going to see you again. And when I picked him up from school today he had felt-tip on his chin. He says he's had a "purse-in just like Pwaige". He was very upset when I washed it off in the bath.'

Paige grinned. 'He's a good man.'

Melanie shook her head. 'Come on then, let's eat. I'm starving. Then I'll go through the plans so far, and you can tell me what you think and add any others in too.'

The way Melanie groaned when she ate the risotto was a little too much for Paige. But soon enough that was over, and they both sat at the kitchen island ready to crack on.

Paige studied Melanie as she got all her things in order. Connie was right about Melanie not looking after herself, Paige had been wondering the same. The skin underneath her eyes seemed more grey, and she had an air of exhaustion around her that made Paige wonder when she'd last slept properly. Which reminded her. 'Oh, hang on I have something for you that might help.' Paige made quick work of running to her car, before getting straight back to the kitchen island.

'Here, it's for you,' Paige said.

'What is it?'

'Nothing special. I just had one about and figured it would be more useful for you. But if not don't worry.'

Well, she sort of had it lying about. Once she'd ordered it. Her reading with Connie had told her she needed to help Melanie, so that's what she was going to do. Well, it hadn't said Melanie specifically, but she knew that's what it had meant.

Looking into the bag, Paige watched as Melanie's eyes lit up.

'Oh wow. Are you sure? I mean this would be amazing, but I'll just borrow it until I get one of my own, if you don't mind?'

Paige looked at the brand-new reinforced rucksack. 'Don't worry. Just take it. I honestly don't use it.'

'It looks brand new. Thanks, Paige. You're sure?'

'It's just a rucksack, Melanie, and you need it.'

Melanie nodded, and with a Melanie megawatt grin she inspected the bag. 'Thanks, Paige.'

'No worries, right let's get back to it.' Paige sat back down, her chest warm as Melanie's happiness infused her every cell.

'Am I right in thinking that Monday's and Tuesday's are our quietest days?' Melanie asked, gently placing the rucksack by her feet and looking at her iPad but not before adjusting her skirt and then her glasses, in other words she was back to all business and Paige wanted to prove she could do that too. So, she opened up her notebook and the to-do list app on her phone. But she would be lying if the sight of Melanie's grin didn't make her feel light as helium. But no, she needed to focus.

'Yep, that's right. Were you thinking of having the artist selection audition thing, on one of those days?' Paige asked.

'Yes. I'm wondering if we could do it as early as Tuesday, so I guess the first task then is to find times we can be available and hope Councillor Houghton can make it too.'

'Did you think we should try and get press coverage for the selection?' Paige asked.

'Yeah, but I think we need to make the choosing panel more diverse,' Melanie said.

'What about Alfie? He's got great taste,' Paige said with a smirk. 'And I can think of a few more people that we could ask too.'

'OK, so if we did it after school next Tuesday, I would probably be picking him up anyway. But where are we going to do it?' Melanie asked.

'We can do it at mine. I'll close one side of the bar down for a private function,' Paige said.

'That would be great. I don't think we could afford to take a hit like that at ours just yet.' Melanie grimaced.

'Is it going OK? Lulu always looks packed whenever I see it.'

'Yeah. Mostly, I — well, no. I mean. Yeah, it's fine.'

'No, go on. What were you going to say?'

Melanie forced out an exhale. 'I'm sure I'm just being paranoid but these reviews, the voicemails. I just get the feeling it's not something we should be ignoring. But anyway, you know how it is with business loans and pressure. We can't afford to slip is all.'

After a soft grimace, Paige spoke up. 'Actually, I don't know about that. Barbarella was bought for me by Connie. It was her living will request after her last husband died.'

'Oh Paige, are you privileged?' Melanie asked in mock horror.

'Yeah. I mean I was raised by my gran while my mum was doing her own thing, does that help?'

'Not much, Paige, not much.' Melanie smiled. 'I imagine being raised by Connie was amazing.'

'Yeah, she's the best.' Paige didn't and couldn't say anything further, but her hand brushed over her phone on the table, half expecting her mum to pick that moment to try and call again. She pulled her hand back and focused on Melanie; it was clear from her face she had more questions.

'Right, well, moving on,' Melanie started. 'Yes let's do it at yours. I mean the call-back thing with the artist not . . .' Melanie's voice wandered off and she laughed nervously.

Luckily Professional Paige kicked in and she quickly moved them on. 'Obviously we can get Sophie to advertise it, but that's sort of global.'

'That's all right, I have some press contacts from when we launched Lulu and I'll get in touch with them.' Melanie added to her to do-list with every action. Paige watched as her app updated, pinging each time an action was added.

'So how many people have applied?' Paige asked.

'Hang on, let me check.' Melanie clicked about on her iPad. 'About a dozen.'

'Do we need more?' Paige asked.

'Probably,' Melanie said before sighing.

'Fine, I'll see what I can do to secure some last-minute contenders.' Paige made a mental note to check with the domestic abuse charity she worked with to see if they would be entering.

'We have the pay arrangements sorted and ready to go. They've been signed off. We need to get the final version of the brief for the judging panel. The thing to be used for scoring the entries. But I guess that's got to be approved by the group.' Melanie put her iPad down and went to run her hands through her hair.

'You can put your hair down if it would help. Does it not give you a headache tied up like that?'

'You just want to see my hair again because of your hair fetish.' Melanie laughed, and her cheeks turned red.

Paige deserved a medal. *Professional!* 'Yes, I think it should go to the group.'

'We have something that we sent out to the entrants, so all the key info, but I wasn't sure how to do this for the judges. Business plan yes, this no. I mean is there a proper way of doing one?' Melanie asked.

'Seb might know. She was involved in something like this before, hence the flyers she could so easily adapt. Let me check now.' Paige grabbed her phone and shot off a text before looking up to see Melanie bite her lip, a tiny scowl visible across the top of her glasses.

'You OK?'

'Yeah,' Melanie said in a not very convincing tone.

'You sure?'

'Yep, so that would be great if, Seb, was it?'

Paige nodded slowly as she studied Melanie picking up some sort of vibe but not knowing quite what.

'If she could share with us . . .'

Paige's phone buzzed on the table.

Seb: *Yeah I'll email something over in the morning? X*

Paige: *Fab thank you x*

Paige looked up and Melanie was looking out the window. Something told her Melanie was looking as far away from Paige's phone as possible.

Could it be . . . ?

'Seb is Bailey's sister. She did all the graphic design at Sophie's wedding.'

Melanie's face lit up. 'Oh yeah, I've seen her on Sophie's YouTube, right?'

'Probably,' Paige said.

'She's gorgeous.'

Paige nodded. Seb was gorgeous, but there'd never been anything there between them on the few times they'd met, and Paige suddenly felt the desire to explain all this to Melanie, but didn't know how. Professional, she reminded herself. She needed to remain professional.

'Anyway, she's going to send us over something in the morning, then we can try and write something ourselves?'

'Sounds good,' Melanie said, but Paige could tell her smile was forced and she had no idea what or how to make it better. In a professional way of course. But then some niggling feeling made her explain further.

'Seb is just Bailey's sister. Not a partner or ex-partner.'

Melanie nodded; Paige could see the scowl disappearing. And there was nothing at all professional about the way that made Paige feel.

CHAPTER TWENTY-ONE

Melanie

Melanie stirred in her bed, and she knew without even opening her eyes that it was around three in the morning. If she opened her eyes it was game over, she'd be awake. The trick was to keep her eyes closed and try to stay still, and then it was just hoping she would fall back to sleep again.

It didn't work.

Again.

She groaned as she turned to grab her phone from where it was charging next to her bed. Sure enough: 3.45 a.m. She opened her schedule for the day. She was opening Lulu as usual, and Sunday was one of their busiest mornings so that was fun. She checked the to-do list, and her brain immediately began to spin; had Louisa ordered the stock that needed replacing from the inventory? Was her sister going to parents' evening later this week? She also needed to get Cleo's latest rota. They needed to sort out these reviews and find out what was going on. Actually, what they really needed to do was start planning for next season's Instagram walls, no that could wait until the art thing was done. Maybe she could get one of the artists in to do one of her walls? Yes. She added that as a possible to-do. And her eyes caught on the one to-do that was all in capitals.

"DO NOT SLEEP WITH PAIGE IT'S NOT WORTH IT."

Melanie sighed and gave up on the idea of going back to sleep. Instead, she turned on the lamp on her bedside table, reaching for her glasses as her eyes could only take so much strain. She grabbed her iPad and began making notes and writing lists. After about an hour she finally put her iPad down, making sure her app synced with her phone. There had been a lot of new interest about the art mural, so Paige had clearly been doing her bit, *and* she had ticked it off the list. It made Melanie smile.

But then she sat in bed, the lamp still on, the outside world still dark, and everything felt really quiet. She looked around her room and saw the boxes that littered the edges. She really should unpack, but she didn't want to see the reminders of what her life had once been. When surrounded by another person's noise, their breathing, their singing, their comments, their grumbles, their shouting, and worse their silence. Melanie knew there were parts of being in a relationship that she missed, and parts that she really hoped she would never have to deal with ever again. The micro-aggressions that chipped away a tiny chunk at a time, the bad feeling, the belief that it had been all her fault. That she hadn't been good enough to keep the relationship going, that she hadn't been enough to stop her from cheating.

But just for a moment her bed felt a little too large, and her flat a little too quiet.

She imagined herself at Paige's. The place where she'd immediately felt at home, felt the warmth. Melanie went to lie back down and her eyes drifted shut, as she let herself imagine for a moment what her life might be like with someone like Paige beside her. All right not someone like Paige, but Paige herself. She smiled softly as she sunk further into her duvet, her body cocooned, still, rested and peaceful.

So, of course her alarm went off on her phone and her eyes opened back up again. It was time to start the day. Great.

The lack of sleep wasn't new and so Melanie cracked on, doing her morning tasks, getting herself ready for the day, going for a run, and going into work early to see where they were up to with the inventory. They had most of the stuff, but the last lot of avocados they'd taken went off too quickly. She made a note to send someone out as soon as the shops were open to try and find some.

She'd had time to sit down and really study the bad reviews and noticed there was a cut and paste pattern about them. Then figuring there was still nothing more she could do about that, she'd made the mistake of looking at the bookings over the month and realised reservations were dropping. The day carried on from there. The avocados had all turned, and nary an avocado could be found and Cleo had not been able to get cover so Melanie was waiting tables and taking orders when what she really needed to be doing was one of the million tasks on her list.

So, it was of very little surprise when Melanie crashed into a customer as they shot back on their chair, and she managed to get hollandaise sauce all down her pencil skirt, and so far, hadn't had chance to change. But the more it dried the worse it looked.

Some of her customers were going hard on the bottomless brunch and they were nearing their time limit, not to mention getting a little too bolshy, and Melanie just knew she'd have to deal with that too.

Grabbing some of the empty plates from another table, she took them back to the kitchen, running backwards and forwards cleaning the tables, taking the orders, while her brain worked a million miles an hour wondering about the bookings being low, but as she looked around the room it was nearing capacity. It was as her brain wondered off thinking about that, that she failed to see the customer's handbag in front of her. Tripping forward she wasn't sure how but she managed to right herself and land back on her feet rather than face-planting.

Straightening gently, muscles in her side stretched, she realised she'd heard a smothered crunching sound. She immediately bent down to put things right for the customer, apologising as she did so. Until she realised she was actually picking up bits of colourful glass coming out of the customer's handbag.

'Wait, are these our glasses? Are you stealing our glasses?' Melanie asked, looking up from the floor.

'No! You can't prove that.'

'I'll just put these pieces of broken glass back in your bag then, shall I, if that's what you choose to carry around with you?'

The eyeball from the customer was enough to send Melanie over the edge. Luckily Cleo came over.

Melanie straightened. 'Boss,' Cleo whispered, 'you want me to handle this one?'

Melanie nodded and walked away to get a dustpan and brush, returning to sweep up the rest of the glass off the floor as the customer held onto her bag on her lap, her voice strong and tone unpleasant as she complained to Cleo.

'I just don't think it's on. She can't talk to people like that. Are you the manager?'

'I am, yes,' Cleo replied, her voice soft and gentle but in no way submissive.

'She called me a thief.' The customer in question pointed down at Melanie, and Melanie sucked her teeth as she continued to clean up. 'I really don't think she can be allowed to say that to customers. I demand you do something about it.'

'Right and what would you suggest?' Cleo said still controlled, face neutral. Melanie took her time clearing up the last of the glass, interested to see how their new manager would handle it.

'I think our meal should be free and she should be fired.'

Melanie looked up and saw the dirty glance thrown her way.

'Let me get this right, so that I understand what you're saying,' Cleo said. 'You would like your meal to be free and for this member of staff to be fired.'

'Yes.'

'I wasn't finished,' Cleo said. 'You would like your meal to be free, for this member of staff to be fired, because you put some of our glasses into your handbag, and then left your handbag in the middle of the floor for someone to fall over.'

The customer's face fell as she quickly realised the manager was not actually on her side.

'Also, this member of staff that you would like fired, happens to be the owner of this establishment, and so let me ask her what she would like to do.' Cleo turned around, her voice not raised once, as she helped Melanie back up to standing. 'Melanie, would you like to call the police about the alleged theft that took place today? Would you like me to get the details of this customer so you can sue her for personal injury? I'm sure in both cases we will have recorded evidence of both, given the camera that is covering this area. Finally, boss, would you like for this customer to be banned?'

Melanie basked for a second in Cleo's awesomeness, and then she turned slowly and dangerously as she looked over at the customer who was now starting to pale as she realised she was in the wrong. Cleo had handed Melanie power on a plate and it felt amazing. The dustpan and brush kinda threw off the vibe a little but Melanie stood tall as she looked down her nose at the customer.

'I'm sorry, OK. I'm sorry. I was careless. Look, here's the cash for the meal and the drinks, we'll just go OK?'

Melanie nodded, as cash was thrown on the table and the two customers fled. Melanie turned and smiled at Cleo. 'You're so awesome Cleo. That was incredible.'

Cleo softly smiled and shrugged as if it was no big deal, and went back towards the bar. Melanie was still amazed as she spun round and strode towards the kitchen, power still coursing through her; she felt unflappable. Maybe her day was starting to turn around.

'Oh my word that was amazing!' A voice she recognised called out to her before she could get to the back.

'Sophie, hi. How are you?' Melanie racked her brains to figure out if she'd missed the fact Sophie was coming today or if she was just randomly there. Sophie gently leaned forward and hugged Melanie, who in turn tried to keep the glass, the dustpan and brush and hollandaise skirt away from Sophie as much as possible.

'I'm really good. I just hadn't seen or heard from you in a while, and was worried I'd offended you with the offer of a makeover.'

Melanie looked down at herself, sure her make-up had mostly sweated off an hour ago. She was covered in hollandaise sauce, which was drying on her black skirt in a really unseemly way, all while holding a dustpan and brush.

'No, the absolute opposite. I'm shocked that you would offer, it would be such an honour. Truly. I just . . . I can't fit it in right now. I'm sorry.'

'No worries, I understand. You're running your own business. I totally get it.'

'No, really. I hope to take you up on it one day and, oh my gosh, we haven't sorted out a time for you to come in and use the walls. I'm so sorry. That's not like me. It must have slipped off my radar.'

Sophie placed her hand on Melanie's arm. 'It's totally OK, Melanie. Paige told us all about this art thing you guys have got going on so maybe after that, yeah?'

'Thanks Sophie, we can definitely sort something out then.' Melanie felt her shoulders relax a little.

'But hopefully we can all meet for drinks before that point?' Sophie asked.

'Excuse me, miss?' Melanie glanced around to see yet another person looking down their nose at her.

'Yes?' Melanie said, trying to keep her voice polite, full customer service mode activated, but it was hard.

'I understand you are the owner?'

'Yes, how can I help you?'

'I'm Chemaine Dalgleesh, from the council. I'm here to inspect your kitchen. We've been receiving complaints.

Do you often walk around the restaurant with a dustpan full of what looks like broken glass? Perhaps we should go somewhere more private?'

Melanie couldn't understand what was being said or the ID badge being flashed around at first. There was a dull clanging in her head. Like her body had realised the seriousness before her brain. But then her brain slowly caught up.

'Er, yes of course, follow me.'

Melanie quickly looked back at Sophie and mouthed 'sorry'. And she was. Really sorry. Sorry that this day was happening.

CHAPTER TWENTY-TWO

Paige

Paige was at the bar waiting for her appointment to turn up, as she looked through the reviews for Lulu. Something was niggling at her that Melanie was right. There was something a little off about them. They read as though someone was jealous rather than genuinely upset about the service or food or whatever. Paige clicked back and forth, but wasn't able to come up with any sort of plan. She was grateful when there was a knock at the bar door.

As she unlocked the main door — they weren't yet open — she realised Belle had turned up at just the right minute too.

'Hi Jenny. Come on in. Hey Belle, you OK?'

'All good boss, you?'

Paige gestured them in then locked the door, leaving the key in the lock for Jenny to see so that she could get out easily if she needed to. Sure enough she saw Jenny glance once and look quickly away again. And every time it twinged at Paige's heart. Paige strode towards the windowed section so that it was nice and bright, hoping Jenny would follow and knowing Belle would.

They got to the seats and Belle didn't miss a beat, but between the two of them they had been doing this routine for a while now. 'I'll go get us all a drink yeah? Has the milk turned up yet?'

'No just run upstairs, it's unlocked. Thank you.'

Belle saluted before dashing away.

'Make yourself comfy. We'll just have a drink and a chat. I'll tell you about the bar, how it works, and then if you want you can tell me a little about you, then if you fancy it you can try out behind the bar before we open. We don't properly open for a little while so we'll just pretend for now. Although you can help me set up for an event we're running later if you want?' Paige sat with her arms on the table, her tone purposefully mellow, and even smiled occasionally. Well, smile was a bit much but she certainly wasn't growling.

'So Jenny, I'm Paige, that was Belle and you know Selena, right?'

Jenny nodded, twisting her hands in her lap. Paige watched as Jenny steeled herself, her spine straightening. 'Yes, Selena said she's had other people work for you before right?'

Paige nodded. 'Yes, we've had a few. Some people enjoy work but don't want to work in a bar, some enjoy bar work and stick around and others get bar jobs elsewhere. I'm more than happy to be used as a stepping stone to wherever you want to go next.'

'What do you want, guys?' Belle shouted from behind the bar.

'Cup of tea, please. Jenny?'

'Tea, please.'

Drinks made Belle rejoined them.

'So how this normally works is that we offer you work of a few hours each day. Once you get used to it you can then pick what hours and days you want. If it's working out that is. You might decide you don't want to work here. If you haven't worked anywhere before or if it's been a long time don't worry. We get that a lot. Just take it easy and see if you like it first, OK?' She hadn't already bolted which was a good sign. 'Do you want to have a go at pulling a pint?'

It wasn't long until Jenny was chatting away to Belle, and they were pouring pints, measures, shots and all sorts. Next was managing the payment system and Paige was impressed to see she was handling that like a pro.

Paige's phone went off, and although she grabbed it, she didn't look, she knew from the sinking feeling who it was trying to contact her again.

'I've got this, boss, if you need to take it,' Belle said, nodding to Paige's hand where her phone continued to ring.

Paige nodded and moved towards the stairs that separated the bar from her apartment. Sitting on the bottom step she looked at the phone screen. The ringing stopped and then before Paige could even take a breather it started up again. Paige stared at it, still unable to actually do anything but recall the last time they'd spoken. It had been about seven years ago. Her mother claimed she wanted to reconnect, to get to know her daughter as an adult. It hadn't been true though. She'd wanted a favour, and no doubt did again.

Her phone finally stopped ringing.

'You could speak to her, you know?' Paige would have jumped but she already sensed Connie at the top of the stairs.

'I can't, you know that. It's not even a big deal. It's water under the bridge. She got bored of me once, she'll do it again.'

'Book, come on, you know that was never the case. And I happen to think I didn't do too badly.'

Paige turned around to look up the stairs. 'You're amazing, Gran, you know that.'

'I do know that. But do you know something?' Paige waited. 'I wasn't talking about speaking to your mum.'

Paige stood up. 'I've got to get back to the bar.'

Connie sighed, the concern evident on her face, but Paige was already gone.

CHAPTER TWENTY-THREE

Melanie

'So, what do I have to do?' Alfie asked from the back of the car, school uniform still on and pen ink all over his hands.

'You just have to look at some pictures and pick the one you like best,' Melanie replied, her voice high and sing-song in a way that she knew placated Alfie but also meant she could hide the stress that she was actually feeling. And she was feeling stressed. The health inspection had taken place there and then on the Sunday right when they were at their busiest. Dan, the head chef had nearly walked out. They'd had to turn some walk-ins away not having the staff on hand or full use of the kitchen. And now they were still waiting on their results, not knowing whether or not they would be shut down for absolutely no reason at all.

On the face of it, Melanie knew she ought not worry, their kitchen was clean, well-organised and documented; complied with all the codes. Dan and Louisa consistently worked hard to make sure that was the case. But a surprise inspection did not make for a chilled-out Melanie. Or indeed Louisa, and when Louisa heard about it, she came to the conclusion that someone was trying to set them up, the same someone behind the bad reviews. Melanie was forced to admit she'd been wondering the same, but if she started thinking that someone had a vendetta against them, then she should probably give up the idea of sleep altogether. Nevertheless, an emergency staff meeting had been called this morning, everyone was updated and reminded on the rules, and it was fair to say, staff morale was low.

Alfie had been saying something in the back of the car and Melanie immediately felt guilty for tuning him out. Good Lord she was tired.

Pulling into her parking spot at Lulu, Alfie cheered.

'I like your work, Auntie Mel. I like all the flowers.'

'I know, but that's not where we're going today. We're going to Paige's bar.'

'Ohhh.' Alfie jumped up and down in his seat which was less than helpful when she was trying to get him out of it.

'Come on dude, help me out, we're late enough as it is.'

Alfie wrapped his little arms around her neck and Melanie breathed in. She loved Alfie more than anything, and so of course the guilt worsened.

'Here's the plan — hold my hand, it's busy, so you and Paige and a few others are going to look at some amazing paintings, and you're going to all pick your top three favourites. Oh, and you'll get some little stickers to put on the ones you think are best.'

So long as Paige got the stickers that is. But in fairness Paige hadn't ticked off a single thing on the list that hadn't been done well, and in some cases, better than Melanie had ever envisioned.

'That's good, 'cos I get a sticker at school if I'm good.'

Melanie nodded as they continued to stroll down the road towards Barbarella. 'You might get a sticker if you're good today too.'

She saw Alfie grin. 'Will there be food too? I'm hungry.'

'I'm sure we can find you something.'

Melanie grimaced. Why the hell hadn't she thought to bring a snack? It was rule number one with kids.

She pushed the door open, and they walked a few steps in before Alfie froze. The interior was much darker than Lulu, and while Melanie thought it was a really cool and gorgeous space all set out with different light fixtures and fittings, she saw it instead through the eyes of a four-year-old. There were a fair few people all gathered around one side and the other side was empty. Melanie wasn't sure which one was more unsettling.

She squeezed his hand tightly and began walking forwards, but she could feel his little feet didn't want to move.

'Hey Alf,' Paige said as she strode towards them. Her usual adult tone to Alfie just like always.

'Hey Pwaige,' Alfie said his hand tightening as they stopped walking and waited for Paige to get to them, and when she did, Melanie watched as Paige quickly assessed the situation.

'Alf, can I pick you up? I need your help with something,' Paige asked bending down so that they were face to face.

Melanie said nothing as Alfie let go of her hand and nodded slowly at Paige.

She picked him up and placed him on her hip as if she'd done it loads of times before and Melanie felt her heart twinge at how cute they were together.

'Come with me, Alf. I need to show you around and you can help me with my problem OK?' Paige turned to Melanie. 'And if you don't mind getting everyone in place, we'll be right there?'

Melanie nodded and watched as they strode off together, Alfie laughing as he felt Paige's undercut, and her heart twisted in panic. Paige and Alfie really were close. It hadn't been her intention but if things went south with Paige, Alfie might unintentionally get caught in the crossfire. She was glad her last relationship was already on the rocks when Alfie was a baby; he didn't remember Laura, and Laura had had no interest in helping look after Alfie. It cemented her decision. Paige was a friend. Only a friend. They could be friends for years and Alfie would be OK.

Hearing raised voices, Melanie turned around to look at the group, grateful for the interruption. Quickly pressing on with the next task at hand, she placed her bag on her shoulder, straightened her skirt and her glasses and strode forward.

'Good afternoon, everyone, I'm Melanie Curzon. Myself and Paige Roberts are in charge today. Are we ready to get started? I need the panel of judges over on the far side near the bar, please, while the artwork is arranged.'

Melanie's tone was calm and confident as she began channelling the control and poise of Cleo.

'We just had some queries,' Councillor Houghton began.

'I'm sure you do and once we have everyone in position, we'll get that all sorted for you.'

'But are we not shortlisting or anything? What if we pick someone unsuitable?' Councillor Houghton asked.

'Define unsuitable,' Melanie challenged not missing a beat.

Councillor Houghton nodded. 'Very well.'

'Right, who's here from the press?' Melanie dropped her bag and got her iPad out as a couple of people made their way towards her. Making sure the media had their info she then corralled the onlookers, some artists in the running, and some of her fellow Neighbourhood Business Alliance pals, to make sure they were stationed out of the way. Then Melanie unboxed all of the collated artwork samples and began placing them on tables, making sure the artist's details were hidden on the back. Once all fifteen pieces of artwork were placed evenly around the space, Melanie coughed to get everyone's attention.

'Judges, if you would all like to come this way, please, and I'll remind you of the brief. We are seeking an artist from our community to paint a huge mural, to celebrate our diverse family ethos and community spirit.'

'And for Tim and Simone from *BBC North West Tonight*, may I present our judges, Councillor Patrick Houghton, Chair of the Neighbourhood Business Alliance that is sponsoring this endeavour.' Melanie looked back down at her notes and waited in case Councillor Houghton wanted to add anything further. He simply nodded and Melanie moved on.

'Paige Roberts, member of the Neighbourhood Business Alliance and owner of Barbarella. Next to her and representing our younger generation is Alfie Curzon.'

'I'm four,' shouted Alfie, and Melanie noticed he was still firmly holding onto Paige's hand, but then she noticed Connie was stood beside them, pointing to herself.

'Paulo Hennessey, owner of Tatt This. We also have, Kazim Hussain, student and manager at All the Beans.' Melanie's attention was taken by Connie waving frantically, pointing to herself.

'And finally Connie Roberts-Bowles representing our more experienced community.'

Melanie paused while Connie took a bow. Trying not to laugh at Paige's expression, she carried on. 'Judges, you each have a copy of the full brief to remind you of what has been asked, along with points you may wish to bear in mind when scoring. You have also been handed three stickers. Once you have made your considered decisions, please put the stickers on your three favourite piece of artwork. Thank you. And please begin.'

Melanie heard Paige lean down to Alfie and say, 'You want to walk around with me?' At the same time, Councillor Houghton leaned down and whispered something to Connie that made her laugh and playfully slap his arm.

What the . . . ?

Choosing not to look into that too much, Melanie watched on as the judges circled the room, the rest of the place quiet except for the occasional murmur. Melanie had seen some of the work in the emails but hadn't seen the sample pieces properly. Each artist had been asked to produce one A3 image that they felt best reflected the brief and a write-up of how it would be achieved, and the meaning behind it.

She knew there had been two colleges submitting group entries, a few quite big named artists had entered, a charity organisation and some first timers. Melanie smiled, it all rested entirely on their understanding of the brief and their community. It had been the fairest way to ensure everyone that entered was on the same playing field. They had toyed with asking people to bring examples of their work but that meant those desperately seeking the opportunity for the first time, would be excluded.

Alfie broke the near silence. 'I love that one, green is my favourite colour. Can I put all my stickers on that one?'

Paige shook her head. 'No, but you can put one sticker on that one. And then we can keep looking, yeah?' Alfie struggled with his sticker and Paige waited patiently by his side. Melanie was itching to get over there and peel it off for him. 'I did it myself,' he finally said. Paige nodded seriously, and Alfie placed his sticker down.

It took twenty minutes, and surprisingly it had been Connie and Alfie who had taken the longest to decide which artwork deserved the last sticker.

And finally they were done, and Alfie ran up to Melanie as she scooped him up to give him a big cuddle.

'I did it. Was I a good jug?'

Melanie grinned. 'Amazing. Can you help me see which one got the most stickers?'

Alfie nodded as she put him down. 'I hope it was the green one.'

They went around each one, Alfie shouting out to the room the number of stickers on each.

'So, Alfie which one got the most stickers?'

'The green one got six.'

'That's right, the one with the most stickers is . . .' Melanie held up the artwork to everyone and looked to see the name on the back. 'Selena and co.'

Connie thankfully started the clap that saw the bar break out into full applause. Melanie looked around unsure if Selena had been watching or not. 'Selena if you are here, come and say hello, and if not, then I'll guess I'll see you over email.'

The press took a few more pictures and asked the judges to gather around the winning entry before they took off.

'Alfie my dear, you were an amazing judge and you have such great taste — it must run in the family.' Connie caught Melanie's eye, as she tried and failed not to squirm. 'Alfie, what's your favourite food?' Connie asked. 'Mine is spaghetti bolognaise.' There was a sly smile on Connie's face.

'Oh that's mine too.'

'Great, I have some cooking upstairs. Let's go and eat. Come on, that's you as well, Melanie. And don't worry, Paige will join us in a minute once she's reset the bar.'

Melanie was helplessly pushed along by Connie towards Paige's apartment. 'You don't need to. I mean we weren't expecting you to . . .' And the other question, when did Alfie tell you what his favourite meal was? Or was that just a guess?

'Not at all, there's plenty and I had a feeling our young man here would be building up an appetite with all that hard work he did downstairs. Besides, who doesn't love spag bol hey? I might even have a chocolate brownie with your name on it, if you eat all your food.' Connie grinned at Melanie, a look in her eyes that suggested she knew full well that was Melanie's favourite too.

It had been a long day in a strange week, and Melanie was more than a little bit moved that someone was cooking for them both.

CHAPTER TWENTY-FOUR

Paige

Paige had known the judging was going to go well, and she hoped the press reported on it favourably. And yes, that was maybe a 'known' in a 'mojo' sort of way — *please let it be back!* — but she couldn't and wouldn't say for certain, worried it would be scared away again. One thing she definitely *didn't* 'know', but would soon find out about, was her gran's involvement with Councillor Houghton. Paige couldn't help but wonder if he was the one the mushroom risotto had been for.

Paige had cleared the artwork away, safely stowing it away for pick-up and had straightened out the bar, just as the after-work crowd began coming in. She went upstairs to her flat. Or should she say home? Because that was the feeling when she saw Connie dishing out spag bol and Melanie and Alfie both sat on the bench at the table. This was so different to how the flat had felt before, not that Paige had noticed that there was anything missing. She'd always liked her quiet, her solitude, and actually if she had this twenty-four seven then she probably would miss her peace. But the smells, the chat and the laughter were all things she hadn't realised she'd been missing, and so she sat down ready to join them.

'You did good today, Alf. You gonna come work for me when you get older?' Paige asked.

'Auntie M, I made a pint,' Alfie said, a huge grin on his face.

Ah yeah, probably not great to let a four-year-old serve behind the bar, but he had asked and Paige found she couldn't say no. Melanie raised an eyebrow in clear disapproval and Paige felt the responding smile tug at her lips.

'Can I have some food now, please?' Alf asked with a big smile at Connie. Charmer.

'Of course, sweetheart. Here you go — but be careful, it's still hot.'

The garlic bread was passed around, and everyone tucked in.

'I imagine you guys still have lots of work to do now that you've a winner? Who is Selena and co. anyway?' Connie asked.

'Yeah, it was one thing organising the judging, which you were all great with, by the way. But now we really need to get a wriggle on,' Melanie said before she frowned, and then Paige knew what would be next. And there it was, the glasses pushed up. Melanie was anxious. It was still on the lower end of Melanie's anxiety scale, and only when it was combined with the skirt straightening and legs crossing were they really in trouble.

'Well, after dinner, why don't Alfie and I watch a movie while you two crack on with work?' Connie suggested. Paige studied Connie and knew she was up to something.

Melanie looked to Connie, her eyebrow raised. 'Are you sure?' Then Paige watched as she cast the same unsure glance her way. 'Is that OK with you? Do you have time?'

Paige nodded. 'I think the bar has enough cover but I might need to nip down and check.' Paige turned to Alfie. 'You want to watch a film with Connie after dinner?'

'With Mr Higgins too?'

'Sure, he seems to like you.'

'Yay.' Alf celebrated with a huge grin. 'Is Connie your mum?' Alfie suddenly asked.

'No, she's my gran.'

'Why did you call her Connie?'

'Cos that's her name.'

Paige, foolishly believing that was the end of it, watched as Alf bent back down to his food.

'Pwaige, are you going to marry Auntie M?'

Paige nearly choked. No matter if she thought her mojo was slowly returning, that one came out of nowhere and she had no idea how to answer it. She quickly looked at Melanie who'd also frozen to the spot. Shifting her gaze, she looked to Connie for help, but all she did was smile deviously, before turning towards Alf.

'I don't know, Alfie. I don't know if Paige is the type to get married. What do you think?' Connie was clearly in the mood to stir the pot.

'If she married Auntie M then she would be my Auntie too, right?' Alf asked between slurping and biting his spaghetti, his whole face now covered in sauce.

Paige did not know what to do. But she found she didn't want to let this little man down. When and how had he carved his way into her stone heart like that?

'Do you think she would be a good auntie?' Connie asked him directly while both Melanie and Paige sat frozen.

'Yeah, but not as good as Auntie M. Because she's the best and lets me eat chocolate for snacks.'

'And is chocolate your favourite?' Connie asked, moving Alfie along as if that whole interlude hadn't just happened.

* * *

It was a little while later that Alfie was sat snuggled up with Connie and Mr Higgins that Paige and Melanie were able to begin their work, but Paige was distracted. Yes by Melanie, but this time by the obvious signs of Melanie's discomfort.

Paige knew how stressed Melanie was, how much she was trying to do in one go, and Paige knew that Melanie needed her help, even if maybe Melanie wasn't quite sure herself. As if on cue, Melanie pulled off her glasses and started rubbing at her temples. Paige got up, made a cup of tea for the grown-ups, grabbed a milk for Alf and a water for Melanie. Drinks sorted, she put the glass of water and the brew on the table for Melanie, pulling out some painkillers from her pocket.

Paige tried not to sigh. Melanie looked exhausted, the grey under her eyes sometimes partially hidden by her glasses, now painfully obvious. Her skin colour wasn't looking right either and Paige was genuinely concerned with everything going on, including the surprise health inspection that Melanie was going to topple over. Grudgingly Paige could also admit the idea of looking after Melanie appealed. She didn't want to say that she was falling hard, but it wasn't just the attraction and the sex, it was the care and comfort, it was the place feeling like home.

It was problematic.

Because Paige wasn't worth it.

So now she had to prove that she was. But she also had to make sure that she didn't hinder Melanie either. Melanie put her glasses back on, turning to check on Alf.

'Don't worry, he's fine. What do you want to work on first?' Paige asked, thinking the sooner they got this done the sooner Melanie might get some rest. Paige nearly scoffed out loud. Melanie did not know how to rest.

'So, who is this Selena and co. anyway? Wait, it's not Selena Dante, is it?' Paige asked.

'Yeah, it is — do you know her?'

Paige smiled. 'Yeah I erm, well we've worked together on some projects before. I hadn't realised that's what she'd called her art programme.'

Melanie looked up expectantly.

'I'll bore you with that another time, but I'm thrilled that she got the contract in that case. Is she doing it with the women she's been working with?'

'Yeah.' Melanie looked down at her emails. 'In her application, Selena says that she supports some of the Women's Aid shelters.'

'Yeah and the LGBT one too,' Paige said.

'Do you know about the art therapy then?' Paige shook her head. 'Apparently some of the women she's been supporting over the years keep up the art therapy and so here we are. Not only will this count towards the therapy but it also means the money being paid will go towards the charities that she's working with.'

Paige nodded. 'That really is great. I'm glad Selena went with so much green.'

Melanie chuckled, before she took the painkillers and drank some water. 'Thanks,' she said.

'Don't worry. What do we need to do first?' Helpful not hindrance, Paige reminded herself.

'So next, we have to set up a meeting. Find out what she needs to get it done, and we also need to get a final wall selected. Councillor Houghton said there were two in our community up for grabs, he just needs to see if there has to be any Council sign off. And then I guess she can get started.'

'So does that mean it gets a little easier then?' Paige asked, unable to hide the hope in her voice.

'I'm not really sure. I keep toying with the idea of whether or not there should be a presence on social media to keep people updated. I suppose wait and see what Councillor Houghton has to say.' Melanie exhaled deeply.

'So email Selena now. Get availability off her to meet up,' Paige suggested, 'then turn the iPad off for a bit and we can all watch the end of *Mary Poppins* together.'

'I wish I could, but I have too many other things to do.'

'Can I help?'

'I don't think so,' Melanie replied.

'Have you heard any more from the health inspector?' Paige asked softly.

'I don't want to talk about it,' Melanie said firmly, before wincing, as if she'd just realised she'd been more abrupt than she meant to be.

'I'll go sit with Alf and Connie, at least let's watch him until the end of the movie and you can work at the table, yeah?' Paige watched as Melanie smiled, her eyes watering a little as she did.

'Thanks. That would really help.' Melanie's voice wobbled a little before she looked back down at her iPad and tapped furiously at the screen.

Paige stood up and moved towards the sofa. She wanted so desperately to wrap Melanie up in a nice cosy blanket and have her sleep next to her for as long as she possibly needed. But instead she went and sat with Alf, taking it in turns to check both on him and on Melanie.

CHAPTER TWENTY-FIVE

Melanie

Melanie couldn't push her glasses up any further. Her headache that had been coming and going for the last week was now more of a low-key guest that had already overstayed its welcome and seemed to have now moved in. Not to mention that at this point she needed a to-do list for her to-do list.

She was sat at a table at the back of Lulu sipping her cold latte. Cold because she'd left it too long before drinking it, as opposed to purposely iced. Her iPad was on the table in front of her and her phone hooked into her bra. And she was knackered. Her usually immaculate make-up wasn't quite right, and she could admit her first instinctive reaction to anything was emotional; she had already had three small cries today, almost all about the health inspection. The first cry in case they failed. The second cry was if they had to find money to make mandated improvements. The third over the fact it had happened at all. She had to believe that not having been immediately shut down was promising. But she didn't want their scores on the doors to be affected. They really needed that five. Not just for them but it was a condition of the lease. Something else that the Neighbourhood Business Alliance had a say in.

Her headache intensified as Paige walked in the bar. Melanie was envious at the almost careless way she strolled towards her and she had to bite her tongue and remember not to get arsey at her friends.

'What's up?' Paige asked as she sat down.

'Nothing. You all right?' Melanie asked.

'Connie might be preparing for her next cruise soon, and it would seem my psychic, for psychic night, double-booked. And I can't help but wonder, how is that even possible?'

Melanie couldn't help the small smile that played on her lips, her mood mellowing.

'So how are you really?' Paige tried again. And just like that Melanie was emotional. It wasn't that her sister wasn't constantly asking her the same question. It wasn't even that Louisa wasn't asking. They were. But they needed her to carry on. They needed Melanie to be OK. When Paige asked, it hit different. It hit right in the chest if she was honest.

Melanie remembered her ex hardly ever asked how she was. And if she did, it was only to make sure Melanie was OK to do something for her. Like the time she was having a party; Laura had made sure Melanie was good, because Melanie had wanted to clean the flat from top to bottom right? And maybe organise the catering because she loved her and wanted to help her succeed right? The orders phrased like questions. The chipping away. For the longest time after the break up she had believed Laura, when she said the fault was Melanie's for not being more attentive, for not catering to her every whim, for not giving enough. For getting it wrong when she did.

Hindsight and all that.

But God, now certainly wasn't the time to be striding down unpleasant memory lane. Swallowing and sitting up straighter, she pushed down the emotions and carried on, getting another to do ticked off her list. 'Alfie has asked me to tell you it's his birthday soon and that you're invited to his birthday party.'

'Cool. Do you have the details on you now? I can let you know.'

'Sure.' Melanie sent the details over to Paige's phone.

'Yeah, I'll be there. What's he into? I would normally bring booze but he's not into that yet, is he?'

'Not quite. Think more *PAW Patrol* or books or something.'

'Disney?'

'Of course.' Melanie nodded and ticked the fact Paige had been asked and was coming to Alfie's party.

'What time was Selena due?' Paige asked as she locked her phone and checked the time.

'Erm, five minutes ago,' Melanie said.

'I've updated the list, but Seb has said she's happy to design any flyers or promo stuff for the big unveiling.'

Wait what? The big reveal. Oh, well of course there would need to be a big reveal. Before she could sink any further into it, Melanie's eyes were drawn to a whole lot of colours as a large flowing kaftan came into the bar. Melanie watched in fascination as the rainbow sensation floated in on a breeze towards them. The person wearing it was barely visible as she swept closer. Melanie cast a look at Paige, who appeared equally as bemused.

'You must be Selena,' Melanie said, standing up to welcome their guest.

'Indeed, I must.' Selena swept down and kissed Melanie on both cheeks. Paige had stood up to greet Selena and Melanie was surprised to see them smile at each other and even more surprised when Paige permitted Selena to wrap her arms around her for a hug before kissing her on both cheeks too. 'How are you, Paige?' Selena asked as she pulled away.

'Good, thanks. You?'

'Of course.' Selena sat down, moving the fabric about her until she was settled.

'Can I get you anything to drink?' Melanie asked.

'A whisky sour, please,' Selena said quickly, and Melanie looked up at Paige.

'I'm good, thanks.'

Melanie nodded and got up to speak to one of her staff. She could do with another coffee anyway, given that caffeine was the only thing keeping her going. She quickly asked Cleo for the drinks and when she got back to the table, saw that Selena had managed to produce a large handbag from somewhere within the kaftan and was going through it.

'Selena, it's so lovely to meet you and congratulations on being the judge's choice.' Selena looked up at Melanie and smiled before placing a crystal on the table.

'Don't worry, it's just to help us get to know each other and send creativity our way. Although . . .' Selena grabbed her bag and began rummaging around again, and all Melanie could see was the rainbow pattern of her head wrap until her head shot up again.

'Here. No offence, sweet, because you are absolutely gorgeous, but I get the impression you're not sleeping so well at the moment. Take this crystal, put it on the windowsill in your bedroom. It helps unblock and allow for more rest. Go on, take it, I insist.'

'Erm, thanks.' Melanie reached forward for the cloth pouch that presumably held a crystal within.

Selena's smile was wide-open, her deep brown eyes warm, her brown skin smooth, her hair neatly wrapped in a head scarf. But whether it was the kaftan, the crystals, her smile, or the kiss on the cheeks, Melanie felt an immediate warmth from Selena that made her shoulders relax a little. Maybe she would try and use the crystal, see if it helped.

'So, perhaps I should tell you a bit more about the project and where we're up to?' Melanie suggested.

Selena nodded. 'Yes please. We're so excited.'

'Well, we're waiting to hear back from Councillor Houghton about which wall will be used, but we should have that in the next day or so, complete with necessary risk assessments and insurances etc. Or so I'm led to believe.' Melanie momentarily panicked; it had said that in the last email right? God, she could barely retain information any more either. She quickly added a note in her list to check, while mumbling her apologies.

'So, yes,' Melanie continued. 'The project, the mural, is being sponsored by the Neighbourhood Business Alliance, the NBA, which is basically a group of business owners in the neighbourhood and around this area all working together with Councillor Houghton as the Chair.'

Selena interrupted. 'What streets specifically are included in the NBA?'

'Erm, I'm not really sure. Why?'

'There are some shelters, and women's centres, and an LGBTQ+ centre around here. While certainly not business in the traditional sense it would be a good idea to join in on occasion, share resources and information etc.'

Paige nodded.

'That would be really great. We can mention that to Councillor Houghton and maybe get some seats on the group made available?' Melanie asked.

'I'll do it,' Paige said.

Selena nodded at Paige, then turned back to Melanie. 'Anyway, you were saying.'

Melanie smiled before continuing, 'So what I think we need next is a list of what you need and when you need it by, based on your brief, like the paints etc.'

'Of course, like the scaffolding and so on,' Selena said, nodding.

'The what?'

'What?'

Melanie and Paige had both spoken at the same time.

'Have either of you ever planned something like this before?' Selena asked softly.

'No,' Paige said.

Melanie shook her head.

'Well, that's all right. We'll figure it out between us. But yes, there might need to be some scaffolding. It's easier to sign off on than cherry pickers.' Selena patted Melanie's hand. 'Don't worry.'

But it was too late, Melanie was already full of worry.

The drinks arrived at that point and Melanie took a sip of her latte, and felt it land in her stomach with an acidic splash.

'I'll pull together a list of all the equipment that we need, including things like scaffolding.' Selena chuckled. 'I'll get that sent over. We also need to think about lone working and safety. For instance, we will need to make sure there's always at least three people on site . . .' Selena's voice dropped off as she clearly began thinking it through.

'But all being well, and the weather staying dry' — they all grimaced, dry weather not exactly Manchester's forte — 'it should be done in two to three weeks. But I would say four to be on the safe side.'

Now this did cheer Melanie up. Four weeks. She could do four weeks. Four weeks was temporary. She needed to check her forecasts, but her business should still be around in four weeks. She would be able to refocus then.

Selena went for her bag again. 'So shall we pencil in the eighteenth then . . . For the big unveiling?'

'Erm OK.' Melanie added the details to her iPad.

'But you should know that as well as the therapy work I also have two more large commissions, so if it's not done in the next six weeks, then I can't help you.'

Melanie nodded, again adding more info into her app.

'Now, will the wall be primed and ready?' Selena asked.

Melanie looked up at Paige.

'What do you mean ready?' Paige asked.

'Will it be paint ready?' Selena said.

'I don't know.' Melanie was feeling completely incompetent.

'You'd best find out, else you might be up the scaffolding painting a base layer.' Selena laughed like it was the funniest thing in the world.

Melanie tried to smile, but she could already see it in her head. Please God let Councillor Houghton have the answer to this one.

'Right, my lovelies.' Selena grabbed her drink and downed it in one go. 'I'll get that list together for you by the end of the day. Oh, actually you'd best give me your number Mel so I can contact you if anything comes up.'

Numbers were exchanged and before Melanie could really comprehend what had just happened, her cheek was kissed and Selena floated away, leaving behind a slightly citrusy scent, and that crystal for Melanie.

Melanie sat back down and played with the fringing on the cloth bag.

'What can I do to help?' Paige asked.

Melanie was about to respond with, 'I don't know,' but a voice she hadn't heard in two years interrupted.

'Melanie! Is that you?'

Melanie felt her skin freeze, her heart slow to a solitary beat. She hadn't even turned around yet, because she already knew.

CHAPTER TWENTY-SIX

Paige

Paige watched as Melanie shrank. Melanie had her back to whomever it was that was shouting, and while Melanie couldn't see who it was, Paige could see who the shrill voice belonged to. She was leading a group of about five people and somehow Paige immediately knew who she was. She watched as Melanie turned around, and stood up, straightening her skirt and pushing up her glasses as she did so.

'Melanie, it's so good to see you.'

Melanie didn't reply with words but allowed herself to be pulled into an embrace and her cheek kissed. There was a chorus of hellos from the rest of the entourage, but still Melanie hadn't said a word.

'I'd heard you finally got your business set up. You've been talking about it for years. You must be so excited. Louisa's done such a great job, she always was a dedicated one. Is she here? I'd love to say hi to her too.'

Paige watched the interaction, looking out for clues and insights. The first thing she was picking up was the tone; she *almost* sounded sincere, but Paige had trouble believing it.

'Did you hear? Pru and I are engaged.' The woman that Paige just knew had to be Laura, Melanie's cheating ex, thrust her hand under Melanie's nose, as Melanie forced a smile.

'Congratulations.' Melanie's voice and facial expression were neutral but her posture had changed and now Melanie was statue still.

'After we parted ways, Pru and I reconnected and gosh when you know you just know.' She looked back at Melanie, her smile all tucked in cheek, scrunched up nose and expressionless eyes.

'Anyway, we were nearby and thought we'd stop in. We didn't expect to actually see you in here, but now we have I'm sure you'll be able to find us a table, right? It would be so good to catch up and find out how you've been since . . . well . . . you know.'

Paige had had enough. The Melanie that ran a business, cared for her nephew, that had a devoted staff team, that had won around Paige's own ragtag group of friends in no time at all was nowhere to be seen. The Melanie that Paige knew had vanished, and it stung to witness this; a sharp pain right in her chest. Paige stood up, deliberately scraping her chair back and standing tall.

'I'm Paige, who are you?' She was deliberately arrogant in her own tone.

'Oh, erm, hi.' She'd faltered for a second but soon enough that big grin was back, the one that was all teeth and no eyes. 'I'm Laura. A good friend of Melanie's.'

'Really? She's never mentioned you.' Paige's tone sliced straight through the thin veneer of pretence.

'Who are you to Melanie then?' Laura asked, her smile nowhere to be found.

'A good friend.'

'And yet I've not heard of you either.' Paige glared, unaffected as Laura's shark-like smile returned. 'But it has been a while. Why don't we all sit together? It would be so lovely to catch up and to find out more about you, Paige.'

'I don't think—' Paige began.

A polite cough interrupted them all. 'Hi there, I'm Cleo the manager. I couldn't help but overhear and I'm so sorry but unfortunately we're all booked up today.'

Paige watched as Laura made a point of looking around the room, noting the empty tables with a raised eyebrow. 'I'm sure Melanie can fit us in.'

'I'm afraid we can't. The tables are all booked.' Cleo's tone was completely professional, but brokered no debate. 'And I apologise for the disruption, but if you reserve a table online, you can use this special code here' — Cleo pulled out a flyer that had a written code on it — 'and that will get you a thirty per cent discount when you come back again.' Cleo had, unbeknownst to the group, subtly shepherded them out towards the door.

'In that case we'll see you again soon then, Mel. Lovely to see you.'

The group left and Melanie collapsed onto the seat. Cleo came and sat next to her. 'You don't want them back, right?' Cleo asked softly.

Melanie shook her head. 'I don't think so.'

'Good.' Cleo nodded.

'But you just gave them a discount code,' Paige said. But the way that Cleo looked at Paige had a very much 'you're next' vibe to it.

'It's fine, we can make it so the code never works and that we appear completely full every time she tries to use it. She'll never try without the code because she'll want the discount.'

'You're amazing,' Paige said in wonder.

Cleo didn't even acknowledge her, but turned to Melanie. 'Was that OK?'

'Yes.' Melanie cleared her throat. 'Yes, that was great. Thank you so much, Cleo. It was the perfect thing to do.'

Cleo nodded once and turned on her heel, going back to the bar.

'Cleo's amazing,' Paige whispered in awe.

'I know, an absolute godsend.'

'What happened, Melanie? I lost you there for a minute,' Paige said as she sat down.

'Laura is my ex.'

'I figured as much. The one who you still haven't unpacked because of, right?'

'It's no big deal.' Melanie stood up abruptly. 'Right, where were we? Yes! Planning for the big reveal.' Melanie had already pulled out her phone.

'Melanie, you can talk to me, you know?' Paige said.

'Can I, Paige?'

'Yeah, of course.'

'I don't even know if we're friends.' Melanie sighed before looking back down at her phone. 'It doesn't matter, look it was messy. I'm glad it's over. I'm even glad that today happened because I was waiting for it and now it's done.' She continued tapping and scrolling. 'I might even be able to unpack now. But right now, I need to plan the big reveal, or I need to do my forecasting.'

She knew when she was being dismissed. Mostly because it hurt. 'Sure. I'll leave you to it.'

'Great, thanks. I'll see you later.' Paige watched as Melanie strode with deliberate purpose to the back.

And Paige felt like shit. Melanie didn't even know if they were friends, and all Paige wanted to do was spend every minute of every day with her. How could she not know that they could be that and so much more. She got up and strode down the road, determined to make this better.

* * *

Paige spent her afternoon taking drinks orders. She wasn't on shift, not strictly needed but she enjoyed doing it and on more than one occasion guessed the drink order before she was told it. She had the slightest glimmer of hope that at least part of her could be returning to normal. Well, normal for Paige at least. And she strongly suspected it had something to do with Melanie. But the reality was, the more time they spent together the more she felt her mojo might be starting to return. The only downside with that was her heart. Her mojo might be getting stronger, but Paige would be foolish to ignore that as her mojo grew so did her feelings. And really how could they not? For all that Melanie was going through she was a badass in her own way.

Distracted by thoughts of Melanie, again, Paige tried to empty her mind once more and focus on the tasks of running a bar. As she took orders, collected empties, and just did her job, her mind ran over different ways she could be more helpful to Melanie. To show that she cared in her own way. To maybe show Melanie that actually she was worth it. There was also the reading from Connie, and she knew that being a help was the answer.

What they really needed to do was go back to Councillor Houghton and explain that they needed additional support.

Yes, and with that in mind, Paige looked at her watch and saw it was just before five. She might catch him if she called now.

Rushing upstairs to her flat, phone in hand, Paige would later recall she had missed the signs, and there had been several. She had missed them all.

As she unlocked and pushed open the door, her phone was already at her ear. As she strode through the door, the dial tone was just about to start. Then she heard the thumping noises, the groans.

'Gran!'

There was a bang as Connie shot up, shoving Councillor Houghton and his bare arse onto the floor.

'Paige! It's Connie when we're in company and did you not see the sock on the handle?'

'Good Lord.' Paige averted her eyes. 'I'll just go out.' Keeping her head down she tried to grab her wallet and keys.

'Oh, my phone is ringing,' Councillor Houghton said and by the sounds of it he began rummaging through his pile of clothes.

Paige realised that it was her. She still had hold of her phone.

'No, that was me. Never mind.' Keys, wallet and phone, Paige grabbed her leather jacket by the door and ran downstairs.

Sitting down at the bar, she opened up the girls' WhatsApp group.

Paige: *Anyone around? x*

Sophie: *I can be — why what's happened? x*

Polly: *Oh me too, shall we go and have an impromptu dinner? X*

Sophie: *Why don't you all come to mine and I'll order takeaway x*

Polly: *Yay see you soon x*

Mya: *I'm just at the airport, I'll grab a taxi and be straight over. Be there in forty-five-ish don't start without me x*

Sophie: *Mya you're back! x*

Polly: *Yay Mya! But you OK Paige? x*

Paige: *Glad to have you back Mya. Thanks girls x and I've just seen Connie being introduced to Councillor Houghton's voting pencil!*

There was silence on the group as they all clearly tried to process this news.

Connie: *If you must know Patrick and I were making love.*

Wait what? When had Connie been added to the group? Paige sighed, she actually wasn't that surprised; Mya probably added her.

Paige: *Cancel dinner, I don't think I can eat ever again x*

Connie: *Oh Paige if anyone should be upset it should be me. You ruined the moment and we were so close x*

Nope that was it. Both her eyeballs and her phone needed to be ended.

Connie: *Does that mean I'm not invited tonight? X*

Paige: *No. Also you owe me a new sofa! Sophie I'm on my way x*

Sophie: *x*

Mya: *Go get some Connie woohoo x*

Paige locked her phone and went to talk to her team, and found India. 'I'm going out. I'll be back later.'

'No worries, boss — you OK?' India spoke as she restocked.

'No. Call me if you need anything.'

Paige got in her car and drove straight to Sophie's house.

* * *

The first words from Marcus were: 'Well at least someone is getting some action in that flat. Come on, it's been a while for you, right?'

'They were on my sofa,' Paige deadpanned.

Marcus started laughing again. 'Come on, I'll make you a cuppa and you can begin therapy with Sophie.'

'Wait.' Paige grabbed his arm and stopped him from turning.

'What?' Marcus asked, but his eyes looked away from hers quite quickly.

'What are you keeping from me?' she asked.

'Nothing at all, let me make you a drink.' Marcus all but ran off.

Paige knew — *yes in the mojo sense!* — she knew that something was amiss and the first thought that went through her head was that Sophie was pregnant, but no that didn't feel quite right.

Paige walked through the immaculate Instagram-worthy house and into the front room. It made Paige smile every time. Every inch in Sophie's house was Instagram worthy, not a single wall that you couldn't film in front of, the light was resplendent, the garden perfectly designed, obviously. But the front room was a mess and Paige loved it.

There was an old corner sofa piled high with throws of different colours, all the cushions you could ever need. Half-burnt candle jars on the cluttered coffee table, accompanied by non-coaster ring stains. A TV hung on the wall above the fireplace, a PlayStation connected to it, which had originally been Marcus' but had since been commandeered. Paige collapsed into the soft sofa and rested her eyes until Sophie arrived, mugs in hand.

The room while messy was essential and Paige could see why. Sophie had struggled at first with the influencer fame. Of course they had all been there to help her out. Keep her grounded and generally just take the piss as only the best of friends can. But Sophie had struggled with her work-life balance. Everything was for show. Every minute could be content and at first Sophie couldn't switch off.

Now she had the opposite of an office. It was Sophie's anti-office. The place where she literally could not work. The blinds meant the light wasn't great, the mess meant it wasn't all that photogenic; it was bliss. On the coffee table and down the side of the sofa were magazines, books, almost all about either make-up or business models and entrepreneurism.

Paige sipped her brew. 'My mojo is starting to come back,' she said, finally voicing the biggest thing that was doing her head in. 'I think it's to do with Melanie.'

As soon as she heard the words out loud she knew it was absolutely true. She actually didn't care that she had walked in on Connie and Councillor Houghton; she wished she hadn't, but actually Marcus was right. It was time that sofa saw some action. The real issue was Melanie.

'How do I know I want Melanie for Melanie or because she might be able to fix me? Because one of those isn't fair. How can I be something that Melanie needs in return?' Paige grumbled into her hands.

'First of all, how do you know your mojo is even coming back?' Sophie asked.

Paige sat up and studied Sophie for a solid ten seconds.

'You and Marcus are wondering whether or not to come off the pill. It's a big decision. You've had lots of conversations about it but neither of you are sure it's the right time yet.'

Sophie stared, her jaw open.

'Did Marcus say . . . ?'

'You know he didn't.' Paige collapsed back into the sofa.

'Are you back to full power or . . . ?'

'No . . . not yet.'

'When did you notice it come back? Wait, no, hang on, we need to wait for everyone else. Here.' Sophie found the remote lodged under the cushion next to her and stuck the TV on, both of them quietly trying to enjoy their tea. But

Paige's brain was a mess and Sophie was biting her lip and twirling her engagement ring around.

One by one everyone arrived and cheered and hugged, welcoming Mya back into the fold. Whenever Mya returned it was like she'd never been away.

Everyone got comfy and started chatting and catching up but Paige couldn't stay quiet any longer and without warning, interrupted. 'What if my gift only came back because Melanie and I had sex?'

The room fell silent, and Sophie quickly turned the TV off.

'You and Melanie did it! Woohoo. About time. How was it?' Mya leant forward, her hands on her chin, eager for the details.

'It was . . . well, it had been building for a while. And we both agreed to get it over and done with so we could move on,' Paige replied.

'Jesus.' Sophie groaned.

'How romantic,' Mya said with more than a little sarcasm.

'That's not right,' Polly said shaking her head.

'It was hot and a great time was had by all, I made sure of it,' Paige said.

'I'm sure you did.' Mya grinned briefly. 'But I, that is to say we, thought Melanie was more than that.'

Paige said nothing. Mya hadn't even been in the country as this was developing; they'd clearly been discussing this behind her back.

'Yeah, I have to say I thought you two were going to be more serious than a one-night thing,' Polly added.

'I feel weirdly sad about this,' Sophie said as everyone nodded, and Paige looked at them all in shock.

'We're not angry with you,' Mya added, 'just very disappointed.'

'What's happening here?' Paige asked.

'Well, we were shipping you two and . . . you blew it,' Sophie said.

'I did not. It was hot as hell.'

'Nobody is doubting that, we just assumed this was the start of a relationship. So now what, you're just friends?' Sophie asked.

'Well that's just it. How do I know I want Melanie? Is it real, or is it because she can fix me?' Paige said.

'You don't know that she did fix you,' Sophie pointed out. 'It could just be coincidental. Your bigger issue is whether or not she'll have you anyway.'

'I . . . Well . . .' Paige couldn't speak.

Mya wrapped her arm around Paige's shoulders. 'Bang again and see if you're fully healed.'

'I can't do that to her. I'm not using her like I would paracetamol,' Paige all but shouted.

Mya grinned. 'So you do want her then. Shame that you fucked it up really, isn't it?'

'I haven't . . . have I? How do I . . . ? What do I do now?'

'We're going to have to come up with a woo plan,' Sophie said. 'Hang on, I need a notebook for this.'

'I can't do that. She has too much on her plate as it is. She's going to have some sort of burnout soon. But then I suppose I could . . .' Paige started. 'Although I was thinking, I have access to her to-do list so I could help clear off some of the things on there. That might help.'

'You mean for the art stuff, right?' Polly clarified.

Paige slowly shook her head. 'No, for everything. The bar, the childcare, all of it. I . . .' Paige hesitated. She might as well let it all out now anyway. 'I don't think she knows she gave me access to all of it.'

The silence in the room had its own heartbeat.

'You don't think or you know?' Mya asked.

Paige shrugged. 'I was going to talk to her about it but we've just been too busy and I didn't want to add more for her to deal with.' Paige's voice ended on a whisper.

'That was weak, Paige,' Mya said.

Paige nodded. It was. But Paige had loved having the insight into Melanie's life. She didn't go on unless it was to update, but she would be lying if she said she hadn't looked at the other lists on there. And if she was going to be really super honest, then she was looking to see if that one action had been removed. The "DO NOT SLEEP WITH PAIGE IT'S NOT WORTH IT" action. But no that was still there.

Well that said it all really didn't it?

But still, even if Paige took the attraction out of it, she wanted to help. She could use her access to the lists to do good. She'd been mulling this over for a few days. It made sense. She could look after Melanie, show her she cared, and actually make Melanie's life easier in the process.

'You're going to look at it again now, aren't you?' Mya asked. 'I want it noting down that we all disagreed with this.'

They all nodded. Then they all gathered around Paige. 'Well go on then,' Mya instructed. 'What? We oppose this but seeing as how you're doing it anyway then obviously, we're going to help.'

Paige literally felt each of her friends curl around her so they could see her phone, and she hesitated. How many times had they all sat together like this? When Sophie was upset about Marcus that time. When Polly had hidden her career and they'd all crowded around her on the bed. They'd done something similar for Mya in Vegas when she wasn't sure what to do about Smithy. It was clearly Paige's turn to be looked after by the girls and she didn't hate it. She didn't like it, but she didn't hate it.

Smiling at them all, she opened up the app. Sure, maybe this wasn't fully 'right' but her intentions were honourable. She wanted to help. Melanie had been looking more and more exhausted of late. If she had a look she could maybe find a way of helping. That was her first priority.

'OK. Here goes.' Paige opened up the to-do list and of course it was on the last list she had looked at. The one labelled personal. Someone tutted, Paige thought it might have been Mya. Then she heard them all suck in a breath.

'Ouch,' Sophie mumbled next to her.

'I thought you said, you showed her a good time,' Mya said.

'I did, she means not worth it as in me, I'm not worth it. Not worth the time. Not the sex.'

'How can you be sure?' Polly asked.

'Because I know my way around a woman's body, OK?' Paige snapped back.

Paige looked back down at the phone and continued to click through the lists.

'Business! Surely there is something you can help with there? You already run a successful bar?' Sophie pointed out. 'Oh, look she's concerned about promo. I told her I would help with that. Hmmm.' Sophie opened up her own calendar. 'I get that she might not have time for a makeover, but I could just film an IG story or something in there. That might help initially. She wouldn't even have to do anything,' Sophie suggested. 'I'll text her now. Polly, are you free Saturday? We could all go for brunch.'

'Oh, me too. Connie has told me all about it and I really want to see it,' Mya said.

'Oh yeah with us three all sharing on our socials that will be a massive help.' Sophie nodded as she began to strategize. Paige watched on, her brow slightly furrowed. Yes, that was helpful, but that wasn't something Paige would be able to help with.

'Hang on, what's this about Alfie?' Polly asked.

'She helps look after him. Her sister is a single mum and a surgeon, so she does a lot of childcare, some school run stuff and like three nights a week or something she picks him up from school and puts him to bed, that type of thing.'

'But that could be time spent doing something else, right?' Mya asked. 'And you know this kid, yeah?'

'Yeah, he's one of the best dudes I know,' Paige said.

'Great, so why don't you offer to babysit? If you need help at the bar, Sophie will go back. Won't you, Soph?' Mya suggested.

'Erm, well actually . . .' Sophie began.

'I think that Sophie would rather help me babysit, for research purposes,' Paige said.

'What do you mean?' Mya asked.

'Hang on, are you and Marcus!? Oh my God!' Polly started shouting.

'No, we're not, we're just talking about protection at the moment, that's all. Calm down. But yeah, we don't exactly have lots of kids in our group so it would be nice to hang out with one for a bit.'

'Alf is good,' Paige said.

'I'll help at the bar,' Mya said.

'No! Sorry no, thanks Mya but it's OK. I'll sort it. Worst case, I'll get Connie down there.'

'So are we best asking or . . . ?' Sophie started. 'No, she'd say no, right?'

'Yeah, she wouldn't want to put us out.'

'Right then, we'll go to hers.' Sophie nodded.

'Her sister's,' Paige clarified.

'Her sister's. We'll rock up, say we're there to help. Tomorrow works, it says she has him then? That way either you and Melanie get to spend some time on your project, or else Melanie can spend the time on . . .' Sophie looked through the list. 'Forecast versus actual. Oh, actually I'd quite like to help her out with that as well really.' Sophie sighed. 'What even is this app? I might have to get it.'

Paige rolled her eyes at Sophie.

'Go back to this art project that you're both doing. You're allowed access to that one anyway, right?' Polly asked.

'Here.'

'So why don't we all plan the big reveal stuff together. We could take that one completely off her plate?' Polly suggested. 'I'm sure I can find someone willing to do some music.' She laughed. 'Sophie and Mya will be there to help us cover it. Between us we can get press coverage. Paige, you could do the drinks, right? And get some free advertising? Done and done.

Paige was about to ask why they would all do that for Melanie. But she knew the answer already. They were doing it for her. Just as she would for any of them.

Sentimentality, however, was not something Paige was comfortable with. So instead she just nodded and mumbled, 'Thanks.'

'I'll order some food,' Polly said eagerly.

'I'm going to start writing out some plans,' Sophie said just as eagerly.

'Melanie's texted back, she'll find us a table for Saturday brunch. Yay!' Sophie said.

'Bottomless mimosa's you say, I can't wait!' Mya shouted and then groaned. 'Actually no, I still can't stomach mimosa's, I'll just stick with prosecco.' Mya and Polly both grimaced, the memory of Mya's food poisoning in Vegas still fresh in their minds.

CHAPTER TWENTY-SEVEN

Melanie

'Right, little man, come on, tea's ready.'

'What is it? Can I have pudding?' Alfie asked as she helped him onto the barstool at the kitchen island. Melanie's mind wandered, again, back to the interaction with Laura, imagining how it could have gone differently. What it would have been like if she had been in boss mode. What it might have been like if she introduced Paige as her girlfriend. What would have happened, if she hadn't had cared? She didn't care, not like she once had, but disinterest would have been her preferred emotion of choice. A chilled not-bothered Melanie; she wasn't sure she could remember what that was like.

'Dinner first. How was school?'

'Good.' He continued to demolish his food with gusto before pausing again. 'Auntie M, is Pwaige not here?'

'No, why? Did you want her to be?'

Alfie nodded. It made Melanie smile just how much he'd fallen for Paige.

The knock on the door interrupted her thoughts. 'Stay still, don't move. I don't want you falling off, I'll be right back.'

Melanie ran to the front door, ready to quickly tell who-ever it was they weren't interested. But when she opened the door that wasn't quite true.

'Yes? Oh, er hi. Are we meeting tonight?' Melanie was stunned. Alfie clearly had summoning powers.

'Can we come in?' Paige asked, striding purposefully towards the kitchen. Melanie still held the door open even more confused when Sophie walked in too.

'Hi, really sorry to arrive uninvited — hope you don't mind?' Sophie asked as she began taking off her coat.

'Sure, is everything all right?'

'Oh yeah, it's grand. Wow, this house is lovely!' Sophie said as she craned her neck, taking in all the details of the hallway. 'Original tile? Very nice.'

'No idea. Come through.' Melanie gestured before fol-lowing Sophie into the kitchen.

Paige was already sat next to Alfie on a barstool, her hand on the back of his stool and they were chatting away, Alfie with a huge grin on his face, and actually Paige's smile wasn't that far off either. Which for Paige was saying a lot.

'Alf, this is my mate Sophie.' Paige nodded her head towards Sophie.

'How do you do?' Sophie asked, hand outstretched.

Paige frowned and quickly shook her head at Sophie. 'He's not a prince, Sophie, just be normal.'

'I am being normal,' Sophie replied, blushing furiously, as she placed her coat on the side.

Melanie was at a loss.

'So Alf, Sophie here wants to learn what it's like hang-ing out with kids. I told her you were the best kid to hang out with. So here we are. We also thought we could help watch you tonight if that's OK with Auntie Mel, so she can get some of her super important work done. What do you think?'

'You're pretty,' Alfie said to Sophie. 'Do you really not know any other kids?'

Sophie shook her head.

'Not even Jacob in my class at school? He told me he knows everyone.'

Sophie shook her head again. 'Erm no. I don't think I know Jacob.'

Melanie made her way around the kitchen island, pausing on the other side of Paige.

'You want to practice being around kids by using my nephew?' Melanie whispered towards Paige.

'Sophie does, yeah. But I figured we could help out with some babysitting. You can sit at the island and do some work? Would that be OK? You'd be really helping us out, and you'd be here the whole time.'

Random, but how could she say no to that? They needed her help, well more precisely they needed Alfie's help. 'Alfie, can Paige and Sophie hang out with us tonight?'

Alfie nodded and carried on eating his food. 'I missed you today, Pwaige.'

Melanie saw Paige's shoulders tense up and her eyes widen with shock. 'You did?'

'Yeah. I'm glad you're here now.'

Paige clearly had no idea what to do with that. Sophie looked like she might cry. Melanie had no idea what was going on so she walked back around the island towards Sophie.

'Why do you need Alfie's help?' Melanie asked quietly.

'Well, Marcus and I are wondering whether or not to stop using contraception. We're not sure either of us are ready, or if it's the right time work wise. We don't have any friends in our groups with kids, and we've none of us really been around babies, and honestly, I thought Paige was going to be the worst with kids. You know how grumpy she can be. But I guess I was wrong.'

Melanie was shocked and knew it must show on her face. She couldn't believe Sophie Bowman, *the* Sophie Bowman, had just confessed to maybe thinking about starting a family. Melanie could still not get to grips with the idea that she was maybe sort of friends with a celebrity. It continued to blow her mind.

But she was going to be chill. She wasn't going to fan girl.
'Cool.'

Too chill. Now she just sounded odd.

'So . . . what's the plan, does he have a routine?' Sophie asked.

'Yeah, normally after dinner we read his school books.' Melanie looked over and saw Paige and Alfie were once again in serious conversation. 'Then it's bath, milk, more books and bed. But tonight, I guess, I'll do his bath, get his PJs on then you guys can do the rest. Or try to.' Melanie looked over at Paige.

'Oh, don't worry. Paige will totally take the lead. I have no idea what I'm doing.'

Melanie was not full of confidence, but she'd be here if there were any problems, and Alfie seemed happy, and if she got the forecasting done tonight, then that meant when she got home later she could do some planning for the art project. She looked up and saw Paige frowning at her.

'What?'

'When did you last eat?' Paige asked.

'I had some lunch leftovers. Why?'

Paige had all but snarled. Great they were back to snarky Paige, only one step up from the nods.

'When did *you* last eat?' Melanie retorted wondering if Paige suffered from being *hangry*. It would explain a lot.

'Why are you doing that face, Pwaige?' Alfie asked.

'What face?'

'Monster face grrrrr.'

Melanie grinned, he was spot on, and Sophie laughed too.

'Right, finish your tea, we're going to do bath first, then you can read your school book to Paige and Sophie and then they'll tuck you in and read you your other books. How does that sound?' Melanie was using her optimistic overly positive child friendly voice.

Paige shook her head. 'Wanna hang out with me and Soph?'

'Yeah!'

'Cool, go get a bath, and shout us when you're done, right?'

'Yes,' Alfie said before finishing his last bite.

'Right, Alf, have a nice bath,' Paige said, picking him up off the barstool. But as she went to put him down, Melanie watched as he pushed his arms over her shoulders and wrapping them around her neck.

'Up, up.'

'You have no chill, Alf.' But Paige lifted him back up again until he was sat on her hip. 'Here, this is yours,' Paige said, tickling his ribs so he'd let go of her neck, as she passed him over to Melanie.

Melanie pressed a kiss to his cheek. 'Come on then little man. Let's get you ready for bed.'

* * *

The bath time had been highly energetic simply because Alfie was so eager to play with his new friends and Melanie knew that actually getting this kid to sleep was going to be hard work tonight. She'd try and get some work done while they did the book reading but she strongly suspected she'd be stepping in.

But he was in his PJs now and studying his bookcase, picking out the books to read. There was already a pile ten high.

'That's enough, Alfie. You'll be up all night.'

'Two more? Pwease?'

Paige stepped in at that point. 'I'm OK with two more if Auntie Mel is, so long as they're Disney stories.'

Alfie cheered, Melanie shrugged, and mentally wished them all good luck.

'Don't worry, we won't need it, we'll be fine, but we'll shout you if needed. Have you got the monitor on?' Paige asked.

She must have said that out loud. 'Yeah, I'll have the monitor. Night night, little man, give me a cuddle.'

'Night, Auntie Mel. Love you.'

'Love you too. Sweet dreams and be good, OK?'

Paige sat down on the floor and Alfie pushed back to be let go of, and sat down next to his new best mate and Sophie followed.

Melanie made it five minutes downstairs before she heard, 'No, Sophie, that's not how you do the voices. Do it like Pwaige.'

She opened up her laptop and iPad and began looking for all the information she needed; she'd loaded up the forecast that went along with the business plan. Then she opened up the app with their earnings.

'Sorry to interrupt, Alfie wants his milk?' Sophie said.

'Oh yeah, hang on.' Quickly pouring milk and getting him a biscuit, she passed them back to Sophie. 'Is it going all right up there?'

'Oh yeah, he's just gorgeous, isn't he?'

Melanie smiled. 'When he wants to be.'

Sophie looked disbelieving but Melanie thought it might not be all that long until they saw the other side.

Sure enough, two minutes later, Melanie could hear them trying to find wet wipes as Alfie's biscuity fingers were about to cover Sophie. Paige was laughing, which of course meant Alfie wanted to do it more.

'Ah. Quick, get some towels,' Paige shouted as Sophie yelped.

Melanie shot up, grabbing the kitchen roll and some tea towels before running upstairs.

Once she'd cleaned up the milk, she said goodnight and headed back downstairs again.

Two minutes later and, 'I need a wee.'

Melanie shouted up, 'He can take himself, don't worry. Go on, Alfie, off you go. Don't forget to wash your hands.'

Two minutes later. 'Ah the water has got me.'

Melanie shot upstairs to get him into dry pyjamas.

'Right, dude, come sit down. Let's get some stories read, yeah?' Paige said. 'You wanna sit on my knee?'

'Pwease.'

Melanie left them to it again.

Deciding to check her emails before starting on the forecast she immediately clicked on the one from her prosecco supplier. Skimming through it, she read it again. Twice more. And then sent a message to Louisa.

Mel: *Have you seen the email from the prosecco ppl? I'll sort it but something needs to be done.*

Someone had tried to cancel their order and possibly not for the first time. After the last issue with missing prosecco, the company had agreed to email for confirmation of orders and cancellations. And what she was reading was that someone had called them to cancel all future prosecco orders. She immediately emailed back explaining that it didn't come from herself or Louisa, that it shouldn't be acted upon and asked if they had details of who made the cancellation.

Her fingers were a blur as she typed furiously. She sent the email and added to her list to ring them tomorrow to follow up. Given everything that was going on, she couldn't shake the sense that the other suppliers needed to be checked out too. She drafted an email which she sent to them all, hoping it was just paranoia and that someone wasn't purposefully going out of their way to end their business. She also hoped that it wasn't one of their staff. But how else would they have known who their suppliers were? Then again if someone was camped out watching they'd be able to see for themselves. Melanie wasn't sure which was worse, so instead she put all her hopes on paranoia.

Except then she saw a response from her greengrocers.

'Shit!'

Her fears confirmed, someone had also contacted them. Glad she'd managed to catch them on email so late in the day she explained that her standing order should not be cancelled and she'd be contacting them in the morning.

Problem-solving mode activated, she called Louisa. They agreed to email all their suppliers again just in case any other random cancellations had been made and planned to conduct their own investigation first thing.

After furiously typing, for what must have been close to an hour she finally sat back in her chair, not having realised her whole body had been completely tensed. She closed her eyes and breathed deeply; there was nothing else they could do right now. She just hoped they'd caught the cancellations in time. But who the hell would do this to them?

But it really was sabotage.

Her heart was pumping furiously when she suddenly realised it was too quiet, that no one was talking, that she couldn't hear anything over the monitor. Melanie looked at the time. How long had they not been talking for? Where was Paige and Sophie? Was the monitor broken? Adrenalin still pumping, she raced upstairs. Then she quickly ran back down, grabbed her phone and ran back up again. Out of breath she took a few pictures. Paige was sat cross-legged just like last time. With Alfie in her lap. Paige's head had fallen back against the wall behind her, her breath slow. Alfie had fallen asleep holding onto a lock of Paige's hair that she must have pulled out of a bobble for him. His other hand was barely holding onto the book.

And Sophie had grabbed the bean bag and rested her head on that and fallen asleep too. It looked like the end of a really fun night, people just passed out where they landed. She sent the picture to Paige and Sophie, as well as to her sister, with the message, *I'll explain when you get home.* She carefully picked up Alfie and got him into bed; he didn't even stir. And neither did Sophie or Paige. Melanie was still trying to calm down as she sank slowly to the floor, watching Paige's chest gently fall and rise. She felt her own breathing ease . . .

CHAPTER TWENTY-EIGHT

Paige

'Cheers,' Mya shouted out, a glass of prosecco raised in the air, as Polly, Sophie and Paige all shouted out too.

'Hang on, let's do that again but this time I'll film it to loop,' Sophie said, as they all groaned, but then immediately raised their glasses. This was life with Sophie; they were all Instagram girlfriends and knew what was expected, even if they did sometimes take the piss.

It took several shots before Sophie was happy. Then she disappeared to one of the Instagram walls and did a quick filming there. Paige rolled her eyes because they were trying to be subtle. They were supposed to be helping Melanie out without her realising it.

Sophie came back and sat down. 'Right, I've tagged you all in.'

Mya and Polly took out their phones and began tapping away. Paige didn't need to, her social media presence practically invisible. She wasn't an internet sensation like her friends.

Paige looked around, and there. Those two. They would be coming over for a selfie with Sophie in three . . . two . . .

one . . . Paige watched carefully as they both nudged each other and decided to go for it.

'Hi, we're really sorry to interrupt but we're huge fans. Is there any chance of getting a selfie with you?'

Paige smiled, happy her mojo was returning. Happy wasn't the word. She was borderline ecstatic. If she only knew why it had gone and why it was now returning, she would feel a hell of a lot better though. She couldn't shift the feeling it was something to do with Melanie.

Selfie taken, Sophie shouted out, 'Don't forget to tag me and Lulu, OK?'

'Of course, thanks, Sophie. And Mya, can I get a quick photo with you to show my boyfriend? He will freak out!'

Mya grinned. 'Of course.'

In true Mya style she pushed her arms into her sides making her boobs more prominent as she blew a kiss.

'Thank you.'

And both women walked away back to their table.

'She's not showing that to her boyfriend. In fact, I think you may have given her some straight confusion,' Paige whispered.

But then Melanie appeared and frankly whatever Mya was going to say or did say, was lost on Paige. All her focus was on the woman stood next to her. She immediately wanted to hustle Melanie back to her apartment.

'Hey guys, thanks for coming. Do you know what you'd like to eat?'

'Hi, I'm Mya.' Mya stood and offered her hand.

Melanie took it, her jaw dropping. 'My God, you're gorgeous.'

'Thanks,' Mya said with a grin. 'Right back at you. I can see why Paige fancies you.'

Paige gritted her teeth. Mya was beautiful, there was no doubt, and she radiated confidence and yes Paige had seen first-hand people stop in their tracks when faced with Mya's full-on attention. And her lack of filter almost always made Paige smile; they were really similar in that respect. But this might well be the first time it had been used against her. She felt awkward. Who says fancy anyway? They weren't at school.

'Oh well. Erm. Lovely to meet you. Do you want to order, or shall I give you a few more minutes?' Melanie asked, her cheeks red.

'I think we're ready,' Polly said.

Orders were taken, and Paige watched as Melanie smiled, and dazzled her friends.

'Are you all right? Did everything turn up OK?' Paige asked.

'So far so good, but as it's the weekend we're not going to know for sure until early next week. But we're good for now. Right, I'll go and get your order placed.'

Paige waited until Melanie was far enough away. 'Mya!' she whispered angrily.

Mya shrugged her shoulders and tossed back her hair. 'What? I'm just trying to help. She needs to know you still like her, that she wasn't a one-night thing.'

Sophie and Polly both nodded.

'If anything, I think I was too subtle. I should have told her you were drooling over her, that you needed her.'

Sophie and Polly shook their heads. 'No.'

'I really like it in here, it has a really good vibe,' Polly said, always the peacekeeper.

'Yeah, it's good, isn't it?' Mya agreed.

Sophie picked up her phone. 'Notifications are already crazy. Should I add in a swipe-up link so they can book a table? Can they do that on Lulu's website? Let me check.'

Sophie had her head down.

'Right onto the next stage of the plan,' Polly announced, her eyes wide with mischief.

'Yeah, well I can't say the first stage went all that well,' Paige muttered as Sophie snorted, her eyes still on her phone.

'Why, what happened? How can you get babysitting wrong?' Polly asked.

'We were terrible! Alfie spilt his milk everywhere and Melanie had to come and sort it. Then he managed to get water all over himself. Melanie had to come and sort it . . .'

Polly and Mya were both laughing. 'Right load of help you two are.'

'It gets worse,' Paige added.

'Yeah, Melanie had to wake us both up. Turns out we all fell asleep during story time. We didn't even manage to get Alfie into bed — he was asleep on Paige.' The whole table were laughing now.

'Melanie took a picture. Look.' Sophie was chuckling as she passed her phone around.

'Aw. You all look so cute. Look at that little dude. He's so handsome,' Mya said affectionately.

'I had no idea you were so nice towards kids,' Sophie said.

'I'm not. But that one is a cutie. Takes one to know one, you see.' Mya grinned.

'So, Sophie — are you broody now?' Polly asked. 'Because being an Auntie would be so nice. Please try for a baby.'

'We're still discussing it,' Sophie said, as Paige's mind flooded with an image of Sophie and Marcus' house no longer Instagram-ready and instead covered in toy detritus.

'Well, keep us in the loop.' Polly grinned.

'Right, but stage two, the big reveal. Oh, I've added a swipe-up, by the way, and sent the link to you both.' Sophie looked at Polly and Mya, who in turn dutifully did their own social media stuff. Sophie tapped her screen. 'Right, I was saying, stage two the big reveal. I've broken it down into areas rather than tasks so we can each do one, OK?'

'Wait, hang on. Are you using the same app as Melanie?' Paige asked.

'Of course. She knows what she's doing,' Sophie said. 'Right, so Polly, you're on music. So, I guess just bring yourself and some musicians, yeah? Paige, you're on refreshments. I mean I couldn't have made this any easier for you. Mya, you're on press. I'm on logistics so like a little stage, lighting and things like that. And all of us are on promotion. Invite everyone, tell everyone. Right then, the only thing we need from Melanie is the date and the go-ahead. And here she is.'

'Here's your food, ladies.' Melanie began placing the meals down.

Polly glanced at Paige who'd become tongue-tied, and then went for it herself. 'We're going to organise the big reveal of the mural. You can leave it entirely with us. We just need to know what date to go for and for you to OK our plans.'

'I'll have the full plan sent over to you in an email. Once you've agreed it you can leave it all to us,' Sophie said, tapping on her screen.

Melanie didn't say anything.

Shit, had they overstepped?

Melanie finally said, 'Why?'

'Huh? I was just expecting a thank you,' Mya grumbled, tucking into her food.

'Why are you all helping like this?' Melanie asked again, clearly bewildered.

'Because we're your friends, and Paige thought we might be able to help.' Sophie gave Paige the eyes, as if to say, speak now, it's your turn. But Paige was lost.

'We can help, so we're offering to help. Paige was explaining how hard the first two years in a business are. If we do this, it gives you more time to focus on other things? Maybe things you enjoy doing, maybe things outside of work?' Sophie said with a definite look towards Paige.

Right, enough Sophie — reign it in now.

Melanie still hadn't said anything, and her face was giving nothing away and Paige was getting no sense of where she was or how this interaction was going to move forward, and even her mojo was at a loss.

'Do you have a date for the big reveal?' Sophie asked.

'Yeah, erm, yes. Selena texted me to confirm the eighteenth.'

'Great.' Sophie typed some more. 'This really is a great app. It's colour-coded me a time-line now.' Sophie grinned. Mya ate. Polly observed.

'Are you sure?' Melanie asked.

'Yes,' Sophie said. 'Look, see it's blue right there.'

'No, I mean about helping.'

Paige nodded as Melanie looked towards her for confirmation.

'Then thank you, I guess. Thanks.'

Paige was studying Melanie's response and something was off, but Paige had no idea what. 'Is that all right?' she asked softly and watched as Melanie hitched her smile slightly higher.

'Erm, yeah of course. Thanks.'

'We should have a night out to celebrate!' Sophie said.

'Oh let's do tonight!' Polly said.

'Thanks, but I can't, I'm on open tomorrow,' Melanie said.

'Just a few drinks and maybe dinner at Paige's?' Sophie pleaded. Paige's eyebrows shot up before her frown softened and she shrugged.

'Yeah, maybe.' Melanie smiled. 'Right, eat up before your food gets cold.'

'I'm nearly finished — this is lush,' Mya said talking with her mouth full.

Melanie laughed as she walked off, and Paige saw her get a phone out of her bra, clearly going to update the app. That girl needed pockets.

Paige had just put her fork down, belly full when Melanie returned, her cheeks red, her eyes wide open.

'You really didn't have to do all the social media stuff, you know? I wasn't expecting you to do that.' Melanie shook her head.

'We know. I still want to do a full makeover in here, but like I said, that can wait. For now, we're just happy to tell people about Lulu and how great it is.'

'Our booking system crashed. Louisa just called to tell me. Thank you.' Paige watched as Melanie's eyes watered. 'And . . . we've just had the health inspection report back and it has a glowing review.'

Paige grabbed her mimosa. 'Here, you need this — congratulations!'

Melanie grabbed the drink and necked it. 'I can't believe it,' she said before handing the now empty glass back. Paige could see Melanie was shaking and before she knew what she was doing, she'd stood up and wrapped her arms around her, stroking her back. She was relieved when Melanie leaned right into her, her heels putting their faces almost side by side. Paige took in a deep breath and then slowly let go.

'Better?' Because Paige was. That gorgeous mango scent, the heat and feel of Melanie's body; the fact she was leaning on Paige for comfort.

'Yes. Thank you. I have so much to sort out. Your brunch is on me, by the way. Thanks, ladies,' Melanie said as she dashed off.

'We'll see you later at Paige's,' Sophie called out.

'I'll need to wipe down the sofa,' Paige mumbled.

Melanie smiled again as she carried on with her work.

Paige sat down, but could feel eyes on her. She looked up and sure enough, Polly, Sophie and Mya were all grinning at her.

'What?' Paige asked.

'It's going to be a good night!' Sophie nodded.

Mya winked at Paige. 'Put the good knickers on.'

'Does she even have any of those?' Sophie asked.

'Do we need to go shopping?' Polly asked.

'No. Absolutely not,' Paige said.

CHAPTER TWENTY-NINE

Melanie

As the brunches drew to a close, Melanie found herself sat at a table with Louisa, mimosas in hand, toasting their health report. In fact, Melanie was so delighted with the turnabout in events that she'd almost forgotten about the sabotage.

Almost.

And it was sabotage. The other suppliers had all confirmed cancellations had been requested over the phone. They'd managed to put a stop to those and establish new processes to prevent it from happening again but enough was enough.

Talking it through with Louisa they both agreed this was targeted and they needed to get to the bottom of it. Which was great, but Melanie didn't know where to begin.

Louisa sighed and relaxed back in her chair. 'I hadn't realised how stressed I'd been about the health report.'

'I know what you mean.'

'That kitchen is one of the most spotless and organised I've ever seen. But even so, it was scary, wasn't it?'

Melanie nodded her head.

'What we need,' Louisa continued, 'is to spend some time figuring out who the evil mastermind is.'

Melanie nodded absently. When the hell were they supposed to fit that in? 'Let's get the art thing out of the way and then perhaps we'll have time to look into it,' she suggested.

Louisa straightened. 'Yeah but what other damage could be done by then?'

Melanie sighed and knew Louisa was right. The celebratory mood from the health report, now soured. One step forward and two steps back every single time, and they were running out of energy trying to constantly jump the random hurdles. Did every new business go through this? She wasn't certain, but knew who she could ask.

Melanie still wanted to believe all their bad luck was just that, bad luck. If not then some sort of *outside* malevolence would be preferable — *anything* but an employee. As she thought about their staff betraying them like this, she felt sick to the very pit of her stomach. Unfortunately, she'd had that sensation before, and her heart had only just healed. She wasn't sure she could take a hit like that again.

Melanie paused her thoughts. Healed? No longer mending?

Despite the chaos and the uncertainty surrounding the business and the mural, and there was a hell of a lot of uncertainty, and pressure, and stress, her heart was definitely on the mend. She thought of all the people in her life that strengthened her heart every day — Alfie, Emily, Louisa, Sophie, Polly and even Mya, and yes, Paige. She could in fact, feel very strongly about Paige. If she had the time. If she could afford the focus a new relationship took. She could already picture it, and it was a little scary how easy it was to imagine.

* * *

Melanie was back in the flat that made her feel settled and calm. She wondered if it was the place, the layout or the person, or maybe a combination of all three that made her feel that way. Round the table there was in-depth discussion regarding what food they were going to eat. Melanie nearly suggested Greek but that was purely because she couldn't help but remember what had happened the last time. As if her mind or perhaps her body could be read, Paige looked up from her phone and smiled at her. Though her eyes said something much more sinful.

Putting a halt to that, Melanie remembered that she needed Paige's help. While the rest of the group argued about the merits of gyoza over pizza, Melanie leaned towards Paige.

'All these things that are happening to the business, the health report, the complaints, the attempt to cancel all the suppliers. Is it normal for a new business to erm . . . Did you . . . ? It's not . . .' She didn't know how to put into words, her worst suspicions.

'In my experience it's normal for a new business to fluctuate. To have some teething issues with suppliers and some customers that miss whatever was there before. Doreen used to come into Barbarella every week demanding I do her a blue rinse.'

'Awww, I miss Doreen,' Sophie said, jumping in. 'She used to let me try my make-up out on her when I was training.'

Paige smiled, and turned to Melanie. 'Getting her hair and make-up done helped Doreen with her dementia, she used to find it really relaxing. Apparently she was in here every four weeks for the full works before they closed down and I turned it into a bar.'

'Why are we talking about Doreen?' Sophie asked.

The room had quietened down now, and Melanie forced herself to get some outside opinions. 'Louisa and I think someone is trying to sabotage Lulu.'

'No, surely not,' Polly said.

'Really? Why?' Sophie responded.

'Yeah, I've been thinking the same to be honest.' Paige's tone was surprisingly soft, like she didn't want to be the bearer of bad news.

A moment of calm washed over Melanie, despite the words. It was like everyone around the table was holding her hand, telling her she was right, wrapping her up in a duvet and—

'Right, let's get cracking. Where can we get evidence? Is it an inside job?' Mya asked clearly ready for action.

'I don't think so. I think someone's been watching. Louisa has checked through our CCTV but nothing really stands out, not that we were sure what to look for.' Melanie said.

'An alarmingly high number of crimes are committed by those we know. Like the time Sophie stole a bottle of marsh-mallow flavoured vodka from Paige,' Mya explained.

'Mya! Shut up! I didn't take it. It was going out of date,' Sophie said, her voice high and shrill.

Paige's eyebrow slowly rose as she stared daggers at Sophie.

'It was stock management.' But Sophie crumpled. 'Mya told me to.'

Mya rolled her eyes. 'My God, Sophie, you cracked so easily.'

'You would too if you were under the Paige Glare of Death,' Sophie replied.

'You two should totally work together on this,' Polly said. 'Melanie, with your knowledge and Paige's Glare of Death, you could have this case cracked in no time.'

'Why don't we go downstairs and have a look at the CCTV footage?' Paige suggested. 'We're not too far away, we might have picked up something.'

'Yeah, you guys go do that,' Mya offered up far too eagerly.

Melanie shrugged. Paige led the way and Melanie distinctly heard Mya say, 'Great, now they're gone we can order pizza.'

Once downstairs they walked through the busy bar, and into the tiny, and boy was it tiny, room. Melanie had to squeeze past Paige just to get in, and when Paige closed the door, it immediately quietened but the next problem quickly presented itself. There was a laptop on a small table, a filing cabinet and a single chair. It was basically a wardrobe.

Paige pulled out the chair, and sat down. 'You wanna . . . ?' Paige pat her leg. 'I think it's the only way we can both see the screen, sorry.'

Melanie awkwardly made her way round, almost taking out the filing cabinet with her bum, until she was lightly perched on the very edge of Paige's lap. Paige's strong arms hoiked Melanie further onto her lap. Making sure they were both settled, chest to back, Paige reached over and booted up the old laptop.

'I think you're right, by the way but how can you be sure it's not an inside job?' Paige asked as they waited for the software to load.

'If you've got the Glare of Death then Cleo is the Blinking Assassin. I know we can't rule it out for sure, and honestly it would break my heart if it was, but I guess let's try and rule out a super villain first.'

'Then let's go be superheroes.' Paige smiled, and Melanie was glad to have Paige's help. It was a miracle how far they'd travelled from the surly nods. Instead, she was being treated to a smile that made her chest feel completely full.

They quickly discovered that the CCTV didn't cover as much of the street as they would have liked. In fact, playing superheroes would have been boring as they didn't have a timeframe to pin it on either. If it wasn't for the sensation of Paige's breath on her neck, the feel of Paige's arms bracketing her waist as she navigated the screen, the accidental skin to skin touches that lit her up causing goosebumps and her breath to quicken, it would have been quite dull.

'Will you stop wriggling,' Paige said softly, what with her mouth being so close to Melanie's ear.

'I must be hurting you.'

'Trust me when I say I could hold you on my lap for a hell of a lot longer than ten minutes.'

Melanie had to swallow. Paige's voice, proximity, heat, and suggestions were too much. She shivered and had no doubt Paige knew it.

'Damn it,' Paige whispered.

Yes, damn it. Melanie turned her head away from the screen and towards Paige.

Which was a mistake.

Their faces were only an inch apart. Melanie looked into Paige's stormy eyes. Her pupils were wide, her dark eyelashes outlining her green eyes. She involuntarily licked her lips, and Paige took in a breath.

All the reasons Melanie absolutely shouldn't be doing anything like this with Paige flew through her mind, but she couldn't seem to hold on to any of them.

Paige blinked and moved her face a little further away. 'It's like looking for a needle in a haystack. What we need to do is look at the CCTV for the stores that are closer to you.'

Melanie should be glad that Paige was keeping this professional. But it actually stung when she jumped up and Melanie nearly fell to the ground.

'Whoops, sorry about that. Come on, with a bit of luck Paulo's tattoo shop might still be open.'

Paige grabbed Melanie's hand and led them back through the bar and out onto the street.

'We can go through the CCTV, but we'd be best asking our neighbours if they've seen anything, too. We might get more luck that way.'

CHAPTER THIRTY

Paige

They all but ran down the road hand in hand to Paulo's tattoo shop. Paige experienced a sense of urgency she couldn't quite shift, and an energy she needed to syphon off before she did something unprofessional.

'Paulo!' Paige shouted as they walked through the first door, maybe a touch louder than she anticipated. But there in the entryway, Paige's eye went to the same framed tattoo design she was always drawn to. The woman with the long flowing hair, her back on display, looking over her shoulder, like she had emerged from bed covers. She was going to get that on her arm soon. Her mojo was telling her it would happen.

Good, they needed her mojo tonight to get to the bottom of all this.

'Yo,' Paulo called out. 'I'm just about to close. Oh, it's you Paige, you all right? Finally, here for me to finish that sleeve?'

'Not yet but definitely soon. Listen, we have a weird favour to ask.'

'Oh, and how weird is weird?' Paulo studied them both, his eyebrow raised.

'It's a weird one but stick with me. We think Melanie's place is being observed or like stalked or something. You seen anyone hanging around?'

'Oh man, I thought she was a tattoo groupie.' Paulo shrugged. 'It happens.'

'Does it though?' Paige asked, eyebrow raised.

'Does to me. There's been someone that hangs about here for a while each day. Like I said I thought she was here for me, so I really wasn't paying all that much attention.'

'Wait, really?' Melanie asked, her glasses almost falling off her face in shock.

'Why, what's going on?' Paulo asked throwing down the cloth he'd been cleaning up with and bringing his arms over his chest.

'We think Melanie's business is being targeted. Someone is putting in cancellations with her suppliers, calling the council about her kitchen hygiene.'

'Inside job,' Paulo said immediately.

'We don't think it is. Tell us about this woman.'

'She's here at random times. Sometimes when I'm opening, sometimes when I'm closing. I thought she was looking across the road to avoid making eye contact with me.'

'Hang on, why were you so sure she was here for you?' Melanie asked.

Paulo looked bashful for a moment and ran his hand through his hair. 'She looked familiar, and I wasn't sure if she was someone I'd inked or someone I had, you know . . .' His voice trailed off but they all knew to what he was referring.

'You don't sound worried about it.'

'No, because now that you think she was scoping out your place, Melanie, it makes more sense,' Paulo reasoned.

'You got any CCTV we could look through?' Paige asked.

'It doesn't cover outside. I've only got the insides done and the front door.'

'Can you tell us what she looked like at all?' Melanie asked, and Paige could hear her spirit starting to deflate when just moments before it seemed as though they may have had a lead.

'White woman with pink hair, sometimes purple, sometimes blue. Usually tied up in a bun, skinny jeans type. Nothing really remarkable; she looks like she's in her mid to late twenties if I had to guess. But I don't know.'

Melanie sighed, and Paige knew how she was feeling. They were back to needle hunting again.

'Listen, I'm locking up, but I'll give you guys the key if you want to hang out here for a bit to see if she rocks up? I haven't seen her yet today so you never know?'

Paige looked at Melanie, and they silently communicated. Paige raised her eyebrows: *why not, we've got nothing to lose.* Melanie's lip bent slightly at one side: *fine but I'm not convinced.*

'That would be great, Paulo, if you're sure you don't mind?'

'It's fine, just throw us a beer next time at yours. Right, follow me and I'll show you where the alarm box is.'

Paige followed Paulo as he went through the process of locking up, arranging for Melanie to keep the key so he could get it from her on his next day in. Lights off, they pulled the sofa from further inside the shop to the window overlooking the street. Across the street to the right they could see Lulu. It was still shining brightly as people ate bar snacks, drank prosecco and took selfies.

Paige turned to look at Melanie as she stared out the window, the lights of the street reflecting on her glasses. She was stunning, and Paige knew she was falling hard. She wasn't sure how much more she could help, how much more she could give that would make Melanie realise she was a serious contender, that she was *worth it.*

'I guess we're on a stakeout,' Paige whispered.

'Why are you whispering?' Melanie said.

'Isn't that what you're supposed to do on a stakeout?'

Melanie smiled. 'You done many of these before?'

'That would be telling.' Paige smirked.

'I actually don't think you're as mysterious as you let on,' Melanie said.

'Oh?' Melanie leaned a little closer and Paige wondered if maybe Melanie did know, maybe Paige's feelings were freaking obvious for everyone to see? Her friends already knew. Connie knew. Her staff knew for the most part if the daily ribbing from Belle and India was anything to go on. Even Jenny had started. Paige's heart warmed as she realised how much Jenny was coming into her own.

'Yeah, I think that underneath the leather, the jeans and the piercings, you're a Disney-loving cat parent.'

Paige quietly laughed. 'You got me. But tell me something about you that I don't know about.'

'Are we taking this in turns?' Melanie asked and then paused. 'Shouldn't we be doing something else? I feel like I should be working, or something. Waiting around here, I don't know, it just feels . . . ?'

'We were just gonna hang out anyway. It'll be worth it if we can figure out what's going on, right? Come on, tell me something, and we can absolutely take it in turns.' Paige was desperate for any crumb of Melanie's life.

'I used to have a drawer full of Post-its.' Melanie let out a sigh of relief, as if she'd been holding on to that secret for years.

Paige on the other hand, was underwhelmed. 'That's not surprising. But I would bet good money it wasn't just a drawer.'

Paige stared at Melanie, who immediately looked down with a blush. 'Oh my days, that Glare of Death really is powerful. Yes, all right it was a storage box full.'

'Not good enough. Tell me about Lulu. Why now, why here?' Paige hoped the desperation she felt to gather every little piece of Melanie wasn't too obvious.

'Because Louisa and I got our loan approved and we'd done our research. Of course, we would want to be here. Anyone would want to be.'

Something in Paige's brain pinged, probably her mojo, asking her to pay attention.

'Sure, but why now? Did you want to build experience in bars, did you want your own place before this point?'

'Well, I wanted to do it a few years ago. I was just building up my funds, writing my business plans, getting everything together. Louisa and I had been talking about it for years, ever since we worked our first bar together when we were students. But then . . . for various reasons it didn't quite work.'

'What reasons? Oh hang on.' Paige's phone was vibrating, and she cursed whoever it was, for interrupting them.

Mum.

Of course it was.

Just that one word was enough to make Paige pause. Maybe she should have changed the contact name to Fiona. Put some distance between them, but no it still said "Mum", and besides, her mum was the pro at putting space between them not her.

It stopped buzzing and Paige put her phone in her back pocket. 'Where were we? Oh yeah, what reasons?'

'Nope, it's my turn. What's going on there?'

'What do you mean?' Paige asked, focusing intently on the people scurrying past the window.

'You don't have to tell me, but we're friends, I hope. I saw that it was your mum ringing. Is there a reason you're not answering it?'

'We are friends, Melanie. No matter what else, we're friends.' Paige looked at Melanie, making sure she understood. There could be no confusion here. They absolutely were friends. Hopefully they could be more, but at the very least they were that. She waited until Melanie slowly nodded.

Paige continued, 'It's just my mum, she's trying to get in touch with me about something and it's really not noteworthy.' Paige wasn't sure why she didn't share with Melanie. But she didn't. It really was something or nothing. Either her mum would get bored and stop calling, or else at some point they'd have the same conversation they always did. It happened every three to five years. Her mum would want to get in touch to say hello and try and reconnect without any effort or apologies for leaving her with Gran. She'd keep up contact for a couple of months and disappear again. And every time Paige swore to herself that she wouldn't fall for it. And this time she was adamant. But yeah, it wasn't really anything that she needed to bother Melanie with.

'OK,' Melanie said with some reluctance. 'Well, come on then, in that case tell me something about yourself that no one else knows.'

Grabbing the change of topic like it was the last seat on the tram, she ran with it. 'I can do that. Here, see this.' Paige shrugged off her jacket and lifted her T-shirt sleeve up. 'See this gap here . . .'

Melanie nodded, her eyes studying all the ink on Paige's bicep. 'Well see that image on the wall over there. The black and white with the woman's back? That's going right here.'

'That's going to look great. But how come no one knows? It doesn't feel all that secretive.'

'I just get them done for me. If I have a really obvious one done the girls might ask me about it. But I think you're the first person I've ever told about a tattoo before I got it.'

'Hmm.' Melanie didn't add anything further to her sigh and Paige couldn't quite translate it. Maybe that had been a rubbish thing to share. 'I erm, would love to do more charity work. I'd like to be able to use my business more as a way of helping other people, maybe getting other businesses to do it too.' Paige would swear to all that she didn't blush. That it wasn't in her ability to do so. Her cheeks were warm for some other reason.

Melanie smiled warmly, her eyes glowing, and Paige's cheeks reddened further.

'I don't have any. Tattoos that is,' Melanie said, clearly taking pity on her.

'I know,' Paige said knowing full well her grin was wide. It widened as she watched Melanie's cheeks blush. 'Or had you forgotten?'

'I'd definitely not forgotten. That was . . .'

Melanie paused and Paige wanted to grab the words from her. 'That was what?' Paige prompted as she edged ever so slightly closer.

'You know what it was, you were there.'

Paige knew that it was unforgettable, that it had rewired her brain, that she would give anything, *everything* to repeat it, not just once but over and again forever.

'It was the hottest night of my life,' Paige said, hoping Melanie would pick up her sincerity.

'I doubt that. Had it been a while for you? Maybe you've forgotten.' Melanie's blush was visible even in the relative darkness.

'It had been a while actually but that doesn't make it any less hot.' Paige laughed as Melanie's eyebrows shot up over her glasses. 'Why is that so surprising?'

'Cos you're you.' Melanie waved her hand up and down. 'You're a hot badass. I just assumed you'd been very busy.'

Paige smiled. 'No, sorry. Why? Had it been a while for you?'

'Oh, I don't think we need to go into all of that,' Melanie said. Now it was her turn to look outside.

Paige placed her hand gently on Melanie's thigh. 'Was it Laura?'

Melanie sighed. 'Yes.'

Paige waited, not so much patiently but she waited, hoping Melanie would share, but not wanting to push. Too much.

'I . . . we . . . It got complicated. I can't say it ended well. But at least once it ended me and Louisa could crack on with our business plans. Eventually.'

'So, she was the reason you didn't do it sooner?'

Paige watched as Melanie took a deep breath, seemingly preparing herself.

'In a nutshell, it was your classic girl meets girl. Girls start a relationship. One of them believes it's love. The other is maybe a narcissist. Until three years later only one of them is still standing and thriving, the other no longer knows what's real and what's manipulation. One of them is now engaged to one of the friends she swore nothing was going on with. The other has a business that is being sabotaged and probably some trust issues.' Melanie let out a little laugh and shrugged her shoulders as if it was nothing. 'It was why I wasn't jumping for joy when you all offered to help with the big opening. My initial assumption was that you all thought I wasn't good enough. That I needed help, else I would fail on my own. I'm sorry about that. I'm usually good at catching those moments but I guess I'm not completely there yet.'

Paige didn't know what to say. She could hear the pain in Melanie's voice and wanted to take it all for her. She wanted to remove every last shred of doubt and hurt, every single painful memory and paint over them all with new ones. At that moment she saw what their future could look like together. A hundred precious occasions. A thousand cherished memories. A million magical moments.

'I'm sorry you had to go through that.' And she was sorry. 'But I'm glad you're here now.'

'What about you? I can't imagine you have a bad relationship in your past?' Melanie asked.

'No, not really. I erm, don't tend to have them.' Paige winced, knowing she needed to be honest, but also that it didn't show her in the best light.

'None at all? That's a red flag. You know that, right?' Melanie said with a small smile.

'It might be to some but' — Paige leaned closer — 'I actually just think I've been waiting for the right one.'

Melanie burst out laughing. 'Paige! That was nowhere near as smooth as you thought it was.'

Paige pulled back but kept eye contact. 'I know, but I meant it. I think I might be worth taking a risk on.' The images of their possible futures together continued to flash through her mind.

'What are you saying?' Melanie asked, soft and low.

Paige still had her hand on Melanie's thigh, but with her other she stroked Melanie's jaw. But truthfully Paige didn't know what to say. She wanted to profess that she was all in. That their future together could be gorgeous. But she also knew Melanie was overwhelmed, and possibly still shaky after seeing Laura the other day. That her to-do list had put Paige on the do not touch list.

In the end Paige didn't have to say or do anything. Melanie was the one that rushed forward, her kiss hungry. Her hands wound around Paige's neck holding her close. Barely able to breathe, Paige tried to tell her everything with that kiss.

CHAPTER THIRTY-ONE

Melanie

Melanie woke up and immediately realised she was sore in the best possible way. Paige's arm was still tight around her middle, holding her close. Melanie smiled, never guessing Paige was a big spoon kind of person.

A kiss to her neck, alerted Melanie to Paige being awake. Melanie really needed to check what time it was; she couldn't be late for work when she was the one opening up.

'I set an alarm on my phone. It's just gone nine o'clock. I'll make us some breakfast and then you can get showered and go to work, OK?' Paige whispered in her ear.

Firstly, Melanie couldn't believe that she'd finally managed to sleep. Then again, several orgasms given and received will tire a girl out. Second, she couldn't believe Paige was such a big cuddler. And finally, that Paige had offered to get out of their warm cosy bed and make breakfast. Melanie hadn't been looked after like this before. Wait, not *their* bed. Just the bed they'd both slept in. It was Paige's bed, not theirs. Melanie frowned, her brain a complete jumble this morning. She clearly needed caffeine.

Paige kissed her cheek. 'Don't worry if you fall back to sleep, I'll come and wake you up again.' Paige's hand was moving up and down Melanie's thigh, circling her hip and Melanie knew she had a very intentional way of waking her back up again.

'Your glasses are on the side, throw anything of mine on you like.'

Melanie grabbed her glasses first, wanting to watch as a dishevelled and completely naked Paige got out of bed. It wasn't disappointing. Until she started getting dressed.

'Keep looking at me like that and I can guarantee you will be late for work.' Paige pulled on a T-shirt and shorts, before turning around with a grin, opening the door and presumably heading to the bathroom.

Melanie was grateful; she needed a minute to reground herself. There was something more than a little bit lovely about waking up with Paige. Something that if she could, she would love to get used to. And that right there, was why she needed a minute. She was getting very carried away with herself. It really couldn't be more. Not right now and she didn't need to go through all of the reasons again. She had them recited by heart. But yet here she was in Paige's bed. So . . .

Ripping off the duvet as if it were a plaster, Melanie got out of bed and searched around for clothes. She found a hoody and some shorts and took one step out of the bedroom, before jumping out of her skin.

'Good morning, dear. I trust you had a lovely night.'

'Connie's back home, by the way,' Paige shouted from behind and somewhere nearer the kitchen.

Melanie didn't really know what to do, where to look, or what to say. 'Morning.' That was the very best she could come up with.

'And was your night good?' Connie asked eyebrows jumping up and down.

'Erm yes.'

'Excellent. That means Paige will be in a good mood today. Come on, don't be shy. She's going to make us both bacon butties, just what we need after an energetic night. I hope you don't mind but I folded up your skirt and pants? They're just over there on the arm of the sofa.'

The normalcy was what was throwing Melanie. They could be talking about the weather. The fact was, Melanie was mortified that she'd left her skirt and knickers scattered across the flat for Paige's *gran* to find.

But neither of them seemed to care in the slightest.

Melanie chuckled, her brain deciding to find the whole thing hilarious.

'That's better,' Connie said with a pat on her arm. 'I'll go make you a cup of coffee, you sit down.'

Melanie sat herself down and a minute later a cup appeared in front of her, along with a quick hand placed on top of hers, and a lovely warm smile. The smell and sound of the bacon cooking was incredible, and before long a bacon buttie was placed in front of her, just as she liked it. Crispy bacon, on toast and with ketchup. Perfection.

Paige sat down beside her and Connie opposite.

'So, what's the plan for today, my loves? Do I need to make myself scarce again?' Connie asked.

'You would if it was up to me, Gran but no. Melanie and I both need to work today.'

'Shame,' Connie said.

Wait, what? Did that mean Paige wanted more? She'd hinted at that last night, but Melanie hadn't been certain Paige's cheesy lines had been sincere. They needed to talk. This was unclear. It was just that Melanie didn't know quite what she wanted to say or how she was going to say it, or quite what she wanted. She concentrated on her food, ignoring as best she could all the wonderful and scary thoughts going around her brain. But all too soon, her bacon buttie was finished and she was none the wiser.

'You go jump in the shower and I'll pull you some clothes together for work,' Paige said. 'Go on. Use whatever you like in there.'

Melanie did as instructed, grateful to Paige for the direction. Stepping in the shower Melanie deliberately chose the scent Paige used. It was a terrible mistake. Melanie was basically Pavlovian to the smell and every time she caught it her body responded. Stepping out of the shower tightly wrapped up in a towel, she saw her black skirt from last night, her black heels, her bra, a T-shirt of Paige's that was black, and a fresh, as in brand-new fresh, pair of knickers, a new toothbrush and bobbles and grips of various sizes.

Oh, Melanie had questions, so many questions.

Once dressed, and teeth clean, she re-emerged to find Paige dressed, and cleaning up the kitchen.

'Hey, I'll walk down to yours with you if that's OK? Here, I've made you a latte.'

Melanie smiled. When had she last been so well taken care of? She couldn't speak as she strode towards Paige and reached out for the coffee, in its own insulated travel mug. 'You look gorgeous,' Paige said, placing a kiss on her cheek.

Melanie felt like Alice in Wonderland. Whatever world she had woken up in, it wasn't hers, but she wasn't sure she wanted to leave it.

'Come on,' Paige said moving towards the back door.

'Bye, love. See you soon,' Connie called out.

'Bye, Connie.'

Melanie was careful going down the fire exit steps until they were on the street.

'Are you going to be OK in those heels? Do you want to borrow some Converse? I'm not sure if we're the same size though,' Paige said.

Melanie shook her head. 'I've some ballerina pumps at work if they get too bad.'

They took a few steps in silence, but then both spoke at once.

'Why did you have knickers in my size? My arse is way—'

'Can we do this again?'

They both fell silent as they continued to walk.

Wait, what? Had Paige just asked if they could do this again? Hook up? Or do the whole morning after thing with a care and consideration, that was completely foreign to Melanie. She looked down at her travel mug that Paige had given her for a walk that would take less than two minutes. To a bar that had its own coffee machine.

'Ah yes. Well, the knickers thing you could just say was wishful thinking,' Paige said. 'Obviously I guessed your size and got them, just in case. Is that too weird?'

'I'm not sure.' It had certainly never happened to her before. 'You want to do this again?' Melanie asked. 'Which bit exactly?'

Paige didn't say anything at first and Melanie worried.

'Not that I don't want to. I just . . .' Melanie hesitated.

They'd arrived at Lulu already as Paige turned to face her. 'I know you're busy and may not be able to find time for me. But any of it. You ask me which bit I want and I want any and all of it. If it's just hanging out the two of us, if it's all hanging out together, if it's the sex, or the sharing a bed. Any of it.'

Melanie thought that through. Nowhere in there did Paige say anything about a relationship. And that was good, right? That was the one thing Melanie couldn't and shouldn't offer. So why did it sting?

'So, a friend with benefits type thing?' Melanie asked, impressed she'd managed to keep the hurt or whatever it was out of her voice.

'If that's what you want?'

'OK sure.' Melanie nodded. 'We can do that.'

The grin from Paige was worth the momentary twang of wanting things she couldn't have and that weren't necessarily being offered.

Paige cupped her face with her hands and kissed her softly. Melanie immediately leaned in closer. They were just starting to really get into it, when a polite cough interrupted them.

'Morning.'

'Oh, sorry Dan. Here, let me get the door and alarm.'

'See you later, Mel.' Paige waved, and nodded at Dan before turning away.

'Yeah, see you later, Paige.'

'Sorry,' Melanie said completely flustered.

'Are we still cool to go through the new menu options this week?' he asked, professional as always.

'Yeah of course. I'm looking forward to it.' Melanie opened the door and got them inside, trying to reactivate the work side of her brain.

'You want some breakfast, boss?' Dan shouted from the kitchen.

'No, I'm good, thanks.'

Was she good? Melanie wasn't sure. But she opened up her app to see what she needed to tackle first of all and saw a message from Louisa.

Notification: I was going over the figures you pulled together, we may need to look at new suppliers for the prosecco after all. It's eating our budget far more than we anticipated. It's not great news. I'll try and have a shop around on Monday.

Well shit. Of course, it wasn't going to be straight forward.

OK, but she didn't have the big art project reveal on her list any more thanks to Paige and co. But she still had scaffolding and sourcing of other resources. And with a click, Melanie felt her work brain engage. And she suspected it may need to stay that way for the time being. But it *was* temporary. The art project would be over in just a few weeks. Her life would be back to her normal, which fine, was very busy, but it wasn't usually this level of overwhelming. She could do this. For a few weeks she could manage. She would just need to prioritise. The first thing she did was add to the list to go through their CCTV again to see if they could see anyone lurking around near the tattoo shop, but she already knew that their CCTV wouldn't quite reach. So, in that case, Melanie needed to go through the figures again and see if it was just the prosecco that was a problem or any of their other goods.

Which just unnecessarily reminded Melanie of how little time she had to offer to Paige. Friends with benefits was an all right idea, in theory, but Melanie couldn't help but feel that at some point she was bound to let Paige down with her absence. And she would never, ever, want to make Paige feel how Laura had made her feel. Melanie could admit that some of her relationship fears could no longer be applied to Paige. She didn't think Paige would belittle anyone. Melanie honestly felt in her gut that she could trust Paige, that she was rock steady. Grumpy at times, yes. But she didn't play games. Her friends also reflected well on Paige and Melanie took all that in. But what Melanie would not do was put Paige in a position where she felt second best, worthless by default, because she knew how much that stung, how much it tore away at your confidence until there was very little left. So, yes, she wanted Paige, she was madly attracted to her and could admit she trusted her. But she would be cautious, and clear. It was a friends with benefits situation and that's all it could be for now.

CHAPTER THIRTY-TWO

Paige

'You always knew there would be no psychic for psychic night, didn't you?' Paige asked as she started making a Tom Collins for Connie, her actions deliberately chill and nonchalant. 'In fact, I would bet you headed on up here because you knew you'd be needed.'

'Don't even try it,' Connie said, her back to the bar as she perched on the barstool, deliberately choosing to look around the room rather than at Paige.

'I'm not trying anything. But you suspected, didn't you?' Paige asked again as she poured the drink.

'I know your plan, too,' Connie said shifting her head only slightly. 'You're trying to butter me up, trying not subtly I might add, to suggest I am better than the fraud you had booked. Now you're making my favourite drink, and you'll make it well, in the hopes I'll agree to be your psychic for the night.' Connie finished the sentence with a pfft type noise and Paige knew, just like they both knew, Connie would do it — all Paige needed to do was ask.

'Not at all, Gran. She's already contacted me to say she can do it, that the other place fell through and she was right to double-book in the first place.'

'Oh, she did not!'

'Yep, so I guess she really is good. Here's your drink.'

Connie slowly turned on the barstool, her nostrils flaring, the tiniest of scowls on her forehead as she made that balloon exhale sound again. Paige had to wait it out. Oh, and she knew this, because it would appear her mojo was working just fine today.

Connie took a sip of her drink, the atmosphere between them so heavy it needed a drink of its own, until Connie nodded in satisfaction.

'I know you're lying to me. I know you know. I know that you know, that I know, you know. I also know that your mojo is fixed. Although I know why it's fixed, do you?' Connie paused, eyebrow raised, and Paige said nothing; in fact she didn't move a muscle. 'And we *both* know that I'm the best. So, let's cut the crap. What time do you need me?'

Paige smiled. 'Thanks, Gran, it starts at eight tomorrow night.'

'Shhh. It's Connie in public, I've told you.'

'Oh I've gotta take this, it's the scaffolders about the wall.' Paige grabbed her phone and sure enough, within minutes arrangements were made and the site would be ready to paint from tomorrow.

Connie took another sip before putting her drink down and pinning Paige with a look. 'And you're going to add that into the app, are you?' Connie sucked her teeth.

'Why, what's wrong with that?' Paige began typing exactly that.

Connie put her hand on the phone and pulled it down, and Paige had no choice but to look at her gran with undivided attention.

'You need to tell her about the app. About the rucksack, about the prosecco. About the girls' brunch social media plan. About the conversation you were thinking of having with Patrick, sorry, Councillor Houghton. About the work you were planning on doing with Selena. I know your heart is in the right place, but this isn't the way to do it.'

'To do what?'

'Paige.' Connie said her name in such a way that Paige looked down at the bar top, not sure she wanted to hear what was coming next.

'You're not her knight in shining armour. You can't debit her into love.'

'Love?!'

'Paige, that's not how relationships work. You can't make someone love you with countless acts of kindness. There has to be a real connection there. You're creating a debt that you have no intention of ever letting her repay.'

'I don't know what you mean. I'm just trying to help out — she's running on fumes.'

'I agree. And the occasional meal, the running of a bath, these are all lovely things. But swooping in like you are. And using the app like you are. It's not the same. Let me put it this way. How can she ever make things better for you? For example, have you even told her about your doodah, your mojo as you call it? What about your mum?'

Paige was stunned silent. Since when had doing nice things for someone become something wrong?

'You and your mum—'

'Gran, that has nothing to do with this thing with Melanie, whatever it is and no one, *no one* ever mentioned love. I'm simply helping out someone I like. I think you're overthinking this whole thing.' Paige hadn't mentioned love. Not out loud but she couldn't deny the idea had been floating around her brain.

'I think you need to tell her about the app.' Connie's voice was stern.

'She gave me access to that app,' Paige said defensively.

Connie said nothing, but her face said it all.

'OK fine. I'll tell her about the app.'

'And maybe open up to her a little more in general?' Connie's nose was scrunched up.

'Huh?'

'Look, all I'm saying is that princesses can defeat their own dragons and become stronger for it. Just like you did, and now you're a badass. You're not the knight in shining armour, but you can hold her sword until she needs it.' Connie slowly nodded, a small smile on her face as if she'd just bestowed the most amazing piece of knowledge.

'I'm holding her what now?'

'Ah, forget it.'

'Oh, wise Connie, please do tell me more of your tales,' Paige said with a bow.

'She could love you, Paige, *you*. And guess what? You are deserving of love just as you are. But you have to share yourself with her in more ways than one, and I know you, Paige. You don't share. I bet you don't even tell the girls what's really going on for you, do you?'

Paige said nothing, neither wanting to confirm nor deny. So instead, she nodded. 'I'll tell her about the app.' But she did share with her friends. Granted only in the last week or so had she really started. And even then not completely. But she'd told Melanie about the tattoo. Which was . . . Rubbish, it was rubbish.

'Good.' Connie looked around. 'It's quiet so you could go tell her right now.'

'Now?'

Connie nodded. 'And if it gets busy here, I can always slip behind the bar and—'

'Oh no. Nope. Not after what happened the other night. No way.'

'It's not my fault I didn't know a slippery nipple was a cocktail,' Connie replied with a shrug.

'We both know you knew full well.'

'Just go.'

'Fine, but I'm going because I know it's the right time, not because you told me.'

'Oh and Paige, I won't be here—'

Paige cut her off, not ready to hear what she was about to say. 'I know . . . Just . . . I know, OK?'

Paige ducked around until she was back on the punters' side. 'I'll be back in a minute.'

As Paige hit the fresh air and drizzle of the Manchester air her mind reeled with what Connie had said. She hadn't been trying to save Melanie, she was simply helping her out. And she had shared plenty of herself. Fine she'd mostly been either grumpy or they'd been having sex but still.

'Eurgh,' Paige said out loud. She knew better than to argue with Connie. Her gran had been the only one able to get through to her. Paige had tried time and again to get some common ground with her mum, but they clashed, and yes on some level Paige could see how her gran might think Paige equated love with gestures. But that wasn't the case at all here.

But then Paige stepped into Lulu and saw the woman in question.

'Shit.' Paige felt like a plaster had been ripped off her heart. It stung and it felt strangely exposed. Connie had been right. Again. As usual. Paige wondered for a moment if it might just be powerful lust. She didn't discount it, but her instinct or gut whatever, was pulling her towards Melanie heart and soul, and at that moment Paige saw two scenarios play out in her head. One where they were both back in Paige's flat, and Melanie was working at the kitchen table, Paige was watching Alfie and everywhere she looked she saw signs of Melanie. The other was Paige as her life was like before Melanie, but where before Melanie she had been quiet and content, now it felt empty and disrupted. Paige wanted to turn around, to go back to her flat and lie down with a Disney film, maybe *Tangled* this time. She went to turn.

'Paige? Is everything OK?' Melanie walked towards her.

And Paige couldn't talk, well she could but she found she couldn't open her mouth. She was suddenly afraid that a declaration of love might fall out. But then she remembered why she was there, and realised Gran was right again. And now Paige was getting wound up.

'Yes, just wanted to let you know that the scaffolding will be put up today. Should be ready for Selena and co. to get started tomorrow.'

'Thanks, Paige. Yeah, I thought I saw a notification on the app. Are you sure you're OK?'

'Yeah. See you later.' Paige nodded once and took off.

CHAPTER THIRTY-THREE

Melanie

'Right, ladies, I know you're all eager, so let's get you lot done before I get too busy and then too tired. Paige, will you get me a Tom Collins please?'

'Here you go.' Paige offered Connie the drink the same moment she asked, and Melanie smiled, they were so in sync.

'I should . . .' Melanie said as she realised what was about to happen.

'Nonsense,' Connie said. 'Sit down, come on now.'

At a table at the back of the bar, with absolutely no fuss but a small amount of quiet, Sophie popped open the prosecco and made sure everyone had a glass, as Connie sat down at the head of the table and gestured first for Sophie.

'I'm not doing the whole kit and caboodle for you guys. Just give me your hand.' Connie looked down and inspected Sophie's hand.

'Yep, there's the ambition. It shows me you still have a lot you want to achieve professionally, and you will. Whatever you set out to do, you're going to get done one way or another. There's another bit here that says watch out for your friends. It's not in a bad way, more a reminder to check in on one another.' Connie closed her eyes for a second, before opening them and studying Sophie's face. 'Personally whatever big thing you're pondering, the decision you're discussing . . .' Melanie grinned behind Connie as Sophie tried to contain her gasp. 'The decision will be made soon, but the outcome while glorious will not happen the way you initially expect. But your planning and resourcefulness will come into its own.'

'Wait, but what do you mean?'

Connie smiled and held onto Sophie's hands with both of hers as she leaned forward. 'It will happen, Sophie. I see a few more people in your family yet, and when the time comes you will understand. Persevere and it will all be worth it. I think maybe twins and then one more.'

Sophie grinned, her eyes welling up.

'You already knew the answer, Sophie,' Connie said with a nod that made Paige roll her eyes at the same time as a tear rolled down Sophie's face. 'It'll be tricky at times but get to it.'

Sophie reached over and kissed Connie on the cheek. 'Thanks, Connie.'

'Right, Polly, come here ,my love. Let's hope we don't see me running off with your man hey?' Connie laughed and Polly smiled but if Melanie had to guess it looked a little forced.

'Let's have a look at you,' Connie began as she did the same thing again with Polly's hand. Polly could barely sit still.

'Oh well then. No Bailey for me.' Then Connie laughed. 'My, you really keep each other on your toes, don't you? He adores you to the moon and back. With that in mind I see a lot of travel for you two and something rather spontaneous that will tie you both together forever.' She bent down further and appeared to really study a line on Polly's hand that had them all trying to lean forward to see what Connie was finding so fascinating.

'Hmm OK. There's something quite big with one of your songs. You're reluctant to believe it will pan out, but

I strongly suspect it will.' Melanie watched as Polly's face flushed pink. 'Same here as well though for you, you're going to be moving about a fair bit in the future, but your girls are going to be as important as always, and you'll need to look out for one another as you always have done. In fact, I don't see that bond you all have weakening anytime in the future but it will grow stronger and stronger as long as you all continue to nurture it. You'll love each other always. It's quite a thing actually,' Connie said her eyes bright and her smile full. Polly was returning the look.

She gave Connie a quick hug and then went around and hugged all of them in turn, even Melanie who wasn't expecting to be included.

'Right, Mya, get over here.'

Mya grinned at Connie, and Melanie felt like she was looking at two kindred spirits.

'Don't worry, Connie, I know my future.'

'You do?'

'Yep, world domination and lots of sex.' She tossed her hair and blew Connie a kiss.

'I'm sure you're right, isn't that what I said last time?' Connie laughed. 'Let's have a look then.'

Mya held her hand out with nothing but confidence and a small smile.

Connie burst out laughing. 'Vegas really doesn't know what to do with you, does it? Oh Mya you are fab, don't ever change. Oh look here, you won't. You're right, lots of domination and lots of sex. You have been and will continue to rock the world. I see a TED Talk in your future, your loyal feminist fan base continues to grow. Oh and' — Connie did laugh — 'no I think I'll leave that one for you to find out on your own.'

Mya's eyes narrowed. 'Connie?'

But Connie was laughing too hard, and Melanie could have sworn Paige was smiling a little too.

'Right, Melanie, come on, girl,' Connie said as Mya reluctantly got up off her chair, kissed Connie on the cheek and whispered something in her ear that had Connie doubled up laughing again. Melanie was nervous. She hadn't expected to be included in this, had felt like a voyeur already. But then she realised that she'd been included a lot, and each time she'd been surprised. Maybe it was time to accept it. But that felt a bit scary, purely because she wanted it so much.

As Connie caught her breath, she thought she saw a look pass between her and Paige but it was already over before she sat down. Connie grabbed her hand and her skin was hot around hers, and Melanie could've sworn she felt a little electric shock. Melanie looked around at all the faces at the table, all looking eager to hear what Connie might have to say.

'Yes,' Connie said. 'I know what you want to know, and the answer is yes. Nothing is ever set in stone and there will be trying times. In fact, if you get a letter about a noise order, my suggestion would be to have Councillor Houghton check it out for you.'

'Wait, what? I got one this morning!' What? How the hell could Connie be *that* good?

'Yes, it's not real.' Connie nodded.

'But that's so specific. How could you possibly know that?'

'Well, I am good, but Patrick may have mentioned about someone unsuccessfully trying to put one through but there was no evidence to support it. I figured that if someone was persistent they may try and fake something. Anyway, share it with Patrick. He should be able to help you get to the bottom of it.'

'But the business . . .'

'Yes, the business should be fine, not without a couple of hiccups but I can't see anything stopping it from succeeding. But like I said nothing is set in stone. There are a few things I need to make you aware of—'

'Gran,' Paige cut in.

'There will be a little bit of turmoil in the near future and you will find yourself wondering how many chances is too many. Only you can know the answer for sure. Some truths will be revealed. But, and I can't stress this enough, however and whatever you decide, this hard time will pass soon. It will start to get easier and you will have more time for a life. You'll just need to decide what to do and who to include within it.'

'Erm, thanks, Connie,' Melanie said as she ran all that information through her brain. Business should be OK, chances with the prosecco supplier or something else? Maybe the Instagram walls?

'No problem, love.'

Melanie got up slightly dazed and gestured for Paige to take the seat.

'Oh no, I don't need to, I . . .' Paige began.

'Paige, we need you a second, sorry,' India shouted out from the bar and Paige ran off. Like, literally ran off, and Melanie was left with a strange vibe. Seriously strange; something was off. Polly smiled up at her but it wasn't real. Sophie was tapping away on her phone and Mya was staring after Paige, but that horrible feeling was settling through her body and she could almost see it working its way around the group. Everyone was avoiding her eye. And Melanie felt like an onlooker again. Would it always feel like this? Included one minute and pressed up against it and trying to get in the next? Melanie realised she might not have a gift like Connie, but it didn't take a psychic to feel this tension. They all knew something, or something was said that she didn't know about and Melanie could admit her heart broke a little, and she felt more than a little bit jolted at the sudden turnabout. Wow Connie was good! That turmoil she'd predicted had landed quickly.

Connie stood up and put her hand on Melanie's shoulder. 'It'll be grand, Melanie. And I'm saying this not as a psychic but as a gran. Paige will try and keep herself at arm's-length. Oh she loves, fiercely and protectively, you only have to look at her friends to see that. But she needs coaxing sometimes; a relationship has to work both ways, don't you agree? But I see the possibility for real happiness, Melanie. I really do. For both of you.'

'Right, I think we all need a cocktail. Come on girls, let's debrief at the bar. The boys will be here soon.' Mya slung her arm around Melanie's shoulders, and Mya was right to do that, because Melanie was tempted to leave them to it at that point. She thought that maybe Paige was avoiding her, and she couldn't shake the ominous feeling that Connie's reading had left her with. Her heart inexplicably ached, and she had a terrible sense that tonight was not going to go as well as she had hoped.

CHAPTER THIRTY-FOUR

Paige

Paige was keeping herself busy behind the bar. She knew it, and she had a feeling Melanie knew it too. How had everything gone from so amazing to so shit in a day? Paige wanted to blame Connie but she knew that would just be shooting the messenger. Luckily the bar was busy and the psychic bookings through the roof. So she really should be behind the bar. It made sense, but she knew she was avoiding facing her mistakes. She should have told Melanie sooner about her mojo and about the app, but really her heart was and remained in the right place.

Shit, she was coming over.

'Hey, you all right?' Melanie asked but Paige could hear the reluctance in her voice.

'Yeah, just busier than I thought it was going to be,' Paige said.

'Oh, come on boss,' Belle said as she passed over the dirty glasses. 'You knew today was going to be awesome. Everyone loves a psychic. At least you managed to get Connie to do it. Otherwise, you would have been the one doing the readings.' Belle laughed as she turned around to go and collect some more glasses.

Melanie went to laugh, but Paige's face must have betrayed how she felt because Melanie's laughing smile quickly dropped. 'What? Wait, are you psychic or something?' Melanie asked.

'Erm. Well, I've never called it that, and well, no, not really see, a little bit for my friends sometimes. More like gut instinct.'

'Why do you look so uncomfortable? That's got to be cool, right? Oh, that's why you didn't need a reading from Connie. You can do your own then or something?'

Melanie looked relieved, and Paige felt worse.

'Am I missing something? What's wrong?' Melanie rightly asked and Paige didn't know what to say. 'Why not tell me sooner, I mean it's not like a big deal or anything, is it?'

Well, no, it wouldn't have been if it hadn't been broken. Paige strongly suspected it had been broken so she couldn't interfere with her own love life. She suspected that her gut instinct, mojo or whatever had taken a holiday so she could meet and develop strong feelings for the person right in front of her. The same person who had fixed her, and knew absolutely nothing about it. The person who had shared so much, who continued to share so much, and who Paige had shared with so little. Her gran was right and Paige felt like hell. All together it was not going to make her look great. But Paige would not run scared. Again. Like Connie had always said, if something needs saying then say it.

She looked around and realised there was only one person that could help her out now.

'Soph!' Paige shouted.

They waited until Sophie approached the bar.

'I need you to cover for me for a minute?'

'OK but I've been drinking.'

'You were always drinking on the job, why would this be any different?' Paige said as Sophie ran round to get behind the bar.

'Can you come with me for a minute?' Paige turned and asked Melanie.

Melanie swallowed before answering, 'Sure.' And Paige felt even worse for making Melanie feel like something was wrong. But something was wrong and a conversation, or rather several conversations were a little overdue.

And then they were walking up the stairs to her flat and Paige could honestly say she had no idea how this was going to go, her mojo having left her once again.

'Sit down. Please,' Paige said. Great start there by barking out orders.

Melanie sat on the edge of the sofa. 'What's going on? What aren't you telling me?'

'A few things. But not on purpose. I'm not sure where to begin.'

Melanie sat and waited but her posture had stiffened, her facial expression overly poised.

'So yeah, I have a strong gut instinct, an intuition. I'm not psychic but my gut instinct, well Connie calls it my doo-dah. I call it mojo. It sounds like a bigger deal than it is. Well, except I lost it. And it made me very grumpy. And I figured out it had something to do with you.'

'Me.'

'Erm yeah, I'm not explaining myself very well and I'm sorry because I should have said this sooner. But honestly it just . . . We've just happened so fast. I just . . . Yeah, well, remember I was grumpy when we first started bumping into each other?'

Melanie's eyebrow raised. 'Hard to forget.'

'Yeah, well, I was grumpy because I'd lost that part of me. But finally it's back, I think because of you. And hopefully you can see I've been a lot less grumpy lately.'

'Right,' Melanie said slowly.

'There's more.'

'Great.'

If Paige's gut instinct was working it would have been blaring at her that this was not going as smoothly as she thought.

'The other thing is I've not really been as open with you as I could have been, as I would like to be. I want to be. But it's not easy for me. As you can tell.' Paige let out a sad little laugh. 'The app,' she continued.

'What app?' Melanie asked, her tone sharp.

'The one you use to organise everything. Well, I don't think you meant to, but you gave me full access.'

'I gave you access, of course. You needed it for the art project. I told you that, you've been working on the list, updating it.'

'No, you gave me access to all of it. Not just the art project list. I saw all the tasks for your bar, for Alfie, your personal list. I can see it all.'

'What? No, there's no way I would . . .' Melanie quickly grabbed her phone from her pocket and Paige watched as her face fell. 'Why would you not tell me this sooner?'

'At first I didn't know it was a mistake.'

Melanie wouldn't look up from her phone, but Paige could see her hands were white where she gripped it so hard.

Melanie uttered something but Paige couldn't make out what it was. 'Sorry?'

'What else? There's more still, isn't there? So, tell me.'

'I knew you were under a lot of pressure and I used the info on the app to try and help you out. Well, not all of it was from the app. The prosecco for example when you ran out and needed more, that was just timing, same with the rucksack. Well, I was going to grab you one before you added it to the list.'

'Why?'

'I just wanted to help.'

'Then why not tell me? Why keep it a secret?'

It was on the tip of Paige's tongue to tell her that she thought she was falling in love with her. But what kind of an answer was that?

'I didn't mean to lie. It all just happened so quickly, and I just wanted to help.'

'Oh . . .' Melanie's voice caught but she cleared her throat and carried on. 'And the brunch with the girls and their social media. They knew too, didn't they? All the concerns about the business, all the things on my lists . . .' Melanie stood up and didn't say anything further.

'No, wait you don't understand. I can explain better. I . . .'

'No, I get it. You used me to make yourself feel better, to be fixed again. When that worked you felt guilty and had to pay me back in some way for using me. Helpless Melanie can't do anything and so you and your friends took pity on me. And Alfie, he fell in love with you and I—' Melanie cut herself off and sucked in a breath.

Paige heard what Melanie said and realised it sounded way worse than she had ever intended, and she desperately wanted to know what Melanie was about to say. 'No, that's not true, I . . .'

But Melanie was already out the door and Paige didn't know how that sentence finished, or why her legs wouldn't move, or why her chest stung. But this was bad and she didn't need her gut instinct to know that a piece of her heart had just walked out the door and she wasn't sure she would see it again.

CHAPTER THIRTY-FIVE

Melanie

'Right so the noise order we've received is a fake. I've checked online and yeah it's not real. Councillor Houghton said he's going to come in later and let us know what's going on.' Melanie spoke as she looked down at her list on her iPad. She'd been tempted to delete the app last night but seeing as how she ran her life off it she'd instead triple-checked to make sure Paige was no longer included. On any of it. The art project she'd sort by herself. She didn't need Paige fixing her problems in some misguided attempt at payment. Not when . . . No she couldn't think about it or else she'd realise her ridiculous heart was breaking.

'The good reviews are now vastly outpacing the few bad ones,' Melanie continued. 'I did some work last night on our costings and I think I've found some ways we can recoup our costs slightly differently but also, where we can make some savings. The Instagram walls need thinking about next and—'

'Stop. Mel, just stop.' Louisa's hand rested on Melanie's arm.

Melanie hadn't realised she could no longer see her iPad, that tears were slowly and silently rolling down her face. But when she did notice she quickly and roughly wiped them away. She wasn't helpless; she wasn't some weak person that needed to be looked after, to be coddled. She quickly looked around the bar to make sure she hadn't been seen.

'Come on, let's go to the emergency meeting room,' Louisa said. 'Don't worry, nobody's paying attention to us.' Louisa led the way out the back of the restaurant, past the bins and round the corner to their tiny patch of land where they tended to park, and got into Louisa's car.

Once settled in the front seats, Louisa turned to face Melanie, who carried on as if nothing had happened. 'So I guess, I think the business will be OK, but as always we will need to keep a close eye.'

'Mel . . . stop. It's not the business that has you upset. Tell me what's happening. Was it something to do with Paige?'

Melanie chewed on her lip, almost making it bleed as she tried to physically hold in her emotions. 'I refuse to be that helpless girl again, Louisa.'

'You never were, Mel. Laura just made you feel that way. It wasn't real.'

'Yeah, well.'

'My God, Mel, you're an absolute legend. You're part owner in a successful business. A business that has been reviewed by *Manchester Confidential*, I might add.'

Melanie shot a look at Louisa. 'Are you serious?'

'A glowing review calling us a wonderful fit to an amazing community, and a must-see venue for all wannabe influencers. The food was paired so perfectly with the drinks that the reviewer said they will come back to sample more.'

'Why didn't you tell me?'

'I only found out yesterday and I wanted us to really be able to celebrate. But I think you need to know now. You did that, we did that, well, the whole team. But we are co-owners of Manchester's newest and most loveliest bar. You did that, Mel. You are not helpless. You practically co-parent Alfie. You navigate the relationship between your mum and your sister like a goddam miracle worker. Not to mention that bloody art project and the way you handle the Neighbourhood business stuff. Mel, I . . .' Melanie was surprised to see Louisa's eyes water. 'I couldn't have done any of this without you and that miracle app of yours.' Louisa sniffed. 'But no crying, that's not my style. You can go for it though.'

Melanie smiled. 'Gee, thanks.'

'Come on, Mel, tell me what's wrong so we can fix it and start celebrating.'

'Oh that bloody app,' Melanie said, and just like that the floodgates opened and the tears flew and so did the words. 'I accidentally gave Paige full access to the app, not just the art stuff — everything. She had access to our work one, to my personal one. Oh, and the best bit, she was broken, and I somehow fixed her, and so she used all the things on the app that she could do and fixed them. The prosecco fairy, was her. The rucksack; I knew it was new. The social media boom from Sophie, Polly and Mya was because Paige had seen we were struggling. All because she felt guilty.'

'I'm not understanding — what on earth did you fix?'

'She's a psychic or some shit, or she was, then she wasn't but then I fixed it. But the point is I knew none of it. I knew absolutely nothing of any of it. What do I actually know about Paige? I know that her mood changes faster than we get through prosecco. She's been grumpy, or she's been trying to get in my pants. I know nothing of any importance. She never really opened up to me, in any meaningful way. And yet . . .' Melanie finally slowed down to catch her breath. 'And yet I know enough that my heart is breaking and I feel betrayed, but worse than that, I feel like helpless Mel again. Like I need to be saved. That's not who I was, and it isn't who I want to be.' Melanie sniffed.

'What should she have done?' Louisa asked.

'She should have told me she was broken, she should have told me when I accidentally gave her full access to my whole entire life with that app.' Melanie felt the hurt turn to a more powerful and hot anger in her belly.

'And what would you have done?' Louisa asked, her tone level and calm.

'What?'

'Well, we both know what she should have done, but no one's perfect. So, I'm interested, what would you have done? Would you have told a person you didn't know that you were broken in some way?'

'Well, no.'

'Hmm.' Louisa raised her eyebrows.

'Whose side are you on?'

'Yours. Of course. But I've never seen you as happy as when you're with Paige, and I don't even get to see it all that often. But when I see you at work I can tell when you've been with Paige or when you're about to see her. And yes, you don't need rescuing, you're not helpless, but you are terrible at looking after yourself, and from what you've told me there has been at least three occasions where she's made sure you were eating properly, and I have to say I'm a little bit grateful to her for that. I'm always trying to get people to feed you here, but you scare them away.' Louisa laughed, but Melanie scowled.

'I'm an adult. A fully grown up, tax-paying adult.'

'Who sometimes makes questionable decisions just like the rest of us.' Louisa nodded.

Melanie's phone rang and for a split second her heart expanded at the thought that it might be Paige, but it wasn't. And Melanie didn't have time to mull over her reaction. She picked up. 'Hey.'

'Mel, sorry to mither you but Councillor Houghton and Selena are here. I've shown them to a table.'

'Thanks, Cleo, we'll be there right now.' Melanie hung up her phone. 'We don't have time to unpack all of this. You need to go and make small talk while I try and sort out the mess that is now my face.' Melanie sighed and held her face in her hands for three seconds. 'Right, come on then. Business mode.' Melanie put her phone in her bra and stepped out the car. She got to the staff toilet and saw herself in the mirror. Sophie was right that really was a good waterproof mascara.

But the concealer was no match for the dark circles under her eyes.

'Shit. Shit!' Melanie's head was a mess and she just hoped Louisa would be able to get through this meeting because in that moment, Melanie wasn't sure how much more she could take. Taking a deep breath, she straightened her spine and tried a smile. Yeah, forget the smile. Professionally neutral was probably the best she could manage. And so Melanie stepped out the loos and made her way to the table where no doubt some new drama was about to unfold.

'Ah Melanie. Good to see you. I don't have long so I'll just cut straight to it.' Melanie nodded and then looked around until Cleo caught her eye and non-verbally she asked for a drink.

'Selena, have you and Councillor Houghton met?' Melanie asked.

'Oh yes,' Selena said laughing, 'we've met a number of times to discuss funding, haven't we?'

'Yes, and I'm still looking over your latest proposal.'

'Of course.' Selena's nod was serious but Melanie got the sense there may be no love lost between the two of them.

'Anyway, two things. The first one, this noise order is absolute nonsense. Ignore it. The other contender for these premises has a bee in their bonnet about being unsuccessful and instead of moving on they keep contacting me and trying to make completely unfounded accusations. This is just their latest attempt.'

'What?' Melanie and Louisa said in shocked unison.

'Yes well, I'm dealing with it.'

'Not very well, this person had the health inspector pay us a surprise visit and they've been trying to tag us in fake negative reviews.' Melanie's anger was way too near the surface after earlier.

'Whatever this person has been doing to you, they've been doing to us too. They've made this personal. It could affect our business — it very nearly did, it still might!' Louisa explained.

'Sounds like harassment to me,' Selena said, folding her arms.

'Yes well, like I say this is a very popular area and for good reason, we have to make sure we vet all possible applicants. I will be speaking to this person and making it very clear they will never be considered for a property in this community again if they don't stop. But please let me know if you have any more incidents. I will take this on myself.'

Louisa and Melanie were both stunned into angry silence.

'Now as for the second thing I need to talk to you all about, the scaffolding has gone up on the wall, I believe. And I was able to secure one of our housing associations to base paint it. So from tomorrow it will be ready. However, given that the scaffolding has caused some minor inconveniences to the units and the foot traffic round there, the council are asking that this is done within a week.'

'A week!' Melanie exclaimed.

'Yes, I'm aware it's not ideal. But that's what we have and I've tried my hardest but my hands really are tied with this one. But I have to say you've already done such an incredible job, Melanie, that I'm sure you can pull this out of the bag. Right, I need to be off. I have a scrutiny to prepare for.'

'Councillor Houghton, I'll be in touch with you about the funding,' Selena reminded.

'Yes, yes, of course. Have a good day.'

And with that newest of bombshells, Councillor Houghton left the bar.

'A week!' Melanie cried again.

'It's fine, it can be done, but we'll need more volunteers, and we'll need more hours. And weather wise, I'll guess we'll just have to do what we can.' Selena sounded all calm and reasonable.

'Sorry, I've just spotted something I need to help with,' Louisa said as she shot up out of the chair. Melanie looked around and could see that one of their staff was struggling with an iPad next to the till.

Melanie sighed.

'You've not been using that crystal, I can tell. I'd give you another one for heart ache but I'm not wasting my crystals on you.' Melanie looked back at Selena and saw she was smiling warmly. 'You OK?'

'Yeah, no. I'm . . . yeah.' Melanie went with a nod in the end.

'Some of the people I work with at the shelter – you know the shelter where people can escape abusive relationships, families? – well, in some cases they literally have nothing but the clothes on their backs. Their whole lives just completely gone in an instant. It's no longer safe for them so they leave everything behind.'

Melanie's eyes widened, her throat restricted. 'Oh God, that's—'

'Awful, yes. But we do what we can and at least they're safer now and we can all begin again. But don't your worries feel small now?'

'Oh my God, are you allowed to do that?' Melanie said.

'Do what, and I'm not wrong, am I?' Selena said with a shrug.

'Well, no. My problems feel really small in comparison.'

Selena smiled. 'Everyone has hard times, and sometimes it's the small things that tip us over. But sometimes we need perspective too. It's a balance. But I'm not trying to belittle your experience, in my own way I'm trying to help.'

'Yeah, well. It's a lot to process, I guess.'

Selena nodded. 'Well, you'll have plenty of time to process when you're up on that wall, painting. We start tomorrow. Wrap up warm. I'll email you a rota schedule tonight with my folks in it and you can fill in the gaps.' Selena finished her whisky sour and floated out the door. One of these days Melanie wanted to walk away from a meeting. She wanted to be the one setting the demands and just disappearing straight after, confident that her demands would be met.

Instead, Melanie opened up her app to see what hours she could put in to painting a wall, and cursed again at the app as she threw the phone on the table.

But it wasn't the app's or her phone's fault. Picking up her phone she once more looked at her to-do list. She still needed to pick up Alfie's present for the weekend, and double-check the booking with the entertainer for his party, so head down, Melanie did what she did best. She planned and she organised and she updated her app. And if it meant her brain couldn't wander, and she wasn't paying attention to her heart hurting, then so much the better.

CHAPTER THIRTY-SIX

Paige

Paige sat on her sofa, Disney on in the background, Mr Higgins nowhere to be found and Connie helping Jenny downstairs. Really that's where Paige should be too but it was early afternoon and she could afford a few minutes to regroup. Her phone pinged and she saw the email from Melanie asking for help with the wall painting. She knew Melanie hadn't meant it for Paige, but Paige would be there, morning noon and night if it meant a chance to talk to her. She had to make this right in some way, but she just wasn't sure how. She forwarded the email to the girls asking if any of them could jump in and help out at any point.

Her phone immediately lit up; the girls' WhatsApp group had a notification.

Polly: *Girls group assemble. Video Chat in five mins xx*

Paige sighed, her heart heavy and actually, she realised with a shock, she needed her girls. She knew she could ask them to help her out. It was difficult and it didn't come easy; she was the fixer not the fixee, but look where that had gotten her. The video chat pinged and Paige opened the app.

'Hey,' Paige said.

'OK come on out with it, what happened at the psychic night?' Polly asked impatiently, clearly having wanted to ask for a few days.

'Yeah Paige, what's going on?' Sophie said.

'Has Melanie had enough of your grumpy bum?' Mya laughed.

Paige didn't say anything to that, but didn't need to, her silence and no doubt the look on her face telling them all they needed to know. Mya's laughter quickly died as they realised that was exactly what had happened.

'Oh no. Sorry, Paige,' Mya whispered.

Polly sighed. 'Oh Paige, what happened?'

Paige looked at the faces on the screen. Polly was sat in front of some sort of sound desk. Sophie was sat at her kitchen table, her lighting and make-up impeccable. Mya was sat in her home office. 'I wish you were here,' Paige said quietly.

One by one she watched as her girls each disconnected from their real life. She saw Mya shut something down and reach to grab her Mulberry handbag. 'I'm going out Smithy, love you.' Sophie disappeared from the screen and returned a second later. 'All sorted, be there in a few minutes.'

Polly was moving through some hallways, phone still in front of her face. 'Hang on.' Paige watched as she pushed through a door. 'I'll be back later, if not then I'll send over the suggested samples tomorrow . . . Yeah thanks. Polly was back down a corridor again, into another room where she grabbed her coat. 'I'm on my way, Paige.'

'Thank you,' Paige said, her throat rough. The call disconnected and she knew they would all get to her as quickly as they could. She shouldn't have been surprised; she'd ran to the aid of her best friends many times, even travelling to Vegas. But she was still moved with how quickly they'd dropped everything for her.

Connie: *It'll be OK, Paige. You and your girls will sort it. I'll come back up later and will help however I can xx*

Paige untied her hair and lay down on the sofa, surprised when a minute later Mr Higgins curled up by her side, his face nudging into hers.

'How do I make this right, Mr H?'

He continued to head-butt her face. 'You're not all that helpful, you know. It's not just her though, is it?' The head-butting continued mercilessly. 'Yeah, I know it's little Alf too.' The butting stopped, as Mr Higgins looked up at her, with a glare that made her feel like an idiot. 'Yes, I know. I fell in love with her. But it's not going to be reciprocated is it? What have I given her to love?'

Mr Higgins sat down beside her, a look of great concentration in his eyes.

'Do you have an answer?' she asked. The eye contact remained, until with cat speed Mr Higgins reached around and began licking his own arse.

'Yeah great, you know, sometimes I credit you with too much intelligence.' Paige leaned back, her mind racing, unable to remove that image of Melanie's face, the look of betrayal, and it had been. Oh, it had never been malicious in its intent, but the consequences were unpleasant all the same.

The door knocked just twenty minutes later and Paige dragged herself off the sofa, trying not to disturb his majesty as she did so.

'Did you run here?' Paige asked, but Polly threw her arms around her and Paige leaned into it. Polly pulled away. 'I'll get the kettle on, or is this a tequila situation?'

'Let's start with a brew.' Paige sat down at the kitchen table, sliding along the bench. 'But seriously how did you get here so quick?'

'I was in a studio not too far from here. It's going really well actually. They're letting me feed into the production elements of it, I mean I don't get my own way, but they're listening to my suggestions.'

'Are we still forbidden from knowing who you've written it for?'

'Afraid so. They're really concerned about a leak and as the newbie I have to show my worth so that they'll think about using me again.'

Paige smiled, her gut instinct telling her enough that she had a strong clue which mega singing superstar Polly was working with.

'And this mega superstar came to Manchester?' Paige asked.

Polly looked over from setting up the cups. The look on her face indicated that Polly knew Paige may have figured it out. 'Nah we're doing it in two teams, one here, one in LA.'

Paige nodded. 'That's really cool.'

'Yeah, but it's really intimidating. Everyday feels like the first day in a new school. I'm a bit of a wreck several times a day.' Paige waited before saying anything further, giving Polly space. 'But it's too good to give up. I guess I'm just getting more resilient.'

'I think that actually you're just one of the bravest people I know,' Paige said.

'Oh yeah, it's really brave to write songs.'

Paige laughed. 'No it's brave to do something that scares you and then to do it every day.'

Polly finished making the mugs of tea and brought them to the table, sitting down opposite Paige. 'Are you not feeling very brave?' Polly asked.

'I think there are risks I should have taken and didn't, and risks that I took that I shouldn't have. It's all very confusing.'

Polly reached forward and gently held Paige's hand. 'We'll figure it out.'

It was only an hour later and everyone had arrived.

Mya grimaced. 'Really, we're on tea? Did nobody think this was more of a tequila situation?'

'Paige said to start with tea and see where we end up.' Polly smiled into her mug.

'Right, start at the beginning,' Sophie demanded as they all sat at the kitchen table.

'You know most of it. I didn't realise I'd fallen in love until it was too late, and by then I'd already broken her trust.' Paige let out a big sigh, her shoulders dropping for what felt like the first time in days.

Sophie threw her arm around Paige. 'Well, on the plus side, you're surrounded by people that have all made mistakes with the people they loved, and we're the queens of grand gestures.'

'Yeah, but she wouldn't want a gesture. Melanie believes everything I've done to help, was pay back for fixing me.'

'But it wasn't, you were just trying to help,' Polly offered.

'Yeah, and if Paige had told her about her abilities before that point, then maybe. But she found out about all of it at the same time. She's going to assume it's all one and the same thing. It's all one big omission of truth.'

Sophie, Polly and Paige all looked at Mya in shock.

'That was surprisingly insightful for you,' Sophie added.

'I'm choosing not to be insulted. I'm actually a very insightful person.' They all waited. 'All right, fine, it's a poker skill. Like if someone will buy one bluff in a situation they're likely to accept several. But only for a limited time. You over-play it and you lose the lot.'

Polly's mug landed on the table with a thud as she shook her head and muttered, 'Good God, Mya.'

'What?'

'You just basically said that Paige is gonna lose Melanie,' Sophie said, as Polly continued to shake her head.

'Oh well, I'm back on trend. Maybe I shouldn't do the soft people stuff — not my skill-set. But for what it's worth I don't think you're going to lose it all.'

Paige laughed. 'Never change, Mya.'

Mya leaned up and kissed Paige on the cheek. 'Love you, Paige, but let's move this to tequila, yeah? You know I always give my best advice on tequila.'

'Right, so let's go through the options,' Sophie said, pulling out a notebook and pen from her bag. Paige smiled at the familiar gesture. 'You need to talk to her and explain that the two things are separate. That you didn't know she was going to fix you but that the helpful things were just that. You were trying to help.'

'Don't forget us,' Polly said. 'We need to apologise too — we helped. She knows we were involved too, right?'

Paige nodded. 'How did you know?'

'She won't reply to my texts either,' Polly said sadly.

'Right, so we think ambush with kindness and clarity then yeah? Explain it all as a group?' Mya said as she came back to the table and lined up the shots.

'No! We're not thinking ambush. Bloody hell, Mya,' Sophie cried.

Polly frowned. 'We're trying to be sensible here.'

'There's more,' Paige said, figuring they needed the whole story. 'I don't think my feelings are reciprocated. I mean, I didn't give her enough of me. I kept myself at a distance.'

'You were showing her how you felt with the gestures, Paige.' Polly put her hand on Paige's arm.

'But when I wasn't doing that I just . . . She hasn't had a chance to see the best of me yet. The majority of our time together has either been in bed or with me being a grump.'

Polly shrugged. 'That is you, and we love you. But yeah, it sounds like you need a heart on your sleeve type conversation with her.'

'I'm telling you now this road leads to ambush.' Mya took a shot. 'You'll see.'

They all shook their heads, took a shot, and slammed their glasses back down on the table.

* * *

'Right, right. So, right, and so you're going to need to try and spend as much time with her on the art thingy as possible,' Polly said.

'Yeah, that's the one. It's all about cominica . . . comic . . . communication — it always is.' Sophie nodded.

Paige's own eyes were a bit bleary but her heart felt lighter at the possibilities they'd discussed, and Paige had hope. She didn't know the outcome, her mojo not helping in this, but she was grateful for that. It needed to come from Paige. Just her.

'So ambush then. Just like I said. I'm a genius,' Mya said as she dropped her head onto Polly's shoulder.

'We need food,' Polly said as she stroked Mya's hair.

CHAPTER THIRTY-SEVEN

Melanie

'Thanks for this,' Melanie said, pointing to the long-length waterproof coat.

'You got thermals and the like?' Emily asked.

'I'll be fine. I'm sure it won't be that bad.'

'You're painting a wall outside in Manchester. Let me find you some more bits and pieces.' Melanie watched as Emily ran around her wardrobes and drawers throwing clothes all over the show.

'Do you ever think you'll find a partner?' Melanie suddenly asked, more surprised than Emily that she'd voiced the question that had been sat right at the back of her brain, but now it was out there, she needed to know.

'I have to focus on Alfie and on work for the time being. But I am reluctant. It doesn't take a genius to figure out why. We didn't exactly get raised with a shining example. And I don't say this often enough but I really am so grateful that you're raising Alfie with me. He's not missing for anything.

'But I would never rule it out. In fact, there's a consultant. But that would never work. We'd never see each other. Why do you ask?'

Melanie shrugged and looked back down at the raincoat on her lap as she sat on the end of her sister's bed.

'Does this have something to do with the hot as hell Paige?'

'Do you believe in psychics?' Melanie asked.

'Are you OK?' Emily put a hand on Melanie's head, checking her temperature. 'What's going on?'

'Paige seems to think she has some sort of intuition. Some sort of a gift.'

'Huh OK.'

'It explains the knickers,' Melanie said on an exhale as she lay back on the bed.

'I'm so confused,' Emily said shaking her head.

'What if she made the whole thing up? Well, that's an even bigger problem, isn't it?'

'Do I need to get Alfie? Will this make more sense to him?'

'Let's say for argument's sake that there's something, some sort of instinct or something, but it was broken. It would have an impact, right? I imagine it would feel quite odd to suddenly be without it.'

'OK in this hypothetical world, yes, if you had another sense, I imagine it would feel disorientating to lose it, just like it would any other sense.' Emily was clearly just playing along at this point.

'You'd probably do whatever it took to get it back?'

'Is that what Paige said?' Emily asked.

'She said I fixed her.'

'Oh, cool,' Emily said, her tone flat, clearly confused as to the appropriate response.

'I was being used and I didn't even know it.'

There was a pause and Melanie could feel Emily thinking. 'Paige? The woman that was helping you out with the art project? The one spending lots of her free time and not free time trying to help you out? The one that babysat Alfie so you'd have more time to do your work? The same Paige that fed you on numerous occasions? *That* Paige? The one my little boy, who is an excellent judge of character by the way, has all but fallen in love with? You know he's asked for a piercing for his birthday.'

'It wasn't real,' Melanie said, her voice sounding as empty as it felt. 'I have terrible taste.'

Emily pulled out her phone, and scrolled until she found what she was looking for. The picture of Alfie asleep on Paige's lap, and Sophie passed out on the bean bag. Melanie had that picture memorised, just like the picture of her asleep on Paige, or any other of the memories with Paige that had been caught forever. But the picture Emily was still showing, captured the peace and the love that Paige offered — so at odds to how Melanie felt right now. She turned her head away; she didn't want to look at the picture any longer.

'*This Paige*? Go on then. Explain,' Emily said.

'I accidentally gave her full access to the app.'

'The one you run your life on, the one I have access to?'

Melanie nodded, releasing her grip on the coat to fold her arms over her eyes.

'The nice things she did, they were all on the app. She was the prosecco fairy too. And she did all these things because she felt like she owed me. She felt guilty. Or worse because she didn't think I was capable.'

'Right, you can stop that one right there. I know exactly where your head is going. I might not know Paige all that well, but I actually trust your judgement and I trust Alfie's too. Paige is not Laura and if you go into this expecting it to turn out like that then that's on you.'

'She lied to me, Emily.' Melanie could feel the tears building behind her closed eyes, and it made her angry. She didn't want to feel this deeply for someone who hurt her so badly. The anger made the hurt burn even brighter and she realised it was all coated in disappointment.

Emily didn't speak but Melanie felt the bed move as she came to lie down next to her.

'She also did some really nice things too.'

'Out of guilt. Not because she wanted to.'

'Oh so she slept with you out of guilt. Gave you the best night of your life, twice, because she felt she had to?'

'You know what,' Melanie said shooting up into a sitting position. 'None of this matters. I never had time for any of this in the first place. I was really clear about my priorities. They were you and Alfie, and the business. Then the art project got added on. And really that should be that. So I need to go, because if I'm not painting a wall, looking after my gorgeous nephew, then I should be running a business. I'll see you later. Thanks for the coat.' Melanie grabbed her stuff and all but ran out of the house, and straight to her car.

Sure enough she was grateful for the coat in no time at all as she found herself harnessed and hard hat-ted up some scaffolding against a wall in Manchester's finest drizzle. The scaffolding shook a little as each person moved around. Selena and some of her more experienced friends had spent the last couple of days setting up the wall into a giant paint by numbers type thing. It had all been outlined on top of the base layer so as long as Melanie matched up the colour number to the number on the wall she would be of use. They were all split off on different levels and despite the noise and the rain, Melanie could tell that some of the women were all chatting and laughing with each other. Melanie simply wanted to lose herself in the task.

'Hey artists, I've brought hot drinks! I can't stay and help today but I'll try and be back tomorrow. But here, I have hot flasks of coffee, tea and hot chocolate.'

Melanie recognised the voice and refused to look down at Polly, stood on the corner of the street. 'Oh thank you, I'll come down now,' Selena shouted out. Melanie heard her unclip herself from one section and clip herself on various parts until she made it low enough that she could just walk down the last few bits.

'You are a star, thank you so much . . .'

'I'm Polly, one of Melanie's friends.' Melanie would like to say she didn't see both Polly and Selena look up at her expectantly — except she hadn't been able to stop herself from looking in their direction. So she said nothing and turned around and continued to paint. She wasn't all that surprised when Selena decided to station herself next to Melanie not ten minutes later.

'So, things still a bit difficult, hey?' Selena asked.

'Nope. Do you really think we'll get this all done in less than a week?' Yes, it was an obvious subject change but so be it.

'Well, we can only do what we can only do, you know?' Selena's voice drifted off at the end, and Melanie didn't think that was much of an answer. 'And failing that we'll just call it abstract.'

Melanie did laugh at that.

'There's more than one way to see things.'

Melanie tried not to roll her eyes. 'Real subtle.'

Selena sighed happily, almost sounding like she was singing. 'Some things are inexcusable, some behaviours that deliberately hurt shouldn't be accepted. But in art, we tend to draw outside of the lines, we constantly push what's accepted and what's new. Always trying to create something that was never there before. It's almost always messy, but with art we invariably leave something richer behind than was there to begin with.'

'Have you finished?' Melanie said, surprised at her own rudeness.

Selena smiled again and did her little sing-song exhale as they each concentrated on their own areas to paint. It was about an hour later, and Melanie's arm was starting to ache a little, not enough to stop, but she carried on for the time being, knowing she'd need to go and pick up Alfie from school shortly.

That was a mistake. She should have left.

'Hi Paige. Yeah, there's space here. Let me help you get set up,' Selena called out.

Melanie should have guessed it wasn't going to be easy to avoid her. If it wasn't now it would've been at the next Business Alliance meeting. Best to get it over and done with.

The familiar spicy scent of Paige wafted towards her as Selena directed her to work between them. 'Make sure you're always clipped in, else we get into trouble,' Selena said. 'Then it's a simple case of grabbing some paint and a brush and going for it. Let out your creative side.'

That sing-song exhale again and Melanie brought her arm down to check the time on her phone. One hour to go. She could do that.

'Hey Melanie, you OK?' Paige asked quietly.

'Yup. You?'

Paige didn't answer but Melanie heard her sigh.

'So, Paige. I'm trying to talk Councillor Houghton into working with me on more projects. In other words, I'm trying to get him to give me some more money.' Selena laughed. 'I'm going to need your help again, if that's OK?'

'Sure, what do you need?'

Melanie couldn't help but listen to the conversation happening right over her, but to say she was intrigued would be an understatement. But at the same time her stomach soured as this was yet another part of Paige she didn't know about.

'I need some stats. How many of the women I referred have you trained up in bar work?' Selena asked.

'Erm, I'd have to check but I would say close to fifty.'

'How many of them went on to work in bars?'

'I've had requests for quite a few references. They didn't all go to bars, some went into hotels working the day shifts because it was easier for childcare.'

Selena nodded. 'Yes, that make sense.' Selena got closer to Melanie. 'Paige helps me run a programme with some of the women we work with. Some, well most, haven't worked in a long time, or ever, and so Paige gives them bar work, trains them up, gives them a safe space and then after a few months they're able to get new employment.'

'It's not quite as saintly as Selena makes it sound.'

Melanie didn't say anything, didn't even nod. On the one hand she could sense Paige would do something like this, that she'd do it with little to no fanfare. On the other, she had to ask herself just how much Paige was holding back on? Had Melanie really only been deserving of head nods and orgasms? But then she remembered Paige mentioning about doing more charity work.

'She got a lot of other businesses involved too though, didn't you? Maybe when you're set up a bit more, Melanie, you might want to include your bar as well.'

'Yes of course, we'd love to be involved. In fact, we could link up the walls in the bar to your art therapy too.'

'That would be brilliant. But we'd have to work out a fee.'

'Of course.' Melanie nodded, her mind trying to replay the whole conversation.

'I need to go and make sure everyone's sorted,' Selena said as she began the process of unclipping and moving around the scaffolding.

The sound of chatter and street noise, was abruptly interrupted. 'It was Connie,' Paige said softly.

'What was?'

'She had a relationship that was abusive. I looked into it, tried to find ways of helping. Luckily, she didn't marry him. But it was a hard time, and she was so far away I was sure at one point that I was going to lose her for good.'

Melanie stayed quiet, desperate for more. She wanted to know everything. She wanted every last crumb. But that's what her experience with Paige had been. She knew all too well what it was like to want. But Melanie knew better, knew she had to keep herself safe and that in a few more minutes she could be out of there.

'I really am sorry, Melanie. I only wanted to help, I promise. But I should have told you everything. I'm just not used to it. I'm a fixer. I help others. It's part of who I am.'

'Yeah, I was a project to you. I get it.'

'No, not at all. I just . . . I don't open up easily, it takes time. I'm too hard-headed. But I would have. I want to, with you, that is.'

Melanie didn't know what to say, but she'd just finished painting her section and figured it was a good time to go. She could go to the coffee shop and get an oat-milk coffee to warm herself up.

'See you,' Melanie said unable to walk away without saying goodbye. She shouted bye to Selena and skipped the coffee, instead getting into her car and making her way to get Alfie, all the while pretending her heart didn't hurt, while the words from Selena and from Emily made their way around her head over and over. Had she been too rash?

It was hours later when Emily was back to look after Alfie that Melanie's phone went off.

Louisa: *So sorry Mel, can you swing by the bar on your way home please? X*

Melanie sighed, not wanting to but what choice did she have? In her head she was already back at her flat, her not lived in, boxes everywhere flat. In the bed that only made her think of Paige. So actually, yeah this was a welcome distraction. And that's what she told herself on the drive over.

She should have gone straight home.

'Sorry, love, I know this wasn't your plan for the night, but I do hope I can convince you to have a quick chat with me?'

'You had my number, you could have called,' Melanie pointed out.

Connie said nothing, giving a soft smile instead, and Melanie knew this was happening. But not before she gave a pointed look in Louisa's direction. Louisa shrugged and quickly moved away.

Finding the tables full, Melanie pointed to the bar, where they propped it up.

'Would you like a drink?' Melanie asked, gesturing towards Cleo.

'A Tom Collins, please,' Connie said.

'What about you, boss?' Cleo asked, not giving anything away, but Melanie strongly suspected Cleo would kick Connie out on her ass if she moved wrong. The loyalty made Melanie feel a little less frosty.

'I'm good but thank you.'

Cleo nodded and quickly looked at Connie and back again to Melanie. 'Let me know if I can do anything.'

Melanie smiled as Cleo turned around to make the drink.

'I know why you're here,' Melanie said.

'Yeah? Why's that?'

'You think I was rash, that I'm overreacting and that I should listen to Paige.'

'Hmm. Interesting. You sure that's what I think and not what you think?' Connie said. 'But listen, that actually wasn't what I was going to say. I—' Connie stopped as the drink was placed in front of her. 'Thank you,' Connie said, bending forward to take a drink. 'My God. That's one of the best Tom Collins I've ever had.' Connie studied Cleo closely. 'I like you.'

Cleo raised an eyebrow and moved to the other side of the bar and continued to prepare the drinks orders.

'What I was going to say' — she took another sip — 'No, seriously, this is one of the best ever.' She sipped again. 'I'm going to be going away again soon.'

Melanie said nothing.

'But I came back here to make sure Paige was OK. I quickly discovered she wasn't. You know when they say to check on the quiet ones. They mean Paige.'

Melanie snorted at that, she couldn't help it. 'I've no doubt Paige can fight her own battles.'

'She can, in so many ways she's a fighter just like her gran. She probably didn't tell you about the relationship she had with her mum. It was difficult. Paige's mum wasn't a natural care-giver and Paige wasn't a naturally caring daughter. They loved to wind each other up, except Paige would always bend, always try and make it right. To the point she would try and fix things before they became a problem. Sometimes it worked, sometimes it didn't. Until her mum decided it just wasn't going to work. There's more to it, but when you have that over a number of years, well it's tricky. And I do blame myself for being away for some of those years, but hopefully I made up for it in the end, but she wants to help. It's how she shows love. It's the only way she knows how. Acts of service. Well, maybe not the *only* way.' Connie winked.

'Why are you telling me this?'

'Are you always this stubborn? I don't know how to be any clearer. I told you all of this in both your readings. Life's too short to spend it all with to-do lists.' She shook her head and finished her drink. 'Love you, Cleo,' she shouted as she got off the barstool. 'I'm biased because she's my favourite granddaughter, of course I am. But she's the best thing in the world, and she could be the best thing in your world too.' Connie kissed her cheek and took off.

Melanie had just about had enough of everyone telling her how amazing Paige was. Nobody was perfect and frankly she didn't have the time for any of this, she never did.

CHAPTER THIRTY-EIGHT

Paige

'You know,' Mya said, altogether too loudly. 'If this was a romcom, Paige would just need to do a big ol' romantic gesture and all would be well. You would either kiss or tell each other you love each other and then kiss and that would be that.' Paige and Sophie stopped and stared at Mya, as she painted the wall. Paige quickly glanced down the scaffolding aisle towards Melanie and knew this had been a terrible idea.

'Mya, are you sure you want to be here painting? Don't you have somewhere else you need to be?' Paige strongly suggested.

'No, I don't think so. I'm always happy to help out.' Mya grinned and tossed her hair, very nearly getting paint all over it.

'I'm not sure how much you're helping right now,' Paige muttered so that hopefully only Mya would hear her.

'You know we all told Paige to tell you about the app access,' Mya shouted. Paige cursed and glared at Mya.

'What? We did! I'm only telling her so she knows we're blameless in all this.'

'Really?' Melanie said, looking surprised that she'd finally entered into the conversation.

'Yup. We told her to tell you but then she made a plea about how much she wanted to help and so as your new friends we all figured out how we could help. It's what friends do, right?'

Paige watched as Melanie chewed her lip. Maybe Mya's direct approach was helping. 'And that *Manchester Confidential* post helped too?' It was at this point she knew Mya had blown up whatever ground they'd fleetingly gained.

'Was that something to do with you too?'

'No!' Paige jumped in. 'Not the way you think. I have a contact there and they were asking for recommendations for who to review, that was all. I would have done it for any business on the street.'

'Hmm.' Melanie turned back to paint.

Paige pulled a 'what was that?' face at Mya.

Mya shrugged, her face saying, 'I tried'.

Paige rolled her eyes in clear exasperation.

'Oh, Seb's coming tomorrow to help out,' Sophie said having just checked her phone.

'Cool.' Paige didn't miss how Melanie quickly looked their way in interest.

'Right, I'm done. See you later.' Melanie hastily put away the paint equipment, but before she could make her getaway Mya had run towards her, the scaffolding squealing and shaking. She pulled Melanie into a hug.

'None of it was for any reason other than we liked you. We thought you were one of us, a friend. And we still are if you want us to be.' Mya kissed her on the cheek and Paige watched as Melanie turned and walked away.

As soon as she was out of hearing she turned to Mya. 'What was that?'

'What? I like her. I don't need to be dragged down by your bad decisions. Besides, if she's talking to the rest of us, it'll make it really hard for her to ignore you. It's a group charm offensive.'

'Yeah because your operation ambush is going so well,' Paige drawled, the sarcasm clear to all.

'Are you opening up like we discussed?' Sophie asked.

'She's not talking to me! It's like baring my soul to a brick wall,' Paige snapped.

'Do you even want to win her back, Paige?' Mya asked, in a way that suggested she was really at the end of her patience.

'Yes, of course.'

'You need to communicate!' Sophie cried.

'I'm trying but is there not something else I could be doing instead?'

'Would it hurt to try a little charm?' Mya said, focused back on the painting.

'I'm rubbish at that too.'

'I know.' Mya sighed and placed her hand on Paige's arm. 'Maybe you should write to her instead?'

'Oh, I know!' Sophie cried out. 'I've got it. You need to get the app, write your own lists and invite her to see it. Why the hell did we not think of this sooner?'

'I'm not sure that's a great idea,' Paige said. 'Besides I need your advice on something. So Alf invited me to his birthday party on Saturday. Can I still go? Would that be weird? I don't want to let him down and I've really missed him.'

Mya and Sophie looked at each other and shrugged. 'I've absolutely no idea of etiquette there.'

'I'd suggest checking with Melanie,' Sophie said.

'Unless you go undercover,' Mya suggested. 'You know like Mickey Mouse or something?'

'I'd rather do the app,' Paige said.

'I can totally see Paige rocking up as Goofy,' Mya said as she and Sophie burst out laughing.

'Nah, with that blonde hair and the cold attitude, she's an Elsa for sure,' Sophie said.

'Apart from the operation ambush, have you actually tried to speak to her?' Mya asked.

'No, I was trying to respect her wishes,' Paige said softly.

'Right, well, here's your chance. You are respecting her wishes but you also don't want to let the little guy down. So go ask,' Sophie said pointing with her paint brush.

'What, right now?'

'Yes!' Sophie shouted, nearly covering them all in paint.

'Yeah, OK yes. I can do this,' Paige said, the uncertainty clear. 'I'll be right back.'

'You better had. We need details,' Mya shouted as Paige all but legged it off the scaffolding.

Paige was out of breath when she ran around the corner and into Lulu.

But then Cleo was stood right in front of her. 'Stay there. I'll check if she wants to talk to you.'

'Cleo, right? Of the Tom Collins fame. You know my gran all but fell in love with you.'

'It happens.' Cleo walked off. Paige was grateful as she tried to get her breath back.

'She's coming. Follow me.' Cleo's expression was non too friendly. In fact, as Paige looked around she saw more than one staff member subtly giving her the stink eye. Trying to ignore them she opened up her phone, got to her notes and started writing some bits and pieces down.

'Hey,' Melanie said, and Paige's face shot up quickly.

'Hey. Sorry for mithering you at work, I know how busy you are.' Paige studied Melanie and could see the dark circles under her eyes were back with a vengeance. Paige would bet money that she wasn't sleeping and hadn't been eating well either, but still Paige's heart fluttered wildly in her chest, and she wanted desperately to wrap Melanie up in her arms. Making a decision, she refocused.

'I just need to ask you a quick question. Well, really, I'd love to sit down and properly talk, but you're busy and now probably isn't the right time. But it's about Saturday. I want to know if it's still all right for me to come to Alf's birthday party? I mean I don't want to make it weird or awkward. If you prefer, I have a gift I can drop with you. But . . . I'd really like to see him. I miss the guy.'

And she did. She missed them all hanging out in her flat watching Disney films. Or reading him books before he went to bed. She'd lost her heart twice over in the last week and this was step one to getting it back. Step two she would begin later tonight.

'I don't know . . .' Melanie began. 'He has really missed you too.' Melanie sat down.

Paige held her breath, feeling this was significant.

'He's not the only one I've been missing,' Paige said quietly.

Paige watched as Melanie looked around the room. 'Yes, you can come. Alfie would love to see you. I think you're practically the guest of honour.'

Paige couldn't stop the smile spreading across her face. 'I can't wait.'

'You've clearly never been to a kid's party before.' Melanie gave a small smile.

'What drink do I need to bring? I'm thinking tequila?'

'I hope you're not joking, because I'll be needing it.'

Paige didn't want to push her luck. 'OK so I'll see you Saturday?'

'Yeah,' Melanie said. 'I guess you will.'

Paige got up and out of habit or desperation she wasn't sure, bent down and gently kissed Melanie's cheek. Quickly moving away in case that was the wrong thing to do she'd almost made it to the door when Melanie shouted, 'He's asked for a piercing for his birthday, by the way.'

Paige was smiling all the way back to Barbarella, thinking about how well it went and revelling in the hope building in her chest. She thought about the things she'd written down and between selling drinks, she wrote them all up in the app.

So when her phone rang, Paige felt more hopeful about her future then she had in a long while, and when she saw it was her mum, she figured now was the time to answer it.

Walking towards the stairs to her flat she braced herself and answered the call.

'Hi Mum.' She winced, great start. She proceeded up the stairs.

'Paige it's so lovely to hear from you, finally. Anyone would think you were avoiding me.' Paige didn't even know where to begin with that one. And she had to bite her tongue down hard to not retaliate, along the lines of reminding her of who had left who. Instead she sat down at the table and moved the conversation on.

'How can I help you?' Paige asked, hoping to move it along quite quickly.

'You sound like you're in a call centre or something. I just wanted to get in touch and see how you are?' Yes, Paige had suspected as much. Every five years her mother's guilt would suddenly kick in and the calls would begin. Unless her mother needed something in which case it would be a little sooner. Paige had contemplated cutting her out of her life altogether. But she knew that would break Connie's heart. And so instead of the usual antagonistic phone conversation, Paige tried something new.

'I'm really well. How are you?'

Fiona was clearly surprised at the response. 'Are you sure you're OK? Are you drunk or something?'

'Nope. I'm just fine.'

'Is work going well?' she asked with more than a little trepidation in her voice.

'Yes, what about you?'

'Yes, fine. I've erm, got a new doctor and some new medication. But what's new with you?'

'Listen Mum you don't have to do this call thing if you don't want to. I know we both have separate lives and that's fine. I genuinely hope yours is going well.'

There was a big sigh and a pause. 'You sound different Paige. Is this Mum's influence?'

'Probably.' Paige smiled, it was all the amazing people in her life actually. She wanted for nothing when it came to love and affection. She had more than most. And with that realisation a weight she hadn't realised she'd been holding onto lifted.

'I do love you, Paige.' Fiona sighed again. 'It's just never easy between us, is it? But I'd really like to keep trying. Maybe I could try and call more often. Maybe even one day I'll come over and we could grab a coffee?'

Was that it? Her mum wasn't after anything? A favour? Some money? Paige was cautious.

'You can ring, I'll try and answer when I can.' Coffee was a long way away, but Paige didn't say that.

'I'm always rooting for you.'

'Thanks, Mum.'

'OK, well, give Mum my love. Take care. If you ever wanted to ring me you know I'd really like that.'

That was new.

'I'm running my own business so it's not always that easy.'

'Oh, I know. Mum won't stop going on about how brilliantly you're doing.'

'I'll try.'

'Bye, Paige.'

'Bye, Mum.'

Putting down the phone, Paige felt her eyes water. It was the nicest conversation they had possibly ever had. Connie appeared at the kitchen table, brew in hand as she passed it over to Paige.

'You heard that huh?' Paige asked.

'You did good, Book.' Connie nodded.

'It's always going to be hard with her though, isn't it? I'm always going to have to be the one that bends.'

'Your mum clearly has her own stuff going on that she's working through. So, it might get a little easier, but yes, it's never going to be straightforward. And I'm so sorry for that.'

Paige stood up and wrapped her arms around Connie. 'It's not your fault, Gran. Parenting clearly isn't for everyone. And I never lacked, I always had you.'

Connie crushed her a little harder. 'I love you, Book. And you turned out pretty amazing thanks to me. Drink your tea. Then you need to head off. Aren't you supposed to be doing something?'

'Shit!' Paige shouted, and Connie chuckled.

Paige ran out of the bar as quick as she could, back to the wall to share her new plan with Mya and Sophie.

CHAPTER THIRTY-NINE

Melanie

Friday was the day things finally started looking up. Melanie took a seat opposite a woman she now knew quite well, except she had turquoise hair today. She didn't say anything as Melanie sat down, but that was fine, Louisa was due any minute, and Melanie was more than happy to wait in the tense atmosphere. And it was tense. Even the bar, filled with people on a Friday afternoon, seemed somehow quieter. The background music softer. The lights laser-focused on this table at this moment.

Melanie was not going to give in. Her brain to mouth filter was fully engaged. Not a word was going to pass her lips until she was good and ready. The woman in front of her squirmed in her seat as Melanie continued to study her. Her face was locked in a forced nonchalance that wasn't convincing. Her stare was anywhere but at Melanie. It kept moving around the room, appearing to stop every now and again to take it all in. A group of bottomless drinkers were getting rowdy in the corner and as they all shouted an enthusiastic cheers, the turquoise terror flinched in her seat and for a second the neutrality dropped and in its place a frown and that felt more real to Melanie.

When Melanie found out from Councillor Houghton that this person had been forced into coming today, she'd spent her time researching and planning. This table and the seating choice was no accident. Just a quiet enough corner that they could hear each other, but Melanie was facing the flower wall, making sure her guest could see the whole place, see how they were thriving, how business was booming.

The seat next to her was pulled back and Melanie turned and greeted Louisa with a smile.

There was a moment before Louisa sat down where she looked down her nose at the person opposite, but then she sat back slowly, crossing her legs.

Melanie took a moment to soak in how she felt. She wasn't a confrontational kind of person by nature. But in the moment she had the control. There was nothing more the person in front of them could do. Nothing she hadn't already done. But now it was their turn.

'Shall I do introductions?' Melanie began. 'I know you already know us. You've been paying very close attention from what I understand. But let's be polite. I'm Melanie, this is Louisa and we are the co-owners of Lulu. The M.E.N. has recently reported that we're, what was it, Louisa?'

'Not to be missed. That people need to reserve their spot now because there's a two-month waiting list.'

'Oh two months is it now? That's amazing,' Melanie said. Indicating the woman before them, she said, 'Louisa, this is Sabrina. She works in, well erm Sabrina is an aspiring beautician? It's the lack of the property preventing her from making it big, right?' Sabrina continued to not say anything but her jaw was tight and her face turned to the side, the petulance strong.

'Anyway, Sabrina has joined us today because Councillor Houghton asked her to pop in and apologise.'

Louisa brushed off imaginary lint from her knee as she waited for a response. Melanie clasped her hands and leaned forwards, eager to hear what would come next. Something behind Melanie must have caught Sabrina's eye as she sat up straighter and looked around a little more.

'I . . . I will apologise but come on, you can't prove I did anything. I *didn't* do anything.' Melanie could just about make out that the bar seemed to have quietened further. Had someone turned off the background music?

'We have a list of the things you've done. But these are just the ones we know about. Shall we start there?' Louisa said, her tone one of rage hidden under layers of smooth slow moving silk. 'You cancelled our orders of prosecco. You had several orders including our napkins redelivered elsewhere. You put a series of fake reviews all over our social media. You had the health inspector pay us a visit. They gave us a glowing review, did you know? Complimented us on having one of the cleanest and most well-organised kitchens they'd had the privilege of observing. You made up fake noise abatement orders. You emailed all suppliers to try and cancel our orders. They're just the ones we know about.'

Sabrina scoffed. 'Right. And you can prove all that, can you?'

Melanie thought of all the amazing women in her life. There were so many and each with their own power; Cleo's control, Mya's confidence, Polly's sensitivity, Sophie's creativity, Emily's resilience, Louisa's support and Paige's strength. Melanie realised at that moment she was not on her own, not only that but that she had a power of her own. She would not be made upset by this person. She was not worth her anger, her sleepless nights. 'Yes, most of it we can. We are more than happy to share what we have with the rest of the Neighbourhood Business Alliance to ensure that you never get a spot in our community.'

Sabrina's face paled and her eyes widened. 'As if I would want to be here anyway!'

'Well, that works out for us all then, doesn't it?' Louisa said evenly.

Sabrina went to push her chair back but Melanie raised at the same time and leaned closer to speak.

'Sabrina of Sabrina Mobile Beauty and Cosmetics. Your Facebook has over ten thousand likes, your Instagram has stalled out at eight thousand followers. Your reviews are mixed but you've, rightly so, put a lot of time and energy into your socials. We know first-hand how hard that is. But understand this, if you make any more bad decisions when it comes to Lulu, myself or any of my amazing team, we will make sure that when you do get a new premises, to share all of our proof, and our suspicions to your new neighbours, and your customers. On that basis, if I were you, I'd admit what you did, apologise and we can then shake hands and say no more about it.'

There was a shuffling sound behind them but Melanie didn't look away from Sabrina. This was it. And once again she would wait. Sabrina was looking at something behind them, and chewing on her lip. The room was so quiet now, somehow she knew the customers were watching what was happening.

'I'm sorry. For trying to sabo — for what's happened.' Sabrina grabbed her bag and dashed for the door. And from right behind there was an almighty cheer. Melanie and Louisa swung around. The entire team had gathered behind them. Dan the head chef, Cleo the general manager, Ari, Tempy, Trav, everyone from the kitchen and from front of house, all of them stood behind them. Even the customers were cheering. And the next thing she knew they were all hugging and jumping, people shouting *we did it* and *best team ever*. The plan had been simple. As soon as Councillor Houghton got in touch, explaining that he'd demanded Sabrina rock up and apologise or else face a permanent ban they knew what they needed to do and had researched what they could.

Cleo moved through the group, phone in hand. 'I got it, it's all recorded!'

Melanie smiled so much her cheeks were sore, but she pulled Cleo into another hug.

'Right, back to work!' Louisa shouted across the room and then addressing their customers. 'Thank you everyone for your patience and we apologise for the disruption to your service today. We hope you'll accept a complimentary drink from us.' The cheers continued as the staff dispersed. Melanie watched as each one of them walked with a slight bounce, a huge smile and a straightened spine. They really were the best team ever. She turned to Louisa. 'Is that really the end of it?' Could the sabotage really be over?

'I reckon so. Do your shoulders feel lighter? Mine feel lighter. I feel like I've been carrying that around for weeks.'

'Same.' Well almost same. She definitely felt lighter for this, but there were other things that she could maybe put right and maybe forgive and ask for forgiveness for, so that she might continue to feel joy in her chest for hopefully a very long time. She quickly pulled Louisa into a hug. 'We're going to do this,' she said in her ear.

'We're going to absolutely smash it.' Louisa pulled back slightly. 'Maybe we need to start looking for our second venue? Shall I add it to the list?'

'Not just yet, hey?'

CHAPTER FORTY

Melanie

She'd got all the food wrapped and ready to go. She'd made
sure the party bags were ready — actually that had been fun
and she'd kept a bouncy ball and some Play Doh to the side
for herself — all they needed was to add slices of birthday
cake at the end. Luckily, she hadn't needed to worry about
the cake as her mum had brought that. And the icing on
the cake? Mum's 'you could have made different choices'
lecture she always gave Emily hadn't emerged because Alfie
had charmed his grandma and they were busy swapping party
hats around, waiting for the rest of the guests to appear.

Melanie looked at her app again. All appeared to be in
order. She quickly glanced at the work app, and no longer
had the same sense of dread.

The squeals of excitement quickly brought her back to
the here and now as Emily appeared and quickly hid the
pass the parcel in one of the kitchen cupboards near where
Melanie was stood.

'Just got it done in time.' Emily smiled.

'I think we're all ready. The entertainer is due in the
next thirty minutes and the first guests should start rocking

up' — there was a knock at the door and excited giggles could be heard — 'right about now,' Melanie said.

'Come on, Alfie, let's welcome your party guests.' Emily grabbed his little hand. Melanie eagerly looked down the hallway and didn't want to admit to herself that she was disappointed when she saw that it wasn't Paige.

Ten minutes later and she was starting to get neck ache from the amount of times she'd checked every time the door went.

Melanie had spent time over the last few days and reckoned she could forgive Paige, and they could perhaps find a way to move on from here. Key was sitting down and talking it out. She loved Paige, and it had hurt beyond belief to think that she was nothing but a first aid kit. But she knew that wasn't quite right. They needed to talk and maybe they could . . . Her phone started vibrating. She answered but it was so loud she couldn't hear what was being said so she ran out to the front of the house.

'I'm so sorry I can't get there. I'll of course give you a full refund . . .'

'Wait, what?'

'I'm in A&E. I'm so sorry.'

'Oh God, are you OK?' Melanie asked.

'Yeah, I tripped over the hair and landed funny on my wrist. It's not quite the right size or colour. I'll send over the refund now. I'm sorry again. Ow!'

'No, of course, erm . . . take care of yourself. Bye.' Melanie ended the call. 'Shit, shit, *shit!*'

'Not really the language I was expecting at a kids' party,' a voice said behind her.

Melanie spun around. 'Oh hey, hi.' She wanted to give Paige her attention but she needed to find an entertainer and fast.

'What's wrong?' Paige asked, the concern evident.

'Oh nothing. The Rapunzel due in the next ten minutes tripped over her hair and has probably broken her wrist. We have a Disney-themed party with no Disney character.' She was still scrolling her phone as she spoke. 'Oh, who am I kidding? I'm not going to get an entertainer this quickly. What am I going to do?'

Melanie looked down at her flowery dress and knee-high boots. Nope she wouldn't pass for a Disney princess. Then she looked up at Paige. No, she couldn't ask. Besides Disney had yet to create a Disney character with ripped jeans, Doc Martens, side cut, and piercings although perhaps they really ought to.

'We need a costume,' Melanie said. 'Can you ring round some fancy-dress shops? I'm going to look online and see what I can order and get like right now.' The pair of them perched on the wall as they scrolled and rang. Melanie couldn't get anything right away. By the end of the day yeah. And the supermarkets only had kids' sizes in.

'Is that the only one you have? What size? OK, hang on.' Paige pulled the phone from her ear. 'I can get a Rey costume.'

'Yes! He loves Rey.'

'Who doesn't? But it's in large,' Paige said.

'Get it, I'll make it work somehow.'

'Mel! I need you. They're getting wild in here. Oh, hey Paige, how are you?' Emily waved.

'We have a slight problem,' Melanie said.

'Which I will sort now,' Paige said.

'I can't ask you to do that,' Melanie said.

'You can. I'll even wait until you ask this time,' Paige said softly. 'And not to make too big a point of it but this really isn't for you. It's for Alf.'

'Well if you grab it, I'll throw it on when you get back.' Melanie paused. 'I'd really appreciate your help, Paige, if you don't mind?'

'I'm happy to help. Back in a bit. Oh, and here, this is for you. Don't get them the wrong way round. Back as soon as I can.'

Paige legged it presumably to her car and Melanie looked down at the gift bags. One with a Disney-wrapped present and the other . . . Sure enough it had top shelf tequila in it. 'Come on, sis, I reckon we both need one of these.'

'What's the problem?' Emily said.

'No entertainer. But Paige has been able to get hold of a Rey costume and has gone to grab it now.'

'Oh God. I was kinda pinning this whole thing on a princess.'

'Me too,' Melanie said. *I still am* she said to herself.

CHAPTER FORTY-ONE

Paige

She tried the front door and saw it was on the latch. Gently pushing it open and tiptoeing down the hall towards the open plan kitchen and den area, Paige could see that a rather serious game of pass the parcel was taking place. There was only one thing for it really and she'd known it was going to come to this. She'd just hoped that it wouldn't.

But, it was a large and it would fit Paige more than it would fit Melanie. Not to mention that Melanie was knee deep in sugared up five-year-olds. Nipping into the downstairs loo she got changed and hoped her Doc Martens would finish the look off. She found some bobbles that she assumed were Emily's and styled her hair. Leaving her wallet and phone hidden underneath her regular clothes, she slowly pushed the door open. She caught a glimpse of herself in the hallway mirror. She looked like an absolute badass. Too right. That's exactly what Rey was. This was so far out of Paige's comfort zone she wasn't sure she'd ever be able to find it again. But she quickly dipped back into the loo and grabbed her phone. There were two things she needed to do and quickly. The first was to take a selfie in the mirror and send it to the girls. Better that she was in charge of PR then they find out later. The second was to press send on the thing she'd worked on last night and hope for the best. Figuring she was already nervous anyway. And as Connie always liked to say, 'might as well get hung for a sheep as a lamb'.

She put her phone back away, picked up her staff and walked out and down and round to where pass the parcel was finishing up. Emily caught her eye first and positively beamed, beckoning her further into the room.

'You look so cool. Thank you for doing this. He's going to freak out!' Emily whispered as the music stopped and the pass the parcel winner was announced.

'You're up!' Emily whispered before shoving Paige towards the crowd. 'Everyone, look who came to Alfie's birthday party. Everyone say hi to Rey!'

The kids were screaming and crowding her and pushing her into the middle of the room, until she was knelt down and could talk to them all.

'Er, hi everyone.' Oh she had no idea what she was doing, but then she spotted Alfie.

'Hi, birthday boy.' And before she'd even really finished speaking, two little arms were flung around her neck and it was cute, until she actually couldn't breathe. She tickled his ribs to get him to let go. His arms relaxed but he lent towards her ear.

'I knew you were cool, Pwaige, but I didn't know you were Rey!'

Not having any clue at all how to answer that she gave him another little squeeze. 'Happy birthday, Alf.'

'Why don't we see if Rey wants to play musical statues?' Emily shouted with frankly way too much glee in her voice.

But then Paige caught Melanie's eyes. She mouthed, 'Thank you,' and Paige nervously smiled back.

CHAPTER FORTY-TWO

Melanie

Melanie had been taking lots of pictures and hadn't seen the email notification. She'd made herself a promise not to check her work stuff today, but the notification on her app caught her attention.

Paige has invited you to join her To-Do list.

What? Paige had done what? The place was loud, the kids were wild, and although she suspected Paige would never admit it, she looked like she was having fun as she answered all their questions about being Rey.

She caught her sister. 'I just need to check something, I won't be a minute.'

'Everything all right?'

'Yeah, promise I won't be long.' Melanie moved towards the hallway.

'I wouldn't worry, the entertainer seems to have it under control. How much do you think she charges?'

Melanie smiled and disappeared into the front garden where she leaned on the wall. She couldn't explain why, but her heart was racing and her hands shook. What had Paige done? Her heart now pounded against her ribs.

She opened up her app and saw a new list on there that wasn't hers.

She quickly scrolled through the items, and then her breath caught as she realised what she was looking at.

She tried to read them again but her eyes were watering. She quickly brushed her tears away and swallowed, willing her brain to focus.

Paige's to-do list

1. Write up a to-do list — tick

2. Share it with Melanie — tick

3. Tell Melanie I'm in love with her

4. Tell Melanie that I've always been in love with her, that all of it was because I fell for her from the first moment. The grumpy nods, the not knowing how to behave. It was all because Melanie had spun my whole world around

5. Tell Melanie that I was never broken, but that my mojo had disappeared so that I could find her. So that I wouldn't get in my own way, which I still managed to do

6. Figure out a way of getting Melanie to fall in love with me

7. Figure out a way of getting Melanie to forgive me

8. Figure out a way of opening up more, hopefully this list will help — tick

9. Tell Melanie I love her — I know this is on here already but it feels the most important so I've put it on twice

10. Ask Melanie to help me with my to-do list

As gestures went, Melanie considered this one to be epic. If only Paige wasn't currently dressed up like Rey, actually that didn't hurt her case, but better if she wasn't in the middle of a kid's birthday party. This would have been the perfect opportunity to kiss and make up. But the party would be wrapping up soon.

Melanie laughed and went through the list again.

Paige's to-do list

1. Write up a to-do list — *tick*

2. Share it with Melanie — *tick*

3. Tell Melanie I'm in love with her

4. Tell Melanie that I've always been in love with her, that all of it was because I fell for her from the first moment. The grumpy nods, the not knowing how to behave. It was all because Melanie had spun my whole world around

5. Tell Melanie that I was never broken, but that my mojo had disappeared so that I could find her. So that I wouldn't get in my own way, which I still managed to do

6. Figure out a way of getting Melanie to fall in love with me — *Consider this one done* — *tick*

7. Figure out a way of getting Melanie to forgive me — *done* — *tick*

8. Figure out a way of opening up more, hopefully this list will help — tick — *definitely tick*

9. Tell Melanie I love her — I know this is on here already but it feels the most important so I've put it on twice

10. Ask Melanie to help me with my to-do list — *Always*

11. Melanie to tell Paige that she loves her too

12. Don't forget to take the Rey outfit back to the shop — but maybe tomorrow

13. Melanie to explain how she is desperately in love with Paige too. This is important and does need to be on the list twice.

Grinning she looked up and saw some of the parents making their way towards the house. Waving and smiling still, she ran back inside to make sure the cake was cut up and in the party bags.

Alfie ran over and between them they began offering the bags out until only one was left. 'Don't worry about that one right now. Go say goodbye to your friends.'

She saw Paige and Emily chatting in the corner and smiled at Paige as she disappeared, presumably to get changed.

Then finally it was quiet, except for the ringing in her ears and the excited pounding of her pulse. She still wasn't really believing the list on her phone. The very best list she had ever seen.

'Did you have a great party, dude?' Emily asked, as Melanie wiped chocolate off Alfie's chin.

Alfie nodded. 'Can I have more cake?'

'Of course,' Emily said. 'Auntie Mel has to go and make sure Paige gets her party bag, then we can have more cake and open up your presents!'

Emily whispered in Melanie's ear, 'She's in the spare room. Go for it.'

Melanie grabbed the little party bag and slowly made her way upstairs. Her hands were shaking as she pushed her glasses up her face and wiped her hands on her dress. She knocked on the door.

'Come in,' Paige said.

Melanie walked in just as Paige finished getting dressed. She spotted her phone on the bed and knew she hadn't looked at it yet. Melanie's mouth dried, and as Paige turned around, she saw the nerves all over her face. Paige had no idea that Melanie had seen the email notification, no idea that she'd seen the list, no idea that she'd added to it. And Melanie had no idea at all what to say. So she bought herself some time.

'Alfie made you a party bag. It's pretty cool.'

Paige grinned as she grabbed it and looked inside. 'Play Doh, cool!'

Melanie had seconds probably until Paige would grab her phone and see the notifications on the lock screen. She could leave it for Paige to see. Let the words there do the talking for her. But Paige had been brave and now it was her turn.

'It was Laura, she erm, she made me feel useless. I would have had a bar years ago if not for her. She kept me at her beck and call, to fulfil her dreams and ambitions. She deliberately made me feel small and incapable because it suited her. It took a long time for me to build myself back up. I'm proud of who I am now. I know I'm far from perfect. I've become too self-reliant. I put too much pressure on myself. I'm always busier than I ought to be. I hog the bed, and I'm a morning person. I've never actually sat down and watched all the Star Wars films. I'm almost always on my phone or an iPad, to the point where I can often be really rude. But I would hope that those that I love know I would drop any-thing for them. I'd drop everything for you, Paige. Whatever you needed I would be there. I love you. I love you so much it's terrifying.' Melanie quickly gulped down a breath to continue. 'I'm terrified that I'm not good enough for you. Or that I won't be able to see you as much as a new relationship needs. I was hurt, but only because I cared so damn much. So much for such a short period of time. Is that not crazy?'

Melanie finally ran out of breath, her chest was tight, her throat sore and she felt like she would cry or run, or freeze or combust she wasn't sure which.

Paige stepped forward. 'It is crazy, which is why it took me so long to realise what was going on. It's absolutely terrifying but I know that I love you and you make me happy, and really everything else we can figure out in time. I already know you're a bed hog. I know that I don't always share as much about myself as I should. My love language is definitely acts of service. Connie raised me, and my relationship with my mum is complicated but I will tell you all about that if you want? I'm used to helping people and fixing things, but I promise I can do more than that. I can listen to what's going on, but I also know you'll be there for me when I need it too and I will need it. I want to share everything with you. I love you, Melanie.' And they reached for each other in a move that looked well rehearsed. Melanie's hands on Paige's hips, Paige's hands gently cradling her face as their lips met and they kissed, and they whispered endearments and declarations of love over each other's cheeks, necks and lips.

'I love you, Melanie,' Paige said holding on to her face and looking into her eyes.

'You can definitely cross that off your to-do list now. Both entries. I love you too, Paige.'

CHAPTER FORTY-THREE

Two weeks later
Melanie

It was finally happening. Melanie was stationed in front of the flower wall. Dan was in the kitchen preparing the food for the day as well as extra samples for later. There was a bright ring light and a rather expensive looking camera pointed at her.

'Just close your eyes for me a second,' Sophie said.

And honestly for the fiftieth time in the last two minutes alone, Melanie could *still* not believe this was happening.

'So where did you get the idea for Lulu?' Sophie asked, as Melanie felt the gentle sweep of the make-up brush over her eyelids. 'Oh and before you answer that, Melanie wears glasses so I'm making her eye make-up extra fierce so it can be seen. Sorry, Melanie, go on.'

'Well, Lulu was the girl I always thought I wanted to be. She was creative, strong, beautiful. She was independent; she didn't need anybody. Louisa, my best friend, she totally understood and helped further design that vision until we were able to create Lulu. It's a bar for people to feel creative, to have happy times, to of course eat delicious food and drink lots of prosecco, but it's also a space for people to find out who they really are. Find out what they really need.' Melanie smiled, and when Sophie moved away, she opened her eyes to look behind the camera where Paige was sat. She could see the cling film around the top of her arm where her fresh tattoo was healing, and she couldn't help but smile as she remembered Paige asking her to pose for it. Paige telling her that the space had always been saved for her, she just hadn't known it.

'I have to say, Melanie, I love it in here. I'd work from here every day if you'd let me. I'll add all the details in the notes so do make sure you check it out and make sure you book, because this place gets busy!' Melanie watched as Sophie smiled at the camera.

'And it's a special day today as well, isn't it?' Sophie asked.

'Yes, today Lulu and Barbarella along with our fellow bar, shop and trade owners in our little community are unveiling a huge piece of wall art. The artists are all volunteers that have either worked with or benefited from Selena Dante Art Therapy. We're talking members of the community that needed support when fleeing domestic abuse, or people who were homeless, to those that have been helped out by the LGBT centre. We've all come together to create a piece of amazing art that captures our community spirit and today it gets its first official unveiling.'

Sophie paused what she was doing and looked directly into the camera. 'Melanie, it's safe to say that you and Paige — come on, Paige, get in on this for a second.' Melanie grinned as Paige grimaced but did as she was told. 'It's safe to say that you both did a lot of work for this project, isn't it?'

Melanie shrugged, her cheeks now flush with embarrassment, but her gaze intently staring at Paige, wanting to see her reaction for the next part.

'We all worked really hard on it,' Paige said.

'Any way, I have some contacts as you know. And well, not to blow my own trumpet, but Sophie Bowman

Cosmetics along with Universal Sound Studios and The Suits have heard about the work you've been doing and have all donated, generously. £500,000 will be given directly to the Selena Dante Art Therapy programme to continue the amazing work they do.' Melanie grinned as she watched Paige's mouth drop open in shock.

'You did what now?' Paige asked.

Sophie grinned at Paige and then back to the camera. 'That's not all. A further £350,000 will be given to the new Voluntary Committee arm of the Neighbourhood Business Association that has recently been set up by Paige here, with the aim of matching up local businesses and charities.'

'I have?' Paige asked.

'I'm going to edit your reaction out there,' Sophie said.

'Yeah, but what?' Paige looked blindsided.

'Well . . .' Melanie started. 'You mentioned to me how you wanted to work more closely with local charities, that you were starting to pull some ideas together. I bumped into Councillor Houghton to sound him out about it and I may have mentioned it to Sophie when we were prepping for this. But the money . . . I swear I had no idea about the money.'

'Well I told the girls,' Sophie said simply. As if it really was that simple.

'And what? You magic'd up how much?'

'£350,000. Technically Universal Sound Studios is actually payment from a very famous musician who wished to remain anonymous and who coincidentally is flying Polly out to LA right now so they can, and I quote, "hang out". Then a chunk from my business, and a chunk from Mya's. See, no big deal, it's a tax thing for most of us. But you'll be able to help loads of people with that, right?'

'There's going to be lots to do setting up an official organisation, Paige, and I've already started on a to-do list,' Melanie said. 'Although obviously I had to keep this one separate so you couldn't see what we were planning. It'll need updating now that there's a budget. I wonder if I should get a new app for finances . . . ?'

'I . . . really?' Paige was clearly having a hard time comprehending what was happening.

Melanie stood up and pulled Paige up too. 'I know you can do anything you want. And if this isn't what you want then we'll just pretend like it never happened. I'm sorry I didn't talk to you about it, but I wanted it to be a surprise.'

'Well, this is going to keep me busy,' Paige said, before pulling Melanie into her arms.

'Not too much with the hugging, please, I haven't finished her face yet,' Sophie said.

Melanie reluctantly pulled away from Paige, and Sophie jumped up to give Paige a huge hug. 'You're amazing, now go use your scary grumpy ass powers for good.'

'Oh my reading!' Paige shook her head. 'Connie said that I needed to aim my help in the right direction, she knew all along.'

'Duh,' Sophie said. 'She always knows.'

They let go and Sophie sat back down. 'You stop that right now. You can't be crying, we don't have time to fix it. Sit now!'

Melanie did as she was told, but not before checking Paige was really OK with it first. Her heart all but melted; Paige was beaming. Her eyes glowed with excitement.

'So, if you would like to donate, I'll add a link to the notes. But I've no doubt that myself, Mya, Polly, Marcus, Bailey, Smithy, Paige and Melanie will all be on here talking more as the charity grows and develops. Now as for Melanie, I'm going to have to redo the bit under her eyes because she was crying.'

* * *

Paige

Canapes were handed around, non-alcoholic drinks were shared, as they all stood before the wall, temporarily covered in a huge sheet. Paige was really excited to see it.

'Why has the wall got a big curtain?' Alf asked as he held on to both Paige's hand and Melanie's.

'You'll see in a minute,' Paige said.

'Ladies and gentlemen, erm, folks, members of our community, and guests. I am Councillor Patrick Houghton, Chair of the Neighbourhood Business Alliance, and proud sponsor of this art mural.' Councillor Houghton paused and a smattering of applause broke out.

'Did he make it sound like he personally paid for this?' Melanie whispered.

Paige nodded. 'Yep.'

'We pride ourselves in having strong links with business, charitable organisations and community projects. We look after one another and it shows — and that ethos is now embodied for all to see as they go about their daily lives, through this magnificent piece of artwork. Thank you to Selena and co. for their design and execution. Selena Dante is an art therapist who works with many of our local organisations, supporting some of our more vulnerable community members. Restoring where she can; their confidence, their creativity and their ambition. A special thank you to Melanie Curzon, and the rest of the Neighbourhood Business Alliance for pulling this together. And now without further ado, I present to you your art mural — simply called "Connections".'

'Really? No mention of the business whatsoever?' Melanie mumbled.

'Don't worry, Mya is already sweet-talking the press.' Paige nodded towards the back of the crowd.

'It's a shame Polly and Connie couldn't be here,' Melanie said.

'Yeah but when pop royalty calls, you have to answer. As for Connie, she'll be back soon enough. I have a horrible feeling she's not finished with Councillor Houghton.' Paige grimaced.

'Shh, he's doing it,' Alf said drawing their attention back to the wall. Paige gave his hand a little squeeze as the sheeting was pulled down. There were some gasps as the image was revealed. It was too big to take in straight away and a lot of people tried to take a step back so they could see it. And one by one people clapped and cheered. There were signs of all of them in there. There were golden links running throughout, large in parts and smaller almost hidden in others. There was a very dominant rainbow, coffee beans, and some of the paint somehow looked like tattoo art. As she studied it more closely, she could see all of their businesses represented on the wall. An image of a woman, dominated the top right hand corner. She was green, and to Paige she looked a lot like Te Fiti from Moana. But she was powerful and she was fierce and she was smiling. Her gaze looking down at the links, at the images, at the community.

'I like green,' Alf said.

'It's beautiful,' Melanie whispered.

'Which bit did you do?' Alf asked Paige.

'Erm.' Truthfully she wasn't sure. Up close she had no idea. She'd definitely used gold paint at some point.

'I think you chose really well, Alfie,' Melanie said.

'Yeah, I'm good at choosing. Like I chose Auntie Pwaige too.'

'Oh you did, did you?' Melanie grinned at him and picked him up, so that he was resting on her hip.

'Auntie Pwaige, can I get a purse-in now?'

'Not quite yet, dude.'

Mya and Sophie chose that moment to come up to them.

'It's amazing,' Sophie said.

'I'm an artist. Is there no end to my talent?' Mya shouted.

A little hand reached up to Mya. 'Shiny,' Alf said trying to get at Mya's hair.

But before he could get anywhere near, Melanie and Alf were called over by Councillor Houghton.

'So, I believe Sophie told you the news. That you're now a philanthropist,' Mya said smugly.

'I didn't even know you could keep a secret, Mya! And you gave the money so doesn't that make you the philanthropist?'

'Philanthropist *and* artist? It's a big day for my CV.' Mya grinned.

'And so modest too,' Sophie added.

'It's pretty exciting.' Paige forced herself to carry on where normally she would have stopped. 'And really terrifying.'

Sophie nodded, and Mya put an arm around her. 'And you will tell us when you need help,' Mya commanded.

'Or else I'll get Melanie to add us to the to-do list app and we'll give you a taste of your own medicine,' Sophie said sternly, before Marcus, Bailey and Smithy turned up and even more cheers and hugs were shared.

After a couple of minutes of being hugged and congratulated, Paige took a step towards the wall, looking for the bit, trying to find the spot. There. Right underneath the profile of the woman, was the word "Friends". Paige had snuck it on there and was glad to see that Selena hadn't covered it up. But then she saw that underneath someone had added "and partners". Yikes that was Paige now wasn't it. She had a partner. She had no idea how to do that properly, but luckily she was in love with a woman who had a to-do list and wasn't afraid to use it.

EPILOGUE

Two years later

'What do you mean married?' Sophie asked.

'Well, you know we just, well, we were here and looking into it. And then we realised how easy it would be. And the day was just so glorious and it just felt so right and, yeah, we're married.'

'Hi. Hey, wait, what did I miss?" Mya asked as she joined the video group chat.

'Yeah, tell her, Polly!' Sophie cried out.

'We should wait for Paige,' Polly said, her face slightly flushed with excitement, her smile wide.

'Why are you so late anyway?' Sophie asked.

'I was throwing up in the bread bin. Not recommended,' Mya said.

The silence that followed spoke volumes.

'Why the hell did you throw up in the bread bin?' Sophie finally asked.

'Because I couldn't get anywhere else in time,' Mya said as if that was obvious. 'Don't worry, the bread in there had already started to go off.'

'But Mya, what the hell?' Polly asked.

'Oh it's not like you've never done it before,' Mya said, as Polly shook her head.

The chat pinged as Paige joined. 'Hi everyone,' she said as she sat back on her sofa.

'Are you drunk?' Polly asked.

'Erm no,' Paige replied.

'Not you — Mya,' Sophie said.

'No, not right now. Why?' Mya asked clearly looking at her own reflection on her device.

'Why throw up in the bread bin then?' Polly asked, starting to sound exasperated.

'Oh Paige, you can give Connie my love and tell her very freaking funny.' Mya shook her head.

Paige grinned, already knowing what was about to be revealed.

'What the hell is going on?' Sophie groaned.

'So the bread bin is because I'm pregnant. Connie guessed that there'd be a happy little accident for us. So, there you are.'

'Oh my God, congratulations. Wait, is it congratulations or . . . ?' Polly asked, her enthusiasm tapering off slightly at the end.

'It's congrats. We have to have an heir to carry on our legacy. No, actually, we're quite excited.' The look on Mya's face was soft and hopeful and honestly not a look any of them had seen before. 'It's really early days but yeah. Smithy says he can tell it's a girl.'

The girls all took turns to offer their congratulations and well wishes.

'Polly, you wanna go ahead and tell everyone the other reason we should be celebrating tonight?' Sophie said, her voice tight.

Polly threw her hands over her face in what Paige thought was embarrassment but then she caught the new piece.

'Ahh, is that a wedding ring?' Mya shouted.

'Yeah, well we just, it just felt right. So, we did it.' Polly was grinning, her eyes glistening.

Again, there was a round of congratulations and Sophie held up her prosecco glass to the screen.

'Well, seeing as we're all sharing big news tonight, Marcus and I have been approved. We are now able to officially adopt. In fact, there's talk of newborn twins but we're not going to know for a little while and we may need to foster them first. But yeah, we're going to be parents too.'

There was no longer a dry eye in the house, or houses.

Paige grinned. 'Alfie is going to be such an awesome cousin to your kids.'

And they all cried a little more.

'These kids have got the *best* ever aunties too. The song-writer, the poker-playing entrepreneur, the one with the MBE and the mega celeb.' Polly's smile was still so wide.

'God, it's so weird to think that only four years ago Sophie and I were squabbling over that tiny garden,' Mya said.

'I got you mate's rates on that garden!' Sophie shouted in response.

'It also got you a mega successful business and a husband but sure,' Mya retorted.

It was a shame they weren't all together in person, Paige thought. But they had big plans for Christmas this year. They were all, as in partners and family and everyone, coming to Paige and Melanie's for Christmas dinner and she couldn't wait. She could admit she'd gotten soppier in her old age, or maybe it was Melanie's influence but yeah, she was excited. Melanie had even added a new to-do list to her app so she was obviously excited as well.

'I wish we were all together in person right now,' Polly said.

'I know,' said Mya. 'One of you could be holding my hair back for me.'

Polly rolled her eyes. 'Now that I have definitely done before.'

'I have to go now, I think I actually do need to go throw up. Love you girls, see you same time next week, yeah?' Mya said to a chorus of agreement. 'Congrats again, Sophie and Polly.' With a belch Mya signed off.

'Eeeek,' Polly squealed.

'I need to take my wife away now, ladies. Sorry, love you all. Come on, Mrs Polly Johnston,' Bailey demanded, a huge grin on his face.

'I told you I'm keeping my name.'

'Come on, we can argue about this in bed,' Bailey said.

'Love you, girls. Bye.' Polly signed off with a sigh that suggested things had already started.

'You're going to be an awesome mum, Soph,' Paige said.

'Don't, you'll set me off again. But come on, as always you haven't told us what's going on with you.'

'Well, the return-to-work scheme with the Domestic Abuse agencies is all going well, and the work with Selena is . . .'

Paige looked up as the door to the flat opened and Melanie walked in. She smiled at Paige, and Paige's heart did that leap thing it always did. She watched as Melanie took off her work rucksack, putting it on the table, kicked off her shoes and then she did the bit that Paige tried her hardest to witness each night. Melanie took the ties out of her hair and shook it free. Then Melanie would do what she always did; she would turn around and go and make herself a drink, unaware Paige was watching the whole thing with complete adoration.

Paige looked down at the screen and saw Sophie had been watching Paige the whole time.

'I'm really happy, Soph. Just really happy.'

Sophie smiled again, and Paige swore she could feel the warmth.

'Love you, Paige.'

'Love you too, Sophie. See you soon, yeah?'

'Of course. Love to Melanie. BYE, MELANIE!' Sophie screamed.

'I'll text you later, Sophie, there's a new organisation app you're going to love!' Melanie shouted back.

'I'm going now. Bye.' Paige quickly disconnected, knowing that when Melanie and Sophie got started they would keep going for a long time.

She put down her iPad on the coffee table and walked towards Melanie in the kitchen area.

'What you making for dinner?' Paige asked.

'Oh ha ha. Are you ever going to let that go?' Melanie asked.

'Nope. Because it was the best Greek food followed by one of the best evenings of my life. I'm going to be reminding you all the time.'

'You don't need to remind me. Happy anniversary, Paige,' Melanie said wrapping her arms around Paige's neck. 'I got you a present.'

'We said no presents, but I have one for you too. Happy anniversary, baby.'

Their lips met, and Paige quickly felt to make sure the ring box was still in her back pocket. She'd wanted to do this two years ago, but knew she had to wait for the right time. Two years in and she couldn't wait any longer. She'd even had a consultation from Connie, who confirmed it was an excellent idea. Yes, Connie of the now six husbands, but still.

Melanie pulled away first. 'I want to give you the present now because, well because, honestly I'm a bag of nerves and I . . .' Paige watched as Melanie dove for her rucksack. Paige grinned while Melanie's back was turned and dropped to one knee, ring box outstretched. It may not have been the most romantic spot, but for them it was perfect. Melanie was home to Paige, she was love, she was sexy, she was everything and it was here that she felt it the most. Not in some fancy restaurant, or some big fundraising event. Their love was theirs and it was real and it was honest and it was this. Paige took a big deep breath and willed her hands not to shake.

Melanie was still rummaging about in her bag as she spoke. 'I know this might seem, no, wait, this might not be the most romantic place, or setting, or, no, wait. I'm not doing this right.'

'You're rambling,' Paige said with a patient smile.

'I just. I know this is right, Paige, and I—' Melanie spun around, a ring box in hand. She burst into tears as she spotted Paige, and dropped to the floor on one knee too.

'Are we both really doing this?' Melanie said, tears continuing to fall.

'Melanie, you are everything to me. Everything I never thought I needed, everything I never thought was for me. You are my home. Wherever you are I want to be next to you. I will happily do all the cooking. I'll do everything, no, wait, I'll do anything you ask and support you in any way you need. Will you please marry me?' It was only when she finished talking did the lump in her throat become released and her own eyes watered. But then she was gifted with a Melanie megawatt smile.

'You stole all my lines. Not to mention that I couldn't even add "buy a ring" to my to-do list. How can I say anything as lovely as that? Paige, I just want you now and forever. Please marry me because I would love nothing more than to marry you.'

They fell into each other's arms, rings temporarily forgotten as they smiled, laughed, cried and kissed to their future.

Melanie suddenly pulled away. 'Wait, did you know I was going to do this?' Melanie asked.

'No, not at all. Honest.' Paige wiped away her tears. 'But I'm really happy you did.'

'Me too, Paige. I love you.'

'I love you too.' Paige held Melanie as close as she possibly could.

'I can't wait to set up the to-do list for our wedding,' Melanie whispered into her ear.

'Now that I did know,' Paige said before they kissed again.

THE END

Milton Keynes UK
Ingram Content Group UK Ltd.
UKHW040214160324
439374UK00004B/242

THE CHOC LIT STORY

Established in 2009, Choc Lit is an independent, award-winning publisher dedicated to creating a delicious selection of quality women's fiction.

We have won 18 awards, including Publisher of the Year and the Romantic Novel of the Year, and have been shortlisted for countless others.

All our novels are selected by genuine readers. We are proud to publish talented first-time authors, as well as established writers whose books we love introducing to a new generation of readers.

In 2023, we became a Joffe Books company. Best known for publishing a wide range of commercial fiction, Joffe Books has its roots in women's fiction. Today it is one of the largest independent publishers in the UK.

We love to hear from you, so please email us about absolutely anything bookish at

choc-lit@joffebooks.com

If you want to hear about all our bargain new releases, join our mailing list here.

www.choc-lit.com

THANK YOU

Dear Reader,

Thank you. You're awesome.

Thank you for choosing *Just Friends for Now*. I really hope you enjoyed it, and thank you so much for being a part of the 'Friends' group. This is the final book in the series and I'm really quite sad to be leaving these girls behind.

If you've enjoyed *Just Friends for Now*, please leave a review for the book on the website where you bought the book. You can also follow me on Twitter, Facebook, Instagram or the ol' TikTok.

As this is the last book, I do just want to say thank you again to every single reader. I appreciate every last one of you.

Take care,
Lucy K
X